COBBLE CAVERN

BOOK 1 OF THE FLIN'S DESTINY SERIES

ERIK OLSEN

Cobble Cavern
Book 1 of the Flin's Destiny Series
Copyright © 2019 by **Erik Olsen**. All rights reserved.

Library of Congress Control Number: 2019916022
ISBN: Paperback   978-0-578-59023-3

CONTENTS

Chapter One

FLIN'S BIRTHDAY THE CHATTERING RINGS

It was growing late as Flin and the rest of the Newby family sat around the table in the petite but tidy kitchen. They were anxiously waiting for their father to return home from a long day's work to celebrate Flin's birthday.

"What's taking him so long…?" moaned Craven with his elbows pressed against the table and the palms of his hands propping up his head from under his chin.

"You know your father gets home about this time every night from his second job," his mother said with a smile as she folded clothes on the kitchen table. "You're just excited is all; that's why it seems like it's taking forever."

Flin's older sister, Valour, was the first to hear the family's car as it made its way down the street and let out its customary "welcome home," backfire. She ran to the kitchen window and pulled back the faded yellow curtain to see the old car engulfed in a big, blue cloud of smoke as it rolled down the road and into their gravel driveway. The brakes let out a dreadful screech as the car came to an abrupt halt and let out one last, loud *"BOOM!"* that shook the entire house, from the loosened bricks at the top of the chimney, clear down into the deep dark crawlspace below where the spiders ran for cover. This caused an even bigger plume of smoke that departed from the Newby yard, infecting the entire neighborhood with a blue cloud that soon blended in with the night air.

"He's home!" shouted Valour over her shoulder, clapping her hands and bouncing up and down on her toes.

A moment later, a tired looking Mr. Newby casually walked through the front door and gave his wife a gentle kiss on the cheek, then turned to the anxious spectators which were all standing behind him.

"Well, what's all the fuss about?" he asked nonchalantly, trying not to smile as he took off his tattered jacket and hung it on a bent hook nailed to the back of the kitchen door. He turned and stared into the eager eyes around him. "Okay, okay," he laughed. "Let's get on with the celebration. I'll go and get the bag from its place of hiding." Moments later Mr. Newby could be heard up in the attic removing floorboards just above the kitchen ceiling. A minute later he entered the kitchen holding a dusty green cloth bag while brushing himself off.

"I'll turn out the light," shouted Craven, Flin's older brother, as he jumped to his feet and excitedly scrambled for the skewed light switch by the front door.

The kitchen light was a single bulb which hung from the ceiling by a cord and swayed in the slightest of breezes.

Craven hit the switch, and an immediate mysterious aura filled the darkened room. Only two flickering mismatched candles on Flin's homemade chocolate birthday cake remained to faintly light the room. It was an unseasonably, warm fall evening, and the warped kitchen window had been pried open to let in the cool night air. The gentle breeze lightly drifted into the room and across the tips of the candle flames tickling them and causing the family's silhouettes to dance about the ceiling and walls like mystical spirits that had come to join in Flin's long- awaited celebration.

With excitement, Flin's family members quickly encircled him.

"Happy Birthday, dear Fli-in, Happy Birthday to you!" They concluded singing, and the room immediately fell silent.

Flin knelt in front of his father, shaking with anticipation. He took in a deep breath that seemed to get stuck in his throat, and then looked apprehensively around the room as his dad carefully untied the frayed old rope from around the legendary emerald green bag and gently placed it on the table. No one really knew how old the bag really was; it was timeless looking and appeared frail and tired.

"So, no one really knows where the bag with all the rings came from?" asked Craven with much enthusiasm, looking down at his own destiny ring on his finger he'd received just a couple years earlier.

"No — and, yes," responded Mr. Newby with a befuddled look.

"Well it can't be both!" replied Craven, wanting a resolute answer.

"What I can remember from what my dad told me so many years ago, is that they may have come from, well, you're probably not going to believe this, but he said the rings were made in some old Leprechaun village by, leprechauns."

Repressed laughter broke out amongst the siblings, however, Flin didn't laugh.

"As a matter of fact, I remember my father mentioned to me that this old bag here was actually made from some leprechaun's jacket."

The laughter soon seized and the room fell silent as all now stared intently at the tattered plaid green fabric.

"At least that's what his father, my grandfather told him," continued Mr. Newby.

"Is that why there's a funny looking pocket in the shape of a clover on the side of the bag?" Craven said reaching out, now wanting to touch it.

"Shh . . . Craven, we'll talk about that after," whispered his mother with her finger pressed up to her lips and looking over at the gradually expiring candles on the cake.

"I always just thought that pocket was to keep the rope in when you took it off the bag," pondered Mr. Newby, now a bit perplexed himself.

As Mr. Newby tilted the bag oh so slightly to the side a hint of sparkling gold dust filtered out of the clover pocket and down onto the table.

"Whoa…." came a mutual response.

"That, that could just be dust from up in the attic," said Mrs. Newby, trying to keep things on a real note, but not too convincingly, especially now things started to become too real with all the leprechaun talk.

It was October 13th, Flin's thirteenth birthday, and for this meager boy, a ring was to be his only and most treasured gift.

Flin was a good-looking boy of average height, sandy blonde hair, and deep blue eyes. His clothes, although neatly pressed daily

by his mother, were tattered and patched hand-me-downs from his three older brothers.

As Flin knelt patiently waiting, a beam of light from one of the flickering candles danced upon his father's ring, reflecting off of a red stone and shooting a red beam of light into Flin's eye, making him even more anxious as his dad carefully opened the aged bag. Mr. Newby reached under the green fabric and gently began to jiggle the few remaining rings, caressing the bag as he spoke.

"From the weight," he said in a heightened expression, trying to make the most of the generational family tradition, "I would guess there are now eight, no, no, hold it — wait a second — possibly nine rings left," he said, smiling down at Flin.

"Now Flin," said his mother, trying to suppress a smile. "Clear your mind and focus on choosing the ring you feel inspires you to grasp hold of."

Flin clenched his eyes closed and carefully placed his hand in the bag. He was the last of seven siblings to finally get to select the ring that was **destined** only for him. His hand slowly reached half-way down and then suddenly he seemed to have frozen in place. Moments later, he moved it over to the other side and again proceeded downward.

"Watch out, there might be spiders in that dusty old thing!" blurted out his oldest brother Tom, who was always at the quick to tell a joke.

"Tom, Shhh! don't ruin it for him," rebuked his mother, shooting him an unfavorable expression.

Flin seemed unaware of any outside disruption. His eyes remained tightly closed; his mind was solely focused on selecting that one ring that was destined to be his. His hand again hesitated. His eyes began to dart back and forth under his eyelids as if he were visualizing something in his mind or having an extremely vivid dream. Seconds later, his shaking arm plunged deeper into the bag.

"What's taking him *so* long?" murmured Craven, looking over his shoulder at the cake. "Why doesn't he just hurry and pick one?"

"Shush!!! That goes for all of you!" chastised Mrs. Newby in a low whisper, her eyes doing most of the talking with an all too familiar glare.

A faint sound of rattling from the rings slowly grew louder and began to fill the air within the small kitchen. Quickly it grew into a startling clatter as Flin's hand now neared the bottom. The bag looked as if it had come to life and was now jerking madly back and forth as if it were trying to free itself from Mr. Newby's grasp. Flin's father now looked greatly concerned as he looked down into the bag. There was no way of stopping the ceremony, the bag seemed to have come to life and had now taken over. Mr. Newby gripped the edges of the bag with both hands as tight as he could.

"I've never seen it do that before," muttered Valour in dismay to no one in particular. Her eyes widened with fear as she glanced around to see the others horrified at the site as well. Bit by bit, the family backed away, leaving all but Flin and his Father in the center of the room.

Somehow, through all of this, Flin was oblivious to all the madness that was happening right in front of him.

A sudden surge of energy shot out of the bag like a gust of tempered wind accompanied with lights of all the colors of the rainbow brushing back the tips of Flin's hair. However, Flin's eyes remained closed. His dad continued to lean as far away from the bag as possible. Just then a bright green flash of light shot out of the bag and smacked against the ceiling sending trails of sparks in every direction.

The sound of countless years of pent-up static electricity quickly grew louder and louder from inside of the bag as Flin reached for the rings. There came another abrupt pop from within the bag, like that of a large firecracker, accompanied by a bright red flash of light that bolted into the air and lit up the entire kitchen in red for a brief moment, while leaving a pale red cloud behind. There came a few more crackling pops and radiant flashes of light, startling the already alarmed family and causing them all to duck for cover.

Then, out of nowhere there came a sudden smile that stole across Flin's face. He pulled his hand upward. The instant his hand was free from the bag, his eyes popped open and quickly widened as they focused on his new ring.

"Whoa… that was amazing!" he said as if he'd just experienced the biggest thrill of his life. He stared down at the oversized ring as it dangled around his thirteen-year-old finger.

His family stood several feet away, frozen and speechless.

"Wow!" he said lifting his hand closer to his face. "I didn't know what to expect, but the further I reached into the bag, the more I could picture the ring, and this is exactly *it!*"

The ring's stones sparkled with brilliance in the candlelight. After a couple of minutes of being mesmerized by the ring, Flin finally noticed the uncomfortable silence that surrounded him; he glanced around the room to see all but his father pinned to the walls.

"Why's everyone so quiet?" He turned to Craven who stood motionless until he finally blinked; at least he was still alive. "Craven, Cra-v-e-n, you can turn the light back on now," he said, looking back at his ring. "What's wrong with everyone? Can't anybody hear me?" he asked. He got up and turned the kitchen light back on, which was swaying furiously back and forth to the point the bulb was nearly hitting the ceiling.

"That stone looked purple in the dark," he mumbled as he studied the ring more closely. "Hey, you should see this! It's actually a dark red."

The ring was a yellow gold, with five distinct stones that encircled the band. Three stones were set in the center — a deep blue, a blood red, and a bright emerald green, and at opposite ends, there gleamed a pearlescent white stone, and an ominous dull black stone. All the rings that had come out of the bag to this point were all unique, but nothing like Flin's. Some had raised symbols with stones, while others were simple only caring engravings.

"Flin?" asked his bewildered mother who had finally regained somewhat of her composer and could be heard panting heavily with one hand over her heart and the other pressed up against her lips as she spoke.

"Yeah?" he answered, now daring to touch the blood red stone.

"Are you — al-right?" she asked, now batting her wide eyes and trying to regain her composer.

"Yeah, sure, why?" he mumbled.

Inspecting the room for damage, she again spoke, "You — didn't notice a bright red flash of light, or any, loud — *noises?*"

"Nope," he replied, disconcertingly. "Wow, that's a cool stone!"

"Well, it was — *quite* — *disturbing!* I thought you might have gotten hurt." she continued, batting her eyelids wildly.

"No, I'm fine," he said. "You know what's neat?" he asked with a relentless grin. "The ring just slid up and onto my finger! I didn't even have to grab hold of it. It's kind of like the ring chose me instead of me choosing it."

Slowly other family members began to move and regain their consciousness, joining in on the peculiarity of what had just happened.

"Don't tell me, Flin, that you didn't hear the rings clanging against each other!" his brother Dane said accusingly. "Or, or that static noise coming out of the bag with all the crackling and bright flashes of light? Come on… Flin. There was one bright flash of red light that shot out of the bag and practically took off *your face! Not to mention all the others that shot out of the bag and left burnt marks all over the ceiling and walls!*"

Flin shook his head, starting to feel more like he was on trial. "I've waited a long time for this birthday," Flin said studying his ring happily. "I thought it would never come."

"Yeah, yeah… we know," snapped Craven, who was obviously tired of hearing Flin talk about it every day for the past year.

There was a moment of silence, until Flin's mother again spoke. "Well, that was really…" she paused, baffled. "…interesting, I guess," she looked around. "Everything seems to be —in order I guess," she sighed, blinking her eyes several more rapid times and trying to clear her thoughts. She looked around the room. "Oh yes, cake! Who wants cake?"

"Meeeee!" came a unanimous plea from the entire family, with the exception, Flin, who sat silently at the dinner table admiring his new destiny ring.

"We'd better hurry and eat it before the frosting's nothing but candle wax!" she said looking over at Flin.

Valour turned to her mother. "Can we turn the light back off so Flin can make a wish and blow out his candles?"

"NO!" came an abrupt response out of Mrs. Newby, as if another loud firecracker had just gone off. She tried to regain her composure by running both of her hands up and down the front of her apron. "I, I think we've had enough excitement in the dark for one night, thank you!"

"Your mother's right; we've had enough excitement for one night," said Mr. Newby in an unnerving voice, picking up shredded pieces of fabric from off the ground.

A line quickly formed as Flin's mother dished them all up a piece of homemade chocolate birthday cake. But Flin didn't get in line, instead he sat silent at the kitchen table, still captivated by his new ring.

"Mom, how many years have we lived in this house now?" asked Craven as he took his last bite, then glanced over at the last piece still on the cake plate which was Flin's.

"Oh . . . let's see now... Your dad and I moved in right after Grandma Newby passed away. That was . . ." she started counting fingers. "What, twenty-three years ago? Has it been that long?"

"It has, honey," replied Mr. Newby, casually overhearing as he now studied the bits and pieces of shredded fabric more closely.

"'Think we'll ever move?" chirped Valour, running her finger across her empty plate and then licking it.

"But didn't Great Grandfather Hovgard build this house? I mean that would be kind of sad if we moved, I mean it's been in the family forever," said Valour sentimentally.

"Yeah, but people say he was crazy," blurted Tom.

"Well, people are sometimes strange. They get these ideas in their heads, about —"

"You mean like how our family can supposedly read minds?"

"Dane!" reproved Mrs. Newby, her nerves far from spent, giving him a sharp glare from the kitchen sink as her head whipped around in his direction.

"Well, Dane," said Mr. Newby, "see, people around here still assume that our family's a bit strange because of some old legend left behind by your Great Grandfather Hovgard, well his first name was really Flinnigan, but he went by Hovgard. Anyways, apparently, he went around claiming to everyone that he could read minds. He also spoke of a, a land so unbelievable, filled with all kinds of other creatures. If I'm not mistaken, he said he had these hybrid pits and seeds he and his partner had concocted, some guy by the last name of, Root, I remember hearing this because I thought it was funny he played with pits and seeds and his last name was, Root. Anyways, they had cut these seeds and pits up into several pieces and then attached them together with other types of pits and seeds combined with some bizarre, crazy fertilizer they had made up. Supposedly they had come up with these plants and trees that could grow all kinds of different fruits and vegetables on them. He claimed some of the trees could walk and move around."

"No kiddin'!," said Craven, now dropping back into one of the chairs around the table.

"You know the ones Flin, from down in the cellar, in the old cigar boxes. Some of those I believe were part of their experiments. But the best was the story of some, some old treasure, and that if he could only get to it, it would make him the richest man in the world," he paused for a moment dwelling back on his childhood memories. He shook his head.

"Treasure?" sparked Craven. "Go on about the treasure!"

"That was years ago, and a lot has changed since then," Mrs. Newby said dismissively, now over at the kitchen sink scrubbing away at the dishes. Mr. Newby went on, but this time he stared blankly at the wall and spoke in a quiet and more serious tone, "He spent his last days in a prison cell where he ended up dying, I believe at the ripe old age of eighty eight."

"Dying? What do you mean, he ended up dying while serving his sentence in prison?" asked Valour, now on the edge of her seat, cake long gone from her mind.

"They say he killed his wife," he shook his head wearily. "He was a good man, never any real evidence. He denied it to his dying day, but then again he wasn't all there at the end — but they never could find her body," said Mr. Newby.

Flin started to become confused as to why he too carried the same name as some psychotic relative. "Then why'd you and mom name me after some, crazy old man?" he asked confused, now for the first time chiming into the outside conversation.

"He wasn't *crazy*, just misunderstood mostly. I have fond memories of him. Anyway, it was more out of tradition that we named you after him than anything else, really. It's gone on supposedly for countless generations that someone has named their fourth son Flinnigan Hovgard Newby, and, well you, just so happened to be, that fourth son. Not to mention the fact that we promised your dying grandfather that we would carry on the tradition. Anyways, so now you can see why your mother would rather not talk about it."

There was a moment of silence – all eyes glanced at the back of Mrs. Newby. Who was scrubbing rampantly on one of the dishes hoping the subject would come to an end.

"Do you think any of us will ever be able to read minds?" asked Craven.

"No!" sparked Mrs. Newby, "and that's about enough of this conversation. I'm going to bed," she said as she threw her apron down onto the counter and stormed out of the kitchen.

Minutes later, the kitchen was about empty.

"Lucky," said Tom, punching Flin in the shoulder, as he was about to file out of the room. "You get to go to Ireland in the morning. None of us have ever even set foot outside this crummy little town —"

"Tom!" reproached his father with narrowed eyes. "Now you know how hard Flin and his friends have had to work to win this debate excursion."

"Yeah, I know . . ."

"And trust me," continued his father. "It wasn't an easy thing for your brother here to raise that money to *go*. He had to sell those strange looking seeds and pits he found down in the cellar, not to mention, help out with Custodian Crane up at the old pris —"

"*School!*" belted out Mrs. Newby, returning to the kitchen in blue fluffy bathrobe and curlers in her hair; clearly far to frazzled to sleep. "You keep referring to that school as a *prison*. You know how I feel about our kids attending some old prison that's been converted into a school. Not to mention the fact that it's said to be *haunted*. It's been a school for over a decade now," she said as she ran the tap water into a bent up, copper kettle to make her a cup of tea. Immediately there came a clatter as she began to put the dishes away.

"Sorry dear, helped out up at the — *school* after hours and on weekends to come up with the other half of the money," concluded his father.

"Just kidding, Flin," said Tom ruffling up Flin's hair. "Have fun with your friends in Ireland." He slid the tip of his finger across the top of Flin's untouched cake and poked it into his mouth. "See ya in a week. Oh!" he turned on a heel. "Bring me back somethin' from Ireland," he said brightly.

A moment later, the chattering sound of dishes came to a halt, and Mrs. Newby made her way over to Flin and gave him an enormous hug while handing him a paper bag.

"Here's your lunch for tomorrow. Now I've made you two of your favorite sandwiches with a few diced up carrots and two pickles. Now do be extremely careful while you're gone."

"I will, thanks mom," said Flin, as she grabbed both sides of his cheeks and kissed him on the forehead, before shedding a tear at the thought of Flin leaving. She briskly turned to her husband. "I think I can finally sleep now," she said with a look of exhaustion. "I'm off to bed."

"I'll be there shortly," responded Mr. Newby.

Awhile later, Flin looked over to see his father still studying the old emerald green bag that was now shredded in several places. He carefully placed his hand under the bottom of it and raised it to the light.

"Are you all right, Dad? I thought you were going to bed?" asked Flin, noticing his dad's peculiar behavior.

"Hm, what? Oh yeah, sure, I'm fine." Carefully he retied the frayed purple cord around the bag and bounced his hand against its bottom jingling what sounded like a six to eight remaining rings.

"Hey Dad, what's going to happen to the last rings now that we all have one?"

His dad sighed, "I don't know. Tom's the oldest, so I guess they'll probably be for his kids. Well...." he sighed, with both mental and physical exhaustion. "I guess I'll go and put this back in its place. Oh, and one last thing, Flin, remember, you're never to take the ring off, and you must protect it at any cost," he said with a hint of humor. He gave Flin another ruffling of the hair and then headed out of the kitchen and started his way back up the stairs towards the unfinished portion of the attic.

"Thanks, Dad."

"'Night son, I'll see you bright and early," The sound of footsteps on the dry wood stairs came to a halt. "Oh, Flin! What time was it that you wanted to leave again in the morning?"

Flin hesitated before responding, "Five, if that's alright?"

"Five! You mean five in the *morning*? Kidding, just kidding, five's fine. See you in the morning."

The Newby family lived in an old, run-down orchard house that had been in their family for generations. It was once surrounded by lush fields and endless rows of fruit trees, but due to increased property taxes over the years, the family had been forced to sell pieces of the land until they were left with just enough property for their modest, little house to sit on.

The land around them had recently been developed into a new cul-de-sac with large mansions lining the roadsides and overshadowing their quaint home which sat at the end of the street. Over time, the house had settled to one side and now looked more as if a giant had leaned up against it.

All the neighbors had complained to the city about wanting the conspicuous old house torn down, but due to its age and history, it had become a historic landmark, making the Newby family very unpopular throughout the posh neighborhood.

Late into the night, Flin finally turned out the kitchen light and headed up the wooden planked stairs to where he and Craven shared a room in the attic. Flin lay on his bed, too excited to sleep, envying Craven as he snored and let out an occasional giggle.

The big night that once had seemed forever away, had finally arrived. Flin and his friends from Stockhaus, the private school he attended, had won the state's debate competition, and in the morning, they'd be leaving on a plane for Ireland. Flin had packed his clothes days earlier. Excitedly, he sat up in his bed and squinted through the darkness of the night at the Stockhaus letterman jacket that had been given to him by Principal Vespar. It had been her's long ago and was a bit outdated as well as worn on the elbows and other places. Flin didn't mind, he finally had a Stockhaus jacket like the rest of his friends. She had also given him a uniform, and both were laid out across his bedspread and ready to wear in the morning.

Oh, that's right, he thought getting up and out of bed. *I want to take the rest of those seeds and pits I couldn't sell with me to see if Head Revels knows what kind they are.* He packed up the three cigar boxes full of seeds and pits to take with him. He again lay on his bed, far too excited to sleep, and looked up through the hole in the roof to see a shooting star race across the dark, majestic purple sky.

It was harvest season, and farmers throughout the area were in the process of cleaning off their fields and clearing away the stubble with fires. The smoke in the air made the moon glow Halloween orange with thousands of shimmering stars surrounding it. If ever a witch were going to fly across the sky, this would be the perfect night.

"Wow…! It's hard to believe that in less than twenty-four hours, I'll be in Ireland with the rest of my friends witnessing international debate competitions," he mumbled in the dark.

After several restless hours, Flin finally forfeited the thought of getting any sleep and got up. He put on his school clothes and tiptoed down the stairs and into the kitchen, where he sat patiently waiting in the dark for his father to awake.

An hour later, his father entered the kitchen and turned on the light. "Well Flin!" he said surprised. "Couldn't you sleep?"

"No, I stared at the stars all night. I was way too excited and didn't sleep a wink."

"I can understand," replied his father, grabbing a drink of water. "You'll be the first Newby to ever fly on an airplane." Flin's parents had never been outside of the state.

"I wish the whole family could go," Flin said somberly.

"Someday, someday," replied his father, between gulps of water. "Well, it doesn't look like you want to go back to bed," Mr. Newby said. "What if we go a little early? It's better to be early than late!" smiled his dad.

"Sounds good!" Flin said excitedly as he swiftly snatched up his tote-bag while on the run and dashed out the kitchen door headed for the car.

A minute later his dad got into the car. "Seat belt, Flin!"

"Oh yeah," Flin said and tied a frayed rope around his waist.

The car's engine whined as it reached the peak of the mountain. The headlights shone on the school's gate, which read, "Burlington County Prison, founded 1811." They drove down the winding lane where moments later they sat parked in front of the school. The shadows of the night enveloped the old, leaning school as it sat quietly on the mountain-top and looked down onto the town below.

"Grass looks like it needs to be cut again already," mumbled Mr. Newby, as he looked through the car window into the shadowy night as they sat waiting. "It seems to grow quickly on this mountain top," he continued. "And I noticed when we came through the gate it's already starting to screech again. I'll have to oil it up later tonight when I come back. I noticed rust was starting to show through again too, so I'll put a fresh coat of paint on it this Saturday."

In addition to Mr. Newby's two jobs, he worked on the old school/prison grounds after hours and on weekends with Custodian Crane in trade for his children's tuition.

The car windows were beginning to fog up on the inside from the cold morning mist that surrounded them. Mr. Newby rolled down his window to let in the outside air. A nearby owl gave a pleasant hoot from the grove of trees just a few feet away.

"Well Flin, what do you think, we've been sitting here for forty-five minutes? It's 5:30 and none of your other debate teammates are here."

Flin looked down at the flier that Parcell, one of the other students, had given him the day before. "It says here to be at the school no later than 5:15!"

"Are you sure there wasn't a change of plans at the last minute?"

"Parcell gave me this itinerary just yesterday after school," Flin said, now examining it more closely through the car window in the pail moonlight. "That's interesting," he said, troubled. "Head Revels' name is spelled 'Head Rebels' on the flier here. He wouldn't misspell his own name — DANG IT!" Flin exclaimed, slapping the paper. "Parcell gave me a fake itinerary!" Furious, he crumpled it up and jammed it deep into his jacket pocket. "The last thing I remember Head Revels saying was to meet at the airport no later than 5:15. They've all got to be at the airport!" he said, livid.

"I'll drive as fast as I can, but it's still going to take at least a half an hour to get there," his dad said in a panic as he raced out of the school parking lot and back down the winding mountain road towards the airport.

Chapter Two

THE FLIGHT

After a half an hour of racing through the night, the airport lights could finally be seen off in the distance.

"Finally!" Flin exclaimed, looking out the car window as several airplanes were lined up on the runway, ready for takeoff.

Once the car brakes began to screech, Flin grabbed his tote bag and darted out of the vehicle and raced for the airport's front doors. "Thanks, Dad!" he yelled over his shoulder.

"I'll wait here for a few minutes, just in case the plane has already left!" his father shouted back.

Where are they? Flin thought in a panic as he dashed through the crowds of people. His heart raced with anxiety as he sprinted through the airport. *Please tell me they haven't left yet. Dang that Parcell, I should have never trusted him!* He passed a clock on the wall in the shape of an airplane. *Six o'clock — shoot! They've probably left by now.*

"Flin, Oh... Flin! Over here!" he heard someone shout from over the congested noise of the crowd. He turned to see Principal Vespar with her arm in the air waving him toward the rest of the group. Her lips were pressed tight, and her eyes narrowed beneath the wire glasses perched on her delicate nose. But he knew the face all too well; it was one of concern, not anger.

"Where have you been?" demanded Flowell with grave concern, one of Flin's best friends, briskly making her way toward him. She had long, strawberry blonde hair, bright green sparkling eyes, and as usual, a bright smile.

Flin hunched over and placed his hands on his knees, trying to catch his breath. He took a dry gulp, pulled out his itinerary and handed it to Flowell, and gave it a distasteful, *tap.*

"Hi Flowell, hi Sam," he wheezed, barely understandable. "My itinerary said to be at the school at five-fifteen!" he ignited, turning to Parcell with disgust.

Parcell was a large boy with wavy, rust colored hair. Many thought Parcell was much older than they were and had failed a grade or two. He was standing by Ruel, supposedly his best friend, or maybe just his least hated enemy, both were snickering back at Flin as he glared over at them.

"To my knowledge, Head Revels didn't make an itinerary," said Principal Vespar with a puzzled look, taking the crumpled paper out of Flowell's hands and studying it more closely. Her smooth, brown coif hair was motionless as she glanced around for Head Revels.

"Where did you get this?" she asked Flin and as she turned the paper over to examine its back.

"Parcell!" Flin said, his blood boiling as he listened to Parcell and Ruel as they continued to mock him from behind.

"Well, I'll speak to Head Revels about this," she said in a disturbed voice, then briskly walked away.

Unable to stop his blood from boiling, Flin balled up his fists and made his way over to Parcell and Ruel. "Thanks for the itinerary, Parcell!" he snarled.

Parcell's mismatched eyes were ablaze and his lips curled back into an evil smile that exposed his gray decayed teeth. "Oh, you're so welcome, Flinny — and do let me know if there's anything else I can do for you! Oh… by the way Newby, it was payback for the topic sheet you so cleverlyleft me. Thanks for all the wrong answers," Parcell said snidely.

Flin wondered how Parcell had discovered that he'd been the one who snuck into the school after hours and switched the real debate topic sheet on Head Revels' desk for a fake one before Parcell had a chance to copy it. Confused, Flin started to walk away.

"Oh! And, uh, nice ladies' jacket, Flinny!" Parcell and Ruel both burst out laughing with pointed fingers in his direction. "I think my grandma still has hers just like it!"

Still bitter, Flin slowly made his way back over to his friends and debate teammates from school.

"Why do those bums even get to come?" Pilt asked with disgust, staring at the back of Parcell and Ruel as they walked away, and headed for what looked like trouble. "Everyone knows they only made it to the final debate by cheating."

Pilt was Flin's best friend. He looked pretty much the same every day; his hair was dark brown and had never seen a comb; his school uniform was new, but looked in shambles with the buttons of his shirt mismatching the holes they were supposed to line up with; his shoe laces untied and frayed, stained with dirt.

"Hey!" Pilt exclaimed, reaching down towards Flin's hand. "You got it! You finally got your ring!"

"You got it! You finally got your ring," repeated Parcell in a squeamish mocking voice as he and Ruel passed by; Ruel giving Parcell a forced courtesy laugh as well as an elbow to the ribs. They all waited to speak until Parcell and Ruel were out of earshot.

"So, they all look different, right?" asked Flowell, daring to touch one of the stones on Flin's ring.

"Yeah," Flin replied, unable to hold back a beaming smile.

"Whoa, that's so cool... Do you think it's made of real gold?" asked Sam, running her finger across the band. The crowd huddled around Flin caused Parcell to become curious, swiftly he back tracked to get a better look.

"It's kinda big for your finger, don't ya think?" Pilt said with a befuddled face. "You're going to get it re-sized aren't you?"

"No, it's meant to be that way so I can grow into it. I'm not supposed to ever take it off. At least that's what my dad said about the tradition."

"Good morning, Flin," Head Revels said sprightly as he made his way over. "We were starting to wonder if you were going to make it. Oh, Pilt, your shirt there needs to be tucked in."

"Oh yeah, sorry ..." Pilt said as he set down the bag strung over his shoulder and respectfully tucked in his shirt.

Head Revels was a man around sixty, always impeccably dressed, and never a hair out of place.

"Flin had a little trouble this morning," said Principal Vespar with a sharp eye glaring over at Parcell. She was fully dressed in her Stockhaus school uniform, as always, which was mandatory for the students at the private school, but not for faculty. "It seems that Parcell over there gave him a fake itinerary."

"Oh…" Head Revels said without much surprise.

"Oh, Flin, you'd better hurry and get your luggage checked in so they can load it onto the plane," she said as her eyes swept the floor around him in search of his luggage. "By the way, where is your luggage?" she asked surprised.

"I have it all right here," he said as he held up the old tote bag, he used for school every dayand gave it a good pat.

"That's all you brought?" asked Pilt, pulling a face, then looking over at the luggage counter where he had placed two large pieces of luggage waiting to be loaded onto the plane.

"Yep! This is all I'll need."

"That's it? That's all you'll need for the next week?" Head Revels questioned.

Flin, slightly embarrassed, responded, "It's only a week, right?"

"By the way, Flin, you look very dapper in that jacket," Principal Vespar admired, giving him a tap of approval on the shoulder.

"Thank you, and thank you again for giving it to me," replied Flin as Parcell and Ruel just within ear reach broke out laughing into cupped hands.

One of the debate members, Edgar, a plump boy with snow white hair, was sitting all by himself in the corner with his hand protectively placed on top of the bag next to him. His head was down but his eyes and attention were focused up at the people as they walked by.

Pilt spotted Edgar and noticed his peculiar behavior as he sat all alone.

"Hey Edgar, what's in the bag?" heckled Pilt, but the plump boy quickly turned and faced the opposite direction. "I'll bet you anything it's his bag of hair. They say he's making a rope or something with all that hair he cuts off of kids who aren't paying attention."

"By the way, did you hear? He cut off one of Jenny Forthbright's pig tails in English on Thursday while she was taking a nap on her desk. Then he ran out of the classroom before the bell even rang," said Flowell as the group of them stared at the odd boy.

"The kid's a serious weirdo!" blurted out Pilt, "I don't know why you have to say hi to him every day at lunch, Flin."

"Well, I'd rather stay on his good side," said Flin. "I don't want him cutting my hair."

Overhearing the conversation, Principal Vespar turned sharply. "Are you talking about Edgar?" The only response was frightened faces. "Yes, the child is slightly troubled; if you knew his past I don't think you'd be putting him down. Besides, putting him down isn't going to help the matter!" she scolded. This was unusual for Principal Vespar who was ordinarily very pleasant. "Now I would hope that each of you might go out of your way and try and include him throughout our trip. He could use a few friends."

"Yes ma'am," the group replied.

They all looked slightly ashamed of themselves for the moment; Sam, uncomfortable with the silence, asked Head Revels a question, "Head Revels, do you know how long this flight might be?"

"Oh, let's see now . . . probably eight or ni —" Head Revels began to say.

Just then, there came a jolting, boisterous, man's voice, disrupting the crowd over at the ticket counter. It was Mr. Sump, Parcell's father; his crass voice had caused everyone within earshot to stop what they were doing. He was having a disagreement with the young girl behind the ticket counter. He stood arrogantly poised, pointing his long, dangly finger at her, intimidating looking in his caramel, suede trench coat.

"That is not an answer young lady! That is an excuse!" he bellowed, his gelled, silver streaked, black hair, trembling from fury.

"I'm sorry, Sir, but all first-class tickets have been sold out for hours," the girl explained patiently. "If you wanted a first-class ticket, you needed to have reserved your seat in advance. However, there are still some tickets available in coach," she said, looking down at the computer screen.

"Coach...!!!" growled Sump, his silver sliver of a goatee quivering below his sharp lower lip. "You've must be joking! Me, ride in coach? Ha! You're out of your blinkin' mind! I want to see the person in charge, right now!" he demanded, the tip of his index finger repeatedly smacking the top of the counter. "You heard me, right now!" Red-faced Mr. Sump turned and glared at the observing crowd. "Well... what do you think you're looking at?" he said hastily to a passerby. "You big baboon," he mumbled to the person's back.

An older woman with a pleasant smile made her way to the ticket counter. "Now then, how may I be of assistance to you, Sir?" she asked, trying to remain pleasant.

"Her, she's the problem!" he said leaning over the counter and pointing. "She says I can't purchase a first-class ticket! And, I'll tell you how you can help me! I *must* have a first-class ticket! It's very simple!"

"The only thing we might be able to do is to find someone who'd be willing to give up his or her first-class ticket," she said hesitantly in an effort to settle the matter.

"Then I suggest that's what you both do! Get busy and *find that someone!*" demanded Sump.

"Why is Mr. Sump coming anyways?" Sam asked gloomily, from a distance.

"I'm guessing it's to keep an eye on his rotten son, Parcell, just like he does every other day at school," Pilt said with disgust, scowling at the back of, Sump.

Mr. Sump stood with two oversized suitcases to each side of him, and a carry-on draped over his shoulder, grimacing at passersby.

"You'd think he was going away for a year with all that stuff," whispered Pilt.

"Well, enough with that," sighed Principal Vespar, her permanent smile wiped clean off her face. She was obviously displeased that Mr. Sump had insisted on going with the group.

"I'm a little nervous about flying. Is anyone else?" Sam admitted, her soft brown eyes looking awkwardly down at the ground.

"Well, I, for one, am not!" sparked Parcell. "A little piece of crap airplane doesn't scare me none! As a matter of fact, I've flown lots of times, and on much bigger planes, too!"

"I've never flown before either, Sam," Principal Vespar said, grasping her hand and giving it a gentle pat. "And, I'll admit, I'm a little nervous myself. It's perfectly normal to be a bit frightened. But I think once we get up in the air, it will be quite fun, don't you?"

"Yeah, I guess you're right," Sam said, rolling her eyes and then giggling.

"Flight 512, Flight 512," came an announcement over the intercom. "Due to the unsettling weather, your flight has been delayed."

"Oh... *great!*" erupted Mr. Sump, abruptly dropping his luggage to the floor and throwing his arms in the air. "Parcell! *Parcell!*" he shouted, looking through the crowded airport and spotting Parcell and Ruel over by the newspaper counter. Parcell quickly doused a cigarette lighter and tucked it in his back pocket. "Get over here, *now!*" he said, snapping his fingers in the air and pulling his wallet out from inside his jacket pocket.

Parcell, along with Ruel, reluctantly made his way over.

"Since we have to be here for a while, there's a little shack of a shop just around the corner over there. It sells my magazine, '*The Man in Control.*' I've bought it there before," said Mr. Sump. He casually pulled out several one-hundred dollar bills while staring out of the corner of his eye at the rest of the group, who were all staring back at him as he held in his hand a large wad of money.

"There's one-hundred," he said, licking his thumb and sliding the bills apart. "Two-hundred," he continued, his eyes burning with greed. "And that makes three-hundred." Before he had stopped counting Parcell reached out and snatched up all three hundred dollars and he and Ruel took off running toward the shop.

"*Oh,* and you two go ahead and get whatever it's going to take to keep those mouths of yours plugged shut for the next while," he hollered after the boys with a motion of the hand as if he were shooing away flies at the table.

Minutes later, Parcell and Ruel could be heard giggling mischievously as they ran back through the terminal, darting in and out of people, shooting scandalous glances over their shoulders from behind.

"Parcell!" spouted Mr. Sump, standing by himself and signaling for him to come.

Parcell's eyes dropped to the floor and he grudgingly made his way over to his father. His pockets were overflowing with empty candy wrappers.

"Change!" demanded Mr. Sump, holding out his open palm.

"There wasn't any, I promise," Parcell responded in a gargled voice as he opened his mouth which was full of tootsie rolls.

"You took three-hundred dollars, *Parcell!* Don't tell me there's no change, ya lyin' little sh —" Mr. Sump's mouth snapped shut when he noticed the eavesdropping crowd that had gathered. "What are you all looking at?" he growled as he began to frisk his own son.

"What's this I feel, huh, *huh?*" Mr. Sump's voice rose with fury and the veins on the sides of his head could be seen pulsating. He yanked up the bottom of Parcell's pant leg. "What ya got here, Smokes? Cigarettes?" he hollered as he held up a pack of cigarettes. "You know I hate cigarettes! Oh, and what's this here?" asked Sump, reaching down into Parcell's other sock. "Would ya looky here? Three crisp, one-hundred dollar bills! How'd you pay for that stuff, *Parcell?*"

"I don't know," whimpered Parcell. "I think Ruel might have bought it."

"Bull sh—" spat Sump, biting his tongue to keep from cursing in front of the curious spectators. "You told me earlier that Ruel's money was all locked up in his luggage. And besides, they don't sell smokes to little boys! You stole 'em, didn't cha?" he pulled back his arm with an open hand, about to slap Parcell on the face.

"No, honest. I don't know how they ended up in my sock!"

"Sure you don't! You two get out of my sight and go do something," Mr. Sump said, shoving Parcell in the back. "I'm already tired of the both of you! Just stay out of my hair, got it?"

Finally, it was time to board. Flowell followed closely behind Flin as they got onto the plane. Flin made his way to a window seat and stared out at a flashing light attached to the wing. Flowell quickly sat down next to him.

"Didn't you want to sit by Sam? Because I thought Pilt—"

"Sam's fine," she said, cutting him off and smiling broadly.

Pilt came staggering down the aisle with his carry-on lopped over his shoulder. He stopped and stared down at Flowell, with a look of confusion.

She turned up to him with a smile. "There are lots more seats in the back, you know?"

Pilt looked over at Flin, blankly, and then back at Flowell, "Oh — okay, I guess," he said, shooting Flin a befuddled look. He made his way to the rear of the plane with Sam following closely behind him.

"Would you like the window seat, Flowell?" Flin asked.

"Are you sure you don't mind?"

Flin blushed. "No, I don't mind."

Ruel and Parcell crashed into the aisle seats as they recklessly made their way to the back of the plane pulling faces at others as they passed by. Ruel stopped long enough to give Flowell a greasy smile and a couple of bounces of the eyebrows.

"Hey cutie, would ya rather sit by me instead of loser here?"

"No thanks, I'd rather drink mud!" She turned toward the window and stared out at the blinking light on the wing.

The pilot came over the intercom. "Sorry for the delay, folks, but we're still waiting on a passenger."

"Who cares? Let's just go!" complained Parcell from the rear, barking over the seat in front of him.

A few minutes later, two policemen struggled to carry a disgruntled male passenger down the aisle while the man kicked and screamed.

"Oh, my gosh! That's Mr. Sump," said Flowell, covering her mouth and looking back over her shoulder at Parcell.

"I've never been treated so poorly!" shouted Mr. Sump, dragging his feet behind him. "I'm not happy about this! You'll be hearing from my attorney, all of you! Make no mistake about that! This is far from over!" He struggled to break free as they pushed him into coach seating and buckled him up, like they were placing him in a strait jacket. "I'll make sure every one of you loses your job!" he screamed as the officers walked off the plane and closed the door.

Minutes later, the plane started to taxi down the runway. A stewardess came over the intercom. "We are about to take off. Please make sure your seat belts are fastened."

"Oh yeah, seat belt, Flin," he said smiling and quoting his father as every morning he'd get into the family car to go to school. Without thinking, Flin began to tie the buckle and latch around his stomach into a knot.

"What, what are you doing, Flin?" chuckled Flowell, grabbing his hands.

"Oops, habit I guess." Flin was embarrassed as she untied his seat belt and latched it for him.

In the back of the plane, Parcell could be heard beginning to squawk in panic, "Hey Ruel, Ruel!" he said with his face pressed against the window. "Don't you think the plane's going a little too fast?"

Ruel sat up in his seat and glanced out the window, "It's just barely moving."

"Stop the, stop the plane!" shouted Parcell, struggling to undo his seat belt. "Let me off!"

A stewardess rushed to his seat. "Excuse me, but you need to leave that on," she said, firmly trying to keep him from removing the seat belt.

"I want off!" he screamed as the plane's vibrations worsened.

The stewardess motioned for help. "Come quick! I need your help!"

Parcell began to squeal like a pig.

"Hurry! Get a sedative!" ordered the head stewardess.

A moment later, she ran down the aisle with a glass of water and some pills.

"Take these," she said soothingly to Parcell as she put the pills up to his mouth. Parcell was no longer aware of what was going on. He bit down onto her hand.

"Open his mouth!"

The head stewardess pried open his mouth, and the two of them forced the pills down his throat. Within minutes, Parcell was no longer screaming. Instead there was an occasional soft whimper, or off-the-wall remark about his dog.

Flin leaned back comfortably in his chair and began to relax. It was hard for him to believe that just a few months earlier, his friends had talked him into joining a debate team, and now they were all headed to Ireland. A smile stole across his face as he thought back at how Parcell had ended up locked in the school's elevator overnight by Custodian Crane, because he had been caught trying to break into Head Revels' office to copy the debate topics. *His father probably bought his way out of that one,* he thought.

Flin grimaced at Mr. Sump's belly-aching just a few rows up. The Sumps seemed to have more money than they knew what to do with, yet Flin almost didn't make the trip for lack of funds. He thought back to the three cigar boxes he'd found down in the dusty, spider and mice infested crawlspace. labeled, "DO NOT PLANT!" He eventually sold twenty-five dollars' worth of the pits to an elderly man on the roadside. He seemed to have heard of Flin's namesake and great- grandfather, Flinnigan Hovgard Newby, and gave the impression to know something about the odd pits.

A bitter shout roused Flin from his reverie. "You don't really expect me to eat that, do you?" Sump complained to the stewardess.

"They're really quite good," said Principal Vespar with a smile, looking over her shoulder and sliding another peanut in her mouth. "You should at least give them a try," she said in an attempt to try and change his bitter attitude.

"Oh— well then. If you say it's good. *Are you kidding?* I wouldn't feed those to my dog! No wonder they're free!" He pushed her hand away, knocking the peanuts to the floor.

Ruel had become annoyed with Parcell's heavy breathing and nose wheezing while he slept. He dumped the remaining bag of his airline peanuts in his hand and began shoving them up Parcell's nostrils until they bulged like a squirrel's cheeks stuffed with nuts for winter. People seated around him laughed only encouraging the stunt.

"Another bag of peanuts, please!" Ruel hollered and waved his hand in the air for the stewardess.

Hours later, Parcell woke. He placed his head against the plane window; his eyes slowly widened. "Ruel!" he said, backhanding him in the chest. "Is the wing supposed to be bouncing up and down like that? And is that the ocean way down there? Hurry! Trade me seats," he jumped to his feet.

"You wanted that seat, now you keep *that* dang seat!" said an irritated Ruel, sitting comfortably.

"Trade me, hurry! Oh, I think I'm going to throw up." Parcell placed his hand over his mouth and grabbed his stomach.

Ruel jumped up and stood in the aisle as Parcell fumbled over the seats and ran toward the bathroom. Seconds later, the vile sound of vomiting could be heard from behind the closed bathroom door.

Mr. Sump approached the rear of the plane where the restroom was. He waited a moment by the door, and then impatiently began knocking. "There are others, you know?" he said loudly to the back of the door.

"What?" came a gargled response from inside.

"Parcell, is that you? Get out! Others need to use it," Sump said in a cutting whisper.

"You mean *you* need to use it. I'll be out in a minute!"

"You'll get out right now or else!" hollered Sump, snarling at the back of the door.

Now everyone in the rear of the plane had turned around to see what all the commotion was about.

"All of you just turn back around and mind your own business," shooed Sump with his hand.

The door finally opened. "Well, it's about time!" spat Sump irately as he pushed past Parcell.

Flowell shook her fist and muttered, "Ew . . . He's a real creep! No wonder his wife left him."

"I didn't think Mr. Sump was ever married. I thought he adopted Parcell," said Flin.

"Oh, he was married alright! They lived right down the street from us. She only stayed with him because of the big house and expensive cars. She looked a lot like Parcell—tall and slender. She was really quite beautiful."

Flin grimaced as he looked over the back of his chair at Parcell. One thing Parcell wasn't, and that was attractive in any way.

Flowell continued, "Then one day she couldn't take it anymore and just vanished without telling either one of them where she was going."

"I don't blame her," muttered Flin.

The pilot announced, "We're nearing our approach. Please take your seats."

Mr. Sump came running out of the bathroom still buttoning his pants. He stammered down the aisle complaining, "These pilots ought to be shot. This is the worst possible time for landing."

Head Revels moved his seat back upright. "I quite enjoyed that!"

"I've definitely had better," mumbled Sump, dropping into his seat and buckling his belt.

The plane's wheels touched ground. Parcell clenched the seat in front of him. "See Ruel, that wasn't too bad of a flight," he sighed with great relief.

"What do you mean? You were squealing like a tortured pig until they sedated you!" Ruel's retort earned him a punch in the gut from Parcell as he reached overhead for his carry-on.

The group de-boarded the plane and went to get their luggage. Mr. Sump returned from using the airport restroom and strode over to the group who stood waiting.

"I ought to file a complaint. I mean, just look at that slob there," Sump pointed a portly man walking by. "Some of these foreigners are real pigs."

"That man's no foreigner. He flew out on the same plane as we did this morning," said a slightly irritated Principal Vespar.

Parcell's heavy breathing caused his father to look over at him.

"Why are your nostrils so inflamed Parcell?" asked Mr. Sump, bending down and looking up into the two, swollen red holes.

"Because of Ruel!" Parcell replied in a nasally voice. "He shoved all his peanuts up my nose while I was asleep. Didn't ya, Ruel? Ya jerk!" A shiny, wet peanut fell from his nostril and landed on the floor.

"Make no mistake, Ruel, your parents will be hearing about this!" spat Sump.

Chapter Three

THE BUS RIDE

Their hotel, The Irish Clover was nothing like Flin had ever seen. It was one of the largest buildings in the middle of the city. It's exterior was green with gold embellishments. As they entered the richly decorated lobby to check in, it was all he could do to keep moving toward the desk.

The next few days Flin and his team mates were kept busy as they, along with thousands of other debate teams from all over the world commuted to Ireland's, Dublin University, where they watched the International Debate Finals.

After six days of competition, the next day was to be their last in Ireland. A field trip had been organized to take all the schools on an excursion that overlooked the coast of Ireland. It would give them a chance to observe the ocean's much coveted marine life. It was definitely the highlight of the week

By 6:00 A.M. the next morning, everyone was down in the lobby except for Parcell and Ruel. The lobby was overrun with students standing shoulder-to-shoulder. Even the stairs that lead up and out of the lobby were packed with students waiting excitedly for the buses to arrive and take them on their ocean excursion.

Edgar was the only one who stood silently with scissors in hand, staring at strangers as they passed. Principal Vespar walked by, and Edgar swiftly tucked the scissors behind his back and out of sight.

"There you two are!" Head Revels said to Parcell and Ruel with a sigh of relief. "What do you have in the bag that you didn't want to put into your luggage?"

Parcell stammered for a moment, trying to avoid answering the question. "Oh, just some . . . you know, some things. Come on, Ruel, let's go," Parcell said awkwardly, grabbing Ruel's shoulder.

"Don't go too far; the buses will be here shortly," Head Revels reminded them then looked down at the itinerary in his hand.

Moments later, the buses rumbled up to the curb in front of the hotel.

Sam clapped her hands, "Goody, the buses are here!"

Everyone promptly filed out of the hotel. The Stockhaus School group ended up at the rear of the crowd.

"We're going to be the last ones on!" complained Ruel.

"They've made provisions to take all of us. I don't think we need to worry," calmed Principal Vespar.

"Well, I don't like being last," blurted Parcell.

"Shut up, Parcell!" came an unexpected rebuke from his father.

Within minutes, the last bus pulled into the parking lot. As it backfired, Flin broke into a laugh, because it reminded him of the family car.

"Finally! It's about time!" grunted Sump as a dull, outdated blue bus pulled up to the curb. At the sight of the bus, his mouth slowly fell open. "This can't possibly be the bus we're taking. This thing's way too old! Why couldn't we have gotten onto one of those first buses? They were much newer than this relic!"

An unexpected thud from the front of the bus drew everyone's attention. There stood a tattered looking man, his face hard, more like stone rather than flesh. He had a wooden leg and leaned slightly to his left. His distinct rust-colored beard was parted down the middle and twisted at both ends, making what looked like two long ice cream cones pointing out both sides of his chin. His long, handlebar mustache matched his handlebar eyebrows, and a big, dull earring that looked like a large fishing hook hung from his right ear. A well-used smoking pipe stuck out of the top pocket of his shirt. He took a quick glance around and then hobbled back to the bus. He reached in, grabbed a small broom that was just inside the bus door, and swept the steps. He swiftly replaced the broom and traded it for a floor mat for riders to wipe their feet.

"Mornin' to ya, me ladies, and gents," he said in a strong, deep voice, and then politely bowed. "Sorry I'm runnin' a tad late. I ran into a bit of trouble this mornin' with the—"

"Oh save it!" spat Sump, giving the bus driver a nasty glare as he thoroughly looked him up and down. "We fully understand!"

"Would some of ye lads there mind 'elpin' me load these 'ere boxes under that there bus?" he ignored Mr. Sump's rude behavior and opened up the luggage compartment. He pointed under the bus, revealing several missing tips of the fingers on his hand.

No one moved. They all stood frozen, staring at their peculiar host.

ERIK OLSEN

He hobbled over to the boxes stacked on the walkway. "So, how is everyone this fine day?" he asked, picking up one of the boxes. His leathered face broke out into a smile, a sparkle glinted across his gold front tooth.

Mr. Sump glared at the bus driver from a safe distance.

"You heard him boys! Let's get these boxes loaded," called Head Revels as he made his way over and started to help load.

Mr. Sump hurried onto the bus then popped his head out of one of the front windows. "Oh, and make sure you're extremely careful with my bags, the ones their made of alligator skin! Oh, and another thing, how many others will be joining us on this dilapidated old bus?"

"Others, Sir?" grunted the bus driver confused, carrying two large bags.

"Oh, you know what I mean," groaned Sump loudly. "Others, *the others*," he snapped, his hands flailing wildly in the air.

"Oh, ya be meanin' the Haunsdale students!"

"Yes, them!"

"Oh, I was told ta plan on about thirty or so Haunsdale students, and I believe somewheres around ten from Stockhaus."

"I need to know now, because I want my own seat."

"Ya should be fine sir," politely replied the driver.

Sump immediately picked out a seat just behind the driver's seat and dusted it off.

"I thank ye all for 'elpin' me!" the driver said once the bus was all loaded. "Me and ol' Inga 'ere!" he said, patting the side of the bus, "Welp, we's asked ta take these 'ere lunches for everyone. The ol' girl's the biggest in 'er fleet, she is!" he said proudly.

"Where are you guys from?" Flin asked a boy, as he and the others made their way onto the bus.

42

"We're from Haunsdale!" said the boy with a swift tongue in a deep Irish accent.

"Oh, where's Haunsdale?" Flin inquired.

"It'd be right here in Dublin. And where might you ull be from?"

"A school called Stockhaus in the United States. Have you heard of the United States?"

"Oh sure, who hasn't?" he laughed. "By the way, me name's Cretchit, Cretchit Tronsel. And that there lad, he be my father," he said pointing to an extremely tall, spindly man. "And what might your name be?" asked Cretchit, picking up a bag.

"Flin, Flin Newby!" he held out his hand.

"Nice ta know ya, Flin Newby!"

"You too," Flin smiled.

A smaller and much newer shuttle bus pulled up behind them. The door opened and out came a dozen Irish girls in matching uniforms, followed by six Irish boys.

"Whoa," whispered Pilt, nudging Flin, "Now those are some gorgeous girls, don't ya think?" he blatantly gawked.

"Yeah, Pilt, but stop with the drooling," Flin said, lifting Pilt's jaw closed. "Well, the boxes are all loaded. Should we get on?"

They climbed aboard the bus and looked around. "Hey, let's sit across from those girls back there," Pilt said, quickly shuffling through the crowded bus and trying to get to the seats before someone else did. "Hi!" he said giddily as he dove into the seats across from the two girls, Flin following suit.

The two girls turned their backs to Pilt and giggled. "Wow! You're really smooth, Pilt," Flin whispered sarcastically.

"Hey, a . . . nice a . . . nice day," Pilt stumbled for words, and the girls giggled again. "They do speak English, don't they Flin?" mumbled Pilt.

"Yeah, but apparently you don't," Flin turned to look out the window to hide his amusement.

Parcell and Ruel walked onto the bus a little too casually. Parcell was trying to hide something behind his back.

The bus driver was the last to board. He started to sit, then brusquely stood up, cleared his throat and faced his passengers. "Oh, I almost forgot, sorry 'bout that. My name's Luftin," he introduced himself. "I'll be your bus driver for the day."

"I'm Head Revels, and it is nice to meet you," Head Revels said from the front seat on the right as he stood to shake the man's hand. Mr. Luftin reached out to grasp hands, and the sleeve of his shirt slid up his forearm, exposing a waving pirate's flag with a skull and cross bones.

Luftin started the bus, and the students still standing in the aisle quickly dropped into the nearest empty seat. One of the Haunsdale boys took the empty seat next to Mr. Sump.

"Not a chance! There are other seats in the back; go find one!" scowled Sump, shoving the boy off the seat and onto the aisle floor.

Parcell and Ruel burst into devious laughter from the back seat.

"What do you think those two are up to?" mumbled Pilt.

"I don't know, but knowing them, it's definitely not good," Flin glanced back over his shoulder.

Before pulling away, Mr. Luftin quickly wiped down the bus's gages and began humming.

"You're not planning on doing that all morning are you?" grimaced Sump.

"Do what all mornin'?" asked Luftin, furrowing his forehead, which made his handle bar eyebrows curl up at the ends.

"That awful noise you're making!" barked Sump.

"Oops, sorry 'bout that," he apologized earnestly. "Habit I guess. I usually hum ever' mornin' when I'm out on the sea in me little boat, Ike," he said with a joyful smile.

"Well, yippy," grumbled Sump under his breath and folded his arms, turning toward the window.

It was still dark outside as their bus pulled away from the curb. As they drove toward the coast, the sky turned from a dark blue to a light azure with a hint of teal.

"Don't you think Ireland's pretty?" Sam asked, turning around in her seat to face Pilt and Flin who were in the row just behind her. "And those debates, don't you think they were amazing? I had so…. Much fun."

Flin nodded while staring out the window, but Pilt was busy gazing in the direction of the Irish girls. With eyes glazed, again he attempted to flirt.

"Tootle-loo!" Pilt said, waving his fingers in a row, making a complete fool of himself.

"What do you guys think?" Sam pressed. Once he noticed Sam glaring back at him, Pilt swiftly tucked his hands under his legs and stared out the window. He started to whistle. "Yeah, I can't wait to get home either," played Pilt dismissively.

"What! Pilt, I didn't say anything about getting home. And who were you just waving at?" she looked around suspiciously.

"Oh, you thought I was, I was waving, when I was doing this with my fingers?" he stuttered as he laughed. "I wasn't really waving. I was just, just doing this, you know, like, like when I practice the piano!"

"But, you don't play the piano, Pilt!" her eyes narrowed. "Well, anyways!" she said, now directing all her attention at Flin. "Flowell and I were just wondering, do you think our bus driver dressed up like a pirate, or do you think he really is a pirate?"

Flin sat up in his seat and looked at the back of Mr. Luftin's tattered, striped shirt and fishing hook earring. "I don't know. He seems pretty real to me, and he does have a wooden leg," he added, as if that finalized it.

"You're humming again!" Sump again could be heard whining again at the bus driver.

"Oops, sorry! I'll try hard not to," apologized Mr. Luftin.

"Yes, please do that," snipped Sump.

"Either way, I'm good with him," said Pilt, now curiously watching Mr. Luftin's every peculiar move. "He was nice to us as we loaded boxes on the bus, don't you think, Flin?"

Minutes later, when Pilt could see Flowell and Sam were back in deep conversation, he again turned to the Irish girl sitting on the other side of the aisle. "So, where are you from?" he whispered.

She turned her head slightly in his direction. "We're from right here in Dublin," she replied with an accent, then broke out giggling along with the girl next to her.

Pilt's head turned to Flin but he made sure his eyes remained glued to the back of Sam's head. "Did you hear that cute accent?" he oozed in whisper. "I don't know if I can handle it, Flin!" He turned back to her. "Did you like the debates, *eh*?"

"I'm sorry, what did you say?"

"You know, the debates that everyone attended, *eh*."

Again she and her friend broke out into giggles.

"What's so funny, *eh*?" he asked.

"We're not part of the debate team," she said trying not to smile. "We're an Irish dance team. We won Ireland's dance competition, so we get to go on this ocean excursion with our school's debate team."

"That's cool, *eh*!" responded Pilt, nudging Flin in the ribs. "I too know quite a few dance moves."

"Ya do?" she said excitedly and leaned closer to him.

"Oh, yeah," Pilt said confidently. "Back home I do quite a bit of dancing, *eh*."

Flin jerked Pilt around by the ear. "What are you telling her? You can't dance! You trip over your own two feet!"

"But, don't you remember, Flin? I can do the do-si-do," whispered Pilt.

"Yeah, but that's only a small part of one dance. And what's with you saying "eh" all the time like you're Canadian, *eh*?" Flin mocked.

"I can't help it! They have the cutest little accent," he said, glaring out the corner of his eyes at the girls.

"What happens when they find out your accent's fake, and that you really don't know how to dance? Did you think of that?" Flin was growing agitated.

"Don't worry, after today's over and we head home, they'll never see me again anyways."

"Okay, but you're digging your own grave," Flin paused then asked in a hush looking at the back of Sam's head, "Wasn't it just the other day when you saw Sam talking to that boy alone in the hall at school, and he gave her a hug that lasted forever, and you said to me, and I quote, 'Sam's the girl for me!' You know Sam likes you, too. What do you think she'll do when she sees that you're flirting with other girls, eh?"

Pilt ignored the question, and instead, engaged again in conversation with the two girls.

"Hm," sighed Flin, shrugging his shoulders as he turned back to the window.

"Why do all these foreigners have to dress so funny?" Parcell's loud voice came from the back of the bus. "And what's up with their stupid accents?"

"Great!" said Flowell folding her arms in disgust, "there goes Parcell. It was only a matter of time…."

Parcell got no reaction from the Haunsdale students in the back of the bus. This seemed to infuriate him even more.

"What's wrong with you?" Parcell asked one of the smaller Haunsdale boys. "Your mama forget to feed ya or something?"

Flin spun around. "Parc—" is all that he managed to get out. Flowell had jerked him by the back of his shirt collar.

"Flin!" she scolded. "You know it will only make things worse! You'd just be wasting your breath with Parcell. He's a big, dumb, jerk!"

"But, Parcell's embarrassing all of us!" Flin hissed angrily, jerking his shirt away from Flowell's grip. Uncontrollably Flin turned back at Parcell, "Parcell, why don't you just shut up and leave the other students alone!"

"Ew . . . is that Newby up there?" Parcell asked, getting up from his seat. "If you're so tough, Newby, why don't you come back here and try making me shut up?"

"See, you didn't listen," Flowell muttered. "Now you've only made things worse!"

"Parcell," taunted Pilt, removing his eyes from the Irish girls for the first time. "Flin already cleaned your clock once before outside Mr. Strubble's classroom, or did he hit you so hard that you don't remember, or are you really just as stupid as they say you are?"

"Shut up, Pilt, you whiny good for nothing little pig!" roared Parcell, now fire engine red in the face. With his fists doubled up he quickly made his way up the aisle toward Flin and Pilt.

Flowell shook her head. "Oh, you're good, Parcell. Not! What a seriously dumb answer."

"Like I'd care what you'd think," barked Parcell back at Flowell.

Just then the bus made several unexpected sudden turns, jostling everyone and forcing them back to their seats, including Parcell.

"This is definitely the worst ride I've ever been on!" grumbled Sump, loudly, over the chattering students.

"Sorry!" Mr. Luftin called back over his shoulder. "I'm doin' my best. It's these darned ol' roads. They're jist too tight for ol' Inga!"

"Why am I not surprised to hear you say that?" barked Sump.

"See, off in the distance, that there lighthouse against the shore?" Mr. Luftin hollered back, pointing. "That there'd be my place!" he said proudly, resuming his humming.

Flin glanced to get a better look. The old lighthouse looked abandoned. There were piles of rubble around the foundation that had sloughed off, and the roof was in desperate need of re-shingling.

"Tanight, I'll drag up me nets," said Luftin. "Always lots of fresh crab and lobsters this time a year. Good eaten they are. Oh, and there's these white tail fish that ya—"

Sourly, Mr. Sump turned to the window, "Yippy! Enough! We get it already, but you're being paid to drive the bus, not play tour guide."

Chapter Four

ENGULFED

The bus started to bounce recklessly back and forth across the road.

"Are you intentionally driving as poorly as you can?" whined Mr. Sump, pale-faced.

"'Tisn't me drivin'!" groaned Mr. Luftin, fighting with the steering wheel and trying to regain control. "'Tis possible we 'ave a blown-out tire, or something!"

The bus swerved uncontrollably down the steep hill approaching a sharp curve. The rear wheels of the bus screeched around the tight corner, hanging two of its passenger-side wheels out over the edge of the cliff with the ocean water just a few hundred feet below. Mammoth boulders came plummeting down the steep mountainside towards the bus. One of the smaller boulders slammed into the side of the bus, jarring everyone inside, and shoving the bus closer to the edge.

"Earthquake! Speed up you idiot or you're going to get us all killed!" cried Sump.

"Look out for that, tree!" screeched Principal Vespar, half standing up from her seat and pointing through the windshield.

The bus swerved, barely missing the uprooted tree as it fell across the road. Gradually the larger boulders cascaded down the mountainside toward the bus, like bowling balls headed for pins. With each hit, the bus being forced closer and closer to the cliff's edge. Luftin yanked the steering wheel toward the mountain and gave the bus full throttle. "Everyone hold on! There's an abandoned tunnel up ahead!" he yelled. "If we cun make it into there we should be safe!"

Sump's eyes widened with fear as he slowly sunk under his seat.

The bus screeched as it veered off the main highway and onto a short gravel strip that was heavily infested with over grown brush from the mountainside. The bus plunged through the vegetation and into the darkened tunnel. As the brakes locked up the bus slid sideways and came to an abrupt halt. Blue smoke and the acrid smell of burning rubber filtered through the bus' open windows.

For a moment, there was nothing but silence and an occasional whimper. Then out of the darkness Mr. Luftin soothingly spoke, "We should be safe in here."

The mountain rumbled deeply around them, shaking the bus and causing dust and debris to pour into the end of the tunnel. Mr. Luftin turned on the headlights as well as the interior lights. There wasn't a single eye that wasn't filled with horror as the occupants glanced about the bus frantically.

Mr. Luftin put the bus back into gear and slowly crept deeper into the dusty tunnel and away from the falling debris. Without notice, again the bus began to bounce up and down.

"Now what are you doing?" screamed Sump from under the seat, gripping it tightly.

"It's another quake! An after-shock!" yelled Mr. Luftin, sticking his head out of the driver's window and looking up into the ceiling of the tunnel as several cracks developed from above. "Ever'one hold on! This is far from over!"

There came a thunder from the entrance as the tunnel from the rear began to collapse and quickly move toward the bus.

"GO! GO! GO!" shouted the students seated in the back.

Mr. Luftin stomped on the accelerator. The rear wheels spun out of control in the loose gravel, and then finally caught hold of large, dry rocks, throwing it forward.

As the tunnel ceiling above disintegrated, rocks of all sizes began to shower down on top of the bus. The light at the end of the tunnel quickly dimmed then went completely out as giant boulders of all sizes crashed on and all around them.

"What can we do?" shouted Head Revels over the roaring thunder, staring out the bus' front window, helplessly.

"We definitely can't go forward!" yelled Luftin, now throwing the bus into reverse.

"Hurry then, back up! Back up!" screamed Sump from under his seat.

Boulders the size of small cars dropped on top of the bus, crushing the roof little by little down on top of them.

"Forward, forward you fool!" again spat Sump. "Now back! Back!"

The tires peeled out in every direction, throwing gravel everywhere. There came a loud, **POP! A** large crack had developed in the tunnel floor just a few feet behind the bus and was quickly growing bigger. In a matter of seconds the rift traveled the entire length of the tunnel. The bus was now perched precariously on the edge of a chasm.

"STOP!" commanded Luftin. "Don' anyone move! Don' evin breathe! If we all remain calm, I think I can inch the bus forward if the weight's on the bus' front wheels. I need ever'one to *slowly* come to the front of the bus, one at a time."

Mr. Sump sprang from under his seat and flew to the front, shoving others aside.

"MR. SUMP!" hissed Principal Vespar, glaring bitterly, shocked at his behavior. "He said cautiously, and one at a time!" she scolded, throwing her hands on her hips.

It took a few nerve-racking minutes for everyone to make it to the front.

"Okay, ever'one hold tight!" Mr. Luftin spoke softly. He carefully put the bus back into gear then gradually crept forward.

Another sudden aftershock knocked the bus backwards, this time the back of the bus fell over twenty feet into the chasm and was pinned against the walls. The bus' broke out into screams and people toppled on top of one another as they fell toward the rear of the bus.

The lights of the bus now pointed straight up into the air. The bus squealed in protests as the sharp rocks from the chasm walls cut deep into its sides the further it slid into the ravine. From the rear windows of the bus, sparks could be seen showering down on the bus below.

"Everyone, remain calm," said Principal Vespar, holding tight to the pole next to the door.

Sump yanked on the door handle screaming, "Remain calm? GET ME OUT OF HERE!"

In a flash, all whimpers were drowned out by a riotous thunder as the mountain above collapsed down on the tunnel in its grand finale, forcing the bus even deeper into the earth.

"There's no going back that way!" said Mr. Luftin.

As the bus progressed downward the windows began to shatter from the rear and continued forward, showering all inside with glass. The bus was now trapped several hundred feet below the surface.

The silence was broken strangely by a calm voice. "Does anyone have a light?" Head Revels asked from the dark.

"I'm afraid we're wedged in too tight to get out! The tunnel above has completely collapsed down on top of us. There's nothin' we can do!" grunted Mr. Luftin as he hung tight to the steering wheel to keep from falling.

"Oh, wonderful! Just great! This is your entire fault, *Revels!*" snipped Sump, directing his comment towards Head Revels. "I knew we should have taken one of those first buses!"

Like hundreds of fingernails on a chalkboard, the screeching was relentless as the bus continued to be swallowed up in the Earth.

Just then the rocks let go and the bus fell through the air several seconds before plunging down into a shallow pool of mud. The bus landed on its back with headlights beaming straight up and through the jagged chasm which held it captive only moments before.

"Is anyone hurt?" Principal Vespar's voice quivered. "It seems as if this dreadful ride has finally ended."

Just then, the bus slowly started to tip forward.

"I'm not so sure of that!" yelled Mr. Luftin. "Ever'one quick, grab onta somethin'!" The front of the bus crashed down onto its wheels, sending a large wave of mud in every direction.

The headlights of the bus were now shining into a round, muddy tunnel up ahead. Slowly, with the current of the mud river, the bus on its belly progressively moved toward the daunting downward tunnel ahead.

"That doesn't look good," came one of the Haunsdale students.

Sump popped up from under his seat and ran to the door. "I'm getting out of this death trap before it goes any deeper!" Frantically he began tugging at the door as many others quickly lined up behind him.

"You're doin' it ull wrong!" hollered Mr. Luftin, quickly pushing his way through the crowded doorway.

"What's wrong with this dang thing? Why won't it open!" barked Sump.

"First ya need to lift that bar latch, and then pull the handle instead of pushin' it!" shouted Luftin.

Sump was too distressed to hear a word Mr. Luftin had said.

"Please, Mr. Sump, step aside. I know what's holdin' it up, and why it won'd open!" Mr. Luftin implored, trying to pull Mr. Sump free from the door.

The bus was picking up speed, nearing the muddy tunnel drop off. In desperation Mr. Luftin swiftly hobbled back to the driver's seat.

"Try the brakes!" yelled Head Revels from the rear of the bus.

Luftin stomped repeatedly down on the brake pedal. "It's no good, she's not slowin' down! The mud must be too deep!"

The headlights of the bus illuminated on the unavoidable path ahead of them—a twisting, downward-sloping tunnel with no end in sight.

"Is there no way we can slow down the bus?" Head Revels said panic-stricken, swiftly making his way to the front.

"I've tried the emergency brake! I've tried everthin', but nothin' seems ta 'elp!"

"What happens if you put it into reverse?" Head Revels proposed desperately.

Mr. Luftin rattled the gear shift and thrust it into reverse. "Nothin'! It's not doin' nothin'!"

He stepped even harder on the accelerator with the tip of his wooden leg, throwing a wave of mud in the air all around the bus. The bus crept up to the drop off and then tipped downward, entering the tunnel. Immediately the bus flew down several steep grades, rapidly rounding the turns like an out-of-control roller coaster.

"HOLD ON!" screamed Principal Vespar as the bus went around an extremely sharp corner, then launched off a cliff for what felt like eternity before landing back on its wheels.

The bus thundered around the sharp rocky walls, gouging deep holes in the side of the bus and throwing a trail of yellow and orange sparks behind it.

"I'm going to puke if the bus doesn't stop!" shrieked Parcell.

The bus had picked up enough speed that it had flipped upside down and was racing across the tunnel ceiling then back down onto the tunnel floor.

"Ever'one get under your seats und 'old on!" yelled Luftin. He futilely jerked back and forth on the steering wheel, trying to control the madness. "There's an incline a comin'. *We're goin' flyin'!*"

The bus hit the muddy ramp and projected itself over a hundred feet into the air, only to come crashing down front first into a bed of gravel. Sparks and bus parts flew everywhere as it finally came to an abrupt halt. The bus and its passengers sat dead silent in the pit of gravel.

"Is, is everyone alright?" asked Principal Vespar, after struggling to get up from off the bus floor, her breathing shallow and uneven.

Clambering up from underneath his seat, Sump whimpered, "Well I, for one, know I'm definitely not!"

The elderly head escort for the students from Haunsdale, Voss Yeg, called out, "Is anyone from Haunsdale hurt?"

It took a few seconds before anyone responded. Then came a soft voice from a timid boy, named Lane, "Just some bumps and bruises is all; nothing serious."

"Ever'one, please, jus' try and stay calm for a moment," said Mr. Luftin as he poked his head through a broken window and looked out into the precarious darkness that surrounded them.

Head Revels got up from his seat and attempted to open the door. *"No luck..."* he groaned. "We're going to have to pry it open."

"Here, let me help," said Fig Tronsel, lifting his frail-framed body up off of the floor.

Eventually with the help of Mr. Luftin the door was pried open. Mr. Sump forced his way to the front of the crowd. "I'll be the first to get out of this *nightmare!*" He took one step down the muddy bus stairs and his feet slid out from underneath him. He landed on his back, sprawled out in the mud. *"Piece of trash bus!"* He spastically stood and kicked the front tire, only to fall again.

One by one, they filed out of the bus and into the uncertain darkness. The only source of light was an unbroken headlamp and the flashing hazard lights.

"What is this place?" asked one of the Haunsdale boys, drawn to the safety of the headlamp staring out into the blackness.

"It looks like some kind of underground air pocket from an inactive volcano or something," Head Revels scrutinized the surroundings.

Everyone stood silently; fear of the unknown enveloped them.

"Owoo...ow, ow, Owoooo..." howled Ruel, impersonating a wolf.

"That's pretty good, but listen to this," Parcell also howled, causing an echo throughout the cavern.

"Shut up, Parcell! That goes for you too, Cendlebright!" snarled Parcell's jittery father, who appeared to have had one too many cups of coffee.

"This is no time for joking boys," said Principal Vespar in a serious tone.

"Why can't you just mind your own business, Vespar?" Sump's eyes narrowed as he scowled back at her. "I don't need some, some doddering old fool telling my kid what to do!" he said throwing his hand at her.

Everyone was now huddled around the bus' headlamp. It was Voss Yeg who asked the question they were all thinking.

"What are we going to do now?" she said in her deep Irish accent, looking into the adults' eyes around her.

The cavity grew darker as everyone encroached on the minimal headlight for safety.

"Do you think they'll find m — I mean us, down here?" Sump said nervously, joining in the conversation while looking to the others for reassurance.

"Well, the mountain collapsed down on the tunnel back there," Head Revels pondered aloud looking up above. "Even if they do dig it out, there won't be any trace of the bus. I think we should assume it's up to us to find a way out."

"Agreed!" said Luftin, firmly nodding his head.

"You've got to be kidding!" erupted Sump. "I — I mean, we'll, we'll all die down here if someone doesn't find us soon!"

"Mr. Sump! We have children with ears here, you know? And if we all have that kind of an attitude, we *will* die down here!" rebuked Principal Vespar. "Now, there's no sense in everyone wandering about and getting themselves lost, so until we've decide what we're going to do, everyone please, let's stay close to the bus. Is this understood?"

"Don't tell me what to do!" Sump said defiantly. "I'm plenty capable of thinking for myself, thank you very much! And the sooner these kids realize that death is inevitable, the bett —"

"That's enough Mr. Sump!" exploded Head Revels, finally losing his patience with the incessant whining of Mr. Sump. "You're an adult, so do as you please. No one's stopping you."

"You're darn right, no one's stopping me!" Without hesitation Sump stormed off into the dark unknown, his hands balled into fists. "Parcell, Ruel, COME!"

"I'm not going out into the dark," whined Ruel.

"If I have to go, then you have to go!" threatened Parcell.

"Ruel, you're welcome to stay with the rest of us," said Principal Vespar warmly.

He glanced around at the students staring back at him. "No, thanks," he replied with disgust, and then the two of them crept out into the darkness as well, talking under their breath as they followed Sump.

"How far down that tunnel do you think we traveled?" Head Revels asked Mr. Luftin.

"Oh, let me see 'ere now. Hmm, best I cun figure, oh… I'd say 'bout seven miles or so — give or take a mile either way."

"Well, I guess this is as good a place as any to set up camp," said Head Revels. "The first thing I think we should do is make a fire to provide more light and heat. It's a trifle cold down here," he said, rubbing his hands together and glancing around for something that they might could use to make a fire.

"How do you propose we make a fire? I don't see any wood," asked Voss Yeg.

Mr. Luftin spoke up. "Welp, I don' think thee ol' girl 'ere is goin' to do us much good anymore," he lamented about the bus. "We could strip 'er down and use some of the burnable items for a fire."

He made his way around the bus, gently brushing his hands over its battered sides. "'Tis a shame though. Never once did the ol' girl let me down. Poor ol' Inga." Small tears welled up in his eyes.

Moments later a fire was burning that had been made from the seats of the bus as well as other parts that would burn. There were sighs of relief as the flames grew higher and everyone huddled around the fire, watching the flames flicker off the distant walls of the cavern.

"This cave is much bigger than I thought it was at first," said Flowell with her back to the fire, staring out into the unknown.

"It sure is musty down here," complained Pilt. "'Smells like our old dog Howard when she gets wet."

Sam snickered.

"What? What's so funny, Sam?" Pilt asked briskly.

"Well, don't get mad, but you're starting to sound a lot like Mr. Sump, with your whining," she giggled.

"'Am not!" Pilt answered back furiously.

"And who has a female dog with the name, Howard?" she said incredulously.

"Well at first we thought it was a girl dog," defended Pilt.

Smoke from the fire gradually accumulated above their heads, looking like a heavy rain cloud. Flin glanced up. "Hey, did any of you guys just see that?"

"See what?" asked Flowell, looking up.

"I don't know what it was, but it was pretty big. It dashed right through the cloud of smoke." His eyes now fixed on the cloud, hoping to catch another glimpse of whatever it was.

"He's just pulling your leg!" said Pilt nervously. "There's nothing to be afraid of down — Aaah! What the heck was that?" he screamed as he ducked and placed his head between his knees.

Clear-winged flies the size of seagulls darted in and out of the smoke above, randomly dive-bombing the flames of the fire. Their long wings occasionally buzzed someone's head as they flew by.

"Head Revels, what do you suppose they are?" Principal Vespar asked with concern.

Head Revels placed his glasses to his eyes and studied them for a moment. "They appear to be some species of dragonfly."

"Wow, look how high the ceiling is up there! It's easily three hundred feet, don't you think, Pilt?" asked Samantha, who stood close to him, still a bit frightened.

"Yeah, you're probably close, but I'd say more like . . ." he paused for a moment and counted his fingers as if getting an exact measurement. "Yeah, you're close. It's about three hundred and eighty-five feet," he concluded confidently, looking around to see if any of the other girls were listening.

"Voss Yeg, we're getting hungry," murmured one of the Haunsdalegirls. "Don't we have any food?"

Overhearing, Mr. Luftin sprang from the back of the bus and into the light. "'Twas a good thin' thee ol' girl 'ere was totin' all the food," he said optimistically.

"That's right!" replied Head Revels, with a sigh of relief. "At least that's one thing we don't need to worry about at the moment."

"Some of ya boys there come 'elp me unload this 'ere food from ol' Inga."

Between bites of his sandwich Head Revels spoke up, "After we finish eating, Fig Tronsel, Mr. Luftin, and I have decided to explore some of the cavern to see what is out there. Everyone will need to remain here until we return."

"While you're gone, would it be alright if some of the boys stacked the boxes with the food in them against the cavern wall?" asked Voss Yeg. "They'd stay much cooler there."

"I think that's a good idea."

"Pilt and I will move the boxes, won't we Pilt?" volunteered Flin, grabbing Pilt by the arm and dragging him out into the dark.

"I don't like this, Flin," complained Pilt. "Why is it whenever you volunteer for something, it always means me too? Besides, I thought the boxes were just fine where they were — close if I wanted to eat."

"Oh Pilt, you're not afraid of the dark, are you?" snickered Flin, picking up a box.

"I'm not afraid of the silly dark! I just like being closer to the fire is all," Pilt protested, as he looked over envying those still huddled close around it.

"Did anyone else hear that?" Flowell asked wide-eyed and clumsily backing closer to the reassuring fire.

"Yeah, I heard it," Flin responded as he set down the last heavy box and glared out into the darkness. "It could just be Parcell and Ruel trying to scare us. You know how they are — always up to no good."

Principal Vespar swiftly made her way over to the crackling fire with a grave look of concern. "I know it will be hard, but I think we should all try and get some rest. For the time being, I think it best if the girls sleep on the bus, and the boys sleep out here close to the fire."

"Why? Why can't we sleep on the bus and let the girls sleep out here?" complained Pilt. Sulking, he threw a rock into the fire, sending sparks into the air. Samantha shot him an incredulous look.

Principal Vespar continued on as if she hadn't heard Pilt's complaint. "Boys and men, we'll give you a minute to get what you need from out of the bus."

A bit later, Pilt and Flin lay next to the fire, wildly fantasizing about what might be out there.

"I bet we're in some giant gopher hole," Pilt laughed in denial, a bit giddy from sleeplessness. He tried hard to block out of his mind the frightful thought of what could really be out there.

"Well, I think —" Flin started.

"Hello…!" came an echoing shout from the dark. It was Head Revels and the others, they approached the fire. "Well, we didn't see much," he said in a discouraged tone as he groaned and set down a makeshift back pack he had made out of seat fabric. "However, there might be something we missed at the opposite end of the cavern," he rubbed his hands together and held them over the fire. "It's so dark out there we really couldn't see much."

Pointing at a big pair of eyes rapidly approaching out of the dark, Cretchit called out fearfully, "Look! **Look!** Does anyone else see that?"

"I see it, whatever it is! It's coming quick!" exclaimed Head Revels, shading his eyes with his hand.

"It looks like a man, but why is whatever it is squealing like that?" asked Fig Tronsel.

"It looks like — Mr. Sump!" said Miss Lemons, shocked.

"I saw it! I saw something!" panted Sump looking over his shoulder as he came running over close to the fire. He took a dry gulp and then turned and glared back into the dark.

Overhearing all the commotion, Principal Vespar and Voss Yeg hurried out of the bus. "Mr. Sump! What? What is it? What did you see?" she asked alarmed, now searching the dark.

Sump glared out into the unknown with fear, his lower lip shaking, causing his goatee to quiver noticeably in the firelight. "I, I don't know what it was, but it was freakishly huge, *huge I tell you!*" he said, his body shaking as he threw his hands above his head, "with these, these, big, glowing, green eyes that lit up in the dark. It was just awful! Awful is what it was!" he nearly sobbed.

"I don't see anything," Head Revels said squinting.

"Look! I think I see it," Sump frantically waved his boney finger out in front of him. "Now it's over there! Now over there!"

"I think what you're seeing is just a shadow from the fire," replied Head Revels.

"Well . . . that one there might have been a shadow, but the other one for sure wasn't!"

"Where are Parcell and Ruel?" asked Principal Vespar, looking around with concern.

"Who cares? Besides, they left me high and dry. And it's none of your pesky business anyways, Vespar," replied Sump miserably.

"Is that your big monster?" Pilt asked, pointing at a small rodent that was running back and forth in the flickering firelight. It was jumping in the air and trying to catch the moths that had been drawn to the fire.

Immediately, the surrounding students broke out into a muffled laughter.

"Shut up, every one of you!" Sump scowled, looking around at each one of them. "What I saw was huge, *huge* I tell you!" he gestured with wide arms. He stood silent for a moment, admiring the camp that had been set up in his absence. "Well, I'm exhausted after all that. I'm going to get some shuteye," he headed for the bus.

"Oh, Mr. Sump! I'm sorry, but the bus is where the girls and the women will be sleeping," explained Principal Vespar.

"Says who?" demanded Sump, stomping his foot to the ground.

"We all discussed it after you left," she turned her head in the direction of the other adults for support.

"Wonderful! Absolutely wonderful!" Sump said, throwing his arms in the air. He made his way over to the bus' storage compartment and began throwing the baggage out of the cargo bay. He took loose blankets and clothes and made a little nest inside. He looked around at the spectating crowd and grunted out loud before climbing in and shutting the compartment door.

In the morning, Head Revels updated everyone on the findings of the previous night. "Well, last night after everyone was asleep; we went back out and searched high and low. The only access that we could find leading out seems to be right in the middle of this cavern. It's a funnel- shaped hole that goes straight down. Now, if we ration the food, we should have enough to last for four, maybe even five days."

With the fearful realization of the food only lasting a few days, rumors of starving to death immediately broke out.

"Quiet, please! I still have more to say." The cavern slowly went silent. "Thank you. As I was saying, instead of all of us going in search of a way out and possibly getting ourselves lost, I think we should just send out a few search parties at a time, and they can explore the possibilities," concluded Head Revels.

A disturbing pounding noise could be heard from under the bus as well as Mr. Sump's faint voice, in a panic, "Help! H-e-l-p! Let me out of here! Open this d —"

Flowell sprinted to the bus and pried open the jammed luggage storage compartment door.

"Where am I? Oh, this place still? Great! I thought I'd had a horrible nightmare was all. And why didn't you come the first time I called for help, young lady?" growled a disheveled Sump. He stumbled out of the storage compartment with matted hair and wrinkled clothes.

Flin spoke up. "I'll be in the first search party!" he volunteered.

"I'll go with him!" said Pilt, catching Flin off guard.

"That's nice of you boys to offer, but I'm not sure you're old enough. This could be very dangerous. We're still not sure what's out there," Principal Vespar said in a concerned, motherly tone.

"Well, I for one think that if the boys are responsible, they should go," said Head Revels. "There's possibly a lot of ground that will need to be covered, and time is a huge factor. So, I think that those who are willing and have fresh legs should go."

"Here, here," agreed Luftin, obviously tired of walking, as he sat next to the fire and deeply massaged his aching thigh just above his peg leg.

"Flin and Pilt, if you two go, you'll need an adult to be with you," replied Principal Vespar, more of a demanded.

"We're alright. We'll be fine!" responded Pilt, again shocking Flin.

"Now, each team will need a torch, so go and find something you can make a torch out of," instructed Head Revels.

Flin remembered seeing roots that had grown through the cavern's ceiling where he and Pilt had stacked the boxes. He called for Pilt, then climbed a short distance up the wall and broke off several of the roots. He handed them down to Pilt.

"These aren't going to work, Flin . . ." criticized Pilt.

"Just take them over to Head Revels while I climb down."

Pilt made his way back over to Head Revels. "Will these work?" he asked reluctantly.

"Yes! Excellent, Pilt! Everyone grab some of those roots over there that Pilt found." Pilt stood taller with a big smile.

"We can use the fabric off ol' Inga's seats to wrap around them. It's a heavy fabric, and should burn for a long time," said Luftin, proudly.

"Another good idea!" responded Head Revels pointing.

They took off for the funnel-shaped hole in the middle of the cavern. Once they got there, Head Revels tossed his torch down the hole. It fell several seconds before crashing to the ground.

"Wow! It's much deeper than we thought," he said with concern.

"Once we get down there, how do we plan on getting back out?" Fig Tronsel fretted.

"Well, the only way we'll all be able to get back out is if we help each other when the time comes," replied Head Revels.

One by one they descended down the hole with a rope Mr. Luftin had brought, until they all stood on the ground below. In the torchlight, several tunnels could be seen branching off the main corridor. The walls of the tunnel shimmered with moisture, and were cold and dark.

Head Revels spoke, "Okay, each party will split up and take a separate tunnel; we'll go to the left, and the rest of you take the tunnels to the right. Oh, and if you come to a place in the tunnel where it branches, make sure to take the one leading up. Now remember, the only way we'll all be able to get out of here when the time comes, is if everyone meets back here at the time we previously discussed so that we can help each other. Okay?" he nodded to everyone with a slight look of uncertainty, "Good Luck!"

Each party went its separate way. Flin and Pilt picked the first tunnel to the right and cautiously started their journey. It was hard to imagine what they might find — or better yet, *what might find them.*

"What do you think made all these tunnels?" Pilt asked apprehensively, seeing large gouging claw marks on the walls.

"I don't have a clue," Flin answered. He knew that if he told Pilt what they really looked like to him, some prehistoric man-eating creature, Pilt would likely turn back.

Warily they continued through the tunnel until they came to an extreme drop-off that practically went straight down.

"Well, what now?" asked Pilt, "Should we turn back?" he suggested hopefully, looking from whence they'd come.

"Well, it's a long way back, and we still have lots of time before we need to turn around. I think if we're careful, we should be okay to go down and check it out."

Carefully they edged down the steep drop-off. The dirt floor quickly turning to mud the further they went.

Pilt took several unpreventable falls, sliding further down each time he fell.

"Try holding onto the walls if you can," advised Flin, who was further down into the drop-off.

"Oh yeah, fine! Easier said than done, Flin," roared Pilt, way past frustration, choosing his footing more carefully.

"Maybe we should turn back, before we can't get out," said Flin somberly, seeing Pilt having a hard time even trying to climb down. He looked further into the slimy tunnel, the mud situation only looking more uncertain the deeper the hole went into the earth.

"Turn around? Okay!" Pilt agreed eagerly. He tried climbing back up, only to slip even further down with every step. "Crud! I'm just sliding further down!"

"Stop Pilt! Just — just stop for one second, okay?" shouted Flin up at the frantic Pilt. "Let's think this through. We can get out of here. We just need to think for a minute," Flin tried to calm them both. "What time is it now?"

Pilt scraped away at the mud on his watch. "Way past the time that we should have started back!"

Chapter Five

"SNAZZARDS!"

Okay! Let's see, we're back in this tunnel probably three or four miles, so—"

"No . . . !" screamed Pilt, losing his footing and rolling down the muddy hill, reaching out desperately for anything that might slow him down, including Flin's hand, but with no luck. He slid over a hundred feet down the muddy burrow before his body finally came to a halt.

"Crap! Crap! Crap! Crap!" agonized Pilt, his cry echoing up at Flin.

"You alright, alright,alright,alright?"

"I'm just peachy, thank you so . . . much for asking, Flin," Pilt replied bitterly. "Coming into this one-way tunnel was such a good idea! I'm so glad I'm stuck here almost in the bottom of this giant worm hole, and the top hundreds of feet way up there."

"I'm coming down. Just, just try and stay still, alright?"

After several minutes of slipping and sliding, Flin finally made it to Pilt. The torch's light on Pilt's face told the unnerving story. "Man Pilt, you don't look so good."

"Gee, thanks. We've definitely missed the time we were supposed to be back," said Pilt discouraged. He wiped the thickly caked mud from around his eyelids, exposing the whites of his eyeballs. Any other time seeing Pilt caked in mud would have made Flin laugh — but not in this dire moment.

"We're not getting out — are we?"

Flin waited to respond while he looked around the barren tunnel for what turned out to be, zero options. "I don't know, Pilt. But we won't know unless we try."

A short time later, Pilt spoke, "We've been trying for several hours now, and we're only farther down."

"Well Pilt, don't, don't go and blame m—"

"Shh, shh Flin wait! I think I hear something!" Pilt said looking up the tunnel then back down. "Didn't you just hear that?"

"Ew . . . Pilt, I didn't hear anything, but something all of the sudden really smells bad?" His nose surveyed the air and then landed back on Pilt, giving him a sniff.

"Well, it's not me, *okay?* I didn't do anything, Shees —!"

"Shh— Quiet!" Flin placed his finger to his lips. "Stop moving," he motioned with his hand. "I, I do hear something," he whispered. "Whatever it is, I think it's listening to us. It seems to stop moving when we start talking."

They sat silently in the mud for a moment and stared down into the dark tunnel below. Suddenly, they heard a shrieking hiss off in the distance that was so great it shook the tunnel.

"What was that?" Pilt asked in alarm.

"Whatever it is, it's coming our way, and fast!" Flin said. Again he searched futilely for a nearby refuge.

Another screeching hiss rose from below.

Flin took the torch and held it out in front of him. "I can see something moving down there!" he said, panic thick in his voice.

"I think I can see it too!" Pilt said, trying to scoot farther up, but with no success.

"I can see it better now," Flin whispered his voice cracking. "It's **huge** whatever it is! It has enormous blue eyes that look like they're glowing. Its head's so big that it almost fills the entire tunnel."

"Oh, Oh, Oh! I'll bet I know what it could be," Pilt said snapping his fingers and somehow unaware of the present danger. "In Biology, Mr. Strubbles, he said it was called a, a . . . I remember it was a cross between a giant snake and a lizard. They grow to be about sixty feet long. They're prehistoric though. What were they called, Lazzard, Blazzard, nope that's not it. Oh! Snazzard! That's what they were called, Snazzards —"Pilt said snapping his fingers and glancing down at the beast. "But it couldn't be one of those—they've been extinct for hundreds of years now."

"Oh really, Pilt? You sure about that? 'Cause I could swear there's one down there right now staring up at us, like it wants to eat us!"

"I'm not so sure about that, Flin; I mean if it's a real Snazzard or not."

"Pilt! It's real alright! It's right there! How real do you want it to be!" Flin said fervently, pointing.

Pilt leaned forward and squinted down into the darkness. "Whoa . . ." he said, hearing its hiss and seeing its eyes for the first time. *"Flin,"* whimpered Pilt, trying to back into the mud, *"what are we going to do?"*

"Shh, be quiet!" whispered Flin, staring down at it. "Hearing us is only going to rile it!"

The creature's head was roughly eight feet across. Flin and Pilt could see its large fangs dripping with yellow venom, almost salivating as it hissed up at them. It had sharp talons protruding out the ends of its numerous feet, digging deep into the mud, and allowing it to get good traction. It slowly crept up the slick tunnel toward them, slapping its enormous tongue against the walls and floor as it neared.

"It can climb up the *m, m, m, mud!*" sniveled Pilt, searching futilely for a place to hide.

"Pilt! You said it was a mix between a snake and a lizard, right?" Flin paused for moment to think. "If that despicable looking thing down there's like a snake, it should be practically blind. They sense their way around with their tongue," Flin concluded. "I think I know how it knows we're here— it can smell us as well as hear our voices."

The Snazzard, sensing the vibration coming from Flin's voice, began to come even quicker. It slithered up the steep tunnel then stopped within twenty feet of them.

"Oh crap," whimpered Pilt, covering his eyes with his hand in an attempt to hide. "It's gggetting cccloser," he said through chattering teeth.

"Pilt, I'm going to put out the torch," Flin whispered.

"What? But there's no way to relight it!" hissed Pilt.

"We'll worry about that later," Flin slammed the torch against the muddy wall. Sparks flew everywhere, agitating the Snazzard even more. The reluctant flame finally went out, leaving a few smoldering embers on the torch as well as on the ground around them.

"Hurry, bury yourself in the mud!" Flin said, working his way into the muddy wall.

"I'm already covered in mud!" snapped Pilt, staring helplessly down at the glowing blue eyes of the beast as they gradually got bigger the closer it got.

"I know you have mud on you," Flin replied impatiently. "But you need lots more!"

"What?" Pilt whispered back, his eyes glued to the giant monster.

"You heard me! Do it *now!* If that thing picks up on your scent, you're Snazzard food!"

"Snazzard food!" Pilt desperately began digging himself deep into the muddy floor, like a dog digging for a bone.

"Now don't move. Stay perfectly still, and whatever it does, stay quiet!"

The Snazzard, losing their scent, viciously moved forward. Pilt felt every step the Snazzard made and squirmed to burrow himself even deeper.

"Pilt, stop moving!" came Flin's garbled voice through the muddy wall.

Slowly, the Snazzard crawled up to where they lay hidden. Its long tongue slithered out of its mouth and rabidly licked at the mud. Its head coiled back high in the air as it let out numerous horrendous hisses at the ground below. It struck down at the muddy floor and walls trying to unearth the boys, then repeatedly drove its head deep into the soft muddy wall. Finally, it made contact with Flin's body and threw him several feet into the air. He landed gruesomely on the tunnel floor. The Snazzard lunged down after him, its head ramming him hard in the back. It raised a front foot then thrashed down on top of him stabbing him deep in the back with one of its sharp talons.

"Ahhhhh!!!" screamed Flin in pain.

The Snazzard grasped Flin in a claw. He wrestled to break free. Finally, the wet, slippery mud helped him to escape. Flin scrambled away from the Snazzard and treaded further down the mud tunnel, every movement riddled with pain. The large Snazzard tried turning around in the narrow tunnel to pursue after him, but the tight tunnel restricted its enormous body.

Flin spotted the remaining glowing embers of the torch and yanked it out of the mud. The Snazzard was slowly backing down the tunnel now toward him. Flin frantically blew at the torch's embers until the few remaining embers had spread like a wildfire and were now more a scorching red branding iron. Flin waited for the huge body of the Snazzard to pass, then cocked back the torch like a baseball bat and swung it at the Snazzard's head, hitting one of its eyes. The Snazzard immediately became enraged and jerked back its head, colliding with the tunnel above. Mud debris broke free from the ceiling and came crashing down on top of Flin as well as the Snazzard. Viciously enraged, it stormed after him, letting out a profane hiss. Orange and green blisters rapidly spread across the damaged eye. The Snazzard's head again lunged at Flin, sending him and the torch hurling even further down the tunnel.

The Snazzard now focused on Pilt. It let out an ear-piercing screech that caused the tunnel to quiver and shake as it quickly headed back up the tunnel.

Pilt's heart pounded hearing the fuming hiss as well as feeling the hammering footsteps as the Snazzard quickly approached him.

Again the Snazzard plunged its head under the surface in hopes of uncovering its prey.

"Ow!" Pilt was unable to suppress his cry of pain as the Snazzard's claws scraped across his body, cutting him deep.

The sound of Pilt's weakened plea only enraged the hissing Snazzard. It dove relentlessly down into the mud after him.

Gradually it moved forward in search of him, crushing down on his back with its multiple legs. Unable to find Pilt, it continued its search up the tunnel past him.

"Pilt, Pilt!" called Flin out of breath.

"Oh, my back…" whined Pilt, emerging from the mud. "I think that wretched thing broke my back…"

"Shut up!" said Flin breathlessly. "Just listen—the only way we're going to be able to get out of here is if we grab on to this thing's tail!"

"What? Are you freaking crazy? Grab on to its tail! Did you forget that it wants to eat us?" Pilt protested.

The Snazzard stopped at the sound of Pilt's voice, trying to pinpoint the source. Its twenty-five-foot-long tail swayed back and forth just above Flin's head.

"It's *way* too steep to climb back out," Flin said in a resolute whisper.

"Your idea really stinks, Flin," hissed Pilt.

"The tunnel's too narrow for it to turn around," Flin explained.

Just then the Snazzard unexpectedly took off up the tunnel. Flin dove for the back of its tail and latched on. "Pilt! Grab on, *hurry!*"

Pilt hesitated for a moment, and then hurled himself onto the Snazzard's tail. The Snazzard realizing that they had both climbed aboard began slamming its tail back and forth against the walls and ceiling. Suddenly the Snazzard came to a halt and reversed and now headed toward the drop off.

Flin spotted the glowing embers of the torch protruding out of the wall. He leaned out and snatched it up.

"Pilt, whatever you do, don't let go!"

Flin tightened his grip on the tail then forced the scalding red torch between the armored scales of the Snazzard and up against the hidden tender skin beneath. The Snazzard let out a vile squeal and charged back up the tunnel. In protest again it came to a stubborn halt.

"Hold on!" hollered Flin as he again thrust the torch deep into the already inflamed and swollen tissue. It let out a gut-wrenching screech and like a horse out of the gate it took off up the muddy tunnel even faster this time.

"Pilt!" yelled Flin over the abrupt bronco ride. "When we get to the top of the ravine, *let go!*"

"What?" yelled Pilt, holding on for dear life.

"Just-do-what-I-do!" Flin instructed.

Once the Snazzard reached the top, Flin jabbed it with the torch one last time and let go. The Snazzard continued down the tunnel like a wild mustang.

"Pilt! Let go! Let go!" screamed Flin as he rolled off the side of the beast and landed in the soft dirt. But in all the commotion, Pilt hadn't seen or heard Flin, and the Snazzard galloped away with Pilt holding tight to its tail.

"Pilt!" Flin screamed one last time as the Snazzard departed out of sight. "Dang it, Pilt!"

After several minutes, he grudgingly started his way back up the tunnel. Thoughts of Pilt being crushed against a wall or—even worse—being eaten by the Snazzard haunted him as he walked.

"Ow, my back . . . I think it's broken," came a moan further up the dark tunnel; cautiously Flin approached.

"Pilt? Pilt, is that you?"

"Who else do you know that would be down in earth hundreds of miles in the pitch-black?" he groaned sarcastically.

Flin sprinted up the tunnel until the flickering torch reflected off Pilt's muddy and frazzled face.

"Why didn't you let go? Are you alright?" he asked, helping Pilt up and looking him over with the red embers of the torch.

"Peachy! Just another day with Flin Newby."

Flin reached out and gave him a hug.

"Why all of the sudden are you getting so mushy on me?"

"Why didn't you just let go?"

"What do you think? Did you think I was riding that monster just for the fun of it? It's not that I didn't *want* to get off Flin! My dag-gum shirt got stuck on one of the blasted Snazzard scales!" Pilt saw blood trickling down onto the burrow floor and noticed Flin's back was bleeding. "Whoa, what happened to your back?"

"Oh, claw got me," Flin grimaced as he felt the inflamed tissue. "Let's get out of here."

"I won't argue with that!"

After what seemed like miles of steady jogging, Flin abruptly stopped.

"Why'd you stop?" panted Pilt confused, looking around.

"Please, no!" muttered Flin, sniffing at the air in front of them. "Pilt, do you smell that?" he said fearfully.

"Oh, Flin, that's not even funny!" Pilt gave the air a sniff, "Oh gag, I do smell it," Pilt muttered, putting his hand over his nose and looking for a place to hide.

Flin whispered, "It must have found a place to turn around."

"Yeah, and I'm sure it's even more ticked off now than it was before!"

"A little ways back, I felt a break in the tunnel wall, like some kind of a cavity. If we run, I think we might be able to make it!" Flin concluded.

"*Might* Flin? We *might* be able to make it? Oh… great!"

They both sprinted back down the dark tunnel in hopes of finding the hiding place.

Seconds later, the sound of pounding footsteps came from behind, gradually closing in on them. Flin frantically ran his hand along the wall.

"Where's your so-called cavity, Flin?" screamed Pilt, as the foul stench of Snazzard breath grew stronger.

"It should be coming up!" Flin hollered, blood dripping from his back to the floor.

Pilt hollered over his shoulder, "You're supposed to be extinct, you stupid thing! Get it through your head and leave us alone!"

The Snazzard's tongue picked up on the scent of Flin's blood, only hastening its pursuit.

"Maybe we passed it! And we're nearing that muddy drop off again!" Flin gasped breathlessly.

"That's really not funny, Flin!"

"I'm not trying to be fun— here it is!" Flin shouted as he swiftly grabbed hold of Pilt by the arm and jerked him in.

"That was way too close!" wheezed Flin.

"Now what, we're trapped in here and eventually we'll starve to death?" whined Pilt, looking around hopelessly.

Flin held up the torch, using what little red embers remained in order to see.

"What are you doing? What are you looking for?" Pilt watched Flin make his way around the small cave.

"I'm trying to see if by some small chance there's another way out of here. You don't think that nauseating thing just on the other side of that wall is just going to give up, do you?"

"That's what I was kinda hoping!"

Flin examined the wall between them and the Snazzard. "This wall between us and the Snazzard isn't very thick," he said patting it. "I don't think it's going to hold him out very long! Pilt, do you hear a rattling noise?"

"It's m-m-my t-teeth, okay!" Pilt chattered, wrapping his arms tightly around his upper body.

Flin shoulders slumped to his sides, "We might as well just sit down."

"I'm s-s-starving," sniveled Pilt as he sat down on the muddy floor.

"That's the least of our worries right now. That Snazzard out there, what do you think its thinking? It's smelling you and me in here as if we're Sunday roast!"

"I was hoping it went far enough up the tunnel to have eaten Parcell and Ruel," Pilt said, now sprawling himself out onto the floor. "Well, if we're going to be here for days—" he said, getting comfortable. "What the! What was that?" he squealed as he jumped up from the floor and scurried to the other side.

"What are ya doing, Pilt? Why you doing the potty dance?" asked Flin, startled, staring down at Pilt's fidgeting feet.

"That *thing's* gross, slippery tongue just slid through the crack and licked me!" Pilt said disgustedly.

Flin spotted the end of its long purple-ish tongue as it slowly retracted from out of the small cave. "Hurry Pilt, toss me the torch—it's right by you!" Flin said pointing, keeping his eyes on the ground.

"But it's burned out!"

"Just give it to me!" Flin said sternly. Pilt handed Flin the torch. "Now stand there and let it touch you again."

"What? Are you nuts? You stand here and I'll stand over there where it's safe."

"Just do it, Pilt!"

The long tongue again slithered through the gap in the wall and into the small cavern and began licking Pilt's ankle.

"Oh, Flin, this is *gross,*" whimpered Pilt.

Flin tiptoed over, where he stood hovered just above the Snazzard's tongue. He raised the sharp tip of the torch high above his head and then thrust it down into the Snazzard's tongue, putting a deep hole clean through it and sending blood in the air.

The Snazzard let out a horrendous squeal of anger as Flin repeatedly jabbed down at the tongue with the sharp tip of the torch. The shredded tongue swiftly retracted out of the room, followed by an evil hiss.

"Way to go, Flin! Now you've really ticked it off!" hollered Pilt, backing away from the wall that safely separated them from the monster.

The ground began to tremble as the wall between them began to crumble and small pieces of rubble fell to the ground in their small cavern. The angry Snazzard slammed its head against the outside wall, toppling more dirt down on top of them.

"What do we do? We're trapped!" screamed Pilt, trying to catch his balance from what felt like an Earthquake.

"I don't know! I'm thinking!"

"Well think faster! We can't just sit here all day! Eventually that wall's going to collapse in on us, or worse, that thing out there is going to get to us and eat us!"

"Do you have any ideas, Pilt? 'Cause if you do, I'm all—"

Just then large amounts of dirt fell on top of them, creating a basketball-size hole in the wall of the cavity. The Snazzard went silent for a moment. Seconds later, the tiny cave lit up in a beaming blue glow as the Snazzard pressed its eye against the hole and glared in at them. Seeing the two of them, the Snazzard wildly began slamming its head sideways against the wall, and then again went silent. The cave again lit up in blue as the Snazzard's eye again neared the hole.

Flin quickly crept to the hole and waited. He pulled back his arm with the torch in his hand, like he was holding a spear. When the blue glow was at its peak, Flin thrust the tip of the torch through the hole and deep into the Snazzard's eye. Another wailing echo of pain came from the Snazzard as it jerked its head away from the hole and tore the torch free from Flin's hand. Its head swayed frantically back and forth as if it had lost its balance. One eye was now covered with green and orange blisters, and the other had a huge gash with the torch protruding out of it.

"RUN FOR IT!" screamed Flin as he darted through the hole.

"Are you nuts?" screeched Pilt, following closely behind.

From earlier, big drops of orange and green puss from the Snazzard's eye glowed on the tunnel floor, laying out a perfect trail for them to follow as they sprinted away.

"We're dead! We're dead!" howled Pilt, looking over his shoulder and stumbling out of control as they ran.

"Keep running! It can't see much now, so just run!"

"You know," panted Pilt. "If we even make it to the funnel-shaped hole, we're not going to be able to get out!"

"I don't think you need to worry about that!"

"Why?" Pilt asked, hopeful.

"Because, we'll probably have been eaten by then!"

"Thanks for the *great news*, Flin. That's exactly what I hoped to hear!" belted Pilt.

The sound of the Snazzard running recklessly behind them quickly grew louder.

"How can that thing be gaining on us?" screamed Pilt. "It can't see anymore, right?"

They stopped momentarily to catch their breath. The Snazzard rounded the distant corner, with its head lowered, like a raging bull. The red embers of the torch were getting brighter as the rushing wind reignited the flame. Its tongue smacked wildly down at the floor as it rapidly approached.

"What are we waiting for? Run!"

They took off running through the darkness, the glowing puss on the floor now gone. Seconds later, SMACK! SMACK! They both crashed into a large boulder in the center of the burrow.

"Ow!" Flin said dazed, getting up off the floor.

"I think I've died!" moaned Pilt as he lay on his back.

"You will if you don't hurry and get up. Get up!"

Flin pulled Pilt up off the floor, and they both again took off at a sprint.

"What was that?" asked Pilt.

"Remember that giant rock in the middle of the tunnel, the one that we could see earlier with the torch? That was it!" wheezed Flin.

"That's it! We need to go back!" hollered Pilt as he turned and sprinted back in the direction of the Snazzard.

"What? Pilt! That's the last thing I thought you'd say!"

"Trust me!" Pilt said as he ran.

"Pilt, have you gone mad?" yelled Flin, catching up to him. "What could you possibly be thinking? The Snazzard's this way!"

"I said to trust me! I trust you a lot, right, Flin?"

"Yeah, I guess."

They came to the rock in the center of the burrow they'd recently crashed into.

"You know how you and I ran into this rock?"

"Yeah, hurry, go on," Flin said, making a circular motion of his hand as he looked down the tunnel for the Snazzard.

"Well the Snazzard can't see either, right?"

"Yeah Pilt! Just hurry and tell me your plan!"

Dirt and rocks from the charging Snazzard began to fall from the ceiling and walls.

"Well, you said it yourself— the Snazzard's probably following its own puss trail, right?"

"Right! Get on with it, *Pilt!"*

"So, we need to collect its puss from off the ground and smear it all over this rock!" Pilt finished, patting the rock.

"Pilt, you're a genius!"

"I know! How come you sound so surprised? I *always* have good ideas; you just never listen to me!"

"Well don't just stand there all full of yourself, get down here and help me do this!" Flin demanded as he scraped up the ooze.

Hearing their voices, the Snazzard moved even faster. It lowered its head and opened its mouth, revealing its gruesome fangs then lunged through the air at them.

"Move, Pilt!" screamed Flin as he saw the Snazzard flying through the air at them. He jerked Pilt to safety.

Crack! There was a colossal rumble as the Snazzard's head collided into the rock, followed by the rest of its body.

Immediately, the roof of the tunnel began to collapse in all around them. Flin rushed to the head of the unconscious Snazzard.

"What are you doing?" hollered Pilt over the falling debris.

Flin pulled the torch from the Snazzard's eye, jumped down and the two of them dashed away.

Chapter Six

FLIN & PILT RETURN

"Why'd you go back for the torch?" inquired Pilt as they walked.

"With the glow of the Snazzard's eye puss, I just thought it would make it easier to see our way out, that's all."

"Hey! Look up ahead! Is that the funnel hole we came through?" Pilt asked, elated.

"Yeah, pretty sure," responded Flin, his head cocked back to look up at it.

The two of them took off at a sprint.

"Hello, helloooo!" echoed Pilt's cry for help as they neared it. "We're way too late. They're long gone by now."

Something long and dangly, like a hairy snake was hanging down through the hole.

"What is that?" Pilt approached cautiously.

"It looks like some kind of a rope," Flin replied, daring to grasp hold of an intricately braided, multi-colored rope. "This looks like it's made out of hair. Are you thinking what I'm thinking?"

"Edgar!" the two of them belted out in relief. Pilt's mouth split into a grin for the first time in days.

Loud rumbling came from down the tunnel.

"Hear that? Snazzard!" screamed Pilt. Quickly he grabbed hold of the rope and began to climb up it spastically.

"It's probably just the tunnel still collapsing, Pilt."

"I don't care what it is! I'm tired of almost being something's next meal! That tunnel doesn't like me!" whined Pilt as he struggled up the rope.

"Could you at least hurry, Pilt?" Flin asked, looking around.

"Why, don't you like it down there?" Pilt teased after making it to the top.

Once out of the tunnel, they spotted the far off flicker of firelight.

"We're home!" hoorayed Pilt as they charged the flickering light.

Principal Vespar came running out into the dark with Head Revels right behind her. She gave the two of them a long, hard hug and a thorough look over.

"Thank Heavens you're both alive. Are you alright?"

"What happened to you two?" asked Head Revels. "Why didn't you meet back at the specified time like we had discussed?"

"Well, you wouldn't believe what happened to us if we told you," said Pilt.

"Go on, try me," Head Revels replied, curiosity evident in his eyes as they made their way to the fire.

"Well, we—" Pilt began to say. He glanced around at all the curious onlookers with big bright eyes, listening intently as well.

"Well, go on, tell me what happened," prodded Head Revels.

Flin walked away from all the excitement to get a drink. When he returned, Parcell was laughing, heartily. "You don't really expect us to believe that stupid story, do you?" he asked, holding his side.

Flin was confused. *Parcell and Ruel, they came back? Why?* Flin stood by Pilt, who was still trying to convince the others of his story.

"Then why's my shoe missing? And look, tell them Flin, tell them how your back got cut! Oh, oh! I know!" Eagerly, Pilt grabbed the torch and ran away from the firelight and out into the dark. "See, look!" he said, holding the torch high above his head. "Then how come the torch glows from the Snazzard's eye?"

The students all broke out into laughter. Pilt looked up to see the torch had lost its glow.

"Yeah, just like I thought!" Parcell said with a cynical laugh as he walked away mumbling something about what an idiot Pilt was.

"No! It's true!" Sump yelled, jumping up from a boulder at the opposite side of the fire. "What he just described is exactly what I saw!"

"You're just a crazy old man!" spat Parcell from the dark.

"I am not old, Parcell! Just well-seasoned is all…" Sump said, patting the top of his hair.

"He didn't seem too concerned about the crazy part," mumbled Sam, just loud enough that Principal Vespar overheard.

"That's because, he *is* a little nuts," confirmed Principal Vespar.

"I heard that Vespar!" Sump said angrily as Principal Vespar walked away toward the bus with her chin in the air.

Pilt finally gave up pleading his case and swaggered over to the boxes of food.

"Oh, Pilt," called Principal Vespar, seeing sandwiches in both of his hands. "Everyone's to only eat one sandwich per day. We're rationing the food so it will last longer."

"Please . . . can I have my other sandwich from yesterday too?"

"I'm sorry, but I'd rather you didn't," she said, staring back at him sternly with a half-smile.

"Alright..." he conceded.

Flin, who stood by the fire answering questions from all the curious students, started to make his way toward Pilt and the sandwiches. Flowell reached out and grabbed him by the arm.

"I'm glad you weren't hurt too badly," she said, bouncing on her toes and biting the side of her lip.

"Yeah, thanks, I mean—I'm, just, just fine!" Flin stuttered as Flowell moved in closer.

"Can I see how bad your back is?" she asked, moving around back of him.

"No! I mean—really, it's, it's fine."

"Flin, are you coming or not?" called Pilt frustrated.

"Yes Pilt! I heard you the first time. I'll be right there!" he paused for a moment and looked into Flowell's soft green eyes. "Well, I guess I'd better go and see what Pilt wants."

Flowell lunged at him, throwing her arms around him. Then, as quickly as she'd hugged him, she backed away. Flin stood dazed, and slightly shocked.

"Well, thanks," he said timidly as they both stared intently at one another. He walked backwards, tripping over loose gravel as he made his way over to Pilt.

"Why are you acting all goofy like that?" Muffled Pilt, stuffing his mouth with the last of his sandwich.

Sam dashed over to Flowell. "I saw that!"

"What?" Flowell said innocently, gazing into the fire.

"You hugged him!" she laughed.

"We're just friends—that's all. If you got lost or something happened to you that caused me to worry, when you got back, I'd hug you, too, you know that," she said, dismissively.

"So, you just said you were worried about him while he was gone!" Sam pressed for more details.

Pilt sat on the food box, licking his fingers clean. "Aren't you going to eat, Flin?"

"I'm not sure. I'm really not that hungry anymore."

"Not hungry! You've got to be hungry! We haven't eaten for over a day and a half!"

"Nah, you can have my sandwich if you want," replied Flin, walking away.

"Really? Cool!" Pilt turned to see Principal Vespar who was staring back at him from afar as she was in conversation with the some of the other adults.

"Oh Pilt, I'd rather you didn't," she said spotting Pilt as he raised the sandwich to his mouth. "We need to ration every last crumb."

"Alright," he said grudgingly.

"I'm beat tired, Pilt," Flin said. "I think I'm going to go to bed."

"Yeah, good idea. You need sleep. Hey Flin, before you go, tell 'em about my great idea!" Pilt looked at the group with a big smile.

Flin reluctantly stopped. "What? What idea, Pilt? I told you, I'm *tired.*"

"You *know*, how I saved our lives and everything like that!" he boasted loudly, unable to refrain from smiling.

Flin started to tell what had happened, when Pilt jumped in. "See, told you!" he snapped, cutting Flin off.

"Pilt, can I go on now?" Flin said annoyed. Pilt had turned a deaf ear to him.

"So I . . ." Pilt went on, greatly embellishing his tale of heroism. Flin slowly broke away to go and get some rest. He was awoken several times by Pilt shouting out some of the more climatic parts of their adventure.

Head Revels spotted Flin's open eyes and walked over to him.

"Sounds like quite the adventure you two had."

"Yeah, I'm just glad it's behind us," Flin stifled a yawn as he lay practically lifeless on his makeshift bed.

"The way Pilt's been going on over there, you'd think he might go out and try and find that old Snazzard again!" Head Revels chuckled, looking over at Pilt as he acted out a scene.

"I don't think Pilt's going very far after that," Flin said, returning Head Revels' smile.

"I know. I've seen him pretty squeamish back at school—and over a mouse."

Flin rolled over onto his back and stared up at Head Revels. "So, what did everyone else find?"

"Well, most of the search parties didn't get a chance to make it to the ends of their tunnels, so we're still not really sure what's out there," he sighed. "But, if we stay persistent and continue searching, I'm sure we'll find a way out."

"I'm still a little tired after all that," Flin said, hoping not to sound rude.

"Yes, you get some more rest," Head Revels said then walked away.

A while later, Flin made his way back over to the fire. He spotted Edgar sitting all alone and glaring into the flames. "Hey, Edgar," Flin sat down next to him. Edgar swiftly turned and faced the opposite direction.

"I wanted to tell you thanks for putting that rope down the hole for us."

Edgar stared back into the fire with a stern look on his face as a tear started to well up in the corner of his eye. He abruptly threw a rock into the flames.

"I don't know what you're talking about!" he said bitterly.

"Yeah, well, thanks anyways." He awkwardly patted Edgar on the back and walked away.

For the next couple of days, Pilt stayed close to the fire. "Darn dragonflies!" he muttered, obvious his nerves were wearing thin. "Why do dragonflies have to be down here?"

Since Pilt was determined not to go anywhere, Flin decided to explore the muddy tunnel the bus had come through. He was gone several hours before he returned.

"You find anything?" asked Pilt, looking up from the fire.

"Nope. It's still just a big, muddy tunnel. I'll never know how the bus ever made it through that crack several miles up. It's plugged solid. There's *nooo* chance of getting out *that* way!"

From a distance, Fig Tronsel, Cretchit's father, could be heard hollering, "I think we may have found something!" He came running toward the fire.

"What? What did you find?" asked the elderly Voss Yeg anxiously.

"Well, we couldn't really make out for sure what it was, but we went down one of the tunnels for several miles until we came to a huge drop-off. It was some kind of a cliff that was way too big to cross over, but we could see light off in the distance on the other side."

"That's great news! How long do you think it will take for the group to travel that far?" asked Principal Vespar, who had also been listening.

"Three, perhaps four days is all."

"This will be good news for Head Revels!" said Principal Vespar.

Later that night, after Head Revels returned, the adults held a council. Once all were in agreement, Head Revels stepped over into the firelight and perched himself on a large boulder. "Attention! Everyone's attention please!" he shouted. "In light of this new bit of information, we have decided that, as a group, we will set out in the morning in hopes of finding our way out."

The area around the fire began to buzz with the good news.

"So, tonight everyone will need to make sure all of their belongings are gathered up and ready to take with them come early morning."

Flin lay on the rocky floor that night, unable to sleep. He stared up at the dirt ceiling as thick clouds of smoke from the fire hovered high above. Almost everyone had long gone to sleep. A few feet away he could overhear the whispering conversation between Head Revels, Principal Vespar, Mr. Luftin, Fig Tronsel, Miss Lemon, and Voss Yeg.

Miss Lemon explained the food crises, "At the rate the food has been declining, I've figured there's only enough for two, maybe three more days. If we haven't found a way out by then, well, I—" she paused, her eyebrows raised with grave concern. "I just don't know what we're going to do."

In the morning, Mr. Luftin broke the silence, "Wake up ever'one! 'Tis time ta get up! We'll be takin' off in jist a bit! Make sure ya've got ull yar belongin's together."

A disagreement broke out,

"You carry your own dang bags! They're too heavy!" Parcell shouted at his father. "You packed more clothes than an old woman!" Parcell stormed off and into the dark.

Sump looked around desperately. He spotted Flin who was standing with one small bag strung over his shoulder.

"Oh, my poor old back," he moaned while glancing out the corner of his eye in Flin's direction.

"Flin!" called Head Revels, swiftly walking over. "Would you and Cretchit be in charge of carrying one of the food boxes?" Head Revels' eyes rested on Sump as he gathered up his precious luggage. "Apparently some of us brought more than necessary!" Sump glared back, a snarl on his lips. He bent over and jerked at the handles of his luggage; his chin held high as he drug his luggage across the sharp rocks.

"Pilt!" called Head Revels, "would you get the first aid kit from out of the bus?"

They all left their makeshift campsite and headed out into the dark unfamiliar tunnels of the underworld.

In only a short time, Sump began to tire and complain as he dragged his luggage from the back of the group. He could see Flin and Cretchit up ahead carrying the one box of food with two small bags on top of it. He scurried up behind them then looked to see if Head Revels was watching.

"Well," Sump said with a smug look, "it looks as if some of us don't have as much to carry as the rest of us, do we? So, a little extra weight's not going to hurt two — strong — young boys like yourselves, now is it?" he heaved his heavy bags on top of the food box.

Several hours into the journey, the group stopped for a break. Head Revels made his way to the rear of the group to check on Flin and Cretchit.

"What's this on here?" he questioned sternly, looking in Sump's direction. "Is this *your* stuff, Mr. Sump?"

Sump gave a grunt and turned away.

"If *all* of this is so important to you Mr. Sump, then you can carry it yourself," Head Revels shoved the luggage off the food box and onto the sharp rocks.

"Hey!" spat Sump, briskly turning around. "You have no right to do that!"

"Everyone up! Break's over, time to continue!" Head Revels shouted, disregarding Sump's remark.

Sump again began dragging his luggage across the sharp rocks, slowly falling behind. As the group distanced themselves, silence now surrounded him, making him nervous. "Aaah, to heck with most of this stuff anyways!" He tossed most of his luggage aside and ran to catch up with the rest of the group.

Several hours later, bodies again began to tire. "I believe we're all rather exhausted for one day. This spot here looks as good as any I've seen. I think we should set up camp for the night. Does anyone object?" asked Head Revels.

Sump mumbled something unrecognizable behind Head Revels back.

"Did you have something to say, Mr. Sump?"

"Yeah, as a matter of fact I do!" piped Sump. *"I don't ever remember voting you in charge!"*

Head Revels gave no reply, instead, turned to the general body, "Then it's final. We'll stay here for the night."

"Psst . . . Psst . . . Parcell!" Sump motioned with his hand.

"What?" responded Parcell, begrudgingly.

"Come here!" Sump said with a disciplinary scowl.

"Why?" murmured Parcell.

Annoyed at Parcell, Sump tromped over and grabbed him by the ear. He pulled him away from the others and into the shadows of the tunnel.

"Ow! You're hurting my ear, jerk!"

"Next time I tell you to come, you'd better come. Got it?" Sump peered around the corner to make sure no one was listening. "I don't know if you've noticed, but we're running out of food!"

"Yeah, and—?"

"Well, *I*, for one, am not going to starve to death down here in this, this dung hole. So, after a while, we're going to slip out of here and leave this pitiful bunch of people behind. Then, once they're asleep, we'll come back for the food!"

"What? What's the rest of the group going to do for food?" Parcell asked with uncharacteristic concern.

"YOU IDIOT!" snarled Sump sharply, again tugging on Parcell's ear and looking suspiciously around at the others. "Haven't you heard? There's not enough food to save all of us. We're all going to die down here. At least this way maybe some of us will survive. And I'd rather it be me than any of them, get my drift? I noticed a short tunnel back a ways that branched off. We'll stay there for the night."

Once no one was looking, Sump snatched up a torch and slipped away. Several minutes later, Parcell and Ruel slid out as well.

"Why'd you have to bring him?" erupted Sump, pointing at Ruel with his gangly long finger. Parcell gave a grunt with a casual shrug of the shoulders.

"That's just one more mouth to feed that I wasn't planning on. If food gets low, you'll be first to go!" snorted Sump, poking Ruel in the chest. "We'll go down this tunnel just far enough so that you two can come back for the food later. Oh, and we'll need some more of those torches. Better bring them all," finished Sump coldly.

Chapter Seven

PIT PRICKED & COCKROACHES

Sump, Parcell and Ruel crept back into the tunnel until they came to a small pocket-cavern.

"That's weird—look up! This cavern has no ceiling," said Ruel, staring up.

"What do you mean it has no ceiling?" asked Sump glaring up into the black hole, and scrunching his nose with a squint. "It's probably nothin', so you two can both just stop whining about right now!"

Hours later, Parcell and Ruel silently crept back through the tunnel to where the main group was all sleeping.

"Looks like they're all asleep," whispered Parcell.

"Looks like they've only got the one torch lit," Ruel observed.

"We'll leave our torch here and sneak in," said Parcell. He leaned the torch against the tunnel wall, and they silently crept in.

"Hey, Flin's junky old tote bag!" whispered Parcell. "What do ya suppose he's got in here that could possibly be worth totin' around?" Parcell recklessly began to go through Flin's bag. "Just what I thought, nothin' but garbage!" He reached deep into the bag and pulled out one of the three cigar boxes. "Hey, do you suppose he's got smokes in here?" Excitedly he opened it. "Dang! Just a bunch of crappy old rocks or something!" He picked up one of the pits with the multicolored thorns and studied it for a moment. Curious, he again glanced down into the box and started shuffling through it. "Rocks. Nothin' but worthless rocks and old pits. No money, no smokes, no nothin'. Just garbage!" He went to put the pit back into the box, when he felt it start to squirm in the palm of his hand. "Ruel look, it's alive!" he said in a loud whisper as he opened up the palm of his hand.

"Parcell! Shut up!" reprimanded Ruel, looking nervously around.

"But it's, its moving! Ow! The black thorn on that dang thing just stung me!" Parcell said, tugging at the thorn which was now embedded deep in the palm of his hand.

"Quiet! You're going to wake someone and get us caught!"

Parcell looked down into the palm of his hand. The four thorns had come to life and were moving around, like the tentacles on an octopus. The black thorn however, continued to bury itself deep into the palm of his hand. Frantically, Parcell commenced to pull at it.

"*Ruel, Ruel!*" he whimpered, holding out his hand. "*Hurry and get over here and help me get it out!*"

Ruel tried grabbing at it with the tips of his fingernails. "It's in there too deep!"

"Just hurry and get it out!" Parcell continued to whine as he danced around, tears of pain now rolling down his face. "Hurry, my hand's starting to kill me!"

The more Ruel tried to get at it, the deeper it buried itself into the skin. "How'd ya get it in there so deep?" asked Ruel as he pulled at it.

"I don't know! I was just holding it and it came to life!" Parcell's hand began to turn black and swell.

Ruel was finally able to pull the pit. "Man, that was in there deep!" He held the pit away from his body and the thorns of the pit dangled around. "Look how the thorns move!"

"Yeah, see that filthy black one? That's the one that got me!" Parcell whispered angrily, trying to shake off the pain.

"Look, you can see black liquid coming out the tip of it," Ruel said in surprise.

Angrily Parcell picked up a rock and threw it at the pit, knocking it out of Ruel's hand.

"You idiot! You just about hit me!"

Just then, Flin turned on his side while sleeping. Parcell and Ruel both stood motionless until Flin rolled onto his back and began to snore. Suddenly the white stone on Flin's ring lit up, whether it was from the torch's light, or from something else, it wasn't sure, but it caught Parcell's eye.

"Ruel, did you just see that?" Parcell asked sharply, pointing down at the ring. He reached for it.

"Leave it alone!" warned Ruel. "You've *already* almost gotten us caught!"

Parcell looked up at Ruel, and then back down at Flin and quickly slid the ring off of his finger. He turned the ring towards the subtle flames of the torchlight and admired it.

"Why are you taking Newby's junky ring anyways?" Ruel murmured, confused.

"Shut up, it's his *family* ring, remember? I heard Pilt on the airplane talking to Sam and saying how he'd waited thirteen years to finally get it, and now whiddle Flinnie's ring is gone!" Parcell gave a fake whimper and rubbed at his eyes.

They crept over to the box of food and picked it up.

"That's it, let's get out of here," whispered Ruel.

"Stop! We almost forgot the torches!" said Parcell pointing to the stack of them.

Ruel skulked over to the tunnel wall and gathered up all the torches. "Are you sure we should take *all* the torches?" he whispered as he looked around at everyone sleeping.

"Yes, *all* of 'em!"

He gathered them all up, but dropped one as he crept away.

They returned to Sump in the small cavern.

"What took you so long?" he barked as he hoisted himself up off the floor. He looked over at Ruel whose arms were bursting with torches. "Why didn't you get all of the torches?"

"This is all of 'em. We only left one unlit torch," replied Ruel.

"Then you left one too many, didn't you?" Sump scolded.

~~~~~~~

Flin woke early the next morning and stared up at the flickering torchlight that reflected off the tunnel ceiling. He laid thinking of the vivid dream he'd just had and how they'd found a way out. He rolled over to see who else was awake.

"Ow, what the heck?" he said as he lifted up his arm and examined it. There, buried deep in the back of his elbow, was one of the thorn pits, and the rest of the pit hanging from it.

"How did that get there?" he mumbled in pain. He pulled at it and tried to get it to come out. *How'd it get in there so deep?* He tugged at it, twisting and pulling, finally the tip of the white thorn broke free from the rest of the pit. "Ow!" he whimpered. He raised his elbow to the torchlight. There, under his skin he spotted the thorn fighting to bury itself deeper into his skin. *How'd that get out of my bag anyway?* He looked over his shoulder and at his tote bag, which was strewn about the dirt floor. He began to gather up the scattered items when he noticed his ring missing.

"Where — where is it! My ring, its gone!" Frantically, he jumped to his feet and rummaged through everything close to where he'd been sleeping as well as the ground around him.

"Pilt, Pilt, wake up!" he said, shaking him recklessly. "My ring's missing! Pilt, wake up and help me look for it!"

"I will after I wake up," moaned Pilt, half asleep.

"Where is it? I know it's got to be here somewhere. I was looking at it last night before I fell asleep!" He glanced around and noticed the box of food he and Cretchit were in charge of was missing as well. "The food! Where'd it go?" His eyes made a quick sweep of the cavern without spotting the box of food. He ran over to Head Revels, who was still asleep.

"Sorry to wake you, Sir."

"What is it Flin?" groaned Head Revels with a frog in his throat and unusual messy hair.

"Do you know what happened to the food?"

Head Revels abruptly sat up and began giving the area a thorough inspection. "We had the two boxes of food last night, right? Let's see, there's the one box. Now where'd the other one go?

Where's the other?" he said in a panic. "Well, there's no reason to alarm everyone just yet. However, we need to start looking for it," Head Revels said with worry imbedded deep into his face.

"I'll help," Flin said, and he ran back to get his shoes.

Head Revels woke Principal Vespar. "Varmelda, Varmelda," he shook her. "Do you know where the torches went? And, Mr. Sump, Parcell, and Ruel seem to be missing this morning as well."

She briskly sat up and placed her hand over her heart and with shaking hand placed her glasses on her nose. "And the food?" she asked warily, looking over her shoulder.

"One of the boxes is gone as well," Head Revels responded reluctantly.

"Good Heavens! I was worried about that. Last night I saw Mr. Sump eyeing the food closely." The look of sleep was long gone from her face.

"I'll go look for them. I think I can find 'em," volunteered Flin.

"I should probably remain here to keep an eye on things. Hopefully, they'll return with the food," said Head Revels with a look of despair at Principal Vespar. She nodded. "Okay Flin, you go look for them, but be extremely careful. And, if you haven't found them in a couple of hours, you turn around and come back, understand?"

Pilt could see the resolute stride in the way Flin was walking.

He jumped up. "Flin, where you goin'?"

"Pilt, you don't need to come."

"It has to do with the food, doesn't it!" It wasn't a question. "Then I'm coming with!"

"Wait!" hollered Cretchit. "I'm comin' wit yuz as well. I'm always up fur an adventure."

~~~~~~~~~

It was morning back in the small cavern.

"Well, let's just see how good you two did last night." Sump opened the box of food. "Well, well, what do we have here?" he asked as his greedy eyes peered inside. "You two didn't do too bad! What, what's that clicking sound? Ruel, are you doing that?" Sump scowled over at Ruel.

Suddenly, a giant winged bug the size of a large frog with wings dropped from the ceiling and landed on Sump's arm. "Ahh! Get it off of me!" he shrieked, flapping his arm like a bird and throwing the bug to the floor.

"What the heck is that disgusting thing?" asked Ruel. He squinted as he walked over to it, keeping a safe distance. "It kind of looks like a giant cockroach!"

"I don't think so, Ruel!" Sump replied coldly. "What's it doing now?" asked Sump. The giant brown cockroach reared back on its hind legs and began clicking loudly, beating its wings against its body.

"What's it doing that for?" asked Ruel with alarm.

Sump grabbed the torch and began smacking down at it.

"Stop!" screamed Parcell, showing his first sign of waking as sparks from the torch landed on the back of his bare neck and burned his skin. "If that torch goes out, we can't relight it!"

"Ha! Take that, you disgusting insect!" Sump triumphed as he finally squished it.

A loud buzzing like a swarm of bees came from up above.

"Now what?" Sump wondered as he held the torch up toward the dark sky. "Where is all that wretched noise coming from?"

All of a sudden, thousands of roaches poured down upon them from the ceiling above, hissing and biting at them as they landed.

"They're after our food!" screamed Parcell. He ran to the box and started kicking and smacking, trying to get the roaches away from it. "They're biting me!" He dropped to the floor and hundreds of roaches dive-bombed down after him. "There're too many—I can't see anymore!" he screamed and ran out.

"Parcell, get back in here! We can't just leave! We need to save the food!" shouted Sump as he battled. He trudged his way over to the box of food that was now covered with hundreds of roaches. He plunged his burning torch deep into the box, which caused the roaches to immediately swarm after him.

"I can't take it anymore!" screamed Ruel as his arms flailed wildly in the air, running out of the cavern as well.

Flin heard their screams coming from out of one of the small break-off tunnels ahead. "There they are!" he hollered. They sprinted toward all the commotion. "What's going on?" Flin yelled to Ruel who was standing outside the small cavern with a look of disgust. He held his arms tightly around his stomach and stared down at the ground.

They darted past Ruel and Parcell and into the small cavern where Mr. Sump was engaged in battle with an endless wave of cockroaches that continued swarming down from the ceiling.

"Get out! Get out!" yelled Flin as he looked to see the box of food now infested with dozens of giant hissing cockroaches. "There's no chance of saving the food!" He made his way over to Sump, who was covered in cockroaches and losing the battle.

"We have to get out of here!" Flin shouted. He grabbed Sump by the arm and pulled him toward the cavern exit.

Sump turned and realized that it was Flin who was tugging at his arm. Irately he jerked away. "Leave me alone!"

Flin bolted out of the cavern. An endless wave of profanity came from Mr. Sump within the cavern. Seconds later, Sump gave up the battle and staggered out, his face covered in blood, dirt, and roach droppings.

"The torches!" shouted Flin as he buried his face into the joint of his arm and charged back in. Moments later, he came barging out, again covered with roaches. Pilt picked up one of the torches and began beating them off of him.

Quickly Flin stomped out the glowing embers of the few remaining torches.

Sump briskly walked over to Flin. *"We didn't need your help, Newby!"* he scowled and walked away.

"Think this makes you some kind of a hero now, Flin?" Parcell asked bitterly, pointing with his finger.

"My ring!" Flin said, looking down at Parcell's hand in disbelief. "I wondered what had happened to it. You stole it!"

"Now, what are you accusing my boy of?" Sump stomped back toward Flin as he scraped off the last of the unrelenting roaches.

"Parcell—he's wearing my ring!"

Sump raised Parcell's hand and looked down at the ring on his finger. "If he's wearing it, it must be his," Sump said with a snarl, staring into Flin's eyes. "It's your word against his!"

"It's not Parcell's!" belted Pilt from behind the safety of Flin's shoulder.

"Oh, and just because you're Newby's little tag-along, Brisken, we're just supposed to believe you? Is that the way it is?" Sump accused. He pinched the last roach from his neck, tossed it to the ground and then stomped on it several times.

"I know its Flin's!" Pilt said furiously, stepping in front of Flin. "I've seen it dozens of times on *his* finger. It's his family ring that he got for his thirteenth birthday!"

"Got it for his birthday, did he?" His eyes narrowed; he turned to Parcell. "Why would you steal Newby's worthless family ring? If you'd have told me you wanted a ring, I'd have gotten you a nice, *expensive,* gold one."

"You wouldn't understand!" Parcell said angrily, doubling up his fists. "It has something to do with families—you can't just *buy* it. What would you know about families anyways?" Parcell slid the ring off and threw it down at Flin's feet, then stormed away.

Flin picked it up, cleaned it off, and carefully placed it back on his finger.

Sump, Parcell, and Ruel grudgingly made their way back to the rest of the group. Head Revels was nervously pacing back and forth at camp when he spotted Flin and darted toward him.

"Oh good—good! Flin, Pilt, Cretchit, did you find them?" he called in the dusky torchlight. "And the food, is the food okay?"

"Stop! Do we have to have so many questions?" rudely replied Sump, from the rear in the obscure darkness.

"Mr. Sump, is that you?" inquired Head Revels, glancing over the top of his spectacles and squinting into the dark.

"Of course, it's me! Who else in their right mind would be down here wandering these despicable tunnels with just a torch in their hand?"

"Good, you found them!" Head Revels sighed.

Sump, Parcell, and Ruel remained in the rear as Head Revels neared them.

"Thank heaven you're all alive! Is everyone alright?" He spotted the blood and filth on their faces. "What in the world happened to you?" he asked in alarm.

"It really doesn't involve you," growled Sump.

Head Revels glanced around. "Where is it?" he asked, looking for the food.

"Where's what?" murmured Sump, defiantly.

"The . . . the food, of course!" Head Revels looked about desperately.

"Oh, yes. Well, we encountered a bit of trouble," Sump mumbled as he turned to walk away.

Head Revels briskly made his way over to Pilt, Flin, and Cretchit. "The food, what's — what's happened to it?" he pressed.

"It's, it's gone," responded Flin, hesitantly.

"What do you mean it's gone? How could it possibly be all gone? It was nearly half-full!"

"It's like the boy said—it's gone!" snapped Sump.

"You, Mr. Sump, may have cost us all our lives!" Head Revels said heatedly. He turned to Flin. "Someone will need to be on guard at all times with what little food we have left," he said looking at Mr. Sump's back. "I'm putting you in charge!"

"Cretchit, me lad, 'ow much farther do ya think 'til we get there?" asked Mr. Luftin.

"It can't be much farther. I think maybe a couple more hours is all."

"On we go!" shouted Luftin, taking the lead.

"I don't feel well. I think those cockroaches must have made me sick!" belly-ached Parcell.

"You better stop with that whining, Parcell, or I'll give you something to whine about!" Sump said crabbily.

Flin didn't feel well either. His breathing had become heavy, and he began to stumble as he and Cretchit carried the last of the food.

"Flin, are you alright?" asked Principal Vespar, who noticed Flin's occasional stammer.

"I'll be fine. I think I'm just a little tired," he answered.

"Head Revels!" called Principal Vespar, making her way toward him. "I know we're close, but I think maybe it would be best if we stopped here for a while!"

"But, we should be just about to the cliff!" responded a very anxious Head Revels.

"But, I think some of us may need to rest," Principal Vespar said, glancing with concern in Flin's direction.

"Oh, I see," Head Revels agreed, noting Flin's unhealthy appearance. "Yes, perhaps you're right, Varmelda." He turned and shouted, "We'll stay here for a brief while and rest!"

Flin set the box of food down and immediately slid down the tunnel wall, his breathing still very heavy.

"What's bothering you, Flin?" asked Miss Lemons, the dance teacher, bending down. "You look a bit pale. Are you not feeling well? Can I do anything for you?"

"It's just my stomach—it keeps churning. I'll be fine." Flin took a dry gulp. "And my left hand for some reason keeps throbbing. It feels like a rock got dropped on it!"

"Let me see your hand," she said. "Yes, you're right, it does feel a tad swollen, and the tips of your fingernails look slightly bruised and red. It's probably just an allergic reaction you're having to something down here," she concluded.

A short while later, both Flin and Parcell fell asleep, moaning with pain.

Hours later, Flin and Parcell both awoke and Principal Vespar, Voss Yeg, and Miss Lemons took it upon themselves to pass out what little portions of food remained. After they'd finished distributing the food, Principal Vespar made her way over to Head Revels. He could tell by the briskness in her walk and her tight face that she was going to be the bearer of bad news.

"Well, now there are only three sandwiches and two drinks left," she sighed, looking over her shoulder at the students.

"I know, I know," responded Head Revels solemnly, shaking his head.

A startling scream came out of Parcell.

"Parcell!" barked Sump. "Stop with that nauseating ruckus! How's anyone supposed to enjoy their meal with you screaming every ten minutes?"

After a few bites of his sandwich, Flin felt a bit better. He attempted to stand up but fell flat on his back. He stared up at the ceiling as perspiration accumulated on his upper lip. He went to wipe it off in the shadows of the dark, when he noticed dim colors glowing from his fingernails. "What the—" he shouted, each nail radiating a different color.

"What is it, Flin?" Principal Vespar ran over to see what was wrong. She placed her open palm on his forehead.

Flin quickly tucked his left hand behind his back.

"I'm a . . . I'm just fine, thank you. I, I thought I saw a big rat over there," he said as he gingerly sat up.

"Are you sure you're fine, Flin? You don't look so good," she hunched over and searched his pale face.

"Didn't sleep too well—you know, Parcell's whining and everything," he said, looking into her caring eyes.

"Well, as soon as we get the chance, I want for you to get some rest," she smiled and patted him on the shoulder.

"Yes, I'll do that." He waited until she was gone and then looked down at his fingernails to see five different colors glowing up at him.

Chapter Eight

PLEASE! NOT ANOTHER SNAZZARD!

From the rear of the tunnel, a loud thud shook the ground causing dust to fall from the ceiling. A frightened Principal Vespar spun around and glared out into the dark. "Did anyone else hear that?" echoed her trembling voice.

Parcell let out another bloodcurdling scream.

THUD! The ground shook again, only this time with more force.

"There it went again!" she said, even more alarmed. She placed her hand above her eyes, trying to avoid the torch's glare, and looked deep down into the tunnel they'd just come through.

"What is it, Vermelda?" inquired Head Revels, his voice full of concern as he rushed toward the rear of the tunnel.

"Please, not again," whimpered Pilt, backing into the wall.

"What on earth could have caused that?" muttered Principal Vespar, "An earthquake possibly," she guessed.

"Pilt! Come help me up," moaned Flin. Pilt's eyes remained glued to the rear of the tunnel as he made his way over to Flin and helped him up. Flin was now stiff as a board. "Are you thinking what I'm thinking?" Flin asked, looking into Pilt's non-responsive eyes.

"Yeah . . . another blasted Snazzard."

"Then, we have to do something! Cretchit!" called Flin. "How far do you think it is to the end of the tunnel?"

"That cliff should jist be up ahead, maybe even jist around this next corner 'ere!"

Flin desperately searched the tunnel, his eyes stopping on the pile of torches. "If only we had more rope!"

Edgar overheard and timidly walked over. His shaggy white hair hid his eyes. He reached into his bag and pulled out several short pieces of rope and dropped them in front of Flin.

"That's awesome, Edgar," said Flin. He gingerly hobbled back to Principal Vespar and Head Revels.

"Flin!" said Principal Vespar, surprised to see him up. "You should be resting!"

"I'm pretty sure that 'thud' is coming from a Snazzard."

"Please no, not now. We're so close to getting out," cried Principal Vespar, placing her hand over her mouth.

"Listen, I know this sounds crazy, but I have a plan," Flin reassured her. "I'll need both Mr. Luftin and Pilt to help me." Before he could say anymore, Pilt was at his side. "But, we'll need everyone else out of the tunnel," Flin said nervously.

"You sure you're up to this Flin?" Head Revels asked skeptically. The thuds grew louder.

"I don't know, Flin. This could be far too dangerous," said Principal Vespar, her voice heavy with concern. For the first time since they had been down there, Flin really looked at her. Her soft wrinkles were becoming harsh and her normally well-groomed hair was in disarray. The stress was definitely taking its toll.

"Look," he said soothingly, "Pilt and I are the only ones who have dealt with a Snazzard before. Now, I know we're not—"

"Flin?" Pilt interrupted, tugging at his arm. All of the color drained from his face as he stared apprehensively down into the dark burrow. "Can you smell that?"

Flin nodded. "Look, we don't have much time. We need to get everyone out. Please, trust us," he implored, his eyes red and slightly swollen from fever.

"I think I know where we can go," Head Revels said in a panic, feeling the ground shake like the aftermath of nearby thunder. "There's a small, makeshift cavern just up the tunnel a ways. I think we can all squeeze into it. Mr. Luftin?" called Head Revels.

"Sir?" said Luftin, as if reporting for duty.

"Flin here could use your help."

Luftin looked confused. "Flin, Sir Revels?" he asked, looking down at the young boy.

"Flin here can explain. Principal Vespar and I need to get the others to safety."

"Quick, everyone, follow us!" ordered Principal Vespar.

"Welp, Flin, what might yar plan be?" asked Mr. Luftin, rubbing his hands together and drawing attention to his missing fingertips.

Flin quickly explained his crude plan. "And you'll need to get its attention!"

"Can do!" Luftin replied. "But jus' one thin', once it duz come after me, well, ya know, wit' me wooden leg und ull, I'm not as spry as I once was."

"Once you've gotten its attention, you go up and hide with the rest of the group!"

"I'm not much for hidin', but I guess I cun do that!"

Flin ran back up the tunnel at a sprint. "Quick, Pilt! We need to tie the torches together."

"But we'll never get all these torches tied together in time. And besides, these torches will never hold our weight!"

"Just trust me—you're the one who gave me the idea!"

They hurried and tied them all together.

"Aren't we going to put the torches over the cliff?" asked Pilt, his confidence in the plan diminishing.

"Not yet. We need to go back and help Mr. Luftin get that Snazzard to chase after us."

"What? Why do I ever listen to you, Flin?" They took off down the tunnel. As they neared Mr. Luftin could be heard screaming frantically up at the beast. "Cum und get me ya diseased, ugly, unsightly, forsaken creature!"

The Snazzard's glowing blue eyes stared fiercely back at them.

"Okay!" hollered Flin. "This is perfect! This is exactly what we want to happen!"

"Perfect?" questioned Pilt, staring down at the angry Snazzard. It hissed furiously back at them. "You call this perfect? Your definition of perfect must be totally different than mine!"

"Pilt! Quick, I need some blood!" Flin looked around.

"Not from me, you don't!" Pilt squirmed away.

"Hurry, we need something sharp! Pilt, your belt! Hurry, take it off!"

"What? Why?"

"Just do it!"

Mr. Luftin was busy throwing rocks up at the Snazzard; it was threatening to charge him.

"Ya oversize' slug, cum und get me!" he growled, his pirate persona surfacing.

The Snazzard's head struck down after Luftin. He turned and hobbled away from the creature as quickly as he could. Then, from a safe distance, he continued to antagonize it.

Pilt jerked his belt free from his pants and handed it to Flin, who jabbed the sharp catch deep into the tip of his finger, puncturing a hole in it.

"Ow!" Pilt grimaced, turning squeamishly away.

"Okay, now you run back up to the cliff!" ordered Flin.

Without argument, Pilt took off up the tunnel at a sprint and was soon out of sight. "Run here, run there!" mumbled Pilt. "Whatever, as long as it gets me far away from that Snazzard!"

Mr. Luftin continued egging on the Snazzard. "Hey! Over 'ere, ye stinkin' maggot!" he raised his knife high into the air up at the beast.

"Pilt!" shouted Head Revels from the dark shadows of their hiding place. "What's all the screaming going on down there? Is everything going as planned?" he asked nervously.

Pilt stopped momentarily, "It's just Mr. Luftin screaming at the Snazzard. He's trying to get it to eat him!"

"*What?*" came a piercing scream in the dark from Principal Vespar. "What kind of plan is *that*? I don't like the sound of that at all!"

"Me neither," said Miss Lemons.

"I have to head back up to the cliff! Flin's trying to get it to eat him now, too! I'll tell you the rest later!" yelled Pilt. He took off recklessly running up the tunnel and out of sight.

"What in the world are they doing?" Principal Vespar asked from their place of hiding with great doubt. "They're going to get themselves killed!"

Head Revels poked his head out to see Mr. Luftin and Flin both screaming up at the Snazzard. "I'm pretty sure they know what they're doing. *At least I hope so."*

"Well I'm not so sure," remarked Principal Vespar.

Flin began throwing rocks as well at the Snazzard. It responded by coiling back its long neck and lunging sporadically down after them throwing gravel in every direction as it head collided with the floor.

"Flin, we're going to have to divert from the plan. You get up the tunnel and do what ya need ta do!"

"But you, with your wooden leg, you could get kill—"

"Go!" demanded Luftin.

"All right! Try and keep it here as long as you can!" shouted as he took off up the tunnel, laying a trail of blood for the Snazzard to follow.

"Whoa!" screamed Luftin, desperately trying to retreat on his wooden leg. He could see the beast had grown tired of playing.

Flin sprinted further up the tunnel, squeezing blood from his fingertip as he ran. He looked down to see instead of red, blue droplets of blood fall from his finger and immediately form big circles of frost on the ground around it. "What the—why is my blood blue?" he stammered as he fled for his life.

Mr. Luftin took off up the tunnel at a high-speed hobble.

But the Snazzard stopped long enough to pick up on the scent of Flin's blood. It let out an excited squeal, followed by a loud hiss as it began running even faster following the trail of blood. Flin fled toward the cliff, turning to see Mr. Luftin just a few feet in front of the Snazzard and bearing down on top of him. Without an extra second, Mr. Luftindarted off the main tunnel and out of sight into the small cavern where he joined with the others who were hiding. Those in the tiny cavern watched as Flin rushed up the tunnel with his flickering torch and the Snazzard nipped at his heals.

He ran toward the food box, tore off one of its cardboard corner flaps and smeared blood all over it, then threw it back in the Snazzard's path. The Snazzard stopped and curiously checked it out giving Flin a spare second. Flin spotted Pilt, standing apprehensively by the torches, and staring back at him, clueless as to what to do.

"Now what?" Pilt shouted bleakly, shrugging his shoulders.

"We need to smear blood on the torches!" screamed Flin. He dove into the gravel and frantically gathered up the torches that had been tied together.

"You do it! I'm not touching your blood!"

"No time to argue Pilt, just help me!" Flin began squeezing droplets of blue blood all over the torches. The blood immediately crystallized as it splashed onto the torches.

"Flin, your, your blood, it's b-b-blue."

"Not now, Pilt! We don't have time to waste!"

Pilt slunk to his knees and reluctantly began smearing the blue blood over the torches. "And your blood's freezing cold!"

The Snazzard had given up on the box flap and could be heard making its way around the corner.

"Hurry, we need to slide the torches out over the cliff!" Flin and Pilt had barely slid the bundle of torches over the ravine when the Snazzard's dreadful head peered from around the corner at them. The two of them stood motionless up against the tunnel wall, just six feet away from the menacing Snazzard's face.

Flin tried sliding further away, bumping into the lit torch leaning against the wall and knocking it over. Sparks flew everywhere as it crashed to the floor.

The Snazzard's head rushed down at the fallen torch and was now only a couple of feet away from Flin. Flin could see his frightened reflection mirrored perfectly back at him in the smoky blue eye of the Snazzard. He held completely still, his heart pounding as the wind from its nostrils brushed back the tips of his hair.

"Hold still, Pilt, don't—even—breathe," Flin said under his breath. "Remember, it can only find us if it picks up our scent."

The Snazzard seemed momentarily confused. Its long tongue slithered out of its mouth and slapped against the tunnel floor, hitting the dirt all around them. Slowly, it stretched back its long neck and surveyed the surroundings. A thunderous hiss of frustration vibrated off the tunnel around them sending rocks and debris to the floor. Cautiously, Flin bent down and picked up what remained of the food box corner. He held it in his hand and let the blood trickle out of his finger and saturate the cardboard.

The Snazzard licked wildly at the line of tied torches suspended over the cliff, but Flin's crystallized blood did not seem to fully entice it. Its head swiftly turned at them, gradually moving toward Pilt until its nose bumped into his chest.

"Hold completely still," hushed Flin.

The Snazzard took in deep breaths, sounding like the rushing wind.

Pilt began to shake, and then uncontrollably whimper. *Flin, what's it doing?"*

"Just stay still and keep quiet!"

The Snazzard's mouth suddenly widened, measuring up to the height of Pilt's frame. Its head suddenly jerked back and hissed at him.

"What now?" gulped Pilt.

The beast let out one last evil scream and lunged down at Pilt. Just then, Flin pitched the blood-saturated cardboard out in front of the nose of the Snazzard and over the cliff. It picked up on the scent of fresh blood and leapt out after it and onto the torches. The weight of the massive Snazzard snapped the thin torches and sent splinters high into the air as its body began to plummet down into the crevice. One of its front legs caught hold of the cliff wall. Its rock like talon fought to keep it from falling any further. It struggled for a moment then let out several high pitched shrieks, almost like a bird squawking. Flin and Pilt raced to the ravine and looked down to see into the eye of the Snazzard. For the first time, they saw a look of terror and a plea for help in the Snazzard's eye. The Snazzard let out one last incredible hiss before losing its grip and then spiraled down into the deep, dark chasm below and out of sight.

The rest of the group ran to the cliff's edge, arriving just in time to hear the Snazzard crash to the bottom of the ravine miles below. Shortly, a dust cloud rose up from the pit.

Principal Vespar raced over to Flin and Pilt. "Are you boys alright?" she asked, looking them both over then squeezing them tightly.

Edgar rushed to the cliff's edge, picked up something and quickly put it in his pocket.

"What is it, Edgar?" asked Flin. Edgar unwillingly pulled out a long, sharp talon that had torn free from the Snazzard's foot.

As the dust settled and the fear of the Snazzard had finally ended, there came good news,

"Look! There be light!" hollered Mr. Luftin joyously, pointing across the cliff.

"Yes! I'm saved!" broke Sump's silence, as he started to cry for joy and raced to the ravine's edge.

Everyone stared out over the chasm that separated them at the sunlight they had been longing for.

"Well, there's no sense in just looking at it—let's all get across!" said Head Revels.

"Yes! We'd all love to do that, wouldn't we?" Sump whined, killing the moment of hope. "But realistically now, if that, that, oversized creature fell to its death trying to get across, how do you propose any of us are going to be able to?"

"Well, Mr. Sump, you'll just have to wait and see!" Head Revels responded confidently.

"Oh, get real," Sump moaned, pushing through the crowd.

Principal Vespar leaned out over the ravine and looked down. "It is quite wide," she said with concern.

"Can't see its bottom," said Luftin, leaning out a bit further. Just then the soft dirt he was standing on gave way, causing him to fall slightly over the edge. Cretchit snatched hold of one of his wrists as Head Revels dove to the ground and grabbed his other pleading hand. With help from some of the others, they pulled Mr. Luftin back to the surface.

"Are you alright, Mr. Luftin?" asked Miss Lemons, examining his scraped forearm.

"Trus' me, ya don' want ta be goin' down there!" he sighed, dusting himself off while keeping a safe distance from the ledge. "Surely stupid of me ta even think that sof' dirt wou'd hol' me and my big belly like that."

"Well, it looks like we're going to have to make some kind of a bridge to get across," said Head Revels.

Sump sat crouched against the tunnel wall. "See, told you! But of course no one wants to listen to me, no sir! Go on, just try and find wood in this cave."

Slowly Edgar walked over to Principal Vespar and reached down into his bag. "It took me over six years to make this." He reluctantly pulled out a long, multi-colored rope made of hair and dropped it at Principal Vespar's feet.

"Edgar, you're a lifesaver!" Principal Vespar said with a big smile.

Head Revels hurried over. "Good, Edgar! This just might be long enough. He examined and tested it for durability.

Edgar somberly made his way through the crowd and to the back of the group, passing Sump who was glaring up at him. "Don't even think about it, Edgar," scolded Sump. "If I even catch you lookin' at my hair, you'll be more than sorry. Got it? Now get!"

"Now, if we can somehow lasso the tip of that rock that's sticking up over there on the other side, we should have enough rope to make it across!" Head Revels tried several times to throw the rope across the ravine without any luck.

"'Tis a far throw there, Mr. Revels," replied Luftin, who had patiently been observing. "Do ya mind if I 'ave a go at it?" He spit into his hands and rubbed them together. He rolled up the hair rope and leaned out over the gaping distance. "Now, le's see 'ere, in me little boat back home I've gotten' pretty goo' at lassoin' the dock. So, here she goes—a one a, and a two a, and a three a." The rope flew through the air, unwinding wildly out of his hand and falling short of the sharp rock and down into the ravine.

"Oh, please!" mocked Sump from the distance.

"Welp, let me think this 'ere over," said Luftin, winding the rope back up and scratching at the whiskers on his chin. "Alrighty! I think I've got 'er figured out now." He whirled the rope high over his head several times before releasing, the rope flew through the air and caught the tip of the sharp rock on the other side of the ravine.

"Yes!" hollered Head Revels. "Well done, Mr. Luftin," he said, patting him on the back.

"Thank ye!" responded Mr. Luftin, turning to see a huge smile on Miss Lemons' face.

She turned several shades of red that were visible even in the minimal light. "You're really quite good at that."

"Why, thank ye, ma'am," blushed back Luftin.

"Whoopee," burbled Sump.

"Okay, let's make sure the rope is tied off good on this side," said Head Revels. "Great!" He gave it a stiff tug to make sure it was secure. "I guess I'll go first, to make sure it's strong enough."

"Oh, sure, go on and save yourself! Don't worry about the rest of us!" Sump continued.

"Well—if you'd like to go first, Mr. Sump, you know, you can try it out to make sure it doesn't break," replied Head Revels.

Sump abruptly folded his arms and turned away. "I'll pass! Who knows how strong that Edgar's rope is."

Head Revels cautiously lowered himself down onto the rope and began crossing the ravine hand over hand. The group held their collective breath until he made it to the other side.

"That wasn't too bad!" he said shakily. "Now, who's wants to be next?" Everyone stood silently.

"I'll go!" said Cretchit bravely.

Soon everyone had crossed the ravine, except for Sump and Parcell.

"Well, go Parcell! It's your turn!" Sump practically pushed Parcell over the edge.

"I still don't feel good!" whined Parcell, holding his stomach.

"Stop making excuses and just do it!" growled Sump.

Parcell reluctantly lowered himself down into the ravine and made his way slowly across.

"I guess now that I've made sure everyone else has made it safely across, I'll go," said Sump. He made several futile attempts to climb down to the rope.

"Jump, old man! Something's behind you?" hollered Parcell, pointing and covering his mouth while nudging Ruel in the ribs.

"Oh yeah, I see it too, hurry its gonna get ya!" Ruel said, trying not to laugh.

"Where, where?" Sump panicked and turned sharply. "I don't see anything!"

"It's right behind you!"

Frightened, Sump leapt from the edge and out several feet onto the fragile rope.

"Careful!" cried Head Revels. "You might break it!"

"Don't tell me what to do!" snarled Sump. Once he made it safely to the other side, he glared back across the ravine. *"You . . . idiots!"* There wasn't anything behind me!"

"I know," laughed Parcell, "but, you should have seen how stupid and scared you looked when you jumped out onto the rope!"

"Oh, shut up, Parcell! You too, Ruel . . ."

Chapter Nine

THE ANEMONE UNDER THE OCEAN

T he group eagerly headed down the other side of the tunnel and toward the light.

"Look, it's getting brighter!" yelled an excited Haunsdale girl. Soon the students were all racing down the tunnel toward the light.

"We're saved!" came shouts of joy as they neared the sunlight beaming down onto the floor. Their cries of joy quickly faded into a silent awe as they entered the sun's rays.

"Whoa . . . ! What is this place?" asked Cretchit, looking up in disbelief. "This is *amazing!*"

"Somehow we've ended up under the ocean!" Sam stared up into the ocean's deep blue water as fish and other ocean life swam casually overhead.

A clear, protective dome hovered hundreds of feet above them, like a giant upside down glass bowl, keeping out the ocean's water. The sun's light filtered down onto the cavern floor, highlighting fields of lush grasses and beautiful wildflowers. The border of the dome where it touched the ground was heavily layered in velvety green moss. Off in the distance, there were many other tunnels leading in and out of the dome, just like the one they'd come through.

"Wow!" Principal Vespar managed to say as she entered the light and glanced upward. "How did we ever end up all the way under the ocean like this?" she said, bewildered.

"Wow— is definitely right! This place is remarkable," said Head Revels with a very perplexed look on his face. "That clear dome has got to be some form of giant sea anemone." Seeing blank looks on faces, he elaborated, "It's a concealed sea plant which provides oxygen." He seemed both fascinated as well as perplexed.

"Well, u'll be. Me great-grandpappy told a such a place," said Luftin.

"Head Revels, what's a memory?" asked Sam, looking up.

"Not 'memory' Sam, a-ne-mo-ne! It's a water-dwelling, predatory creature that can grow for hundreds, if not thousands, of years. In this case, this one appears to have done just that in order to become this big! This must be some sort of mutation or rare form not yet discovered. I've never heard of one this big before."

"Look, up there!" shouted Flowell, pointing. The students responded by gawking.

"Dat there, that be a tiger shark!" grunted Luftin proudly, twisting both tips of his pointed beard. "I should know—they come ever'morn' to me place by the shore. I feed 'em broke up crabs that washed up from the night before. They love 'em."

"Lovely story, Luftin," yawned Sump while sitting on a boulder surrounded by flowers. He seemed uninterested in the new world.

"Mmm, smell that fresh air!" said Principal Vespar, taking in a deep breath. "Smells like freshly picked flowers."

"Well, should we see what's further in?" asked Head Revels.

"Not me! I'm for stayin' right here where I know it's safe!" whined Sump, stubbornly folding his arms.

"Suit yourself, Mr. Sump." It was obvious that Principal Vespar was tired of his constant hostility toward everyone, including Parcell and Ruel. She casually headed further in to admire the new underground world with the rest of the group.

"Alright," groaned Sump, picking himself up to catch up with the rest of the group.

"Where do you think all of these other tunnels lead?" asked Flin curiously and a bit concerned as to what might be lingering in them.

"They're all probably similar to the tunnel we've just come through," answered Voss Yeg.

Pilt had climbed a small hill to get a better look. "Wow! This place is *huge*! I can't even see the end of it!"

"I think we should all stay close together, we really don't know what's out there," instructed Principal Vespar, guiding the students into a group.

"Truly amazing!" remarked Voss Yeg in her delicate, vintage Irish voice. "I wouldn't believe it unless I'd seen it with me own eyes!"

"Hey! Look up ahead!" shouted Sam. "It looks like a forest!"

Off in the distance, dark green, lush pines and lofty, leafy trees surrounded several meadows. As the group continued walking, they could see small birds resembling hummingbirds darting in and out of the fields of flowers.

A half-hour later, they were standing on the shore of what appeared to be a giant underground lake with fish of all different colors and sizes jumping in and out of the water. The lake in the cavern traveled under the clear dome of the anemone and back out into the ocean.

Pilt leaned over and cupped up some of the water out of the lake and started to drink. "Ew . . . !" he said, spitting it out of his mouth.

"What's the matter, Pilt?" asked Principal Vespar, making her way over to him.

"It's salty!" he said, vigorously scratching at his tongue.

After another hour of walking, they came to a river that fed into the great lake. Pilt, still thirsty, bent down and cautiously sipped at the water. "Hey, this is good! Its fresh water," he said and then went back to drinking.

"Let's follow the river here and see where it leads us," said Head Revels, setting out at a quick pace. "If it's fresh water it's possible it could lead to somewhere outside this cavern."

Evening was quickly approaching and light within the cavern was beginning to grow dim. They followed the river through several winding groves of trees, where it opened up into a beautiful meadow full of all kinds of oversized butterflies.

Mr. Luftin was the first to emerge from the thickly wooded trees. "Great Scot!" he hollered in disbelief, staring straight up at a mountainous tree that went up and out of sight through the anemone.

Soon, everyone was gawking up at the mountainous tree.

"It appears that, at some point, someone converted that tree into some sort of a cathedral or something," Voss Yeg said, placing her palms to her cheeks.

"That means someone's been here before!" said a bright-eyed Principal Vespar. "But why is the tree petrified?"

"I was wondering that myself," replied Head Revels.

The roots of the tree were exposed and looked as if water had at some point washed away the soil that surrounded them. The roots were long and gnarled and appeared more like twisted legs balancing the tall tree. The coarse, petrified bark of the tree was a cold gray, which gave the tree a statuesque appearance.

There were two stained-glass windows just above a massive pair of front doors, one red and the other a deep blue. Wild ivy enveloped the tree's trunk, traveling hundreds of feet into the air. On the doors were medieval carvings and images engulfed by years of cobwebs and dust. One daunting persona kept the group at bay for the moment. Surrounding the door was a quaint porch with cobblestone steps leading to a pathway that wound down the hill and to a bridge that crossed over the river. The surroundings looked like they'd been well maintained at one time, but now the place as well as the surroundings appeared to be abandoned.

"Ya know, that tree there reminds me of a tale my mother used to tell me of a boy named Jack! 'Jack and a Beanstalk,' I believe she called it," said Voss Yeg.

"It's 'Jack and *the* Bean Stalk' you antiquated dope!" barked Sump, who was sitting. "Everyone knows that!"

"It's mind-boggling to me to think that we're not the first, that someone or something else lived down here before," said Head Revels, staring up at the tree. "I wonder, these carvings here," he said, daring to step a bit closer to one of the doors. "It looks as if they're in some sort of sequence that tells a story. And those carvings on the front of the building covered by all those wild vines, it appears to be a man's face carved into the surface." He rubbed the sides of his chin as he walked around pondering.

Mr. Luftin came from around the back of the cathedral. "Thot there river what we jis' followed, it runs the entire length under this here cathedral and comes out under this porch."

"I think we should camp here for the night," said Head Revels, pointing to an open meadow thirty feet in front of the cathedral.

"But—" blurted out Principal Vespar, "aren't you the least bit curious as to what's inside that tree?" she said, revealing her intense curiosity for the eccentric looking, giant, petrified tree.

"Yes, but I think it would be best if we wait until morning. In the meantime, let's make more torches so that, come first sunlight, we can enter into that mystical cathedral and see what's really inside. For now, I think it would be best if we set camp here for the night."

"What about food? All we have are but a few remaining sandwiches, which is not near enough to feed us all," said Principal Vespar, feeling hunger pains in her own stomach.

Head Revels started to make camp. "We'll have to worry about that come morning,"

As the night grew dark, a harmony of crickets and croaking toads echoed throughout the cavern, and the nightlife of the enormous cavern began to unveil its secrets.

"Look!" Flowell said, pointing out into the meadow at dozens of bright red flashes of light that hovered in the air and lit up the meadow flowers in red. "What are they?"

"Great glowing fireflies!" hollered Luftin. "Have small ones jist like 'em back home." He sat on a far off log, bent over, attending to his wooden leg which was now severely scratched from the journey.

"They're huge! I wonder why everything's so much bigger down here," Flin wondered, glancing about at the peculiar things making themselves present in the nightlife.

"Hey, what are those things way up there?" Sam asked, pointing up excitedly at the ceiling of the anemone. Giant snails and slugs, the size of small dogs, were making iridescent slime trails in stripes and circles on the anemone.

"Isn't it pretty down here?" Sam asked, breathing in the cool night air and lying back on the soft meadow grass.

Head Revels took the opportunity to speak to the group. "Tonight, no one should go wandering too far from camp; we're still not sure what might be out there."

These last words caused Pilt much concern. *We're still not sure what might be out there*, he repeated in his head, taking his eyes off of the anemone and nervously searching the dark shadows of the cavern. He gulped deeply as an assortment of unfamiliar noises answered him.

Off in the distance, a startling, piercing crack came from the heavily wooded trees.

Pilt sat up abruptly. "Flin, did you hear that? Flin, I said did you hear —"

"Of course I heard it, who didn't?" said Flin, who was relaxed with his eyes closed as he tried to get to sleep.

Minutes later, a very unsettled Pilt lay back down. "There it went again!" he said, popping up and jerking back and forth in every direction. "I'll bet that Snazzard followed us!"

Although Flin appeared to be asleep, he couldn't help but snicker.

"What's so funny?" Pilt asked crossly, still searching the darkness.

"You! You're paranoid of everything!"

"And you're not?" Pilt replied bitterly.

"Pilt, I'm sure we're safe here," said Flin.

"Oh yeah, tell that to whatever used to live in that old tree thing over there! I'll bet they thought they were pretty safe, too, huh? What do you think about that?"

"Pilt, stop worrying yourself to death and just go to sleep."

"If I go to sleep, then who's going to watch out for flesh-eating creatures?"

Hours later, after Pilt had finally fallen asleep, Flin awoke from a great pain in his fingers. The stars and the moon were shining brilliantly through the anemone, helping to take his mind off the pain. He thought about his room at home in the attic, and the holes in the roof that also let him see the stars and moon. The night seemed to last forever as Flin lay holding his throbbing hand. He raised it to his face. "What in the—?" he belted out. His fingernails were now glowing brightly.

"You say something, Flin?" yawned Pilt, half asleep.

A rainbow of colors illuminated from his fingernails.

"I don't get this!" he mumbled, then glanced around hoping no one had seen or heard him. *Why are my fingernails all glowing?* He held each nail up to his face one at a time and studied its confusing dim glow. "Blue, and this one's reddish-orange," he said surprised. "Green! Black! White! And why does the white nail glow so much brighter than the others?" he said in a whisper.

Finally, sunlight shone through the anemone and onto the cavern floor.

"What the heck?" shouted Parcell, waking those around him as he leapt up from the ground. Flin quickly glanced over to see what had caused Parcell such concern. Parcell was standing with his right hand above his head, staring at it in confusion. "What in the— how is this even possible!"

Flin raised his hand up carefully, making sure not to let the others see, and again began to study it.

"What are you looking at?" Flowell asked, sneaking up from behind and startling him. He quickly hid his hand behind his back.

"Oh! Uh . . . nothing, really. I just uh . . . haven't cleaned under my fingernails for some time!"

"Ew, that's gross, Flin!" she said, pulling a sour face. Sam called her. "Oop, got ta go and see what Sam wants."

"Whoa, Flin, how come your hand looks so much worse today?" Pilt asked loudly, catching Flin off-guard.

"Shhh, Pilt!" Flin looked around as he quickly put his hand to his side. "I don't know what happened! Remember how my blood was blue?"

"Yeah, and cold. Why was it like that anyway?" Pilt sat up and scratched his head.

"I don't know why!" Flin said puzzled. He looked around and seeing that no one was watching, raised his hand to his face again.

"What did you do to it to make it look so—so, bad? How come your fingernails are all those different colors now? You look like you're wearing fingernail polish," laughed Pilt to himself, a bit giddy from a lack of sleep.

"No! I don't know what happened to them! And I thought you were still asleep, Nosey."

"Hey! I'll bet it had something to do with that red Snazzard licking your back! Remember, when we were running through the tunnel?"

"I know the red Snazzard, Pilt! And no!" snarled Flin. "I don't think that's what caused it!"

"My bet is that Snazzard's saliva had something to do with it."

"I told you, Pilt, it's not from the Snazzard Sali—"

Parcell shrieked loudly, catching everyone's attention.

"Parcell!" barked his father, growing tired of his whining.

"I've noticed Parcell's been acting strange all morning," whispered Flin, to Pilt. "I'm going to find out what they're talking about." He snuck over and hid in some nearby bushes. He could see Mr. Sump examining Parcell's hand.

"But it's my fingernails—they're killing me!" moaned Parcell.

"Black! Why are they all black, *Parcell?* What have you done to them this time?" Sump asked sharply, then slapped Parcell's tender hand away.

"Ever since that blasted pit got stuck in my hand—" Parcell said with tears in his eyes, then stopped as his eyes wandered further up to his father's hair on top of his head. A big grin spread across Parcell's face.

"What on earth could be so funny, Parcell?" snapped his father.

"What did you do to your hair?" asked Parcell, who was now uncontrollably laughing instead of crying. "Ruel, Ruel, look!" he laughed pointing up at Sump's hair.

"Why? What's wrong with my hair?" retorted Sump, reaching back to feel short, sharp stubbles instead of long hair. "Edgar! EDGAR . . . !" he shouted at the top of his lungs, looking sharply around in every direction. "That little brat's gonna pay for this! *I'll kill him!*" growled Sump then wildly he took off running and darted off the beaten path in search of Edgar.

Chapter Ten

WHAT'S REALLY INSIDE THE CATHEDRAL?

Flin was listening intently to Parcell and Ruel conversing about Parcell's fingernails, when Head Revels approached him, catching him off-guard and startling him.

"Oh Flin, there you are. Some of the others and I are going to explore the inside of the cathedral. Would you and Pilt like to join us?"

"Sure!" Flin responded, volunteering them both.

The small group of men made their way to the door.

"Are you sure we should go inside, Head Revels?" Pilt asked with his head buried deep into his shoulders like a frightened turtle.

"Pilt, there's nothing to worry about. This place looks like it's been vacant for years," Head Revels said reassuringly.

"Should we at least knock?" asked Pilt, hiding behind Flin.

"Some of these carvings do kind of look like warnings. Let's see here now," Head Revels said as he did his best to translate the symbols on the door. "Those who enter," he said, squinting and wiping away layers of dust. "Death—Death be—Death be upon those who enter!" he said. "We better not mention this to the others, agreed?"

"Yep," said Pilt. "Someone definitely needs to protect the girls!" he handed Flin his torch and stepped off the porch.

"Pilt!" hollered Flin. "You've got to go in!"

"Ah, no, I don't! Didn't you just hear what Head Revels said? '*Death* to those who enter!' I think that's a no-brainer, Flin."

"Okay, suit yourself. But I thought I heard someone say just this morning that they saw another Snazzard running around here, a big black one with yellow eyes!"

"I guess a little peak inside is not going to hurt!" Pilt said as he bounced back up the steps and retrieved his torch.

They pushed back one of the huge doors and it shrilled as it slowly opened.

"I still think we should have knocked first," muttered Pilt as the door creaked open and sunlight shone on the dark wooden floor clearly for the first time in years. A blanket of dust covered the floor, which was decorated with child-like footprints.

"I hear water!" said Fig Tronsel, his long boney neck, like an ostrich as he craned above the others and peered in.

"I hear it too!" replied Head Revels. "It's got to be that river that enters from the rear of the cathedral and comes out under the front porch there."

Several giant frogs and toads bounded across the floor and quickly took refuge outside.

"Well, we guessed wrong; it wasn't empty," said Fig with a nervous sigh.

Cretchit raised his torch high above his head as he roamed about the room curiously. "There's no ceiling in here."

"That's interesting; it's got to be up there somewhere," replied Fig as he also raised his torch and glared up. "That is strange—every structure's got to have some kind of a roof!"

"Wow! Hey guys, you all have got to come and see this! These stools have funny faces carved into them," said Pilt. The light from his torch shone on several hand carved stools surrounding a low sitting table.

"Can anyone else hear that ticking sound?" asked Head Revels looking around.

"Yeah, I hear it!" responded Luftin.

"Whatever it is, it sounds like it's coming from over there!" said Head Revels, raising his torch high above his head and walking in the direction of the noise.

"Look!" pointed Fig Tronsel. "Up ahead there! Do you see that?" He held his torch out in front of him. The light shimmered on several bridges that crossed back and forth over a wandering stream that ran the entire length of the room and then vanished under the floor.

"Whoever built this place must have been really short—maybe elves or gnomes!" Pilt mumbled, still intrigued by the ornate tables and stools.

"How do you figure?" Flin inadvertently responded.

"Well, just look how low this stool sits. This had to be for a short person," Pilt reasoned. He bent down with his torch and caught the bottom of the table on fire, then slapped out the flames with his hand.

"Pilt!" shouted Head Revels. "We didn't come here to burn the place down!"

"Over here!" called Flin from a distance. His torchlight illuminated on a magnificent fireplace that went well beyond the reach of his light.

"Whoa, that thing's *huge!*" Pilt exclaimed. He stumbled over to where the rest of the group had gathered. "I've never seen a fireplace that big before, not even at our ski lodge back home!"

After examining the intricate workmanship of the ornate hearth, the group walked to the edge of the room. There was a four-foot tall planter box full of white rocks that ran the entire perimeter of the room.

"This is interesting," remarked Fig as he examined the strange looking rocks. "I don't see why anyone would do this?"

"Maybe who ever used to live here grew rocks?" guessed Pilt with a slight laugh.

"Yeah, right, Pilt!" said Flin.

"Where do you think these stairs lead?" asked Head Revels, standing at the base of a stairway made of wooden logs and branches that were woven together.

"'Tis an upper level, I'm a guessin'!" said Luftin, pointing out the obvious as his torchlight flickered upon twisted and gnarled branches that constructed a railing. "I'll go up wit ya ta take a look see!" Luftin, Head Revels and Fig Tronsel all went up the staircase to check out the upper level.

"These rocks are all perfectly spaced apart," said Flin, who was enthralled with the planter box filled with the white rocks.

"That's obvious, Flin," muttered Pilt as he went around the room leaving scorch marks from his torch on practically everything he looked at.

Flin placed his hand against one of the white rocks and started to dust it off to get a better look. The stone suddenly lit up at his touch. Shocked, he jumped backwards, and landed on his back.

"Whoa!"

The room vaguely lit up, Pilt turned to see where the light was coming from.

"Whoa ... !!! How'd you do that?" Pilt quickly made his way over.

Flin again rubbed the rock, only this time with more caution. The rock slowly illuminated.

"Check it out! The longer and faster you rub it, the brighter it gets!" He glanced around the dimly lit room that was now growing brighter. The two of them scurried around the perimeter of the room polishing all the rocks and causing them to light up.

"Nice! How'd you get that one to light up like a rainbow? Except —" Pilt took a closer look, "it's got a black streak in it. How'd ya do that?"

"I don't know what happened. I, I just rubbed it with my left hand is all!" Flin looked down at his multi-colored fingernails. One nail was now a distinct, ominous black.

He tried rubbing out the black streak on the rock with his right hand, but with no luck.

"It's like you killed that part of the rock!" Pilt said, touching the black streak.

"Yeah, I know," Flin replied with a hint of sadness.

The lights throughout the room started to dim as rushing footsteps could be heard from the upper level making their way toward them.

"Light?" Head Revels shouted from up above. "Where's all the light coming from?" he asked in surprise. Rapidly he made it to the railing above and looked down to seethe glowing white rocks below. "Amazing! Truly amazing!" He hurried down the wooden staircase.

"We got these dusty old rocks to light up!" bragged Pilt.

"Rocks?" Head Revels said puzzled. "What did—how'd you do it?"

"We just started rubbin', and they all lit up!" Pilt said boastfully.

"Pilt, quick, I have an idea. Run and get some of that water from out of that stream over there," said Head Revels as he turned back to the stones.

Pilt sprinted back with cupped hands, water trickling out between his fingers. He poured the few remaining droplets of water over the rock that Head Revels pointed to and instantly the rock grew brighter. "See!" Head Revels said. He delicately began rubbing the rock, producing more light.

"How's the water making the rock get brighter?" Flin asked.

"Well, those so called 'rocks' aren't really rocks at all—they're plants! They just look like rocks with that hard exoskeleton shell."

"What's an 'egg-o-skeleton'?" asked Pilt, hovering over the rock as it shone on his face.

"E-X-O-S-K-E-L-E-T-O-N, Pilt! Don't you listen in Mr. Strubbles' class?" responded Head Revels. "See! The plant lights up when touched as a defense mechanism. Truly ingenious, really, whoever came up with all these ideas."

"Wow, look! There *is* a ceiling; it's just way up there!" Pilt could see clearly now that the entire room was illuminated. Up above, there were three more levels of the cathedral, suspended out over the lobby below.

"Whoa!" Flin looked toward the opposite end of the cathedral.

"What is it, Flin?" Head Revels asked. "'Whoa' is right!" he said, glancing up to a towering grandfather clock that had been carved into the wall. The top of the clock was a man's face with a long beard made of twisted roots that hung down approximately seven feet. The face of the clock had two enormous eyes that moved side to side with every tick. A giant upside-down battle axe was used for the pendulum, which could be heard slicing through the air as it swung back and forth. An old rusted chain with an anchor hanging on the end of it was used for the clock's weights.

They both stared up at the colossal clock for a moment. Then, Flin turned to Head Revels, "But, but if, if no one lives here, then, then who wound the clock?"

"You ask a good question, Flin. I only wish I had a good answer to go with it."

"Wow, look at the size of this glow rock over here," hollered Cretchit from the center of the room.

Head Revels and the others crossed over one of the many bridges to Cretchit. As they neared the big glow rock, they saw that a wooden rail surrounded it as if protecting it.

"I wonder why there's a chunk missing out of the top of it?" asked Pilt, touching it.

Head Revels leaned out over the rail and put his glasses to his eyes to study it. "I don't know. Maybe at some time something dropped on it." He rubbed it, and it gradually lit up and then flickered, as if it too, had been deprived of water.

"An' look. Ya see right there below where it's chipped? Someon's gone und marked it ull up," Luftin observed as he joined them, now curious just like the others.

"I believe those are symbols that have been carved into it!" said Head Revels, getting a closer look.

Flin walked over to get a better look at the giant rock when he noticed something in the pond. "Hey, here's more fish like the ones outside!"

Head Revels' attention was immediately diverted to potential food. "Just look at all of the different colors and sizes of those fish! Have you noticed that everything down here is freakish in size and so rich in color? It's got to have something to do with a high nutrient content deeper in the Earth."

"Head Revels?" Flin asked. "Do you think these different colors of fish could be dangerous?"

"On the contrary, I'll bet these fish are probably much healthier than those on the surface, and probably better tasting as well," he said, licking his lips and widening his eyes.

"I smell something sweet!" Pilt turned in the opposite direction.

"I smell it as well. It smells a lot like cinnamon!" Head Revels said, bouncing his eyebrows and taking another deep breath through his nostrils. "Mr. Luftin, why don't you and Fig finish exploring all those other rooms upstairs that we didn't get to see, while the boys and I finish searching out what's down here?"

"Ulrighty, we cun do that," he said with a smile.

"This way!" called Head Revels eagerly to the boys who were having trouble keeping up with his quick stride. He shuffled out of the main entrance hall and down a corridor that split in two. "I believe the smell is coming from . . . that direction!" he pointed excitedly. They entered a room that was filled with all kinds of delicious smells that lingered about.

"And I would presume this to be the kitchen!" he said, his torchlight shining throughout the great room. "Remarkable! Truly remarkable!" He curiously swooped around the kitchen, examining every gadget and knickknack. "Would you just look at all these different types of food! And looky here—hot water!" Several low, wooden counter tops were scattered throughout the kitchen. A stone fireplace was tucked deep in the corner for cooking.

Pilt pulled out a wooden jar, stuck his finger in it, and gave it a lick. "Here's the cinnamon we smelled.

Head Revels pulled out more food items. "There has to be a place nearby where all this is grown!" he glanced around the kitchen with a pleased look. "Well, I think we've seen enough for now. Let's go and tell the others the good news of what we've found!"

Chapter Eleven

"WE MEAN YA NO HARM"

ead Revels had just finished informing the group of what had been found inside the cathedral, when Sump piped up. "You're just saying all that, because you know that we have no other place to go. You're just trying to get us all to go in that haunted place. Everything you've told us is probably nothing more than a bunch of lies! Well, I, for one, can see right through your drivel! I heard you say, just before you went inside, that the symbols on the door read, 'Death be upon those who enter!' And then you told everyone to just keep quiet about it, isn't that right?"

"Yes, but—"

"See! Even the fool admits he said it!" shouted Sump triumphantly, throwing his hands in the air.

"But I had no idea what was in there until we got inside!"

"Then, what's happened to that slob Luftin and Tronsel? Where are they?"

"They're still inside exploring the place."

"And how do we know they're not dead?" Sump accused.

"It doesn't matter what you think, thank you!" Principal Vespar interceded sharply as she made her way through the crowd of people and closer to the door. "The rest of us are going inside to see for ourselves!"

"Well! I'm definitely not going to stay here and get eaten or, even worse, starve to death over the next several days! Who's with me?" Sump glanced around with jittery eyes, but there came no response. "Fine!" he snarled. "But just remember this—*if*, by chance, you're still alive and starving to death, don't bother come looking for us! Come, Parcell! Oh, and you too, Ruel. I said *now*, Parcell!"

"What if I don't want to come?" said Ruel coldly.

"Oh, you'll come! Did I say you had a choice?" Sump threatened, reaching out at him.

"Let the boy decide for himself!" Principal Vespar said assertively, stepping forward.

Ruel looked over at Parcell and then at each group member. "You're right! I'm not staying here with these losers!" he scowled. The three of them made their way down the path, Sump grabbed Ruel by the ear. "What were you thinking? You weren't seriously considering staying with that scum back there?"

They walked down the path and out of sight.

"Well, that was quite interesting," sighed Head Revels, glad to be done with Sump. "But enough with that—is everyone ready to go inside?" He tried to change the recent darkness.

They neared the front door.

"You're sure it's safe to enter then?" asked Miss Lemons, fear evident in her eyes as she hesitantly neared the door.

"You'll be fine, trust me," Head Revels said. He took her by the hand and helped her up the few remaining steps.

"Yes, these symbols are a bit concerning. They definitely don't look like the flowers and butterflies that I have on my welcome mat back home," laughed Principal Vespar, trying to relieve the tension.

Head Revels pushed open the creaky door and stepped in. The rest of the group reluctantly followed.

Outside, Sump, Parcell, and Ruel made their way back and hid behind some nearby trees. "Now go and get what's left of that food!" ordered Sump, pointing his greedy finger at the unguarded box.

"If you want it so bad, you go and get it!" replied Parcell snidely.

Sump raised his hand threateningly. "Do as you're told boy!"

A minute later, Parcell returned carrying very few items.

"Why didn't you get all of it?" asked Sump angrily, looking over Parcell's shoulder.

"This is all of it!" he scowled as he threw it to the ground.

"Why are your fingernails completely black now, Parcell?" noticed Sump.

"I don't know," he said as they snatched up the food and headed their own way.

~~~~~~~~~

"I thought you said there was light in here," one of the frightened Haunsdale students whimpered, clinging to Miss Lemons.

"Oh, just one second; you're going to think this is neat!" said Head Revels as he scurried over to the huge glow rock in the center of the room. He gave it a generous rub, causing it to light up.

An overwhelming "whoa!" came from the group.

Flin, Pilt, and Cretchit rushed around the room, rubbing the rest of the glow rocks.

"You were right, Head Revels," exclaimed Principal Vespar with relief. "This place truly is amazing. In all my life, I've never seen anything so ornate!" The fear quickly faded into a sense of curiosity as the entire group glanced around the room and tried to take everything in.

"This place is absolutely astonishing," said Miss Lemons. Her Irish dance students were now buzzing about the main room of the cathedral.

"Just incredible!" said Voss Yeg. "The glow rocks, the streams with those little bridges, and what an elaborate fireplace!" she said as she turned around. "I've never seen one that comes close to matching its size, or beauty!"

"I wonder who could have possibly lived here and what could have happened to them," wondered Principal Vespar, glancing around the room in disbelief.

"Wow! Voss Yeg, you've got to come and see this!" yelled a Haunsdale girl from on one of the bridges.

Voss Yeg was a plump, elderly woman, but as quickly as she could, she hustled her way over to see what all the excitement was about. She raised the glasses that hung by a chain around her neck up to her eyes. "My goodness child, you're absolutely right! Just look at all those beautiful fish!" she said solemnly.

Head Revels tried speaking over all the whispers of excitement. "We really haven't had a chance to check out the entire cathedral, so until we've done that, I think it would be best if we keep the activity to the main room here." The stern look on his face contrasted heavily with the excited twinkle in his eye.

"There ya ull be!" called Luftin from the upper level. "Mr. Tronsel and meself wandered a little over 'ere, a bit more there, checking ou' this 'ere place. We never did see ull of 'er! Remarkable sight thee ol' girl is. Jus' truly remarkable!" He talked as if he had found a new passion to replace his bus, Inga.

Awhile later, Flin, Pilt, and Cretchit, along with Mr. Luftin and Head Revels, set out to better explore the cathedral.

"Whoever built this place sure put lots of bedrooms in it," Flin said, poking his head into several of the rooms as they passed. Pilt came to a sudden halt. "What was that?" he whispered nervously, taking a couple of quick steps back. "Didn't anyone else just see a black blur run into the shadows just up ahead?" he asked as he stretched his torch toward the dark cavity.

"I see it too! I see two sets of eyes staring back at me!" said a timorous Cretchit.

Two sets of eyes stared back at them intently—one set was a deep purple, the other pale lavender and in the midsection of its body.

"Why is one set of eyes so much lower than the other? And a different color?" asked Head Revels, slightly hunched over and staring at the creature from a safe distance. "Its lower eyes are more in the midsection of its stomach."

"It's got to be some kind of monster!" squirmed Pilt, backing away.

The creature let out a growl, causing everyone to take several steps back.

"What the heck is it?" Cretchit asked, backed against the wall.

"I don't know. But one thing I do know is that I don't want to know!" sniveled Pilt.

"How do we know the thing's even dangerous?" Luftin asked, stepping closer.

Just then, liquid flew from the monster's mouth, hitting Pilt in the face. He jumped backwards, nearly falling over. "That thing's vicious! It just squirted venom on me!"

"That looks more like spit to me," Cretchit said after studying the bubbly fluid more closely on Pilt's face.

Luftin took no heed. Instead, he walked directly at the beast as if he were going to charge it, and then slowed. "What kinda creature wears a long, black cloak?" he puzzled, narrowing his eyes at it.

Now even more curious, they all began to make their way towards the creature, Pilt staying at the back of the pack.

"We men no ham!" came the voice of the creature as it now tried backing further away from them into the corner.

"Did it just say something?" asked Head Revels in shock.

"It spoke! I heard it say something!" said Cretchit as the group came to a halt just a few feet away from the monster.

"Yeah, I heard it say something, too. Something about mean and ham! I think it wants to kill us and then eat us!" Pilt turned to run.

"No, what I think it was trying to say is, 'We mean no harm!'" replied Flin, grabbing Pilt by the collar. Flin moved in closer.

"We men no ham! We men no ham!" it swiftly repeated over and over, trembling.

Flin continued to creep toward the creature with his torch out in front of him.

"We men ya no ham! WE MEN YA NO HAM!" screamed the beast. "Run fur it!" shouted the midsection of the creature as the cloak flew open and two little men appeared. One jumped off of the other's shoulders, and the two of them ran down the hall, pitching the dark cloak over Pilt's head as they passed by him.

"Hurry! We can't let 'em get away! We need ta catch 'em!" hollered Luftin as they all dashed down the hall after them.

"I think they went in here!" whispered Cretchit, pointing his torch into a bedroom off the main corridor. They entered the room.

"It's pitch dark in here," wheezed Flin. "I can't see a thing." He warily made his way further into the room, holding his torch as far out in front of him as he could.

"I hear something," whispered Flin. "It sounds like it's coming from that direction!" He and Cretchit made their way to the corner of the room towards a rattling sound. They heard the startling thud of Luftin's wooden leg as he entered the room behind them.

"There it went again! I'm pretty sure it's coming from that big closet in the corner!" Flin pointed at an old armoire made of a dark, knotty wood. He neared it, his torchlight shining on the doors of the closet as they began to rock back and forth.

"They're definitely in there!" Cretchit whispered as the closet now swayed side to side and nearly tipped over.

"Some 'ow we need ta trap 'em," whispered Luftin, looking at the drapes on the wall.

Head Revels and Pilt finally staggered through the doorway. They were greeted by the loud banging of the rocking wardrobe.

An argument between the two little men came from inside the armoire.

"I see dere torchlight! Dere a comin' fur us! Move out a me way, ya fool!"

"Yur da one who'z in da way, ya winker! Move bifore they catch uz both!"

"I would guess you're right!" Head Revels exclaimed. "Pilt!" he hushed, turning towards the entrance of the room. "Shut the door so they can't get out!"

"What?" Pilt said, slowly backing up, his eyes frightfully focused on the teetering cabinet as he walked out of the room and into the hallway.

"Pilt! Get back in here!" demanded Head Revels. "We might need your help catching these, these things!" Pilt unwillingly made his way back into the room and shut the door behind him.

"Okay, we're ready now. Go ahead, Flin, open the cabinet door," Head Revels said under his breath.

Slowly, Flin reached for the giant wooden handle on the cabinet door, then jerked it open, revealing two dwarfs holding tight to one another. After a few seconds, the plumper of the two spoke in a deep Old Irish accent. "Please, kindly dear sirs, don' be hurtin' uz. We means ya no ham."

Head Revels calmly walked to the cabinet, his torchlight dancing upon their frightened faces. "Well," he contemplated, "they appear harmless enough."

Their clothes looked to be made from curtains and were adorned with polished stones. Head Revels gradually stretched out his hand. Horrified, the two dwarfs recklessly jumped from the closet to the floor, diving between Head Revels' legs in an attempt to get to the door.

Chapter Twelve

MEET THE COBBLES

"Stop!" shouted Head Revels. "We mean you no harm."

The two dwarfs froze. There was a brief moment of uncertainty before Head Revels slowly made his way toward the two shivering forms. "We mean you no harm," Head Revels repeated again as he stretched out his hand in friendship. The little men stared at each other. One quickly dropped to the floor and bowed before Head Revels. The other, seeing the first's response, followed.

"No, that's, that's not necessary—*friends*," Head Revels said in a subdued tone, trying not to startle them. He then pointed to his chest. "Head Revels." He slowly pointed at the two of them, who were still kneeling on the floor before him. "What are your names?"

They paused for a moment and then looked at one another. The intense look of fear slowly abandoned their faces, and then they both spoke at the same time. "FIENZGZEYR!"

"Okay, okay," Head Revels chuckled lightly. "Now, one at a time. Who are you?" he asked, pointing to the plumper of the two.

"Ay'm Fezzy," he whistled a zippy reply through his teeth. Fezzy raised his chin proudly and stuck out his chest.

"And your name is?" Head Revels pointed to the other, who was the taller and thinner of the two.

He stammered, "Ay'm Inger."

"So, you're Fezzy and you're Inger?"

They both nodded. Head Revels again reached out slowly, only this time with both hands. Fezzy raised a shaky hand, which steadily moved forward until he was grasping hands with Head Revels. Inger soon followed.

"Come on! Up off the floor with the both of you," he said, giving them both a lift. Fezzy stood proud and tall after quickly dusting himself off.

"Cool . . . jacket," muttered Cretchit.

"Thank ye! 'Tis me lucky vest!" came Fezzy's sprightly voice. "Ay've had it nearly four hundred years now, wouldn't cha know!"

"Fezzy, did you just say you've had that jacket nearly four hundred years now?" asked Head Revels with raised brows.

"'Tis so! Me 'Eppel made it for me! Nope, I fibbed. 'Til be four hundred years come first sun up of March. 'Tis me and 'Eppel's anniversary thot day!" he said pulling on the tails of his shimmering jacket and straightening it.

"How do ya both know English sa well?" asked Luftin, who had taken an instant liking to the two dwarfs.

"Bin speekin' it fur, oh, some hundreds of years now."

Flin stuck out his hand, startling them. Again, they both went to kneel.

"No, you don't need to kneel—*friends*," Flin said. In turn, he shook each of their hands. "Flin, I'm just Flin," he laughed.

"Flin's a fine name!" replied Fezzy, nodding. "And your name, what might it be?" he asked Cretchit.

"Oh, yeah. Sorry! I'm, I'm a . . ."

"Forgotten yar name have ya?" apparently all fear had left the room.

"No, it's, it's Cretchit," he laughed nervously, as he backed away and stared down at the floor.

"Und I'm Shan. Oops, sorry 'bout that," chuckled Luftin. "Jus' call me Luftin."

"Pilt! Come on over and shake their hands!" Flin insisted, motioning for him to come.

Pilt apprehensively made his way over. He raised his quivering hand towards Fezzy, who swiftly reached up with both hands and roughly shook it. Inger did the same.

"'Tis Pilt then, is it?" asked Fezzy.

"A . . . yeah, that's right. I'd be Pilt," he stammered.

"Why were you two wearing that big, black cloak?" asked Head Revels. He seemed to be enthralled by every detail of the two dwarfs.

"Well, we weren't sure if'n ya'd be friendly ur not—we thought ya'z all might be Grimgoblins," Fezzy explained. His big lavender eyes glossed over and dropped to the floor.

"Grimgoblins! So, you two aren't Grimgoblins?" asked Luftin with relief.

"No, we be Cobbles!" Fezzy responded.

"But the symbols on the front door?" asked Head Revels confused.

"We three Cobbles carved them 'bout a hundred years ago." Fezzy's fear of the trespassers seemed to have vanished.

"Why?" asked Cretchit.

"Fur ta scare enemies away!" Inger replied timidly, still not daring to make eye contact.

"So, there are others beside yourselves that live down here under the earth's surface?" Head Revels was fascinated.

"Oh yis! Most are bad though! Very evul!" said Fezzy.

"Who else lives in the cathedral? You said 'we three,'" asked Flin.

"Jis' Eppel und us two!" said Fezzy, reluctantly.

"Heppel! What's a Heppel?" asked Pilt, squinting with confusion.

"Like uz!" said Fezzy, pointing with his stubby dwarf finger at himself and Inger. "She be me wife. We'z thought you'z waz comin' ta kill ull uz, so we'z ull hid!" said Fezzy. A giant tear rolled down his cheek and splashed on the dusty wooden floor below.

"You thought we were going to kill you?" Head Revels was a bit surprised.

"Eppel hide too," he said thickly. "She don' want ta get kilt!"

"So, you're all Cobbles, and there are no Grimgoblins like the front door of the cathedral said there were?" Head Revels asked, trying to piece it all together.

"Yes, un no," said Fezzy. "There be Grimgoblins, but they not here. They be wit Blade in the dark cavern deeper inta the earth called, Arie Woods! They come long time ago with Zippas—"

"What's a Zippa?" asked Head Revels hanging on to every detail.

"Aaa... aaa... a giant ya know, Lazzard, Ay think ya call it," said Fezzy.

"Snazzard!" sparked Pilt.

"Yes, he got it, Snazzard," Fezzy said with the point of his finger in Pilt's direction. An approving smile quickly covered Pilt's entire face.

"Came with the Snazzards and kilt lots of uz Cobbles." Fezzy's voice quivered, multiple tears now streaming down his face.

"Und ate flesh from stream und cause much harm ta cathedral!" said Inger bitterly, finally daring to make eye contact.

"I don't understand—what are 'flesh'?" Head Revels inquired, looking from one to the other dwarf.

Fezzy grabbed hold of his hand and speedily ran the two of them out of the room and down the long hall, stopping at the top of the winding staircase. Whispers of fright came from below as students from the main lobby spotted them and pointed up at Fezzy. Their eyes followed him closely as Fezzy led Head Revels down the winding staircase and to the alarmed crowd.

"It's alright," Head Revels said in a calming voice as he raised a hand to hush them. "Quiet everyone, quiet! Everything's fine. He's friendly!" At the bottom of the stairs, Fezzy broke free and ran to a nearby bridge. He pointed down into the stream.

"See, Flesh!"

"Oh, you mean fish?" responded Head Revels, smiling.

"Yis! Flish," nodded Fezzy.

"So, you say the Snazzards and Blade's men came and ate the fish?" Head Revels devised.

Flin and Luftin suddenly appeared at the top of the stairs, holding Inger's hands.

One of the Haunsdale girls spotted them and screamed, "There's more of them!" Then, she quickly looked for Miss Lemons for refuge.

"Just three of them," said Head Revels calmly and turned back to Fezzy. "Fezzy, what are the Arie Woods?"

"Arie Woods! Ya know!" Fezzy paused a moment to think. Then he raised his hands high above his head like Frankenstein and walked around the room, pulling faces and growling.

"Oh, Scary Woods, Fezzy?" blurted out Pilt. The students were now very intrigued by the two childlike dwarfs.

Fezzy shook his head and continued walking around, howling and making odd faces.

Principal Vespar spoke up. "I think what he's trying to get us to say is, 'Eerie Woods.'"

"Yis, yis, yis!" Fezzy nodded and pointed in her direction.

"So, Blade's an evil man who lives in the Eerie Woods?" asked Head Revels.

"Yis! Blade's very bad!" replied Fezzy. Just then, everyone turned to the top of the stairs where another dwarf stood. This one was a woman with a look of terror on her face. She stood shaking, staring down into the wide eyes of the group.

"'Eppel!" hollered Fezzy up at her.

She was slightly shorter than the others and very petite. Her dress appeared to be made from bedding, but it complimented her small frame well. Her lavender eyes twinkled as she looked down at the sea of expectant faces. Fezzy stared up at the trembling, terrified Heppel. Quickly, he ran up the stairs to her. He whispered something in her ear and grabbed her by the arm. She jerked free from his grip and scolded him briefly. Then moments later, she started to gradually make her own way down the stairway.

"She's beautiful," came several hushed whispers from the girls.

Head Revels slowly walked over to the base of the stairs and cautiously bent down, trying not to startle her. He looked through her red eyelashes and into her soft lavender eyes.

He pointed to himself. "I am Head Revels," he said in a tranquil voice. "And you must be Heppel. You're just as beautiful as Fezzy described."

Her cheeks flushed, and she looked awkwardly from him to Fezzy. Still smiling, Head Revels reached out to shake her hand. Heppel's eyes filled with fear as she placed her hands behind her back and warily crept away. Fezzy ran up to her and whispered something in her ear. She seemed to be contemplating something as her eyes caught every subtle movement around her. Then suddenly, her eyes rested on Principal Vespar, who smiled back. Cautiously, Heppel began to kneel before her.

"No! No! Get Up!" hollered Fezzy, trying to pull her up off the floor.

"She's fine, Fezzy. Whatever she feels comfortable doing," soothed Principal Vespar.

Fezzy took Heppel's hand. "Frinds, 'Eppel. Frinds," Fezzy said softly.

Head Revels took a couple of steps back, and then knelt down before her. Tears pooled in her terrified eyes, then slid down her cheeks, making two small puddles on the floor. She stood silently, paused for a moment, and then carefully walked over to Head Revels, who held out his hand. Slowly, her trembling hand stretched towards his until she eventually rested it in his open palm. He bowed before her.

Principal Vespar gracefully approached her. "I'm Vermelda," she whispered, as she held out her hand and crouched down to her eye level. Heppel cautiously placed her hand in Principal Vespar's. "How charming it is to meet your acquaintance," Principal Vespar said with a small curtsy.

Heppel looked up at Principal Vespar, her shy grin slowly spreading into a beautiful smile that revealed her sparkling teeth.

The icy tension that had filled the room quickly melted. Soon others gathered around and wanted to meet the three Cobbles.

"No sudden movements," warned Head Revels. "Let them have a chance to warm up to us first. We don't want to overwhelm them in any way."

Heppel held tightly to Principal Vespar's hand as introductions were made. Head Revels made his way over to where Fezzy and Inger stood introducing themselves to the others.

"Do either of you know where we might find food?" he asked.

Fezzy ran to the open cathedral door and pointed out. "Fuuud!"

"Would you mind taking us to this food?" asked Head Revels.

"Tid be me pleasure!" zipped Fezzy joyfully.

As Fezzy started to leave, Principal Vespar could feel Heppel's grip tighten. She gently gave a reassuring squeeze as they walked to the door to watch the men head down the path that led to the lake.

Several of the boys, excited at the prospect of a decent meal, ran out as well. They all gathered at the lake shoreline.

The two Cobbles grabbed onto what appeared to be a vine that went from the shore and into the water. They dug their feet deep into the lake's sandy shore and started to pull. Flin ran down to help. They reeled in several yards of vine, and then a trap woven out of tree limbs bobbed up. It was bulging with hundreds of crabs and lobsters.

They took the food back to the cathedral where Inger and Fezzy busied themselves building an enormous fire in the fireplace. Heppel seemed a little more at ease with something to do as she came scurrying out of the kitchen with an armful of wooden pots. She placed them next to the fireplace and then returned to the kitchen. Upon her retreat, Fezzy came scurrying in from the kitchen carrying an old brass pitcher filled with fresh cool water. "Yuz ull jist wait!" he said excitedly, pouring the water into the big pots. "Me 'Eppel, she luvs ta cook." He smiled and then returned to the kitchen.

A far off melody rang from the kitchen. Fezzy returned. "Hear thot?" he asked with a broad grin. "Haven't heard 'Eppel hum like that fur, oh . . . seventy sum odd years!" he chuckled. "Makes me happy it does, ta see her like thot!" As he spoke, his bushy red eyebrows bounced upon his forehead.

Heppel entered the room and shuffled back and forth from pot to pan, which were hanging out over the flames. She added a variety of spices as she worked her magic, making a delicious aroma that seasoned the air. Principal Vespar, Voss Yeg, and some of the girls helped by carry large wooden plates and utensils out of the kitchen and then placed them around tables near the fireplace. Inger began putting smaller plates and utensils on a table further away from the rest.

"What are you doing, Inger? Why are you setting up clear over there?" Head Revels asked.

"We'z told we worn't ta eat with da others. Cobbles are only ta eat with each other!" Inger replied as he continued setting the table.

"That's silly!" said Principal Vespar. "You'll bring your things over here and eat with the rest of us."

Heppel turned around with a big smile. "Fuud's ready!" she shouted, catching everyone off guard with her unexpected abrupt voice.

The room sat silent while starving mouths were finally fed.

Head Revels, who was just finishing up, leaned over to Heppel. "Heppel, that was definitely, theeee best meal I've had in ages. Thank you!" he said, dabbing the sides of his lips with an old green fabric napkin. Heppel blushed as she peeked over the wooden table.

Head Revels set down his drinking mug and turned to Fezzy. "Fezzy, do you by chance know of a way that would take us back up to the surface?"

"Ay heard tales a da surface, but neber hab Ay been there."

"Do you know of any tunnels that lead up?"

"Yes, some lead up, but neber hab Ay seen one thot goes clear ta da surface," he responded, pouring himself some more berry juice.

"Fezzy, you spoke of others that live in the Eerie Woods. Why didn't they just remain here instead?"

"Fezzy don' know why," he said, now eating a large crab leg.

"Where did you say your family was?" asked Miss Lemons, in her soft Irish voice. Everyone at their table was now caught up in the conversation, staring intriguingly at the three dwarfs as they ate.

"Blade, he took them away. He said he'd kill them if they didn't go with him. He took all our family und made dem prisoners. Inger, Heppel, and Ay hide. They look fur us fur long time, but no can find, 'cause we hide way back in cathedral." Fezzy was overwhelmed with emotion.

Head Revels waited a moment. "Tell me more about this, this Blade fellow?" asked Head Revels while pouring Fezzy his fifth refill of berry juice.

"Oh, he's a bad, bad man! Tall, pointy ears, he look kinda like a . . . a . . . a . . ." Fezzy started snorting and squealing.

"A pig?" piped Sam.

"Yis, pig!" responded Fezzy. "He wears a long, black coat wit heavy boots." Fezzy shuddered as he described the man, and then snatched up another handful of crab legs.

"Where's he putting it all," whispered Pilt, referring to the endless amount of food Fezzy had eaten.

"Quiet, Pilt!" rebuked Sam, clearly taken by the dwarfs.

"Why did he threaten to kill your people?" Head Revels asked.

"Oh, Blade vory bad. He kilt lots uz Cobbles and take rest for prisoners und slaves!" Fezzy paused, trying not to cry.

Head Revels reached out and patted his shoulder. "I'm sorry about your family being taken, Fezzy," said Head Revels. Fezzy couldn't stop the tears. Head Revels quickly changed the subject, "Where did all of these glow rocks come from and why is this one in the middle of the floor have a railing around it?"

"'Tis a giant moon rock!" Fezzy said proudly, turning toward it. "We'z put it in da middle of floor ta keep out da Snazzards!"

"How does that there rock keep ou' Snazzards?" asked Luftin.

"They don' like da light. Dey neber come out in da light, unless Blade makes um come out in da light," Fezzy explained.

"Interestin'," Luftin said, nodding. He sat comfortably with his arms crossed over his slightly bulging belly and his feet propped up.

"Fezzy, where did the glow rocks come from?" asked Voss Yeg.

"Oh, yeah— 'bout one handrid fifty yars igo, me parents pulled it out frum deep down in da Black Lagoon. Dey brought it here when I wus jist a lad. Since then it's multiplied lots of times! These are da only glow rocks we know uf. We call um moon rocks, 'cause they're round und glow like da moon in da dark!"

"You mean to say that you're over a hundred and fifty years old?" Principal Vespar asked open-mouthed, putting down her fork and looking him over thoroughly.

"Yis, Ay'm jist over—" Fezzy calculated, tapping his head.

"Nine hundred und thirty-two, come next April!" reproved Heppel. "Ya know that. Ya reminded me und Inger of thot jist yisterday. Ya remind us practically everyday. Remember, ya said not ta forget ta get ya some'n!" Vigorously she picked up her plate and goblet then headed for the kitchen.

"Nine hundred thirty-two, really?" questioned a shocked Principal Vespar. "You don't look that old!" she said, now raising her glasses to her eyes.

"Thank ye!" Fezzy leaned towards them and looked at the back of Heppel as she stormed away; he whispered. "Heppel, she don' like birthdays. We been celebrating her two hundredth birthday six hundred and sixty-three years now."

"You'll pay fur that, Fezzy Brundlemair!" came her shout as she disappeared around the corridor that lead to the kitchen.

"Got good ears too fur bein' eight hundred and sixty three, jist of dis last Tuesday past," he whispered.

"Heard that too, Fizzy!"

~~~~~~~~~

That night, with the help of the Cobbles, sleeping assignments were made. Since the cathedral was spacious and had many furnished rooms, it accommodated the large number of guests quite well. The men and boys were assigned the rooms on the upper levels, and the women and girls stayed on the main floor.

Instead of using their torches in the dark, Heppel had given them all a tall, thick stick of honey wax and a wooden saucer to use as candles. Flowell and Sam crept slowly down the hall to their assigned room. Sam held her candle out in front of her, turning nervously at every noise. Sam pushed the door open to their room. It made a horrible creaking sound as it slowly opened, and the candlelight gradually filled the room.

"Sam, look!" Flowell said excitedly, pointing at a waterfall and bridge as they both eagerly entered the room. Sam spotted a moon rock and began rubbing at it until the room faintly illuminated. She ran and drew some water out of the stream and poured it over the rock until the room got brighter and brighter, as if the moon's rays had now filled the room.

Upstairs, Flin, Pilt, and Cretchit headed to their room. "Whoa, you guys!" shouted Flin. "You're not going to believe this!"

"Flin, lad, after the last few days, you'd be surprised at what I'd be willing ta believe," responded Cretchit.

"Holy cow!" Pilt shouted enthusiastically as he entered.

"Check it out! We don't even need a candle in our room. The anemone is part of the ceiling!" Flin said, blowing out his candle as the moon's rays filtered down through the ocean's rippling water and onto the bedroom floor. As he stared up through the anemone, the stars reminded him of the last night he'd spent in his bedroom back home.

"Check it out! We have a moon rock in our room," hollered Pilt. "This place is awesome," he mumbled as he scurried about the room. "I dibs the bed closest to the bathroom!"

"Bathroom?" Flin and Cretchit both said with surprise. "There's a bathroom?" Sure enough, behind a small wooden door in the corner of the room was a tiny bathroom with all the accommodations.

Chapter Thirteen

SUMP LOST? IMPOSSIBLE!

"**C**an't we stop here?" whined Parcell, leaning against the tunnel's wall. "We've been walking forever…"

The three of them had been wandering for quite some time, one tunnel undistinguishable from the last.

"No, Parcell!" barked Sump. "With all of that whining you do, it's no wonder your mother left!"

"I think Parcell's right, Mr. Sump," Ruel implored. "I mean, it is getting dark, and we could get even more lost!"

"Dark? We're trapped under the earth! And what are we now? Lost, you moron!" spat Sump. "We'll go through one of these tunnels a bit further, and if we don't see something hopeful then we'll rest. Besides, what are you both so worried about? We have a torch!" Sump declared as he held it close to his side. "See look, a tunnel up ahead! We'll follow that for a while, and who knows, it may be the tunnel that takes us out of this wormhole!"

They traveled further through the tunnel, when finally it opened up into a cavern with an anemone over the top of it; only this one wasn't bright and clear like the cavern above. This one was much deeper under the ocean and dark with gray clouds that roamed about the dead trees and barren ground of the cavern.

"Look! Look over there!" shouted Sump excitedly, pointing with his torch. "It's a cave, and there's smoke coming out of it!"

Quickly they made their way closer, the smoke changed to a dim light.

"Look! I can see movement in there. Come on!" He ran ahead, leaving Parcell and Ruel in the dark.

Once they made it to the cave, they saw two large figures dressed in black cloaks that stood motionless just outside of the entrance like guards. The black-hooded men strongly resembled executioners.

"Hello! Hello in there!" hollered Sump. Parcell wrapped his hand around his dad's mouth to shut him up, but it was too late. One of the hooded figures abruptly turned in their direction.

"Leave me alone, Parcell! Yes, it's us out here in the dark! We're over here!" screamed Sump, waving his torch.

"They don't look friendly, Dad! I don't think you should be waving!" argued Parcell, trying to grab away the torch.

"Nonsense, boy!" Sump pulled the torch further away. "Once I tell them who I am, we'll be treated like royalty, especially down here. And *stop* telling me what to do! I'm in charge!"

The two guards stomped briskly through the dead brush after them.

"Yes! You're getting closer, but we're more over this way!" Sump yelled, signaling with his torch. "Wow! They are rather abnormally large!" Sump said as they drew nearer. They were dressed from head to toe in dark, heavy fabric that hid any distinguishable characteristics. One of them immediately grabbed Sump's arm and forced it behind his back.

"Hey! Ow! Stop that, you moron! You're hurting me!" Sump whined, trying to squirm free.

The other grabbed Parcell and Ruel, restraining them both with just one hand.

"You're going to be sorry you ever treated me like this!" shouted Sump, as the guard dragged him toward the lit tunnel. "I want to speak to your superior, you . . . you . . . imbecile!" he stammered.

A cold chill embraced them as the guards dragged them into the cave and threw them up against the wall. A small, darkly dressed dwarf scampered further up the tunnel and out of sight.

"So, what are your names?" Sump asked the guards, but they made no response. "I guess uneducated imbeciles like yourselves don't understand English," he chuckled sarcastically with a snort.

Just then, an eight-foot-tall man, with a face resembling that of a pig, came tromping down the tunnel toward them. His ears pitched high on the sides of his head and came to a point. What few remaining hairs he had left on his head were wiry gray. His large hands were adorned with roughly made jewelry, and the torchlight reflected on a heavy gold chain that hung around his neck.

"Doesn't look as if pigman there's missed any meals! Looks like he could use a bath," snorted Sump audaciously to Parcell and Ruel.

The pigman turned swiftly, giving Sump a sharp glance that immediately halted his rude remarks. He stomped over to one of the guards and back-handed him, then tromped over to Sump and placed his chest up against his nose, squishing him.

"You really do smell bad!" muffled Sump through his smashed nose.

The pigman stood stiff, and then took in a deep breath. "I could crush your tiny human head if I wanted!" he growled. He suddenly stepped back, causing Sump to collapse to the ground.

"DO—YOU—KNOW—WHO—I—AM?" the pigman boomed. Sump's face turned pasty white as he clutched his bleeding nose.

"Oh . . . so . . . so . . . you speak, you speak English?" Sump laughed nervously as he stood gulping.

"Yes, which is too bad for you!" His wicked smile revealed teeth, which were covered with a green mossy film. "What was all that gibberish you were mumbling about, eating all the time, and needing to bathe?" he asked indignantly.

"I— You thought I, I said that?" stammered Sump, pointing to himself as if surprised. "I, I think you're mistaken. It must have come from one of those boys over there!"

"Do you take me, Blade, for a fool?" He stomped his foot, knocking dirt from the ceiling that showered them. "This is my world! I own everything you see, even the three of you now!" He walked around examining each of them closely. "Ah, I see that you are of some value," he said, stopping at Sump. His eyes grew wide with greed as he looked over the jewelry that garnished Sump's body.

"Hey! Those are mi—" Sump started to say as Blade grabbed hold of his hands and pulled off his precious gold rings.

"We usually just get rid of trash like you!" snarled Blade. "Who are you, and why have you come here?"

Sump nervously responded, "I—I'm Sump, I mean, Mr. Sump, and those fine-looking lads over there are my sons! Well, one of them is my son, anyways."

"You still haven't answered me! What are you doing here?"

"We came from the surface," cowered Sump. "Our, our bus fell through this hole that opened up in the earth, and then it, it just closed up, just like that!" chuckled Sump nervously.

"So, you came from up top, you say . . . Enough chatter, get rid of them all!" yelled Blade, then started back up the tunnel. The two guards began dragging Parcell and Ruel out the tunnel's exit. Then, one snatched up Sump as well.

"Wait! WAIT!" squealed Sump while being dragged. "We can help you!"

Blade fervently continued stomping away.

"We know of a treasure!" shrieked Sump.

Instantly Blade halted. His sharp ears slowly rose up the sides of his head. He turned around.

"STOP!" he ordered the guards and trudged back down the tunnel. "Treasure! What treasure?" growled Blade through gritted teeth. Then, he unexpectedly sniffed at Sump.

Sump nervously blurted out, "It's a huge, glorious, grand treasure! I'm surprised you don't know of it!"

"I own this world down here, and everything *including* treasures!" snarled Blade. "Wealth, gold, diamonds! Now that is true power!" He made a fist and licked the rings on his fingers. "Down here you are nothing more than a slave, unless . . ." he paused and looked over at Sump through the corner of his eye. "Unless, you have gems or food. Without either of those, you might as well be dead!"

He reached into his pocket and pulled out a handful of jewelry he'd taken off of Sump's body. "You had something a moment ago to bargain your lives with, but now you have nothing!" he said, lusting over his new treasures. "You're of no worth to me anymore—any of you!" He glanced over at Parcell and Ruel. "Get rid of them!"

"No wait! Wait! What about the treasure?" hollered Sump. "I said we know of a *grand treasure*! Where do you think that jewelry in your hands came from?"

Blade's ears again slowly rose. "What then, is the location of this so-called grand treasure that you speak of?"

Sump stumbled. "I can't tell you that."

"Bah! You know of no treasure," laughed Blade mockingly. "You're just bluffing to try and save your skins."

"No! No! You said it yourself! If I tell you where it is, I've lost my bargaining chip," Sump said as he glanced over at Parcell and Ruel, who stared back befuddled. "If you don't believe me, you'll just have to kill us then!" Parcell and Ruel's eyes widened and their heads jerked in Sump's direction, now even more confused.

"Hmm . . . So you do know of a treasure," sneered Blade.

"What makes you believe me?" questioned Sump, dabbing at the sweat on his upper lip.

"Because you're hiding something, I can tell! You don't want me to know of this, this treasure you speak of. Only a man who knew of such a thing would not reveal it, because he knows this so-called treasure is worth more than his own life!" roared Blade. "Well, I know of this treasure you speak of, human," he quickly turned and lowered his face just inches from Sump's. "This treasure you speak of—is it the—*Oliblish Treasure?*" Blade spit in Sump's face as he spoke.

"Yep! Yeah! That's the one! Isn't it, boys?" Sump agreed.

A devilish sparkle of greed twinkled in Blade's dull red eyes. "How is it you know of this treasure?"

Sump stuttered. "Every, everyone speaks of it down here!"

"Who speaks of it?"

"Everyone, lots of people, I mean, lots of creatures. And we know where it is, right boys?" Parcell and Ruel stared back blank-faced and then nodded.

"Not everyone knows of the Oliblish Treasure, only some," said Blade suspiciously.

"There are other settlements besides you down here?" asked Sump curiously.

"Of course there are others, you idiot!" scolded Blade. "You just said a minute ago how all the other creatures speak of this Oliblish Treasure!" shouted Blade, his curiosity replaced by anger and suspicion.

"Of course, those people, I didn't know there were others near here, though," cringed Sump, quickly recovering.

Blade went on. "You know, you better not be taking me for a fool. I will give you one week to prove your story true. By the end of one week, if you haven't proven yourself, you're all done for! Now escort them to their cells! " demanded Blade, his cloak brushing against Sump's leg as he stormed off.

The guards shoved them up the tunnel until they came to a heavy wooden door. One of the guards pulled out a key from under his cloak, unlocked it, and shoved the three of them inside. It was even darker than the tunnel. There were dwarfs and giant Grimgoblins milling about, all completely dressed in dark attire. As they made their way further in, they heard a loud hissing. Sump leaned over a ledge and looked down into a big pit that was hundreds of feet below. In it were six giant Snazzards, all different colors, hissing and crawling over one another.

Sump gulped hard as he turned to the dwarf Grimgoblin. "What are the Snazzards for?" he asked hesitantly.

"Blade throws whoever he wants into the pit."

"It's a good thing we're on his good side then, huh?" nervously chuckled Sump.

"Move it! Get going!" grunted the larger Grimgoblin, shoving a sharp spear in Sump's back.

They were led out of the enormous common cavern and down an unlit tunnel, lined on both sides with metal bars and cell doors. At the end of the hall was a colossal guard holding a cell door open. When they reached the cell, he roughly threw them inside. A Grimgoblin staggered in after them and leaned his torch up to one that was mounted on the wall. The small torch lit up, shedding light on scurrying rats and a cold, damp, cavern cell with a glaze of frost that shimmered off the outer walls.

"This is your room for now, and those are your beds," he pointed to piles of straw on the floor.

"Beds! You call this a bed?" Sump complained as he spastically kicked at the straw. "Maybe a bed for a pig!— No! I beg of you— please, don't tell Blade I said that."

"Hmm . . ." groaned the guard. He slammed the door behind him and locked it. Sump waited until the guards had gone. "This won't do!"

Parcell glance around the dank cell and whimpered, "What other choice do we have?"

"Oh, shut up, Parcell, and listen to me! We have no treasure to offer, and once Blade finds this out, we'll all be thrown down into that blasted Snazzard pit! So, before Blade finds out, we have to try and get out of here. Okay, here's the plan," Sump whispered, as they all huddled close together. "We'll tell Blade we're going for the treasure, and that we'll be back with it. As soon as we exit the tunnel, we'll get as far away from this infernal dung heap as we can. Agreed?"

"Agreed," the two boys responded.

Chapter Fourteen

WHO DONE IT?

Early the next morning, Flin went outside to see a giant shadow meandering about the cavern floor. He looked up to see what was causing it.

"Whoa . . . unreal!" A huge whale was brushing itself against the outer layer of the anemone. "Everyone! Hey, everyone!" he shouted as he ran back into the cathedral. "You've got to come and see this!"

"Wh— what is it, Flin?" Head Revels ran out the front door distraught, glancing all over and then up to where Flin's eyes were glued. "Oh, a whale . . ." he said with relief.

Hastily, everyone flooded out of the cathedral.

"You're right, there really is a whale!" Principal Vespar said, staring up and shading her eyes.

"Why's it just laying there like that?" asked Flowell. "Is it sick or something?" she asked Head Revels.

"No, it's probably just tired. Or, it's possible that the whale is about to give birth!" Head Revels said with an emerging smile.

The whale progressively drifted down to the bottom of the anemone, where it hovered against the wall. The students ran to where it had settled.

"Students! Students!" chirped Voss Yeg, briskly making her way over. "Now we don't want to alarm it! Everyone back up and give the whale some space!"

~~~~~~~~~

Deep in the Snazzard pit, Sump, Parcell, and Ruel were finishing cleaning up.

"This stuff's disgusting! Some of these piles are as big as me!" Ruel said as he tried to shovel up an enormous Snazzard dropping.

"That's because that was someone like you, you idiot!" shrieked Sump. He then gestured for Parcell and Ruel to come closer. "Now listen," he whispered. "Instead of returning to our room like we were told, we're leaving here tonight, got it? Guard! *Guard!*" hollered Sump impatiently, as he banged on the back of the locked door. "We're done in here! You can open this do—" The door flew open. "That was revolting!" Sump informed the guard, his face scrunched up tight like an old shriveled apple.

"I'll be sure and tell Blade you said that. I'm sure he'll have you down here again real soon, only next time, with the Snazzards still roaming about!" barked the guard.

"No, no!" chuckled Sump nervously. "It, it really wasn't all *that* bad, was it boys?"

"Yes it wa—"

"Parcell!" Sump snapped, shooting him a sharp glare.

They followed the guard up the dark stairway and into the main cavern.

"Well, I, for one, am dead tired," exaggerated Sump. "I think we'll just go back to our room and get a little shut eye," he said as he stretched and yawned.

The guard escorted them back to their room, where they pretended to shut the cell door behind them. They waited until the sound of the guard's footsteps had vanished then cautiously made their way back down the tunnel toward the cavern's exit.

"STOP!" shouted a guard at the three suspicious looking characters. "Where do you think you're going?"

"Well, we're, we're headed to get some of that treasure we told Blade about," Sump responded tensely with a feeble half smile.

"Blade gave strict orders to only let two of you out at a time. That way, if the others didn't return, the one left behind would be Snazzard food!" grunted the guard with satisfaction as he grabbed Sump around the neck. "You'll stay, and the others can go for now!"

The guard slammed the handle of a lit torch into Ruel's chest. "Now go!" Sump's eyes glazed over in shock as he watched the two of them walk down and out the tunnel's exit then stroll away into the dead trees of the dismal cavern.

"Yes!" celebrated Parcell, falling to his knees. "Finally, we're out of there for good!"

"What about your dad? They'll kill him for sure if we don't return!"

"Ruel! We have nothing of value we can return with. Besides, he'd do the same if he were in our shoes. You know they'll kill us too if we return with zilch!"

"I have an idea," Ruel said. "What if we go back to that old petrified tree where we left the rest of the group? Maybe we can find something of value in there."

"What are you thinking, *Ruel?* You know they have nothing there! All they have is a bunch of banged up luggage and old clothes!"

"We can't just do nothing, Parcell—but . . . on the other hand, you're probably right— your dad is just an, ornery, old, rich man!"

"Hey, watch it, Ruel. He may be old, but he really is rich! We've got to go back or I'll never see a dime of my inheritance. Okay, Ruel, we'll go and check out that old, stupid tree. Maybe we'll find something valuable there."

It was late into the night when the two of them made it to the cathedral.

"This old rock-tree gives me the creeps," whimpered Parcell as the moon's light gleamed down upon the mammoth tree. "We don't even know if they're still alive in there. For all we know, they could be dead!"

"Well, we're going to find out!" said Ruel and headed up the steps toward the front door.

They forced the door open. The inside of the cathedral was pitch black.

"What's that noise?" whispered Ruel. "It sounds like running water? Wow, take a look at this place! There are real fish in here!"

"Big whoop. What'd you think? They'd be fake fish?" Parcell said, stepping backwards and grazing the base of the large moon rock with his shoe. His touch had caused the light to illuminate.

"Whoa, Ruel! Look at this! What do you think it is?" Parcell reared back his foot and gave it a hard kick, causing the rock to pulsate with flashing light. He went to kick it again.

"Stop it, Parcell!" Ruel said angrily, looking around and hoping that they hadn't been detected.

"Gosh, Ruel, you're no fun!"

"We're looking for something valuable, remember? Where do you think those stairs over there go?"

"Like I know? You ask as if I've been here before!" Parcell snidely remarked.

They crept up the wooden staircase and down the hall, poking their heads in and out of rooms as they passed.

"Look at this place. This place is cool. I like all the waterfalls," Ruel said glancing around in the dim light.

"You sure are getting excited about it," Parcell sneered. "Yeah, well I think this place sucks, just like the people in it!" However, his facial expression contradicted his words as he stared around in amazement. "Hey look, it's Edgar's room, and he's asleep!" Parcell whispered, tiptoeing into the dark bedroom. "What's old Edgar been up to lately?" He picked up Edgar's hair bag, untied it, and slowly slid his hand deep into the bag. "Whose hair ya been cuttin' lately Edgar? OUCH!" he shouted, jerking his hand out of the bag and dropping it to the floor.

"Parcell! Shut — up! You're going to wake someone and get us caught!"

Parcell held his hand close to his face with gritted teeth. "Stupid thing!" he mumbled, kicking at the bag on the floor. Slowly, the bag began to move. "What the—?" Parcell muttered, jumping back several feet. "That's not hair!" A long black cobra slithered out of the bag, raised its head, and flared its sides before it fell lifeless to the floor. Parcell nudged at it with the end of his shoe, but the snake lay dead. Bitterly, he reared back his leg and kicked it across the room. It slammed against the back of the door.

Ruel glanced down at it confused. "What do you think killed it?"

Parcell looked down at his black fingernails puzzled, and then stared down at the dead snake.

"Where do you think Edgar got that?" Ruel asked.

"I don't know, but knowing Edgar, it was probably his best friend."

"We're wasting way too much time. We've got to get going!" Ruel exclaimed.

They tiptoed further down the hall. "Hey look, it's Newby," Parcell whispered and then glided into the room.

"What are you doing? You know Flin doesn't have anything of value!" Ruel said in a slightly elevated voice as he continued down the hall, leaving Parcell behind. A moment later, Ruel's face reappeared in Flin's doorway as Parcell swiftly put something into his pocket.

"Hey, Newby's cigar boxes," Parcell whispered, raising his eyebrows and tucking one of the boxes under his arm.

"They're just junk, and you know that," scowled Ruel from the hall, looking both ways down the corridor. "Now, come on!"

After going through several rooms, Parcell barked, "There's nothing of value here!"

"What have I been telling you for the past two hours!" erupted Ruel.

"Oh, shut up!"

They crept back down the stairs. The moon rock that Parcell had kicked earlier was still aglow, but it was illuminating a pulsating red light in the kicked area where it was injured. Parcell walked over to it.

"Come on, Parcell, let's go," hushed Ruel from the open front door.

"Come here," Parcell stood stubborn. "Get over here! Now!"

Ruel begrudgingly obeyed.

"Pull this rock out of the dirt!" demanded Parcell.

"Why?"

"Because I said so, that's why!"

Ruel pulled at the rock. "It's too heavy."

"If you're too weak, then get one of the smaller ones over there!" Parcell pointed across the room.

Ruel shot Parcell a dirty look and then went over and tore one of the smaller rocks out of the ground. The two of them left the cathedral, leaving the door open behind them.

"It's possible we could pass this glow rock off as something valuable," Parcell shrugged as they crept down the path. Parcell pulled the cigar box out from under his arm and opened it up. "Why would Newby be totin' these junky things around anyways? These big colored ones just look like rocks," he said disappointedly, his fingers fumbling through the pits.

He picked out a big, shiny ruby pit, looked at it briefly, and threw it into a nearby pond. The water in the pond immediately began to boil, sending up enormous brown bubbles. In a matter of seconds, the pond looked like a pot of boiling water.

"Do you see that? All that fuss over one crappy pit!" spat Parcell as he reached into the box to throw another.

"Hold it! Stop!" Ruel demanded, grabbing Parcell's arm. "It's possible we could pass some of these off as jewels!"

The corners of Parcell's mouth slowly turned up into a crude half smile. "Ya think? What if Blade can tell they're not real jewels, then what?" Parcell looked down into the box skeptically.

"Trust me, I've never seen pits like these— have you?"

"No—Okay, we'll do it! We can outsmart this Pigman!" Parcell said, slamming the box closed. A loose pit fell to the cavern floor and burrowed itself out of sight.

Ruel looked around in desperation one last time for something of worth. He spotted the giant whale resting against the bottom of the anemone wall and noticed that next to it was a newborn baby whale. "Look at that!" Ruel said in amazement.

They rushed to the wall and stared out into the ocean at the two whales. Parcell suddenly dashed away into a nearby grove of trees and returned with a branch in his hand. He stripped away the limbs and sharpened the tip of it on a nearby boulder.

"What are you doing?" asked Ruel.

"You'll see!" Parcell said proudly with a disturbing gleam.

"We don't have time for this, Parcell."

Both whales lay resting against the anemone wall. Parcell ran up to the wall where the baby whale was sleeping. "Watch this," he said with a twisted smile. He cocked back his arm and rushed the wall, forcing the spear clean through the anemone tissue and deep into the side of the baby whale. Red blood quickly tainted the water as the baby whale let out a painful squeal that could be hear inside the cavern. The baby whale started to squirm, trying to break free. The mother whale seeing what had happened glared in at Parcell. She let out a high-pitched squeal and began slamming her tail against the anemone wall, trying to get at him. Angrily, she swam backwards and then rushed the wall in a fury, slamming against it, and causing it to send concerning ripples up the clear wall.

Hearing the disturbance, Head Revels came running out of his room half dressed, pulling on his bathrobe. "What is that noise?" he hollered, looking around.

"I think it's coming from outside," replied Miss Lemons.

Head Revels dashed out of the open front door as the others followed. Just as they exited the cathedral, the mother whale collided into the anemone again.

"Look!" yelled Cretchit, pointing at two devious figures as they darted out of the moonlight and into a dark grove of trees.

Principal Vespar rushed out of the cathedral and raised her glasses to her eyes. "What's upset the whale?"

Flowell pointed to the base of the anemone where the baby whale was pinned to the wall engulfed in a cloud of red water.

"There's a spear stuck in it!" hollered one of the students, who had made his way over to the whale with a torch.

Head Revels took off running toward the baby whale, then stopped and yelled back, "Quick, we need the first aid kit!"

Hearing this, Pilt sprinted back into the cathedral.

The mother whale, protective of its newborn and now dreadfully agitated, glared in at the crowd and let out an ear-piercing squeal. Then she abruptly turned and swam away.

"What's taking Pilt so long?" said Head Revels impatiently. "Someone go and help him find that first aid kit!"

Minutes later the mother whale returned with several other large whales. They began ramming the walls of the anemone sending major ripples that traveled throughout the cavern.

"I don't think the anemone can take much more of this before it ruptures and floods the entire cavern!" quivered Fig Tronsel.

Pilt finally came running down the path with the first aid kit in his hands. Head Revels unexpectedly took off running into the nearby grove of trees and returned with a sharp stick. He began gouging two new holes in the anemone. Seeing this, the mother whale became even more furious and dove toward Head Revels. She rammed the wall with her head, trying to get at him.

"I need someone to help hold the baby whale!" he demanded.

Flin dove to the cavern floor next to Head Revels. The ocean's cold salty water poured through the two new holes and onto his knees.

"Flin, put your arms through the holes and hold tight to the baby whale. Whatever you do, don't let go! I'm going to try and pull the spear out of its side without breaking it off!"

Head Revels pulled on the spear. "It's stuck in there good!" he groaned. He planted both of his feet against the anemone wall and tugged.

Mr. Luftin fell to the ground and grabbed hold of the stick along with Head Revels and pulled until it finally came free. Blood poured from out of the baby whale's body. The whales were now enraged and continued to strike the wall. Head Revels grabbed several feet of gauze from the first aid kit, made a couple of more new holes in the wall, and stuck his hands through them. He wrapped the gauze several times tightly around the baby whale's body and tied it into a knot.

"Okay, Flin, let go!" Instantly, the baby whale swam up to its mother, who swam several circles around it in a thorough inspection. One at a time, the large whales withdrew, and the ripples gradually subsided. The group stared up silently as the mother whale and baby whale brushed against one another before they solemnly swam away.

Head Revels fell to his knees. "We need to repair the anemone. We don't want it to hemorrhage and tear any further!"

Principal Vespar sent some of the girls to get small vines and sharp sticks to suture the holes back together.

"Who could have done such a thing?" Principal Vespar asked indignantly as she knelt in the mossy mud, busy stitching. "Why on earth would anyone want to hurt a baby whale?"

Once they repaired the anemone, they all returned to the cathedral. Head Revels was the last to cross the threshold. He entered to the sound of whispers and traumatized eyes as the group stared up at the ceiling. He looked up. There, high on the ceiling, shone the words, "DEATH TO ALL WHO ENTER!"

"Now there's no need for panic!" Head Revels said loudly.

"But this place is cursed!" yelled a student.

Tension was thick in the room. Edgar somberly walked to the balcony of the second floor. He raised his dead snake high above his head and hung it out over the rail.

"My snake's dead! Someone killed it!" he cried, then turned and headed back for his room.

Flin made his way over to Head Revels. "I think I know what happened to the moon rocks!" he said. He pulled Head Revels several feet away and then raised his left hand to his face.

"Flin! What on earth has happened to your fingernails! How?" Alarmed, Head Revels grabbed Flin by the wrist and raised his glasses to his face. "Why are they all discolored like that?"

"I'm not exactly sure what happened to my hand," Flin said in a quiet voice. He looked around, concerned about being overheard. "But I saw Parcell in pain, and he was holding his right hand. I then noticed that his fingernails were like mine— only his were all black."

"What do you mean 'his fingernails were all black?'" asked Head Revels, clearly confused and a trifle annoyed.

"Hold out your hand and open your palm," instructed Flin. He looked over his shoulder to make sure no one else was watching.

Head Revels cautiously held open his palm. Flin took his finger with the black nail and touched his palm.

"OW!" Head Revels said startled, jerking his hand away, and shaking it. He looked into Flin's eyes with grave confusion.

"Hold your hand out again," said Flin.

Head Revels reluctantly held it out. Flin placed his blue fingernail on Head Revels hand. Quickly a layer of shimmering frost spread over his palm. He pulled it away.

"That was cold!" He looked down extremely bewildered at Flin's fingernails.

"Hold out your hand one more time."

"I'm not sure I want to, Flin," he said as he held out a slightly trembling hand. This time, Flin placed the reddish-orange nail on his palm.

"Sheez, that one's hot!" he rubbed his hand. "Maybe not quite as extreme as the others, but still."

Head Revels carefully raised Flin's hand to his face and squinted through his glasses, the wrinkles in his face even more distinguished with concern. "What do the white and green do?"

"I'm not sure," Flin said, his eyes full of uncertainty. "This is all new to me—I just noticed my fingernails changing colors a couple of days ago. It all happened just after I got sick, which is why I think I know what's happened to the moon rocks."

Head Revels took a deep sigh. "So, what do you believe happened to the rocks?" he said, folding his arms and looking over the top of his spectacles to make sure they weren't being watched.

"I think Parcell and Ruel broke in, and Parcell spelled all of this on the moon rocks. It sort of surprises me, because even as dumb as Parcell is, he didn't misspell a word," Flin tried to lighten the mood with a joke. Head Revels couldn't help but snort a small laugh.

"So, you're saying Parcell went around the room touching the stones and spelled out DEATH TO ALL WHO ENTER! Why? Why would Parcell and Ruel come back?"

A sickened look suddenly appeared on Flin's face as he stared down at his hand.

"What is it, Flin? You look as if you've just seen a ghost."

"My, my ring—it's missing! It must have fallen off into the ocean when I was holding onto the baby whale."

"I'm sorry, Flin," Head Revels said, patting him on the shoulder. He then walked to the center of the concerned crowd and stepped up on a stool so that he could be seen. "Attention, attention everyone! Please, everyone quiet down. I have something to say."

The room quickly fell silent, leaving only the sound of the running streams and the whistling pendulum of the clock.

"This appears to be Parcell's doing! It's just another one of his little pranks."

"How do you know that? How do we know it's not some kind of curse or omen?" yelled a terrified student standing next to the towering Fig Tronsel, who was fearfully chewing away at the ends of his fingernails and staring up through his eyelids.

"Let's just say a credible source has given me a lot of conclusive information as to what's happened here tonight. So, there's no need to be alarmed or worried!"

"Who would be this credible source?" asked Voss Yeg with a look of concern.

"I won't divulge that piece of information for the time being. It's confidential. Just trust me when I tell you this: It was Parcell's doing, along with Ruel, so everyone can just go back to bed!"

Fezzy came to the top of the stairs and glanced down between the rails. His face suddenly dropped. "One of me moon rocks is gone!" he whined. He sprung down the stairs and fell to his knees, sobbing in front of the missing rock.

Head Revels walked over to Fezzy and knelt down beside him. "I'm sorry, Fezzy. It appears that someone with no respect broke into the cathedral tonight and did quite a bit of damage."

Head Revels spotted the back of Flin, heading back up to his room. "Flin!" he shouted, signaling for him to stop. "I'll be right back, Fezzy." He went to the stairs and looked deep into Flin's troubled eyes. "We'll talk about your hand in the morning." Flin gave a tired nod.

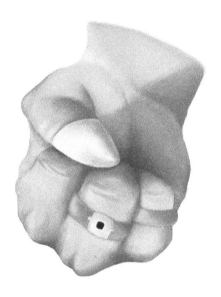

Chapter Fifteen

BLADE'S CRAVING POWER

Early the next morning, Parcell and Ruel made their way into Eerie Wood's cavern. The guard spotted their torchlight from afar and immediately sent for Blade, who was anxiously awaiting their return.

"What have you brought me?" he shouted as he tromped through the tunnel. Sweat dripped profusely off the sides of his face, and his eyes were filled with greed.

Parcell looked over at Ruel nervously, stumbling for words. "We, we—"

"Speak boy, and it better be good!" thundered Blade.

"Oh, it's good!" Parcell said in hopes of lessening Blade's intensity. "We brought back a couple of really good things! But some of the treasure was already stolen when we got there."

"Stolen! By whom?" growled Blade.

"Um, um, we think it was Newby! Yeah, Flin Newby!" nodded Parcell. Ruel began to nod as well. "But we did bring you back some of the treasure."

"Stop wasting my time and show me!"

"Show him the glowing rock, Ruel!" Parcell said tersely.

Ruel timidly pulled the glowing rock out from under his shirt. The warmth from his body had caused the rock to light up brilliantly.

"Interesting," Blade grumbled. "I've never seen anything like it before. This doesn't look like part of the Oliblish treasure. Where did you get it?" he said, jerking it out of Ruel's hands. Curious, he began sniffing it and then tapping on its exterior.

"We, we pulled it out of th—"

"Ruel! Let me tell him," Parcell said cutting him off. "What Ruel was trying to say is, we pulled it out of the treasure box. It's a rare piece, so that's why we brought it."

"I never heard of a glowing rock being part of the Oliblish treasure. Show me what else you've brought me!" Blade insisted, as he cradled the rock in one hand while the fingers of his other writhed about restlessly with greed.

"Well, we . . . we . . ."

"Stop wasting my time! I'm growing impatient!"

Parcell reluctantly pulled out the cigar box from under his arm. He looked apprehensive out of the corner of his eye at Ruel.

"Well, open it up!" barked Blade, vainly reaching for the box.

Parcell slowly pulled back the lid and stared nervously up at Blade.

"What are they?" he said, peeking down into the box with a pessimistic sneer. "They just look like little rocks!"

"Oh no, really, they're not rocks. They're precious stones!"

"Hmm," snorted Blade. He thrust his large calloused hand into the box and carelessly began sorting through the pits. "There's nothing of value in here! Junk, all of it!" He knocked the box out of Parcell's hand. When the pits crashed to the floor, they sprung to life and began to burrow themselves deep into the dirt. "What are they doing? Gems don't do that!" Blade hollered.

"But these, these gems have great powers. Look!" Parcell held up his right hand to reveal his black fingernails, while Ruel quickly snatched up the pits and seeds from out of the dirt.

"Watch!" He dashed out of the tunnel. "See this bush?"

"So, what if I do? Get on with it!" Blade said through squinted eyes.

Parcell knelt down and placed his hand at the base of the bush. Instantly, the bush began to shrivel, turn gray and harden. He removed his hand as the bush continued to crackle then turned to a fine powdery dust that blew away in the gentle breeze. Blade stared down at the ground with great fascination as the last of the bush blew out into the cavern.

"I was told the treasure had great powers, but never did I hear of this," Blade said, his pointed ears perking up so high that the tips touched each other. "How did you do that?"

"See these prickly gems," Parcell said proudly. "They carry a *deadly* liquid venom. The venom will either kill you at once, or... give you great *powers*!"

"Give me those gems! I want power now!" snarled Blade, reaching for the box.

Parcell hesitantly pulled the box out of his reach. "I don't know if I would do that if I were you."

"What? Are you trying to keep me from getting the power?" growled Blade through gritted teeth. "No one, and I mean no one, tells me what I can and cannot do!"

"Sorry, it's just that—"

"Just that what?" roared Blade, glaring over Parcell's shoulder.

"Well, it could possibly have messy effects on people, and, well, you're not exactly a normal person."

"What are you saying, human? You're the one who's not normal," bellowed Blade, towering over him.

"It's just that I think you should try it on someone else first, that's all," Parcell explained.

"Hmm, yes, you make a good point." He turned to his closest guard. "Go and bring me the three men that were to be thrown into the Snazzard pit!"

Relieved that he was spared, the guard ran up the tunnel and shortly returned with three other disgruntled Grimgoblins.

"Now, show me how this is done!" demanded Blade, stomping the ground.

"First, you carefully take the pit," Parcell began, shaking with fear.

"*And?*" hollered Blade impatiently, motioning with his hand.

"Then you put the, the thorn onto the, the, skin," he said with uncertainty, as he gingerly handled the pit.

"Bring him!" barked Blade, snapping his fingers. The Grimgoblin resisted. "Get him over here!"

Two of the guards forced him forward. "Now do it!" he demanded.

"Me?" Parcell gulped.

"Of course, you!"

His hand shook as he raised the thorn pit close to the Grimgoblin's arm. Again, the Grimgoblin began to squirm.

"Stop moving!" yelled Blade, backhanding the Grimgoblin.

Parcell held out the pit so that the reddish-orange tip pointed toward the Grimgoblin's arm. He closed his eyes as he forced it in. The Grimgoblin let out a squeal. Parcell jerked the thorn out and threw the pit to the floor and backed away. Nothing happened. The Grimgoblin looked down at his arm with relief. The guards gradually let go of him. The Grimgoblin took a few steps back up the tunnel then suddenly let out a curdling scream. He began slamming into the tunnel walls, causing dirt to fall.

"I'm on fire!" he shouted as he desperately looked around for water. The skin on his arms began to blister. He scratched at himself frantically. Seconds later, he dropped to his knees and lay motionless. The tunnel reeked of burning flesh as smoke issued from his body.

"Next!" ordered Blade. "Next!"

"No! No!" pleaded the next victim, fighting to break free.

"Hold still!" yelled Blade. "Do it!"

Parcell stared at Blade with a blank look on his face, frightened from the last unsuccessful incident.

"Didn't you hear me?" he hollered at Parcell, who stared down at the dead Grimgoblin. "I said *do it!*"

Parcell finally came to and picked up the moving pit from off the dirt floor.

"Bring him!" Blade said, snapping his fingers.

Again, Parcell nervously took the pit, only this time he pointed the black thorn out. He closed his eyes and jabbed the thorn deep into the Grimgoblin's arm. Immediately, the area where the thorn had been injected began to turn gray and harden, gradually spreading outward. A look of distress overtook the Grimgoblin's face as he tried to scream, but his screams were drowned out by loud crackling and popping noises. He ran up the tunnel a few feet then froze into a statue that crumbled to pieces.

"Enough!" shouted Blade. "You've cost me two of my men due to your foolish idea!" he growled.

The last of the three disobedient guards fell to the ground in relief as Blade stormed past him and back up the tunnel.

Chapter Sixteen

THE WIND TUNNEL

Several days had passed. Head Revels continued to send out search parties in hopes of finding a way out. On this particular day, Flin and Cretchit volunteered to go and search out one of the dozens of tunnels still left to explore.

"Flin, lad, do ya think we'll ever find a tunnel that leads outa this place?" Cretchit asked as they entered the unexplored tunnel.

"I think there's a good chance, but we won't know unless we keep searching, will we?" replied Flin, turning to him with a smile.

"Yeah, you're right 'bout that. Guess we just need ta keep lookin'," Cretchit said, kicking at hard pebbles and making sparks.

They traveled up the tunnel a ways when it branched into two separate tunnels.

"Hey! Hey, Cretchit, look up there!" hollered Flin joyfully. He raised his torch to get a better look. "It's a door!" he shouted, causing a series of echoes.

"It 'tis! I wonder what could be on the other side?"

"I don't know, but why would someone put a door in the middle of a tunnel? Unless, they were trying to keep something out—or in," said a perplexed Flin.

The two of them pushed the rolling door back into its dusty channel. They cautiously entered.

"This is interesting— this tunnel goes straight up!" said Flin.

"Flin, is it jist me, or does it seem overly warm in here?" asked Cretchit, pulling his collar away from his neck.

"Yeah, it kinda feels like we're in a furnace," Flin said as he wandered further into the burrow.

"Hey, Flin, come look at this!" Cretchit called. He pointed his torch high up on the tunnel wall. "It's some kind of a symbol."

Flin turned and stood speechless. His lower jaw fell open and his eyes widened.

"Doesn't it look like a symbol or something?" asked Cretchit, wiping away decades of dust. Flin stared up at the symbols. "What is it, Flinny? What's wrong?"

"I've, I've seen these symbols before, Cretchit!" he studied it closer. "Well, not this tornado here," he said, touching it. "But I've seen all the others."

"Where? Where did ya see it?" Cretchit said, now wiping away at the tornado symbol.

Flin slowly lowered his hand while still staring up at the symbol and pointed down at his finger where his ring had recently been. "It used to be right there."

"All I see, lad, is your finger."

"No, they were the symbols on my ring!"

"That is a huge coincidence!" said Cretchit, now curiously studying the images. "What did you say again was further up the tunnel there?"

Flin remained silent, still mesmerized, his eyes glued to the symbols on the wall.

"Flin, Flinny!" Cretchit yelled, waving his hand in front of Flin's face. "I asked ya, what's farther up the tunnel?"

"Oh, yeah, it's way too steep to climb. I think it's a waste of time to go any further that way."

They turned out of the tunnel, walking past the big wooden door they'd forced open.

"Do ya think we should roll the door closed?" asked Cretchit.

"I don't think it's going to matter either way, since it goes nowhere!" responded Flin. "Let's try this other fork in the tunnel and see where it leads."

Cretchit ran in a bit further. "Hey, look! It's another door, just like the one we just came through!" His torchlight blared on the door. "And there's another one of those twister things."

"Yeah . . . that's weird. Let's check it out—maybe this one leads somewhere," suggested Flin.

They forced back the door. A slight cool breeze greeted them.

"Do you feel that cold air?" asked Flin over a whistling wind.

"Yeah! Let's push the door back a little further and see where all the air's comin' from."

They pushed the door open all the way and entered several feet into the tunnel. Suddenly, a gust of wind raced through the entrance of the tunnel, blowing out their torch and sucking them further in.

"Stop!" yelled Flin to Cretchit, who had been blown in deeper than Flin had. *"We need to go back! The wind is getting too strong!"* Just then the wind ripped his extinguished torch out of his hand.

"What?" Cretchit hollered back through the piercing gusts.

The wind grew even more furious, whipping their clothes and sweeping their bodies up off of the floor. They were sucked even further into the tunnel. Small pebbles and debris flew in from the tunnel entrance, stinging their skin as they tried to hold on for their lives.

"Cretchit! Cretchit!" screamed Flin in the dark, but the howling wind was far too great. Flin tried to make it back out of the tunnel, only to be drawn in further. He dropped to his belly and clutched the protruding rocks of the wall. Slowly, he began pulling himself down into the tunnel in search of Cretchit, feeling aimlessly in the dark.

"Ow, Cretchit! You're stepping on my hand!" The heel of Cretchit's boot had cut deep into the top of Flin's hand. Cretchit held desperately to the tunnel wall. A violent gust of wind tore through the tunnel, ripping rocks and dirt free from the walls. Cretchit was jerked from the wall and sent high in the air. Flin reached up and grabbed hold of his boot and struggled to pull him back to the ground.

"Stay low!" hollered Flin. *"The wind's not as strong down here!"*

They fought desperately for every inch they gained as they slowly made their way back up the tunnel's entrance. Finally, they crawled out the wooden door.

"We need to close the door!" wheezed Flin over the spiraling wind as a small tree from Cobble Cavern flew past them and down into the tunnel.

"What?" replied Cretchit, who was fighting to stand.

"The door! We need to close it!" he repeated. They struggled to push the door closed while flying debris slammed into them. Once the door was finally shut, the wind subsided.

"Holy!" is all Cretchit could manage to say as he fell against the closed door and tried to catch his breath.

"Somehow we created a wind tunnel," panted Flin. "That's why there was a tornado on both of the doors: the one tunnel went up, forcing hot air, and the other tunnel went down, pulling cold air in. We're lucky to still be alive."

"'Tis the truth for certain," gasped Cretchit.

The two of them staggered back down the tunnel with no light.

As they exited the tunnel, damage from the tornado was evident all around them. Large trees lay on their sides. Dirt had been ripped away from small hills and ditch banks, making gullies and ravines.

"We better hurry back and tell Head Revels about this," said Flin. The two of them took off at a sprint for the cathedral.

The next morning, Flin was awoken by the smell of freshly baked Danishes. He swiftly threw on his clothes and ran out of his room. He followed his nose, which led him to the kitchen. There he found Heppel covered in flour, humming a joyful tune.

"What is it that you're making, Heppel? It smells good!"

Heppel turned to Flin with a pleased look on her face. "'Tis sigar und miste!" she said in her sweet zippy voice, followed by a smile.

Flin watched as she rolled out several types of dough with her wooden roller, spread cinnamon and other delectables on top of the dough, and threw them in the oven.

"It smells delicious," he repeated, running his tongue over his lips in hopes of getting a sample. "What's the occasion?"

"No reason really, jist wanted ta do it!" she chirped gleefully as she busily worked.

Flin looked about the kitchen at all the different goodies that she'd already made.

"Heppel, when did you get time to make all this?" he asked flabbergasted. His wide eyes sampling each scrumptious tart in his imagination, making his mouth water.

"Wull, I been makin' it all night!" she said as she began to knead a new roll of dough. "I truly enjoy cookin', ya know." Her smile broke into a spirited hum, and she skipped about the kitchen, as if she had forgotten that Flin was even there.

Flin walked out of the kitchen and into the Entrance Hall where the tables were covered in goodies that Heppel had made. There were candies, cakes, fudges, puddings, and all sorts of mouth-watering treats. Big wooden barrels sat in a circle on one of the tables, filled with all kinds of punch. Flin picked up one of the old horned goblets and tasted a bit out of each of the barrels.

"Mmmm! I've never tasted punch so good," he muttered in his goblet as he drank. Heppel overheard him as she came into the room carrying another tray full of jellies and jams.

"Mmm 'tis right! That be Juli—'tis me favorite," she said with approval, pointing at his goblet with a wooden spoon.

"I like Juli!" He licked his lips, leaving a big red punch mustache above his upper lip.

Others were now trickling in to explore the source of all the delicious smells.

Flowell came running into the dining area, her hair in rollers. "I've never seen so many yummy foods," she said, standing in her pj's.

"Ever'one hep yursef!" shouted Heppel as she left the room.

"I wish my mom could make food this good!" muddled Pilt, his mouth bulging with food. "That's why I don't bring a sack lunch to school," he said, looking over at Flin while shoving another sticky raspberry Danish in his mouth.

"My goodness, Heppel!" said Principal Vespar as she entered the room, dressed from head to toe in her Stockhaus uniform. "How is it that you know how to make all these exquisite foods, and where did you get such a variety of ingredients?"

Fezzy, who was standing close by and eating, responded, "We have a garden und lots of udder crops, too. I cun show ya after we eat if ya'd like," he said. He glanced guiltily around the room as he stuffed a large cinnamon roll down into one of his pockets and a frosted Danish in the other.

"Fezzy Brundlemair!" Heppel entered from the kitchen, both her hands on her hips. "You get thot food ou' of yar pockets right now and put 'em back on da table! You know how the sweets go right to yar belly."

"Sorry, me luv," he replied, emptying his pockets of Danishes and candies.

"Fezzy, you were saying that you have a garden?" Principal Vespar replied in surprise. "And is that milk I see in Inger's goblet and on his face?"

"A moo moo," replied Inger, taking another gulp of creamy milk from his goblet. He was enjoying the spotlight.

After breakfast, Fezzy and Inger took Principal Vespar and Head Revels down to see the garden. They looked over the thriving garden in amazement.

"Wow, this is incredible! I've never seen fruits and vegetables growing on trees before!" Head Revels marveled as he walked around and examined a nearby tree. "Pumpkins, squash, watermelons, and grapes, all growing on the same tree. Fascinating, this world down here . . . And would you looky here— this corn has kernels the size of golf balls," he said, pulling back the husk.

"And everywhere!" said Principal Vespar in astonishment, daring to touch the fruits hanging from the tree. "This strawberry hanging from this branch here is as big as a pumpkin. Fezzy, where on earth did all of these different fruits come from?"

"They've been here fur over a hundred yars now."

The garden appeared to be slightly neglected although incredibly massive in size.

"Yeah, ya should see da corn when it hatches!" said Fezzy excitedly, tearing several ripe cobs of corn full of different colored kernels free from the tree and bundling them up in his arms.

"Hatches?" they both asked confused.

"Ya know, explodes when ya hang it over the fire."

"Oh, you mean pops," Principal Vespar giggled.

"The kids wull luv it! Some taste like raspberry, udders oranges, and the purple taste like, wull, purple!"

"Who takes care of all this?" asked Principal Vespar.

Fezzy pointed to Inger and himself. "Ulso, me 'eppel!"

"Just the three of you take care of this entire garden?" Head Revels asked in disbelief, glancing about the acres of garden.

"Yis!" Fezzy nodded proudly.

Head Revels eyes swept across the land. "But, there are rows and rows of squash fields, tomatoes, and raspberry patches, not to mention the two cows over there that need daily milking!"

"Yis, we know," replied Inger, proud as well.

Principal Vespar spoke, "Amazing, just truly amazing! I would never have thought anything under the earth could be so beautiful and incredible as all this. If we're going to be down here for some time, do you mind if the students take turns helping out with the garden responsibilities?"

"And me!" said Head Revels zealously, "I want to be a part of it!"

"Thot'd be fine und much appreciated, thank ye!"

As they made their way back to the cathedral, a thick murkiness was beginning to crawl out of one of the tunnels, and then quickly change into a threatening storm that spread throughout the anemone.

"We need ta hurry back!" Hollered Fezzy, looking up with concern as he hobbled swiftly back up the path.

"Why?" yelled Principal Vespar, reluctant to run.

"Some'n left the storm tunnel door open. Storm's a comin' quick," came Fezzy's faint voice as he ran.

"You can control the weather down here?" asked Head Revels right on the heels of Fezzy.

"Oh, yis, we open the rain tunnel twice a week ta water the garden, but we must run now und talk later, some'n left the tunnel open!"

At that moment a large lightning bolt struck the ground just a few feet in front of them. The roar of thunder followed, which alarmed them into a sprint for the cathedral. A downpour of rain rushed upon them as they entered the door of the cathedral and slammed it safely closed behind them.

"My goodness! I've never seen such a ferocious storm come on so suddenly!" huffed Principal Vespar, her wet clothes making several little puddles around her on the wooden floor.

Outside, the booming thunder rattled the entire cathedral, showering its outside with loose rocks and debris. Everyone huddled close to the big fireplace as intense flashes of light lit up the stained glass windows above.

Fezzy seemed unaffected by the raging storm outside. He called for Heppel. She scurried from out of the kitchen covered in flour from head to toe and still humming a tune.

"Yes, me luv?"

"Ay've gone und picked some corn from da garden. Ay thought da students might have a go of it. Would ja please go und get da corker cage so we might *pop* it?"

"Yes, me luv!" She gave him a peck on the cheek before returning to the kitchen. She now seemed very at ease with her new guests.

Moments later, she returned carrying what looked like a big birdcage over her head. It was made from tree branches and roots that had been woven together. Fezzy loaded the apparatus with several large, colorful cobs of corn and held it over the fire with a long wooden pole. Suddenly, the kernels began to pop right off of the cobs, sounding like loud firecrackers.

"Holy cow!" chuckled Flin as he and other students laughed at each loud explosion. Kernels the size of large golf balls suddenly burst into softball-sized popcorn. Fezzy pulled the corker out of the fire and placed it on a nearby table. Steam rose up from the corker cage and the aromas of a pie shop lingered throughout the Entrance Hall. Fezzy clapped his hands together and rubbed them with excitement.

"Und jis ya wait til ya taste it!" he said, opening the cage door and taking a blue piece of popcorn almost the size of his head out of the corker. He bit off a corner of it. Soon, everyone in the room was enjoying the delightful treat.

"Mmm! This one tastes like raspberries!" said Flowell.

"Mine's cherry," said Gretchen, licking her lips.

"Mine's lemon," Pilt said, sliding closer to Gretchen. "Want to try some?" Sam, overhearing, shot Pilt a dirty look.

Head Revels picked up the corker by its long stick and walked around the room dispersing what little was left to the others. He spotted Flin climbing up the stairs.

"Oh, Flin!" he called. Flin stopped midway on the stairs. "A word if I may. Excuse me, please, ladies," he said, placing the corker down on a table.

Flin walked over to Head Revels. "You wanted to see me, sir?"

"Yes, Flin. Remember, I was going to take a look at your hand." It wasn't a question.

"Oh, yeah," replied Flin, somewhat embarrassed.

"There's a room just down the hall here where I think we can have some privacy." As they entered, Head Revels hurried over to the corner of the room and rubbed the moon rock. "Now, let's take a look at that hand of yours."

Flin held out his left hand, and Head Revels studied it from a safe distance.

"Do you remember anything happening to your hand before your fingernails started changing colors?"

"I remember it was the morning I woke up in the tunnel and noticed the food was missing."

"Do you remember anything else? Anything at all about that morning?" pressed Head Revels, now daring to touch Flin's nails.

Flin thought for a moment. "I remember waking— and a . . . a pit jabbed me in the back of my elbow. That's right, that pit jabbed me," Flin said, feeling the back of his arm.

"What kind of a pit was it?"

"Just some old pits my great-great-great-grandfather had invented. Hey, wait a minute!" Flin said, his eyes glazing over as if he were on to something. "Head Revels, ju— just a minute, wait here, I'll be right back!" He dashed out of the room and reappeared a couple minutes later with one of his cigar boxes in his hand. "Something's happened to one of my cigar boxes!" he said in a troubled voice.

"Why? What do you mean, your cigar boxes?" inquired a perplexed Head Revels, trying to make sense of what Flin was talking about.

"Well, I used to have three boxes in my closet upstairs and now there are only two. They have these strange pits and seeds in them."

"Let's take a look at those pits," Head Revels said curiously.

Flin carefully opened the box and leaned it out towards Head Revels, who poked his nose down close to the box. The room dimmed, so Head Revels reached over and gave the moon rock another quick rub.

"Fascinating!" Head Revels squinted through his glasses down into the box. "I've never seen such pits! These are very intriguing to say the least." He reached into the box and started to pull out one of the sharp thorn pits.

"*Careful!*" Flin said nervously. "I don't think you want to hold that one!"

Head Revels held it gently, looked at it, and then placed it back in the box.

"See the different colored thorns on those spiked pits?" asked Flin.

Head Revels again leaned over the box and examined the colored tips closely.

"See that white thorn on the big round pit? That's the kind that dug deep into my elbow and broke off under my skin. I tried getting it out, but the harder I tried the further it dug in."

"Is it still there?" asked Head Revels, raising his glasses to his forehead and focused his eyes on the back of Flin's arm.

The relentless thunder boomed again, shaking the cathedral.

Head Revels replaced his glasses to his eyes. "I can see a mark where the thorn entered your elbow, but there's no sign of a thorn."

Head Revels let go of Flin's arm and looked around the room. In the corner, there was a neglected, wilted plant in a planter box. He walked over to it. "See this plant? I want to try an experiment. I want you to touch it with one of your fingers."

Flin walked over to the plant, reached out, and touched the brittle leaf with his blue fingernail. Frost unexpectedly spread over the leaf then down the stem of the plant. The leaf dangled for a moment then fell off. Startled, Flin jerked his hand away. The frost on the plant melted into droplets of water that fell to the dirt.

"Astonishing! Now touch the plant with your reddish nail."

Flin reached out again and touched the plant. It instantly shriveled.

"Whoa!" Flin blurted out, pulling his hand away in fright.

"What happens when you touch the plant with your black nail?"

Flin reluctantly reached out a third time and touched it with his black nail. Seconds later, the plant turned gray and hardened. A crackling sound followed and spread down the stem, into the soil and through the roots as well. Flin stared down at the plant in disbelief. Head Revels stared back at him. He touched one of the plant's hardened leaves.

"Remarkable! It's hard, like glass!" he said, giving the leaf a flick. He bent down and looked closely at the plant and then back at Flin's fingernails.

"Hmm. Try touching the plant with your green fingernail."

Flin placed his finger on the dead plant. Slowly, life began to return to the plant, at first where his finger was touching and radiating outward until the entire plant looked healthy and refreshed. It continued growing several new leaves and big yellow flowers that burst open in full bloom.

"Okay, okay, you can stop!" Head Revels breathed, grasping his chin with his fingers. "Incredible! Let's see what the white one does!" This time he looked uneasy.

Flin was nervous as he touched the plant with his white nail. They stared in anxious anticipation, but nothing happened. There was a moment of silence as Head Revels pulled his glasses from his eyes and dangled them from his teeth. He brooded for a minute then looked deep into Flin's eyes.

"You said the white thorn broke off under your skin, correct?" Flin responded with a blank face and a simple nod.

Head Revels was puzzled. "Hmm, the only thing I can determine is that the pit excreted something into your elbow, and your body had to adapt to the genetic makeup of the pit."

Flin still stared back blank-faced, and then looked down at his hand.

"What I'm trying to say, Flin, is that the thorn must think your arm is soil, or the host, if you will, and it has fashioned your hand to be like a tree. It's created your different colored nails to be the fruit, or so it thinks. Since your body doesn't have the genetic makeup of the pit, and the pit doesn't have the makeup of your body. . . I'm sorry if this all sounds so complicated, but I believe what's happened is that your body and the thorn have reconciled. Whatever your fingernails are doing now is a compromise between the thorn and your body."

Flin was even more confused. "How's that?"

"Now, you said Parcell's nails were all black, correct? I'm just guessing here, but my bet would be that Parcell was pricked by only the black thorn, which only carried the chemistry or makeup of the black or 'death' gene. Whereas you, on the other hand, were pricked with the white thorn. It must carry the complete genetic makeup of the entire pit! I want to try one more thing." He left the room and returned with a wooden goblet of water.

"I want you to place the black finger in the water." Flin put his fingernail in the water. Instantly, the water began to ripple as if it had become agitated.

"Hmm, interesting, now try the reddish-orange one!" Flin put that finger into the water and it gradually started to steam before coming to a boil. He jerked his hand out of the cup.

"Now the green!" Flin put his green finger into the water.

"Interesting— nothing happened. And now try the blue one." The water slowly turned to slush and then froze around Flin's finger, cracking the wooden goblet in half.

"Does your hand still cause you much pain?"

"Not as much anymore. I think it's getting better."

"We'll, let's keep an eye on it. May I suggest that we keep this between the two of us?"

"Sure, I guess."

Later that night, while everyone was gathered around eating, Head Revels made an announcement. "The staff has decided that, until we've found a safe way out, we'll remain here in the cathedral." The majority of the students cheered and clapped. "There will be assignments made to all of the students to help with keeping up the cathedral as well as the gardens. We have also decided that school is necessary while we're here. So Miss. Lemons, along with Voss Yeg and Principal Vespar will be taking turns teaching the classes. They will consist of things from part of our curriculum, thanks to Principal Vespar who brought her manual with her, as well as Voss Yeg, who will be teaching the courses from the Irish manual. We will begin conducting these classes tomorrow for five hours each day. We will continue with these courses until we've found a way out."

The next morning, Flin, Pilt, and Cretchit were assigned the first shift in the gardens. After breakfast, Fezzy led them down the path to the garden area.

"Stop!" hollered Pilt. "Would you just look at the size of that flower over there?"

The enormous flower was from the pit Parcell and Ruel had thrown into the pond the day before.

Fezzy tilted his head and stared in confusion up at the plant growing out of the muddy pond. "I don' eber remember seein' thot there!" Fezzy said, pulling off his top hat and scratching the bald part of his head. They continued down the path until they came to the garden.

"Whoa!" said Flin. "The three of you take care of all of this by yourselves?"

"Oh, yis! Dere be five gardons jis' like dis!" he replied.

"This garden's huge . . ." moaned Pilt after Fezzy had left, his shoulders drooping with discouragement. "How are we supposed to weed this all in one day? And these tools Fezzy gave us to work with—they're so small, they're more like kids' toys!"

"It doesn't look like anyone's really taken care of it for a long time," Cretchit kicked at a weed.

"Well, there's no sense in just standing here!" said an overwhelmed Flin. "I say we start with the rows of grapes first."

They started by pulling weeds and grooming the plants. Flin had a difficult time pulling weeds. Depending on which fingernail touched the weed, it would either die so that he'd have to dig it out by the roots, or grow so rapidly that he'd have trouble pulling it out. After a while, to avoid Pilt and Cretchit from seeing his new freakish powers, Flin decided to only use his right hand. Without thinking, however, he reached out with his left hand and grabbed hold of the base of a grapevine. The vine shot out of the ground, jumping over several rows of pumpkins and large squash plants before stopping and turning the juicy purple grapes into dried up black raisins.

"Whoa!" he shouted in disbelief and jerked his hand away. He looked over his shoulder to make sure no one had noticed.

"Was that you, Flin? Did you say something?" Pilt hollered from two rows over.

"Aaa . . . NO . . . !" replied a startled Flin, wondering how he was going to hide the fairytale-sized grapevine.

They worked for several hours until it started to get dark.

A far off howl came from the dark shadows just beyond the gardens.

"A . . . guys, I think we should head back now!" Pilt glared out into the obscure trees that lined the garden.

Cretchit stood up, brushed himself off, and then looked around. "Yeah. We accomplished a lot today."

"Looks pretty good," Flin sighed, as he picked up the miniature tools and placed them back in the nearby hollowed out log.

On their way back, Flin suddenly stopped. He looked straight in the air in disbelief and his eyes popped wide open. "Wow! Look at how big that flower is now!"

The plant had tripled in size in just a few hours. It now peered down at them from over sixty feet in the air.

"Is it jist me or does it look like that thing's gettin' taller as we stand here?" Cretchit asked awestruck.

"If that thing keeps growing as fast as it is, we could be in big trouble!" said Flin in alarm as several leaves the size of umbrellas burst out of its trunk.

"Where do ya think that plant even came from?" asked a befuddled Cretchit.

"I don't know," Flin said, shaking his head. "I haven't seen any others like it down here."

Curious, the three of them made their way to the murky shore of the pond and stared up at the beastly plant.

"You never know, Flin," stated Pilt, "maybe that's how that kind of plant grows down here. And besides, how's that silly little plant going to hurt anyone?" he said nonchalantly, skipping a rock.

"For one, Pilt, it's not a little plant anymore. I mean, look at how fast it's growing, and how big it is now. It could puncture through the anemone and flood the entire cavern within just a few hours. We need to hurry back and tell Head Revels!"

"I don't know, Flin," Pilt persisted. "I think you're making more out of it than—" Suddenly, the giant plant gave a sudden jolt, shaking the ground beneath them as if it had come to life and it were trying to free its roots from the ground. Its long stalk leaned out over them.

"Aa . . . maybe you're right, Flin," Pilt's voice quivered as the towering plant hovered over them. "Maybe we should hurry back and tell Head Revels."

Within minutes, they burst through the front door.

"Head Revels, Head Revels!" they shouted frantically.

"Now what is it?" hollered Head Revels. He came running out of his second-story room and glared down at them.

"You need to come quick! It's hard to explain, just, please come!" Flin pleaded.

Chapter Seventeen

THE BATTLE OF THE SNAPDRAGON

"Torches! We'll need torches!" hollered Head Revels as they darted down the darkened path in the early part of the night. Cretchit ran back for torches as the rest of their small group sprinted toward the giant plant. Head Revels caught his first glimpse of it. "You weren't kidding!" he shouted as he saw the plant towering off in the distance. "It appears to be some kind of an abnormally large Snapdragon!" he said, staring up through bouncing spectacles. The plant now stood over one hundred feet tall and had grown massive, dark burgundy petals.

They came to the pond's murky shore. Head Revels stared bewilderedly up at the giant plant. "You're right! We need to do something, and quick! That thing is growing at such a rate it will tear through the anemone within a couple of hours!" Head Revels looked around in desperation. "Someone, hurry and go and ask Fezzy or Inger if they have an axe or hatchet. Quick!"

Pilt sprinted back toward the cathedral, screaming Fezzy's and Inger's names the entire way.

Suddenly, the giant Snapdragon unexpectedly dove down after them.

"Back up! EVERYONE BACK UP! It must feel threatened!" screamed Head Revels, his arms spread wide open.

The Snapdragon stretched out its long stem at them and began snapping with its petals. Fezzy and Inger scurried down the trail, both carrying axes, with Pilt following close on their heels.

"Whoa!" yelped Fezzy as the Snapdragon charged out after them. "Out of me way!" he shrieked, turning and knocking Inger and Pilt both to the ground. The Snapdragon crashed into the back of him, tossing him off of the path and into a clump of trees.

Flin darted up the path and snatched the axe out of Fezzy's hand as he lay entangled in a pile of dead branches. The Snapdragon now stood two hundred feet tall and was still rapidly growing. Head Revels snatched the axe from Flin and charged out through the muddy water toward the base of the plant.

A cackling of commotion followed as Mr. Luftin, along with several others, came running down the path. "Wu'll get to thee opposite side und try divertin' its attention!" he screamed. "Pay 'er no mind and jus' concentrate on choppin'"er down!" He hobbled as fast as he could to the other side. Those with torches raised them high above their heads and waved them recklessly in the air in an effort to get the beast's attention. The Snapdragon lunged down at them repeatedly, spraying acid from out of the center of its petals. The acid struck Mr. Luftin in the shoulder and knocked him to the ground. Miss Lemons ran to his aid.

Head Revels chopped desperately at the tremendous trunk, while Flin and the others continually tried to divert the creature's attention. As Head Revels chopped at its base, the plant rushed down after him, colliding with the axe and knocking it free from his hand and into the deep, murky pond. Again, the Snapdragon charged down after him. It pounced on top of him and threw him several feet in the air. Head Revels landed on the shore just shy of the pond. Fig Tronsel and others rushed to drag his listless body out of danger.

Flin grabbed the only remaining axe just a few feet away and trudged out toward the trunk. Passionately, he began swinging the axe at the trunk. However, with every blow, the trunk was now doubling in size. Flin looked over at the shoreline. Head Revels and Mr. Luftin both lay injured, only able to watch from the distance. Again, the Snapdragon lunged aimlessly down after him, causing a big wave that threw Flin and his axe to the shore.

"Flin!" moaned Head Revels, rolling on to his side in pain. "Run and get your pits!"

Flin dropped the axe and raced back up the path to the cathedral. When he returned moments later, the terrible towering plant loomed from the anemone's ceiling, appearing like a giant snake striking down at its vulnerable prey. Flin's heart pounded in terror as he ran back to the pond. He made it to the edge of the pond and hastily picked out of his cigar box a couple of pits with the black-tipped thorns. He was set to charge out after the Snapdragon when Head Revels, who had feebly made it to his feet, grabbed hold of him.

"Flin!" he said, unusually grim. "The only way we're going to be able to kill that thing is to place the black-tipped thorn into the mouth of its petals."

Just then, the plant's root burst through the soil and wrapped tightly around Flin's waist, throwing the box of pits high in the air. The root pulled Flin closer to its trunk. Head Revels scrambled over and carefully pulled a few pits free from the soil. He ran out across the root which held Flin captive and thrust the sharp black thorn deep into the soft new tissue of the root. Feeling the pain, the flower head of the Snapdragon jerked back and spit acid straight into the air. The acid came crashing down onto its own petals, burning holes throughout them.

Its head whipped back and forth, viciously out of control. The root holding Flin hostage turned gray, hardened, and died. Flin was pinned deep into the solidified tissue. Head Revels climbed up the petrified root and desperately tugged at Flin's arms, trying unsuccessfully to set him free. He ran back to the shore and grabbed the axe then returned and began striking at the hardened root until it cracked and fell to the ground in large chunks.

Enraged, the Snapdragon dove down after both of them. Fezzy, seeing what had worked for Head Revels, picked up one of the pits and charged out after the plant. Just as it opened its colossal acid-eaten petals to engulf Head Revels and Flin, Fezzy threw the pit at it in desperation. The green thorn of the pit stuck deep into the plant, just beneath its petals. Immediately, the plant took off growing even more rapidly.

Head Revels ran over to where the pits had scattered in the dirt. "Pilt!" shouted Head Revels, pulling Pilt out of a daze as he stared helplessly up at the beast. "Quickly, run to the orchard and get some fruit!"

"What? Why do you need fruit at a time like this?"

"Just do it!" Head Revels shouted uncharacteristically. Pilt raced for the orchard. "What kind of fruit does he want?" he mumbled repeatedly as he ran around in a panic. Finally, he snatched up several kinds and sprinted back to the battlefield.

"Why'd you take so long, and why did you pick so many?" scolded Head Revels as he picked up one of the pits.

"Well, I didn't know what kind you wanted," Pilt replied.

"I only needed *one*," snapped Head Revels.

"Now you tell me!" Pilt griped back.

"Flin, quick, take one of these pits and place the black thorn out!" demanded Head Revels. "Pilt, fruit!" Head Revels snatched up the nearest piece, knocking the rest to the ground. "Okay, Flin, take the pit and get the black thorn to excrete fluid into the peach," Head Revels instructed in one swift breath.

Flin forced the tip of the black thorn deep into the peach until the thorn stopped moving. The tender reddish-orange peach started to turn gray and shrivel. He looked up to see the giant petals of the Snapdragon peering up toward the anemone, now totally focused on tearing through it.

"Hurry, we need another! It's going to take several!" Head Revels desperately ordered.

Flin grabbed another pit and forced the black thorn into the now hardening tissue. Dozens of sharp metal-like corkscrews began to grow out of the peach and curl.

Terrified, Pilt looked up. "It's getting close to the anemone," he muttered.

"Okay, we don't have time for anymore. Hopefully this will do!" Head Revels was unsure but dropped the remaining pits into the cigar box. He looked up at the soaring Snapdragon. It had grown so high that the light from their torches no longer reached the top of the plant anymore. The vile plant seemed to be no longer interested in the insignificant teachers and students below. Instead, it was spewing acid up at the anemone, just barely missing it, as if it were trying to rupture a hole through the anemone.

"We need to figure out a way to get this peach inside the petals of its mouth way up there," Head Revels said hopelessly, pointing hundreds of feet into the air.

Flin hastily looked around. He spotted Fezzy holding the axe. He snatched the poisonous peach from Head Revels and dashed for Fezzy, tearing the axe free from his grip. He darted out across the roots and headed for the trunk of the Snapdragon.

"What are you doing?" shouted Head Revels as he could only futilely observe from a distance. Once Flin made it to the trunk, he feverishly began hacking away at the beast. Buckets of acid spewed out, eating away at the blade of the axe. Sharp thorns began to protrude from its trunk. Indecisively, the Snapdragon lunged down after him, but changed its mind and again shot up towards the anemone.

Flin continued to hack away at the beastly stalk—only this time, he spotted fresh, fragile tissue deep within its center. He dropped the axe and forced his black fingernail deep into its tender tissue. The tissue instantly turned an injurious gray and quickly spread outward. The flower felt the pain and flared open its giant burgundy petals. It dove down after him. He reached into his shirt, pulled out the peach, raised it high above his head and crouched over. The giant petals of the flower crashed down upon him, enveloping every bit of his body.

The Snapdragon lifted Flin high off of the ground and began recklessly jerking him about. Flin squirmed down the throat of the flower and into its deepest, darkest petals. Once he made it in as far as he could, he shoved his arm down a long narrow passageway and dropped the peach.

Seconds later, there was a loud "pop" from within. Flin did his best to cover his ears as the loud crackling sounds became as thunder, radiating through the plant and into its roots. The creature, now feeling the pain of the deadly toxin within, whipped uncontrollably back and forth. Its aggressive lunges turned into slow meandering sways. The stalk's healthy, green sheen dulled into a deathly gray, which spread from the top of the petals down the trunk, and into the roots. Minutes later, it solidified and stood as a giant statue just a few feet from tearing through the anemone.

"Flin! FLIN!" shouted a distressed Head Revels up at the highest part of the devilish plant.

"FLIN!" shrieked Principal Vespar, but there was no response. "Oh dear, tell me he's still alive," whimpered Principal Vespar, covering her mouth in fright.

Two dangling feet gradually emerged from out of the mouth of the petrified Snapdragon.

"Thank heavens!" sighed Principal Vespar, her hand over her heart.

"Are you alright?" shouted Head Revels.

"I'm fine!" he shouted down, waving his hands high above his head. Cautiously, he climbed down, using the sharp, hardened thorns as ladder rungs.

"BE CAREFUL!" hollered Flowell impulsively, realizing what she had done she quickly covered her mouth and turned red in the face.

As he neared the bottom, Flin leapt from the base of the stem, crashing to the ground. Flowell was the first to greet him. She threw her arms around him tightly and then suddenly backed away. "Are you alright?"

"I'm fine," he sighed, holding his arm.

The rest of the group soon gathered around their new hero. Flin stood, exhausted and covered with deep gashes across his chest.

"When we get back, I'll mend your shirt for you," said Flowell, grabbing hold of the bottom of his torn shirt.

"It's alright," Flin said tiredly as he tried to regain his composure.

"No, it's not alright!" she said loudly. Recognizing her hostility, she picked a more subtle tone before she continued. "I mean," she cleared her throat, unable to conceal a smile. "I want to do it."

"Alright—thanks."

Pilt finally made it through the crowd to face Flin. "Flin, you missed the whole thing! That thing almost got us, and not just once—it was like a hundred times!"

"Oh, really? It almost got *you*, Pilt? And where was I the whole time, huh?"

Fezzy scampered over to Head Revels. "Heb Rebels! Whad wuz those pits?"

"You know, Fezzy, I'm really not sure, and at the moment, I really don't want to think about it!"

Chapter Eighteen

THE BLACK PEARL & FLIN'S NEW POWER

The next morning, the sun was shining brilliantly on the cavern floor. At breakfast, Heppel announced a big dinner she was preparing in celebration of their triumph over the Snapdragon.

Evening came, and Heppel tugged on a long rope, which went up and out of sight in the Entrance Hall. A large bell, like that off of a boat, rang in the shadows of the ceiling. Flin stiffly made his way to the stair rail and looked down at the magnificent banquet she'd prepared. Everything that could possibly be imagined was set out on the tables: simmering hot meats, chilled fruits and vegetables, seafood, all kinds of cakes and pies, and hard candies of every color.

Flin spotted Fezzy who was busy filling his mouth, pants and jacket pockets with candy and glancing around in fear of being caught by Heppel.

Flin slowly descended down the stairs and sat his achy body between Cretchit and Pilt and across from Head Revels, Principal Vespar, Voss Yeg, Fezzy, Inger, and Heppel.

Mr. Luftin, in preparation for the big event, had stacked wood in the fireplace. He teetered over, picked up two stones—one an ominous gray, the other a sparkling white—and struck them together. Sparks flew in the air and settled over the timbers. Soon, flames leapt about the logs, lighting up the room.

The feast had started as people walked around the tables, loading their wooden plates with all kinds of goodies.

Pilt was one of the first to fill his plate and make it back to his seat. His food towered high on his plate and lopped over the sides. He struggled to get an oyster open.

"Finally!" he grunted loudly and raised it to his mouth.

"STUP!" yelled Fezzy, his eyes the size of golf balls as he pointed at Pilt with the tip of his three-pronged fork. "Don' eat thot!"

Startled, Pilt dropped the oyster to the table.

"Don' cha see lad, 'tis poisonous! The muscle, 'tis gone black!"

"What do you mean it's gone black?" Pilt asked sourly.

Fezzy pried the muscle out of the oyster. "See, 'tis like Ay said, black. Und would ya get a load a thot!" Fezzy lifted up the muscle. "'Tis got a black pearl in it, too! Thot black muscle cun make ya real sick! Kill ya in fact!"

Pilt gulped hard. "Well, I'm for sure not going to eat it," he scowled, flicking the oyster in Flin's direction.

Flin was deep in conversation with Cretchit about the Snapdragon. He turned swiftly in Pilt's direction, picked up the black oyster, and slid the muscle—pearl included—down into his mouth.

"STUP! I mean stop!" yelled Pilt, now pointing his wooden fork just inches from Flin's mouth.

"What?" Flin said as he finished chewing and nonchalantly swallowed. "Stop what, Pilt?"

"Chew-ing . . ." muttered Pilt, staring at Flin's mouth. "You didn't just—*eat* that, did you?" stammered Pilt.

"Eat what, Pilt?"

"Tha— tha—that black muscle that was right there. Fezzy said it would make you sick!"

"What black muscle?" Flin took a drink not too concerned.

"The one that was right—there," Pilt said stunned, lifting up the empty oyster shell next to Flin's plate with his fork. "I pushed it to right here, and now it's, it's gone," Pilt stammered, looking down at Flin's stomach then back up into Flin's now startled eyes.

"Well why'd you put it in front of me, Pilt?" Flin said crossly as tiny beads of sweat began to develop on his forehead.

"'Cause I, for one, wasn't going to eat it!"

"Well, thanks a lot, Pilt!" Flin snapped, dropping his fork. "I think I am starting to feel sick!" he clutched his stomach.

"Hey, hey, Fezzy!" Pilt waved his finger at Fezzy, hoping to get his attention. "Flin just ate that black muscle!"

"Whad! Tell me it 'tisn't so?" Fezzy jumped to his feet and ran around to Flin's side of the table. "Flin, tell me ya din't just eat thot black muscle! Please, tell me ya din't!"

Flin's face turned ghostly white as he tried to stand.

"Ah . . . 'e's nut goin' ta mik it very far!" Fezzy said, calling for help as he hovered close by. Flin took a couple steps and collapsed to the floor. Head Revels and Principal Vespar scrambled over to him.

"He's breathing heavily, and his entire body feels cold and clammy! We need to quickly get him up to his room!" Principal Vespar signaled for help.

Head Revels and Mr. Luftin carried Flin up to his room and placed him in his bed. He lay motionless for several days with someone at his bedside at all times.

"Da poor boy isn't lookin' ta gud today is 'e?" a discouraged Fezzy said to Heppel from the doorway. He took off his top hat and gloomily entered the room.

Heppel was busy folding Flin's clothes that she had just finished washing in the stream. She calmly walked over to his bed. "No, not a bit," Heppel sighed quietly. "He looks eben worser taday." She re-stretched his covers and tucked them tightly around his body.

Fezzy stared with droopy eyes down at the thin, pale boy for a minute, and then suddenly scurried out of the room.

"Fezzy, where do ya think yar goin'?" shouted Heppel.

The only response was the sound of speedy footsteps fading quickly down the hall.

Minutes later, Fezzy returned carrying a bent root covered in dirt. He peeked into the room to make sure Heppel's back was to him then quietly tiptoed in. He opened Flin's mouth and began to insert the root.

"*Stop right there,* Fizzy Brundlemair!" shouted Heppel. "Yar not goin' ta put thot dirty ol' root in 'is mouth! He's ulready sick 'nough wifout thot!" she said, jerking it from his hand and placing it on the table next to his bed.

"But 'eppel . . . please, da boy, 'e needs it. Can't cha see thot?" Fezzy said as he again began to slowly open Flin's mouth.

"NO!" Heppel slapped Fezzy's hand away and escorted him to the door.

"Bud 'eppel, surely ya can see the boy needs it," pleaded Fezzy. "Ay'b neber seen unyone sa sik in me whole life!"

"No! Thot there root could kill em—ya know that!" she said as she brusquely escorted him from the room before returning to her laundry.

"But 'eppel, please, da boy's gettin' weaker by da day."

"I said no! Now be gone wit yarself."

Fezzy waited outside the door until Heppel went back to humming, and he knew that she was folding clothes. He silently slid back into the room, looking over his shoulder the entire way until he stood at Flin's bedside. He snatched up the root, broke off a piece of it and placed it in Flin's mouth. Then he quickly crept out of the room.

Awhile later, Principal Vespar came into the room to give Flin his hourly checkup. She placed her hand on his forehead. "Flin!" she said with alarm as she checked for a pulse. "FLIN!" she hollered again, stray hairs falling across her eyes as she slapped at his hand, hoping for a reaction. "Heppel, he's not breathing! What's happened to him?"

"Ay don' rightly know!" She dropped the laundry and rushed over. "Jis a bit ago he was breathin'. It wuz a bit heavy, but least he wuz breathin'!" she said, stripping back the blankets.

Panicked, Principal Vespar yelled for Head Revels and Voss Yeg.

Seconds later, Voss Yeg came running into the room. "What is it?" she asked distressed, her countenance array.

Principal Vespar was red-faced. "It's Flin—he stopped breathing! And I can't get a pulse!"

Voss Yeg placed her ear to his chest. "His heart's not beating!"

Head Revels burst into the room, his glasses askew on his face. "What is it, what's wrong?"

"He's not breathing, and there's no heartbeat!" Principal Vespar blurted out frantically.

"FLIN!" hollered Head Revels, "Breathe!" he said, pounding on his chest.

Fezzy stumbled through the door and landed flat on his face. "Don' touch him!" he muddled; his face glued to the floor as a hand shot up.

"Don't what?" cried Principal Vespar.

"Breathe, Flin!" Head Revels shrieked as he continued pressing down on Flin's chest, oblivious to what Fezzy had said.

Fezzy jumped up off the floor and ran over and grabbed Head Revels by the arm. "'E's fine! 'E's fine . . ."

"He's *not* fine! He's not breathing, and there's no heartbeat! NOTHING!" said Voss Yeg, still attending to him.

Fezzy timidly fell into a nearby chair and pulled off his hat, his hair mussed. "Ay—Ay kinda gave him a bit a Roseary root."

"Kinda! Oh Fizzy, ya din't!" Heppel moaned. "Fizzy Brundlemair, Oh... I told ya not ta!" She stuck her fingers into Flin's mouth and felt around.

"But, da boy's sicker than any Ay've eber seen bifore."

"So, please explain—how is he fine?" Head Revels pleaded urgently, staring down at Flin's lifeless body.

"Roseary root. It turns off da body fur a bit und cleans out yar insides," Heppel replied, finally fishing out of Flin's mouth what was left of the rootand tossing it into a hollowed-out log used for a trash can.

"So, when does he start to breathe again?" Principal Vespar sighed grimly, looking down at Flin with grave concern.

"Hopeflee soon," replied Fezzy. "Hopeflee soon."

Throughout the night, someone stayed constantly by Flin's side.

When morning came, Heppel was again on watch duty. She was busy dusting about the room.

"Heppel?"came a dry, faint voice from behind her.

Heppel dropped her duster and ran to Flin's bedside. "Yar awake!" Her voice was full of relief as tears flooded her eyes. Flin slowly sat up. She reached up and gave him a hug. "Ay'll go und tell da others!" she said with a big smile as tears ran down her cheeks. She darted out of the room. "Come quick! He's alive!"

Ew, dirt in my mouth—how'd that get there? he wondered, raising his hand up to rid his mouth of the foul taste. *My fingernails! They've fallen off!* He was relieved.

Just then, the door flew open, and people poured into the room, led by Principal Vespar. "You gave us all quite a fright! We weren't sure you were going to make it!" she said, holding his hand and stroking it with motherly affection.

"Ay, Flinster," Mr. Luftin said, ruffling up his hair. "Glad ta see yar back ta life."

"Thanks."

"Why'd ya eat that black muscle anyways?" asked Pilt from a safe distance, hiding behind others as he slowly made his way further in.

"Pilt!" is all Flin managed to say and then sighed.

Head Revels spoke up. "Okay, I'm sure we're all glad Flin's feeling better. Now everyone outside, so he can get some rest."

Flin crawled out of his bed and went into the bathroom. He pulled off his shirt to take a shower and noticed an abnormality on his left forearm. *What in the heck? It looks like a twig's growing out of my wrist! And what's this attached to it? A LEAF!* A small leaf was beginning to open. He nearly fainted. "It can't be!" he said frantically, twisting at the twig in hopes it would come off.

CRACK!

"Ow!" The twig snapped in half, and the wound started to bleed.

Just then the bedroom door again flew open. Flin glanced out of the bathroom to see Flowell with a look of concern on her face. She spotted Flin's head peering out of the bathroom.

"I thought I heard a loud scream," she said, looking around curiously.

"Yeah, you did. I mean, you did? It was me. I . . . I . . . I stepped on something sharp crawling out of bed."

Flowell got down on her hands and knees to take a look at his foot. Flin stood holding his arm behind his back as now red blood trickled down his forearm.

"Well . . . I'm not down here for my health! Lift your foot, so I can see what's the matter!"

Flin slowly raised his foot.

"EW…!" Flowell said, springing to her feet.

"What? What is it?" Flin asked frantically, his voice rising with concern as he looked down. "There's nothing growing out of it is there, nothing with a leaf on it?" he asked fretfully as he raised his heel.

"That's a strange question," she said in a nasally voice, holding her nose. "No, nothing's growing out of it. But your foot could use a good washing!" she said with a wrinkled nose. She left the room in a hurry and slammed the door.

Flin quickly took a hot shower and then went directly in search of Head Revels, whom he found in the kitchen helping Heppel with food.

"So . . . Heppel, that's the secret to making the lemon toffee hard like you do—you place it over the fire to let it cure," said Head Revels. He was bent over, glaring into the oven as flames kissed the bottom of the wooden tray.

"Uh . . . Head Revels, can I speak to you for a moment?" whispered Flin desperately, hoping Heppel wouldn't hear.

"Why sure, Flin," Head Revels replied, seeing Flin's alarm. He dipped his finger into Heppel's wooden bowl of raspberry tart as he left the kitchen. "Be back in a bit, Heppel."

"Could we go somewhere private?" Flin asked urgently.

"Sure, let's go into the room we were in before," said Head Revels.

Head Revels stroked the moon rock then swiftly closed the door. "Now then, what seems to be troubling you, Flin?"

"I'm, I'm just a little confused. When I woke up, I noticed my fingernails had fallen off, and the new ones are growing back in their normal color—"

"Well, that's good news, isn't it?"

"Yes, sir, it is, but now I had a twig growing out of my wrist!"

"A wha—did you say a twig? Is that what you just said?" Head Revels inquired in disbelief, quickly raising his glasses to his eyes.

"I think it's a twig or something—see, I've got it right here!" Flin said, placing it into Head Revels' palm. Head Revels' face scrunched. He looked over the top of his glasses. "It does appear to be flesh as well as wood. Where on your arm was it?" he now asked, gravely concerned. "Interesting!" Head Revels sighed, staring down at the twig and then back at Flin's wound. "It could be just a side effect—those things happen occasionally," he said soothingly. "You said your colored fingernails all fell off, but now they're growing back normal?"

"I think so," Flin said, holding up his hand. "There are no more colors."

Head Revels walked over to the plant they'd experimented with days earlier. "See what happens when you touch the plant now."

Flin fearfully reached toward the healthy looking plant. He placed his index finger on it.

"Nothing, nothing happened!" he sighed with a smile.

"Now try another."

He again nervously stretched out his hand. "Nothing again!" Flin said happily as he began touching the plant with all of his fingernails. "I must be better!" he smirked up at Head Revels.

"I wouldn't be too concerned about the twig thing, Flin. It was probably nothing more than a side effect. I think you've seen the last of your worries," Head Revels said, trying to relieve Flin of some of his anxiety.

Flin looked down at his wrist. "Yeah, you're probably right. I'm just glad to be done with that whole fingernail thing!" he sighed heavily.

That night, after dinner, Flin went outside by himself for a breath of fresh air. He was greatly relieved now that his hand was better. He stared up at the anemone as he walked barefoot through the meadow grass that was chilled by an earlier rainstorm. A serene reverberation came from the field's crickets as he sauntered to the center of the meadow and lay back on the cool gentle grass. He pulled out a few long blades and began chewing on their sweet roots. A noise from the outskirts of the meadow startled him. Frightened, he sat up.

"Sorry," said a faint apologetic voice. "Did I scare you?" It was Flowell, and she was now walking more slowly. "What are you doin' out here in the dark all by yourself?"

"Oh, just lookin' up at the stars, as well as the fish above," Flin replied and then lay back down and stared up through the anemone.

Flowell sat down next to him. "It's so dark out tonight, I had a hard time finding you. I don't know how you found your way out here so fast and without your shoes on," she chuckled.

Flin abruptly sat up again and looked around.

"Are you okay?" she asked, looking in the same direction.

Flin looked around frantically in all directions. He hesitated to respond. "Yeah—atleast I think so. Yeah, I'm fine. It was probably nothing," he said, forcing himself to lie back down.

Flowell, sensing thick tension, changed the subject. "Don't you think it's amazing how big the moon and stars are under the water? It's like you're looking up through a giant telescope and seeing every star all at the same time!" she said smiling over at him.

"At night back home, I would lay on my bed for hours just staring up at the stars. Coming out here reminds me of home."

"Do you miss your family?" she asked. Flin sensed deep emotion concealed within her voice.

"Yeah, I miss 'em a lot! How about you?"

"I miss them like you do," she said softly. An uncomfortable silence developed. Suddenly, a giant shooting star rocketed across the sky.

"Wow! Did you just see that?" Flowell asked.

"Yeah, that was amazing!" Flin said as he observed the remains of the dust trail.

"I just can't believe how different and yet so beautiful it is down here. Look at all the pretty iridescent trails the snails have made on the anemone tonight," Flowell pointed. "Flin . . . ?" she hesitated then went silent.

"Yeah?" responded Flin casually, pulling out another blade of grass.

"I . . . I . . ."

"Yeah, what is it?" Flin asked, gazing about the sky and chewing on his fresh blade of grass.

"Well, I noticed your fingernails were all different colors while you were in bed all those days," she said in one stiff breath. "But, I didn't tell anyone."

Flin stared back uneasily and tucked his hands under his legs and out of sight. He wished he could just disappear. He was grateful when a distraction interrupted.

"Look! It's the mother whale with her baby!" he said.

Frustrated, Flowell asked again. "Flin, what made your fingernails go all those odd colors like that? And now, I've noticed they're gone—why?"

"Look, the bandage wrap is off of the baby and the wound looks almost better!" Flin continued, hoping to avoid the subject.

"You don't want to talk about it, do you?" she asked firmly.

"I think the mother whale's trying to tell us something!"

"You don't need to tell me if you don't want to," Flowell said sadly and sighed.

Flin slowly turned to her. "It's not that I don't want to tell you, Flowell, it's just that I . . . I . . . Well, I really don't know what happened to my fingernails, alright? I just know that I'm better now. Hey look, the mother whale's thanking us."

"And how do you know she's thanking us?" Flowell replied with a snicker. She looked up at the great blue whale that gazed in the blue water sky above them.

"I'm not sure how I know. Somehow I just do." Suddenly, Flin realized his senses had somehow been heightened.

Flowell got up and walked to the anemone wall. She placed her hands against it, and stared eye to eye with the baby whale. Suddenly, the mother whale let out a high-pitched squeal that sent several large air bubbles from her breathing hole.

"I guess they're leaving now," Flin said, his nose pressed against the anemone wall.

"And just what makes you say that?" Flowell again chuckled, now even more puzzled. She turned to Flin then back to the whales.

"I told you, I'm not sure how I know. I just do," he said, a bit surprised himself. Just then, the two whales turned and slowly swam away.

"How—how did you know they were about to leave?"

Flin was troubled. "I'm not sure. Somehow I just did."

"I'm sure glad the baby whale's doing alright, aren't you?"

"Yeah, I'm sure that spear Parcell and Ruel stabbed in it didn't do it any good!"

Flowell slowly inched closer to Flin. She stood motionless and indecisive for a moment next to him. She held her hands tensely, balled up tight into fists. Her fingers uncurled one at a time until her hand reached over to grab his. Flin felt their hands touch and quickly pulled away. They stood back to back in awkward silence.

"Well, it's really pretty dark out, so we should be heading back," he said in an attempt to sound as if nothing had happened.

"What do mean its dark out here? Just a bit ago you said it wasn't all that dark," she laughed out of frustration.

"Yeah, well, I guess I changed my mind," Flin said uncomfortably and then started to walk back. Determined not to budge, Flowell remained silent. She folded her arms tightly across her chest and turned in the opposite direction.

"Come on Flowell, please, please come," he said in a teasing tone. Then, he thought he could hear whispering, "*He doesn't care! He doesn't even want to be with me, and now I've made a fool of myself coming out here!*" Flowell looked over her shoulder to see Flin shaking and slapping the side of his head.

"What's wrong? Why are you slapping the side of your head like that?"

"I'm not sure. I've never had anything like this happen to me before. I'll be alright in a minute, I think." He now realized that he could read her most personal thoughts.

"Well, if you keep hitting yourself in the head like that, you're *definitely* not going to be alright."

"I'll be fine," he said, again shaking his head. He stopped and turned to her. "Flowell, are you coming?"

"Maybe, maybe not." She glared at him in confusion and then looked up at the anemone. "You do like me, don't you?"

Flin stumbled for words. "Yeah, of course I do. What are you talking about? We've been friends for, two, almost

Three—"

"No! Not like that. You know what I mean."

His face flushed red and even the dark night that surrounded them couldn't hide the color. "Yes, Flowell, I do like you! Shouldn't we go now?" he said, looking around unsettled.

"Then how come every time I say or do anything nice for you, you avoid me?" she asked, her green eyes glossy with sadness in the moonlight.

"I, I don't do that."

"Yes, yes, you do, Flin!" Her eyes full of pain and tears slowly turned his way. She looked down and cautiously made her way back over to him. Her hands balled up into fists. She again timidly reached for his hand then pulled away. "*Maybe I shouldn't!*" he heard her thoughts say.

"Maybe you shouldn't what?" he asked.

"What? I didn't say anything!" she said, sharply turning at him, and then again making light, with a slight chuckle.

He looked down at her quivering hand as she slowly pulled it to her side. "*He'd probably just push it away again anyways!*" He heard her again think.

Swiftly he reached down and took hold of her warm hand. She hesitantly looked over at him with a hint of a smile. He could sense her relief as the two of them made their way out of the meadow, passed over the cobble bridge, and started up the path toward the cathedral. As they neared the front door, they both reluctantly set each other's hand free.

Flowell turned to him as he pulled open the door. "Thanks, Flin." Her cheeks flushed with color.

He responded with a simple smile.

It was late as they entered the cathedral. The glow rocks had all practically gone out, and there were only a few students huddled close to the fireplace. Flin escorted Flowell to the bridge that crossed over the main stream. They both stopped in the middle of it and leaned over its rail, not wanting their time together to come to an end. They stared down into the rushing water.

Flin abruptly turned to Flowell and stuck out his hand. "Well, good night Flowell," he said, just loud enough for the others in the room to overhear. The room went silent. Everyone watched to see what the two of them would do. They stood there awkwardly. A mellow chant began and quickly grew louder.

"Kiss! Kiss! KISS!" A few days earlier, a girl and a boy had been caught kissing on the bridge, quickly earning it the nickname, "The kissing bridge."

Flin looked timidly out of the corner of his eyes at the chanting students. Flowell started to back away, leaving him standing all alone.

"KISS! KISS! KISS!" they continued chanting, now standing on their feet.

Flowell dashed back up the bridge, kissed Flin on the cheek, and skipped off to her room.

Flin stood dazed as the room hummed with "Oooos" and "Ahhhs."

The next day, Flin awoke to another morning of delicious smells of Heppel's cooking. The enchanting aroma wafted throughout the cathedral, luring everyone down to breakfast.

"Mmm! Heppel's made something really good this morning," Pilt said, his eyes popping open at several turtles swimming overhead through the anemone in their room.

At breakfast, Head Revels announced that more search parties would be sent out during the week.

"Oh, and one last thing! Tomorrow morning class will start at," he glanced up at the giant grandfather clock, "8:45 a.m. If you're not in the Baltic Room by 8:45 a. m., then you're late. Do I make myself clear?" he asked, looking around at the students. The Baltic Room was a huge room carved in the shape of a whale with a clear anemone ceiling overhead.

Flin picked up his empty dish and carried it into the kitchen. Heppel was busy humming a joyful Old Irish tune as he entered. He watched as she poured simmering brown toffee from a pot and mixed it with golden honey swirls. His mouth began to water.

"Heppel!" he called as he placed his plate and cup in the wash water.

"Shush! I con't be interrupted durin' da twistin' stage. The two wull set up und then, well, the honey toffee twill be ruined." She twirled the toffee in a large circle then laid it out on the wooden countertop.

"Now, what was it ya needed, Flinny?"

"Heppel, have you ever been to the surface?"

"Nooo! Don' reckon 'tis for me. Don' think Ay'd like it up dere much. Ulthough dere's a place down 'ere, you've probly neber heard uf dat I could do without as wull." She stopped, broke him off a piece of honey toffee, and stuck it in his mouth.

"Wha, wha pace?" he mumbled, his mouth watering over from the sweet toffee flavor.

"Don' like ta really talk 'bout it."

"Please, Heppel, tell me what it's called."

"Wull, if'n ya must know," she cupped her hands around her mouth and whispered, "'Tis the Devil's Garden!" She quickly glanced around to make sure no one else had heard. "Like Ay said, don' really like ta talk 'bout it. Da stories me's heard uf thot horrid place, oh, jis scares me ta death it does!" she said, shaking her head.

A minute later, she was once again fully engaged with her humming and candy making. Flin walked back out to the Entrance Hall. He could see Pilt and Cretchit standing by the fireplace talking to a couple of the Irish dance girls.

"Pilt," garbled Flin, rolling his eyes. "I should have known where he'd be." As Flin weaved through the crowded room, people's thoughts began to penetrate deep into his mind, eventually getting to the point of causing his head great pain. Confused, he quickly ran for the cathedral doors and exited.

Cretchit, seeing him, tried to get Pilt's attention.

"Uh, Pilt, lad, I think we need ta go and check on Flin."

"A minute, Cretchit!" exploded Pilt. "I'm in the middle of telling these girls how I saved Flin's and my life."

"Uh … Pilt, you've told us this story before, remember," said one of the dance girls annoyed and turned away.

"Yeah, but last time you told it, you weren't carrying Flin over your shoulder and charging the Snazzard with a spear!" Tabatha said piercingly.

"Well, maybe the last time I told the story, I forgot to mention that part."

"Yeah, it's a story, Pilt! Just a big, fat story! Let's go." The two girls grimaced, then got up and walked away.

Chapter Nineteen

WHAT'S FLIN DONE NOW?

Cretchit and Pilt pushed open the front door of the cathedral to see Flin's head tilted to one side and he was busy smacking it.

"Why, lad, are ya doin' that to your head?" Cretchit asked with a painful squint as he went to Flin's side.

"No real reason—I've had a headache since last night and can't seem to get rid of it," he said casually, giving the side of his head one last good *thump*.

"Well, knocking yourself in the head like that is not going to make it go away," replied Pilt. He was still irritated by the girls' rejection moments earlier.

The three of them walked down the cathedral's steps and started along the stone pathway. Flin was busy talking when he accidentally stepped on Gretchen's lavender flower. It had voluntarily grown between two rocks in the pathway, so over the past couple of weeks she had decided to take care of it.

"Dang it! I knew that flower was there!" Flin grumbled as he bent over and tried to stand it back up.

"You just think Gretchen's cute, that's why you're fixing it!" burst Pilt, nudging Cretchit in the ribs.

"No, you're the one who thinks Gretchen's cute, Pilt!" he said as he reached down with his right hand and gently raised it off of the stone. When he pulled his hand away, the flower immediately fell over and back onto the path. He tried propping it back up with small pebbles, but again it dropped lifeless on its side.

"Come on, Flin, let's just go! You're wasting your time. It's dead now. You killed it," Pilt said, tired of staring at Flin's back.

Flin knelt down and stacked dirt around its base. He thought of Gretchen, and how he'd seen her several times a day carrying out cups of water to the plant. He felt overcome with guilt knowing how Gretchen would feel when she saw the crushed flower. He reached down one last time with his left hand and tried to straighten its broken stem. Unexpectedly, the plant shot out of the ground like a cannon ball high into the air, striking Flin in the forehead and knocking him flat on his back.

"Wow!" shouted both Pilt and Cretchit, stepping back and looking up.

Flin's mouth fell wide open as he stared up at the grand lavender bloom which now provided him with shade. Stones and mud littered the ground at its base as the once small flower now resembled a giant tree.

"Flin, what just happened? What made that flower go ballistic like that?" asked a bewildered Pilt, staring up.

"I, I, I don't know," Flin said, rubbing his head where a purplish knot was beginning to form above his left eyebrow.

Rumor of the colossal flower quickly spread throughout the cathedral, and people swarmed out of the front door to see what had happened.

"What in the world?" Principal Vespar gasped, staring up as she exited the cathedral.

Head Revels came rushing out of the front door as well, looking up in the air.

"Wha—Who? Where in the world did that thing ever come from?" He followed the trunk of the plant down to where he spotted Flin, at its base, bewildered and sitting in the dirt, staring back up at him. "Do we need to kill this one as well, Flin?" He asked with disgust.

Flin gave an uncertain shrug of the shoulders.

"Is that a yes or a no?" snarled Head Revels, displeased.

"I'm not sure. But, I don't think so," Flin said, wishing he could hide from everyone who stared at the beastly flower and him in amazement.

Head Revels stared up at the mammoth lavender flower, watching to see if it was going to be another repeat of the Snapdragon incident. "What is it going to do this time?" he mumbled, shaking his head incredulously.

The repetitive thump of Mr. Luftin's wooden leg and his usual early morning humming could be heard coming up the path.

"Holy Bu-gee-bees! Where in creations did thot thin' come from?" he bellowed, stopping dead in his tracks.

Head Revels scurried down the cobble pathway. "Flin, Flin, Flin!" he clucked bitterly. "What is it that's happened this time?"

Flin hesitated. "Well . . ."

"Well, what?" Head Revels insisted. "Flin, it seems that every time there's some kind of a catastrophe, you're there. Now what's going on?"

"I'm not sure what happened, Head Revels," Flin said faintly.

Head Revels grabbed Flin's left hand and abruptly began twisting it back and forth, looking keenly at his fingernails. "They *look* normal anyways. Flin, let's go for a walk," he sighed, his voice sounding troubled.

They walked along the stream for a ways before they turned into a clump of red maple trees.

"What happened to make the flower grow like that?" asked Head Revels, stopping and gruffly folding his arms.

"Well, I accidentally stepped on it, and when I went to stand it back up, it just shot out of the ground at me."

"That's *all* you did?" Head Revels asked incredulously. "That's it? Let me see your fingernails again," he demanded, placing his spectacles to his eyes for a more accurate view.

Flin reluctantly held out his hand.

"Come and touch this plant over here," said Head Revels, indicating a small group of bluebells.

Flin slowly walked over and placed one of his fingers on the plant's petals. "See, it's like I said—nothing."

"There has to be more. What happened just before you touched the flower?"

"Well, I was just about to leave, but then I thought of how bad Gretchen would feel when she saw it, so I tried fixing it."

"Come here again." This time Head Revels squashed the little plant. Flin stared at Head Revels, confused. "Now touch it."

As Flin put his hand toward the small wilted plant, a sense of sadness overcame him; he touched it. Instantly, a huge bluebell flower grew on the branch, bending the branch to the ground under its weight, and causing it to snap free from the rest of the plant.

"Amazing!" remarked Head Revels.

"Uhh!" Flin heaved, startled. He took a deep breath.

"*In*credible! I've never seen anything like it!"

"I thought after I ate that black oyster pearl I was cured!"

"Apparently not. I don't think your powers ever went away. In fact, I would dare say that black pearl gave you much greater power," Head Revels thought aloud. "Maybe it will wear off in time," he added optimistically, patting Flin's shoulder.

"I sure hope so," Flin said as he looked down at his fingers.

"Well, I think we should go back now." Head Revels forced a smile.

Flin was preoccupied with his hands and started to walk away, when he walked directly into the biggest maple tree in the clump.

"Dumb tree!" he grumbled, already a bit fluttered and striking it with his fist.

A sudden abrupt crackle came from the tree as it turned a deathly gray. Its branches began to twist and curl as if in pain. The soft leaves turned dull then hardened and fell to the ground shattering, like plates of glass as they landed on the hard rocks below. After it had completed with the reaction, Head Revels stared in disbelief, a troubled look in his eyes. He finally managed to speak,

"Flin, wha—what just—what just happened?"

"I—I'm not sure. I only wish I knew!"

"I think that's enough for one day," Head Revels said, his eyes still glued to the tree. "A . . . Flin, I think it best if we just kept this whole incident to ourselves, understood?"

"Yes, Head Revels," Flin sighed, gloomily looking down.

As they made their way back, Head Revels spoke tentatively, choosing his words carefully. "Flin, son, this—this strange new power you have—well, it could be very dangerous if misused. If you lashed out in anger at someone, the consequences could be irreversible. What I'm trying to say *is,* that you'll need to be extremely careful around the others now, understand?"

"Yes, sir, I understand." said Flin sullenly.

"You'll need to learn to control it. You may have this power with you for quite some time."

Once back at the cathedral, Flin went directly to his bedroom. As he walked in, Pilt and Cretchit bombarded him with all kinds of questions.

"I said I don't know how or why it happened!" Flin said crossly. "It's nothing personal guys, but I just need some time alone right now, okay?"

The two of them dejectedly walked out of the room and closed the door. Flin lay on his bed and placed his hands on his head trying to stop the pounding.

What's happening to me? How's any of this possible? Maybe in a bad dream or something, but I'm not dreaming!

His eyes were drawn to a peculiar school of tuna that swam overhead. *All of this is so different! I remember just a few weeks ago being at home, playing with my brothers and sisters. Who'd ever have thought I'd be several thousands of miles away, trapped under the ocean, staring up at fish instead of birds?*

The heavy shock from all that had happened slowly put Flin into a deep sleep. Hours later, he awoke to a deep sapphire blue ocean overhead. He crept down the hall to the top of the stairs. All eyes suddenly looked up at him from below, bringing every conversation to an immediate halt. Obviously, his earlier experience was obviously the topic of dinner conversation.

Little by little, Flin slithered down the stairs towards the group. He crossed over the stream and neared the tables.

Principal Vespar broke the silence. "Good, Flin, you're awake!"

Flin could feel all eyes fixed on him.

"We've all just started eating. Come join us," Principal Vespar said, motioning to a nearby seat and giving it a pat.

Flin made his way around the table to where Pilt and Cretchit were sitting. The tension in the air was a thick haze.

"Hey," he said solemnly to Pilt and the others as he passed by, hoping to break the deep strain that lingered in the room.

Flowell sprang from her seat and walked over. "Would you care for some food, Flin?" she asked.

"I'm fine. Thanks, though."

"Are you sure? It's really not a problem!" she said with an unnaturally big smile.

"Maybe just a little something, thanks," he barely whispered. Flowell hurried off to the kitchen.

"What a day, huh, Flin?" Cretchit forced, as the other students stared dumbstruck at him.

Flin waited a moment to respond. "Yeah, I guess," he said, his head still pounding and his sight a bit blurred.

Flowell returned from the kitchen with a plate full of food. "Here you go," she said, handing it to him.

He forced a smile. "Thanks, Flowell, this is more than a little bit," he said softly. He set it on the table and just stared at it.

"I know," she blushed as she turned and walked away.

Flin picked at his food for a short moment as whispers broke out around him.

"Well, I think I'll go back up to bed," he said dejectedly.

"But, you haven't even touched your food!" pleaded Voss Yeg.

"Sorry," he said dispirited. He walked back up the darkened stairway, down the hall, and into his room.

Flin had fallen back to sleep for a few hours when a high-pitched, devilish squeal jerked him awake. He sat up and looked frantically around. The unfamiliar squeal grew louder as Pilt dashed into the room in a panic.

"Flin! FLIN!" he wheezed as he stood hunched over. "Something's wrong! Something's gone very wrong outside. Hurry, I need for you to come!"

"Wrong, wrong with what? Pilt, just tell me what's going on!" pleaded Flin, trying to clear the fog from his head.

"Quick, follow me!"

Chapter Twenty

THE SHADOWING HANDPRINT

The two of them flew down the stairs and out the front door. Flin's eyes were instantly drawn to a disturbingly huge, gray hand print that was growing larger by the second on the domed anemone above. He glanced around to see the surrounding anemone quivering and rippling in pain like the waves of the ocean. The high pitched squeal he'd heard from inside was coming from the injured anemone and was now coming at him from every direction and rapidly growing louder. Flin covered his ears and sprinted towards Head Revels and the rest of the group as the dark gray handprint continued to spread across the anemone's ceiling, like an incessant growing cloud. He finally joined up with the rest of the group, who stood helplessly staring up at the mysterious gray handprint as it infectiously spread across the anemone.

"Head Revels, Head Revels!" Flin shouted from just a few feet away. "What are we going to do?"

"I'm working on it!" Flin could tell by the look of distress in Head Revels' eyes and his helpless demeanor said otherwise.

"Head Revels, where's Mr. Luftin?" Flin yelled desperately.

"He and Fig left hours ago to go and explore the tunnels."

Flin could see there wasn't going to be anyone coming to their rescue. He dashed to the base of the Snapdragon, where the handprint seemed to have originated. He glanced up at the anemone to see several hairline cracks quickly spreading outward through the gray, infected area. Water now fell from the cavern sky and poured down upon him. The cavern was speedily growing darker as the handprint blocked out the moon's rays. Flin recognized something familiar about the crackling and popping noises—they were the same ones he'd heard earlier that morning coming from the maple tree after he had struck it. Frantically, he began to climb up the trunk of giant, petrified Snapdragon.

"Flin! Flin!" Principal Vespar shouted up at him, but the whining of the screeching anemone overpowered her delicate voice. "That boy's going to end up getting himself killed!" She pointed sharply, in hopes someone would try and stop him.

Large amounts of water poured down onto the cavern floor and on top of Flin. He nearly slipped and fell to his death. Flin finally reached the top of the stem, nearly hundreds of feet above the floor. Recklessly, he climbed the highest petal of the flower while the cracks in the anemone rapidly widened. More water gushed through the anemone and down on top of him.

He extended his left hand upward through the pounding water and held it firmly to the damaged tissue. *Nothing's happening! Think, Flin, think! What was it that made Gretchen's flower grow?* he thought as he fought back the relentless wave of water. *Come on . . . please . . . DO SOMETHING! What was it that I did that healed the flower? Love! It was love, Flin! I need to focus on love!*

The cracks continued to widen, and the anemone was now showing signs of collapsing at any moment. Flin thought of his family and how much he missed them. Joy welled up inside of him as he held his left hand unyieldingly up to the anemone. He could feel the hardened, dead tissue beneath his hand begin to soften. Gradually its true healthy clear color spread outward from under his hand, overtaking the deathly dull gray handprint. Flin's body was exhausted from holding back the rushing tide. He focused on his handprint as it devoured up the hauntingly gray handprint that threatened the cavern. The gushing water began to subside, but Flin was now feeling extremely fatigued.

"Please! I just need a little more strength!" he shouted up at the anemone's ceiling. He held his hand there for a moment more, then passed out from exhaustion and slid down into the mouth of the petrified Snapdragon where he lay asleep. It was dawn, and the sun shone brilliantly through the anemone as screams and shouts of joy came from down below, awaking Flin.

"Flin, Flin! Are you alright?" he heard the quivering voice of Voss Yeg shriek up at him.

Tired, he started his way back down the enormous trunk. As he neared the bottom, his weary hands lost their grip, and he crashed into the ocean water below. He lay in a puddle of mud, motionless.

They all ran for him. "Flin, Flin! Answer if you're okay! Please, say something!" pleaded Flowell into Flin's lifeless, closed eyes. He opened his eyes to see her terrified face staring down at him. She tried, but couldn't hold back a smile of relief.

"Flin! Flin, oh ya brave child," sighed Voss Yeg, holding Flin's hand as she crouched her old frame down and knelt next to him in the mud.

"Hey, he's my friend!" shouted Pilt, fighting his way through the crowd. "Everyone can just back off and give him some room to breathe! Besides, I'm his best friend. Right, Flin?" Pilt said once he'd finally made it to him. "Hey, by the way Flin, you should have seen it! There was a giant black handprint that spread across the anemone and almost flooded the cavern, and then it just disappeared."

"Yeah, Pilt, I kind of remember that . . ."

"Hey, hey, Flinny, the lad, 'e's our new hero," chanted Fezzy and Inger with laughter. They threw their hands in the air as they darted between people's legs until they were by his side in the mud. "You were great, laddy! That was some good thinkin'!"

"Thanks Fezzy, thanks Inger!"

Head Revels was the last to arrive. "Well done, Flin, well done. You saved the cavern, as well as all of our lives," he chuckled, rubbing his muddy, matted blonde hair. "Let's take him back up to the cathedral." Flin was lifted high in the air and carried on the shoulders of students.

Later that night, Miss Lemons taught the group how to play a new game. Flin was more interested in food. Heppel strolled over to the table where Flin was sitting and placed a plate heavy with food in front of him.

"Now you eat! Und Ay don' wan' ta see a single crumb on this 'ere plate when Ay come back, understand?" she said, pouring him a large goblet full of red punch as he was already busily eating.

The next day, Flin, Cretchit and Pilt made their way down to the gardens and vineyard for a day of maintenance. Flin and Cretchit were growing tired of hearing Pilt go on and on about all he'd done to help save the group from the incident the night before. As they neared the garden, Pilt's ongoing voice was finally interrupted by the thud of large footsteps.

"What was that?" whispered Pilt, looking for a place to hide.

The footsteps pounded again, only this time, they were more consistent, as if they were charging after the boys.

"Run!" shouted Cretchit. The three of them took off at a sprint down the pathway.

Soon, they arrived at the garden, and the sound was gone. They worked several grueling hours. Then they placed the tools back, excluding Inger's shovel, and headed for the cathedral. As they hiked up the grass-lined trail, the frightening sound of footsteps came again.

"There's that sound again," whispered Pilt, shaking.

"Shhh!" admonished Flin, poking his head between several bushes.

"What are you doing? Don't let it see you! Whatever's out there probably wants to eat us!" mumbled Pilt, backing away.

Flin spotted a fruit tree several feet off the pathway. The fruit on the tree was growing at such a rate, that as soon as a piece ripened and fell to the ground, another swiftly blossomed and took its place.

"There's your monster, Pilt!" mocked Flin. Pilt waited before finally daring to poke his head through the bushes.

The tree was large and divided up into five parts. Each part had a different colored fruit on its branches, as well as different colored leaves and bark.

Cretchit cautiously approached the tree. "What kind of tree's that?" Fruit continued to fall to the ground.

"I don't know. I've never seen a fruit tree like that before, and I grew up on an orchard," responded Flin.

The fruit continued to grow, ripen, and drop before their very eyes. Pilt bent down and picked up an orange-red piece that had just fallen to the ground. He took a bite. "Mmm, hey guys, this is good. You got ta try it," he garbled as juice spewed from his mouth. "It's warm and sweet. It reminds me of my mom's peach cobbler!" he said, taking another bite. "Flin, Cretchit, try some."

Cretchit reached up and pulled off a ripe, dark blue piece of fruit from the tree. He took a bite. "It *is* good!" he said, surprised. "Mine's cold and tastes like blueberry pie, Pilt," he said with a mouthful of fruit. "You gotta try the blue kind—it's the best!"

"How would you know? That's the only kind you've tried!" Pilt wiped the juice from his hands and onto his chest. "No, I think I'm going to try one of these . . . black ones right here, if I can reach it."

Flin looked over at Pilt, who'd just picked a black piece of fruit and was rubbing it against his shirt, anxious to bite into it. Flin spotted a rotten piece of fruit on the ground with part of the pit exposed. He reached down and picked it free from the rest of the pile and gave it a shake, leaving just the pit in his hand. The pit had five different colored tipped thorns and Flin knew exactly what it was. Pilt raised the fruit to his mouth, ready to take a bite.

"Stop, Pilt!" shouted Flin, slapping the fruit out of his hand.

"Hey... what did you do that for?" groaned Pilt, indignantly. "That one was hard to reach!" He looked down at the black piece of fruit and within seconds, the fruit dissolved into black ooze, and smoke began to billow up from the ground where it once had been. Pilt stared down at the rising smoke then rubbed at his lips where the black skin of the fruit had touched him. The skin on his lip turned red and instantly blisters appeared.

"Can you believe that?" he complained.

Cretchit's eyes slowly widened. He dropped the fruit in his hand and stared intently at Pilt's shirt. "P, P, Pilt, your shirt!" The fabric of

245

his shirt was smoking and had holes in it where he had wiped the fruit. The holes continued to get bigger as the embers continued moving outward.

"I think this tree came from one of my greatgrandfather's pits," Flin said with a troubled look. "And, if that's the case, I'm pretty sure the black fruit is deadly. Cretchit, let me see the shovel."

Flin took the shovel and knocked another piece of black fruit free from the tree. He chopped the fruit in half, spewing juice all over. Everywhere the juice landed, smoke began to rise. The tip of the metal shovel glowed a fiery red for a brief moment then dissolved into liquid.

"Whoa! I'm glad I didn't eat that!" Pilt said.

They rushed back to the cathedral and told Head Revels about the tree.

"It will have to be cut down as soon as possible! Tomorrow, I want the three of you to see to it, but do be careful, understood? Besides, we need more wood to burn."

The next morning, they made quick work of cutting up the tree and hauling the wood back up to the cathedral where they placed it against the outside wall. That night, Triston, one of the Haunsdale students, carried in an arm full of the dark blue wood and placed it in the fireplace. Mr. Luftin hobbled over, picked up the white and black stones and struck them together. Yellow sparks fell from the stones and ignited the wood. Within seconds, a bizarre blue flame started to grow around the logs.

The room fell silent as everyone in the room noticed the peculiar blue flames crawling over the logs and leaping high in the air.

"Strange, thot there flame," said Mr. Luftin, poking his head into the fireplace. When he pulled his head back out and turned to the group, his beard and eyebrows were thick with ice crystals and icicles hanging from them.

"Fascinating," said Principal Vespar. Mesmerized, she went over to the fire and placed her hand over its flames. "The flame is cold!" she exclaimed, befuddled.

"Yet, somehow the room is getting warmer!" said Head Revels from a distance, curiously stepping toward the fireplace. "Look, there are icicles developing around the logs. Somehow the blue flames must feed on the cold air, leaving only warm air in the room. Fascinating!" he said, pointing his finger directly into the flames without getting burned. As the flames grew higher, the pungent smell of blueberries filled the room. The fire crackled, throwing out blue spark crystals that landed onto the wooden floor and quickly melted.

Voss Yeg sat on the hearth. "It's different, but different in a fun way!" she said with a childlike smile.

The next morning, Krage came running through the front door, yelling at the top of his lungs, *We found a leaf! We found a leaf!*"

Mr. Luftin, who was busily working in the stream trying to reattach the straps around the waterwheel, quickly splashed his way up the bank and hobbled over. "Thot had ta huv cum frum up top, I'm sure of it! It's off a Russian Oak tree. I have one in me backyard at home. Haven't seen none of these down here, though—"

"Where did you find the leaf?" asked Head Revels reaching for it and looking intently through his glasses.

"Well, Edgar and I, we were headed to explore one of the north tunnels, when this leaf just floated out in front of us."

"Interesting. Has that tunnel been explored yet? Was there an X scratched on the outside of it?" Head Revels said in one swift, hopeful breath.

"There wasn't a mark on the outside of it, so we took our torches in a ways to get a better look, but when we got further inside, it looked like the tunnel went straight down!"

"Give me a moment to get ready, and then I want you to take me and show me this tunnel!" Head Revels dashed away to get supplies, and seconds later returned.

~~~~~~~~~~~~

"Are you sure this is the one, Krage?" asked Head Revels, as he and several others made their way to the tunnel where the leaf had been found.

"I'm positive! We put these two sticks together in front of the tunnel to make an X."

"Triston, let me see your torch for a moment!" Head Revels leaned his head into the tunnel and stretched forth his arm. "Darn!" came his echo a second later from inside the tunnel. He backed out.

"Whad? Whad tis it we're darnin'?" asked Luftin, peering into the unlit tunnel.

"Krage said it looked as if it dropped off—it's practically a cliff!"

"If it goes down, then how could a leaf have blown out?" asked Fig Tronsel, nervously shaking from the possible outcomes.

"There's got to be an access that leads out, and possibly a strong wind pushed it through. Regardless, something had to have forced it out." Head Revels took the torch and held it just outside the tunnel. "See! Look how the torch's flame flickers from the air coming out of the tunnel?"

"So, whad'll we do?" spoke Luftin's eager, strong burly voice.

"I think first thing tomorrow morning, a search party needs to see where this tunnel leads!"

Back at the cathedral, all those who hadn't gone were standing anxiously by the front door as they entered.

"What did you find out? Does the tunnel lead out?" shot Principal Vespar, who was much too excited to wait for the news.

"The tunnel definitely leads somewhere outside, because there's warm air flowing out of it," Head Revels said, taking off his coat.

"So, that's good news, *right*?" prodded Principal Vespar, stepping on the heels of Head Revels as he walked away.

"Most likely. We'll know more in the morning."

At the crack of dawn, Head Revels—along with Mr. Luftin, Flin, Pilt, and Cretchit—entered the tunnel. Several hundreds of feet down, the steep tunnel split into two.

"Which do ya think we should take?" asked Mr. Luftin, glancing impatiently in both directions.

Head Revels again raised his torch to both tunnels. "I can't tell which of the tunnels is forcing the warm air."

"Head Revels, what if Pilt, Cretchit, and I go and see where this tunnel leads?" asked Flin.

"I don't know, Flin, we really should stay together."

"If there's any chance of danger, I promise we'll turn back."

Head Revels paused for a moment. "What do you think, Mr. Luftin?"

"Welp, fresh and younger legs could be better, travel farther if'n they all stayed together—cover twice as much ground that way."

"Alright then, but if you think you might be getting yourselves into any kind of trouble, I want you to turn back immediately! Is that understood?" Head Revels said, giving them all a stern look.

The three of them nodded then anxiously entered into the tunnel on the left. They journeyed for a couple of hours when the tunnel opened up into a dimly lit cavern with a darkened anemone overhead. A colossal octopus the size of a circus tent lay on top of the anemone, blocking out any possible sunlight. The cavern was round and domed inside, a lot like Cobble Cavern, but much smaller and dismal with a darkness that felt as if something were trying to smother them.

Chapter Twenty-One

FLIN IMPRISONED

They cautiously entered the scantily lit cavern. A thick, roaming, gray fog enveloped them within its haze for a short moment then departed and lingered about the cavern floor with no sense of direction.

"That's somethin' ya don't see every day," whined Pilt as he wiped gray droplets of moisture deposited by the fog from his arms and face. "And, why is it so dark in here?"

"Because, we're much deeper under the ocean. And maybe that humongous octopus sitting on top of the anemone up there has something to do with it!" Just then, one of the long tentacles of the octopus reached out and snatched up a sea turtle.

"Look, why do ya think everything's dead in this cavern? Something's wrong with this place—it's givin' me the creeps!" said Cretchit, folding his arms close to his chest and standing firm.

"That's because it's haunted," Pilt responded, nervously looking around. "I say we turn back before we get kil—"

"Pilt! It's not haunted, and we're not going to get killed. Now, come on both of you, we need to find out where this cavern leads."

"Okay, Flin, but I'm going against my better judgment on this, I'm telling you!" Pilt whimpered.

"Yeah, yeah Pilt, I understand. If it was up to your better judgment, you'd have stayed back at the cathedral with the girls!"

"No, I wouldn't! Besides, sometimes they really do need guarding, Flin!" replied Pilt in defense.

"Yeah, yeah, whatever, Pilt. If I hadn't dragged you wi—"

"Light! I see a light! Hey, Pilt, Flin, stop arguing and look!"

"There is a light!" Pilt said hopefully.

They took off at a jog towards it but slowed cautiously as they neared an open tunnel lit by torchlight.

"What is it?" Pilt asked boisterously.

"Shush, Pilt. Not so loud," hushed Flin. "Who knows what's inside there?"

A moment later, two men came down the open tunnel. One was much larger than the other, and both were dressed in black hooded cloaks. They stood at both sides of the entrance, like guards.

"Put out the torches, quick!" said Flin, dropping his torch to the ground and stomping out its flames.

"Did you just see that?" Cretchit asked. "The big guy just hit the smaller guy."

"I'm not sure, but doesn't it look like he's pointing in our direction now?" whimpered Pilt.

"It's because he can see the embers of your torch, Pilt!" scorned Flin, grabbing Pilt's torch and quickly stomping out the remaining embers.

The two guards turned and walked back up the tunnel and out of sight.

"Shees, that was close!" sighed Cretchit. "You almost got us caught, Pilt!"

"Maybe they didn't see us," mumbled Pilt, peeking between the branches of a dead tree.

Through the silence, a piercing howl echoed through the tunnel down after them.

"What's that? Where's that noise coming from?" asked Cretchit, standing tall and looking over the dead limbs in every direction. The frightful noise quickly grew louder.

"There! There's your noise!" shouted Flin as he pointed at the tunnel where the two guards had been standing. A mad cluster of rabid black wolves dashed out of the flickering tunnel toward them.

Pilt was terrified. Where do you think they're headed?"

"Guess!" yelled Flin as he sprang to his feet and took off running back out the way they came. The sound of growling wolves increased as they ran recklessly back through the dead forest.

Pilt began to shout as he ran, "When Head Revels announced that the debate team was going on a fun excursion to Ireland, I had no idea it meant being chased by ravenous wolves in the center of the earth!"

"You're not having fun yet?" hollered Flin as his shirt snagged on a limb and temporarily held him captive.

Suddenly, a log reached up from the ground and grabbed Cretchit by the ankle, sending him crashing hard to the ground. "My leg!" he yelped, grabbing hold of it. "I think I broke my leg!" Flin and Pilt ran back to help him up off of the ground. The vivid snarls caused Flin to turn and see the wolves as they mowed over small trees and bushes. They were quickly closing in.

"They're gaining on us! Pilt, help Cretchit get to the tunnel! I'll try and throw them off! Hurry, go!" As Pilt and Cretchit limped their way toward the tunnel, Flin sprinted directly back at the pack of wolves. *How did I get into this mess?* His heart leapt higher and higher with every beat as the thundering growls grew.

Flin aborted the path that led to his demise and ran toward the cavern's wall which was not much further away. He turned back to see there wasn't much distance between him and the wolves. Flin spotted a clump of trees just ahead and ran for them. He started to climb the biggest tree when the pack of wolves quickly surrounded it and began lunging up at him. One of them caught hold of his pant leg and started scratching him with its paws. The weight of the large, dangling wolf was far too great for Flin. He started losing his grip when the bottom of his pant leg tore free, sending the wolf crashing to the ground. He desperately climbed further up for safety. He looked out over the desolate plain to see the last of Pilt and Cretchit as they limped together into the safety of the tunnel. He wished he could be exiting the cavern and entering the tunnel to safety with them, but the sound of snarling, devilish, bloodthirsty wolves quickly dashed his hopes.

He could hear deep voices rushing toward him. *Great! What now? I'm stuck up in this dead tree!* He looked down at the branch he was standing on. *Maybe, if I can—that just might possibly work!* He bent down, placed his hand on the branch, and closed his eyes, "Grow! Grow branch, grow!" He peeked out of an eye to see if anything had happened, only to spot several large Grimgoblins coming out of the thicket and heading his way.

"There he is!" shouted a Grimgoblin, pointing.

Focus, Flin, focus! Please, you can do this! Flin again closed his eyes and placed his hand on the branch. "Please, branch, I need for you to grow. Please, grow!" Suddenly the limb shot out, growing rapidly towards the cavern wall and tearing the limbs off of other dead trees that surrounded it as it raced above the cavern floor. "Keep growing!" shouted Flin as he held tight to the branch. The weight of the heavy, extended limb was causing the tree to lean to its side. "Come on, please, just a bit farther!" The weight of the branch became too heavy for the tree and there came a loud snap, and the branch he was standing on crashed to the ground. The wolves immediately surrounded it and tore into the lower branches in search of him. Flin jumped to his feet and scrambled up the ledge. The wolves took after him.

"Get him!" a Grimgoblin shouted as Flin neared the ledge. "Hurry, some of you get over there!"

Flin's heart raced as he reached for the top of the ledge and pulled himself up.

"He's getting away!" Flin heard a Grimgoblin yell. He rounded the sharp corner of the ledge and entered into a thick fog where he immediately met a pair of blue electrified eyes glowing back at him from a distance. The eyes narrowed and were accompanied with a deep growl. Then the eyes grew bigger as the creature approached him. It was a wolf the size of a large lion, salivating as it neared. Flin slowly backed away, knocking small rocks over the cliff's edge.

"There he is! Some of you go that way!" pointed the Grimgoblin in charge. The giant wolf backed Flin down to where he'd originally climbed up. Suddenly, the fog parted from behind the wolf and out walked a Grimgoblin holding a huge club.

"Back!" he ordered the wolf, but the wolf seemed non-responsive and totally focused on Flin. The wolf continued inching him. "I said back, you mangy dog!"

The corners of the wolf's mouth pulled back into an evil quivering grin exposing large fangs. The hair on its back was now standing straight up like the quills on a porcupine. It made small lunges at Flin.

"Back, I said!" hollered the giant Grimgoblin as he neared the rear of the wolf. The vicious wolf was now only a few feet away from Flin. It gave one last thunderous growl then leapt high in the air at Flin.

Adrenalin rushed through Flin's veins. "Nooo!" he shouted as his fist impulsively rushed to his defense and hit the wolf in the side of the head. The wolf let out a yelp as its body glided past Flin and flew over the cliff. As the wolf's body soared through the air, its hair swiftly turned a dull gray, and its body stiffened and hardened like a statue. It crashed into the rocks below, shattering into hundreds of pieces.

"Did you see that?" shouted one of the guards in disbelief.

"I don't care—grab him!"

Flin was suddenly surrounded by several guards. "Who are you and what are you doing here?" The head Grimgoblin demanded.

Flin glared at the giant, black-hooded man out of the corner of his eye but made no response.

"So, he won't talk. Take him back to Blade! We'll see what he wants to do with him." None of them dared touch him. "I said, grab him. If none of you are brave enough to grab hold of him, tie that rope around him and we'll drag him back to Blade!"

As they dragged Flin into the entrance of the tunnel, Blade came pouncing down toward them through the shadows, his large belly bouncing.

"Why did you not just do with him as I instructed, Rykirk?" shouted Blade, just inches away from Flin's stoical face.

"He has powers! He killed one of the Daglids!" replied one of the sniveling guards.

"How is this possible?" scowled Blade, sniffing at Flin from a distance. "Such a small human like this couldn't do such damage."

Rykirk spoke, "He struck the Daglid with his fist! It then fell to the ground and shattered into pieces!"

"Tell me, human," growled Blade with gritted teeth and squinted eyes, "how is this possible?"

Flin scowled bitterly directly back into Blade's yellow eyes but remained silent.

Blade walked down to the tunnel's entrance and stopped. "Bring him here!" The guards grabbed Flin by the rope and dragged him just outside the tunnel. Blade kicked at a bush. "Touch that!"

Flin stood still. Blade placed his hand on the back of Flin's neck and forced him to the ground.

"Touch it, I said!" demanded Blade.

Flin could feel anger welling up inside of him. He knew that if he touched the bush at this moment, it would definitely die and petrify. He took his time as he stretched his hand toward the bush. He could feel Blade breathing heavily down on his back, becoming more impatient. Blade cocked back his foot, about to kick him.

Quick, Flin! Think of something funny! Flin forced out a laugh as he stretched his hand toward the bush.

"What's so funny, human?" growled Blade. Flin quickly grabbed hold of the bush then let go and backed away.

"Nothing happened. I thought you said he had special powers!" snarled Blade, turning to the cowering guards. "Get him and lock him up!" Blade said, pointing down at Flin. "And you, you come with me!" he ordered Rykirk.

"Please, no sir, don't throw me into the Snazzard pit! I'm telling you, we saw him kill one of the Daglids!"

Two guards escorted Flin to his chamber. "Enjoy!" the guard laughed as he shoved Flin into a cell and slammed the metal bar door closed behind him.

Hours later, Blade stomped to the cell door followed by Parcell, Sump, and Ruel.

"Parcell! Ruel! Mr. Sump!" Flin said as he jumped up from the floor and brushed himself off, thinking he'd be set free. "We've all been wondering if you guys were alright!"

"That's him alright!" Sump accused coldly in the dim light, pointing at Flin. "He's the one who stole the rest of our treasure!"

"So, the human can talk! Is this true? Did you steal the Oliblish Treasure?" asked Blade.

Flin spotted one of his cigar boxes in Blade's enormous hands. "My box!" he said, pointing at it. "I thought one of you took it!" he glared at Parcell and then back at Ruel. "We found a tree growing from one of the pits you must have dropped in a grove of trees just off of the path in Cobble Cavern," said Flin bitterly.

"Maybe," snickered Parcell from the rear, a dark shadow covering his face.

"Then, it was you as well who threw one of the bigger pits into the pond by the garden!"

"The boy's full of lies!" came Sump's sour voice. "He took the treasure from us and put some of the jewels in his little box here!"

"What's happened to you guys? What's going on? Why are you accusing me of stealing this treasure?" Flin asked, puzzled.

"'Cause you did steal it, ya little liar!" spat Sump.

Parcell moved to the dark corner of the cell and continued snickering in hisses. "Ya forgot to mention the giant handprint I put on your anemone ceiling, Newby.... It wasn't easy climbing that dead giant plant."

"I thought that was you, Parcell!" Flin replied, revolted, trying to get a glimpse of him in the shadows. A wicked chuckle came from out of the corner.

Sump again spoke, "That's why we can't find any more of the treasure!"

Flin suddenly realized Sump's impish game. If Blade found out there was no treasure, Mr. Sump, Parcell, and Ruel would all become Snazzard food.

"That's right! I mean, that's right!" Flin said more forcefully the second time. "I took it and hid it!" A sick look crossed Sump's face as he realized what a foolish thing he'd done. He had just given Flin complete power over this nonexistent treasure that he'd been using as leverage. Blade's ears slowly perked up. He turned to Flin.

"Where, then, is this treasure? Tell me or else!" he threatened, making a fist.

"Either way, you'll never see that treasure, because I'm the only one who knows where it is!" Flin replied poker-faced.

"Guards!" shouted Blade, looking around the room irately. "Get rid of him!" The guards grabbed Flin by the arms and started dragging him out of the cell.

"Stop!" snarled Blade, raising his hand in the air and bending down to Flin's eye level. "Are you sure you didn't want to say something?"

Flin remained silent.

"Fine, leave him in here to rot!" Blade hollered and slammed the door. "And, he is to get no food! Maybe he'll want to change his mind after a while!" Blade put his face to the bars. "You get one day; that is all! If you don't tell me where it is by then, treasure or no treasure, you're dead!" he shouted, striking the bars and shaking dirt from the ceiling and walls. He stomped away with Flin's cigar box clutched tightly in his hand, and Sump and the others following.

"Well, this is a fine mess, Flin!" he mumbled to himself. Exhausted, he slid down the wall and sat in the dry corner. *Once Blade finds out that I don't know anything about this Oliblish Treasure, I'm as good as dead!*

The hooded Grimgoblin that sat on guard duty slowly stood from his stumpy chair and waddled away. He returned moments later. "Water, human!" he said annoyed. He banged the bars with a wooden cup, spilling half of its contents. "You get water, but no food!" he said, dropping the cup through the bars and down onto the dirt floor.

Flin reluctantly reached for the filthy wooden cup and saw that it was now nearly empty and half full of dirt. He drank to the point where the water turned to mud then absentmindedly put his fingers into the sludge and began to swirl it around. The muddy water quickly turned into an icy slush. His frazzled nerves and the chill of the damp cell, along with the fright of what might happen to him the following day, had traveled through his body and out the ends of his fingers. Seconds later, the muddy slush turned to ice, and his fingers were stuck deep in the bottom of the wooden goblet.

"Wouldn't you know it," he said irritated, trying to pull his fingers free. "Just my luck!"

Hearing Flin, the guard curiously stood up from his stump and looked through the cell down at him. "What are you doing to that cup?" he demanded.

"Aaa . . . nothing!" replied Flin nervously, hiding the stuck cup behind his back. The guard stared at Flin for a moment before falling back into his chair.

Flin's fingers finally pulled free and an idea popped into his head. "Excuse me! Excuse me sir!" Flin called to the guard as politely as he dared.

"Quiet! I don't want to be bothered! Besides, I gave you water," the guard said, slouching deeper into his chair.

"I know you did, but could I please have more?"

"No! You're to only get water twice a day. Now leave me alone so I can sleep!"

"Please," Flin persisted. "You spil—I mean—I spilled mine," Flin said innocently.

"Alright—anything to shut you up! But, this counts as your second cup. Give me that goblet!" grumbled the guard, jerking the cup out of Flin's hand.

Chapter Twenty-Two

FLIN'S ESCAPE

"Water!" shouted the guard as he returned. The water splashed again against the bars as he forced the cup in at Flin.

"Thank you," Flin said as he backed deep into the cell and pretended to drink. "Is that someone calling you?" Flin asked as he sat on the floor.

"I heard nothing. Now shut up and drink your water so I can sleep!" barked the guard, again slouching comfortably in his chair.

"Sorry, I thought I heard something," Flin said as he went back to pretending to sip his water. "There it went again! It sounded a lot like Blade. I think he's calling you."

The guard grunted as he got up from his seat and stomped out of sight. Flin scrambled to the cell door. He carefully poured the water evenly over the bars. Then, hearing the guard returning, he dove out of sight and into the shadows next to the door.

"There was no one! I told you I heard nothing! You think you can hear better than me?" he hollered as he came toward the cell door and peeked in.

Flin grabbed the lower corner of the cell door where he wouldn't be seen and focused. "Freeze. Come on, freeze," he whispered repeatedly as he hid on the floor, grasping the bar.

The guard put his masked face up to the cell door and looked in. "Where are you? How come I can't see you?"

Flin jumped up, still holding tight to the cell bar.

"What were you doing down there?"

"I was, I was just resting is all," Flin said casually.

The guard set down his enormous club and fell back into his seat.

"Oh, I'm done with my water," Flin said as he held out his cup from within the bars hoping the guard would reach inside the cell and take it from him.

Lazily, the guard leaned out from his stump and held out his hand. "Well, give it to me!" he groaned. "Stop wasting my time and give me that cup!"

Flin stretched forth the cup within a foot of the cell door. Unwillingly, the guard reached through the bars for it. Flin slowly pulled the cup further away, forcing the guard to stand and reach in.

"Stop pulling that cup away from me!" demanded the guard.

A shimmering frost quickly spread over the bars where the water had been poured.

"I said give me that cup, or I'm coming in there!" He grabbed hold of the bars and began shaking them irately, threatening to tear them free from their hinges. "Gimme that cup!" He tried letting go of the bars but couldn't. "What have you done?" he shouted, looking down at his trapped hands.

Flin swiftly poured what little water remained in his cup over the guard's hands and onto the bars.

"What are you doing? Stop that! I said stop that now!"

He closed his eyes and again focused. The water on the guard's hands turned to hard icicles and rapidly traveled up his arms and under his cloak.

The guard began to growl as he wrestled vainly with the bars. Flin could hear the cell keys dangling from around his waist. He reached through bars, grabbed hold of them, and tore the leather key strap free from the guard's waist.

"Stop! Do you hear me? I SAID STOP!"

Flin reached through the icy bars and unlocked the door. He tried pushing the door open, but the guard stood firmly in his way.

"Ha, ha!" mocked the guard.

Flin knew he was outsized and incapable of pushing the guard out of his way. He could feel his adrenalin racing through his veins in fury. He placed his left hand on the hefty belly of the guard.

"What are you doing now? Ow! Stop that!" yelled the guard as he felt a deadly, electrifying pain shoot through his stomach and travel throughout the rest of his body.

"Back up now, or I'll do it again!" threatened Flin.

A slight chuckle came from the guard and soon turned into a roaring laugh. "I'm not moving!"

Flin placed his left hand on the guard's stomach again.

"Ow! Stop! Stop, or I'll tear you to shreds!" shrieked the guard. His eyes suddenly glazed over and rolled back into his head as he fell to his knees and passed out with his hands still frozen to the bars.

Just then, Flin heard another guard enter the cell area from up above and slam a cell door. "Why are you resting like that?" he shouted in Flin's direction at the guard on the floor. "You're supposed to be on duty. Get up or I'll make Blade aware of your slothfulness! Hey! I'm talking to you!" the guard barked. Then, he snorted and lazily stomped away.

There was silence. Flin looked out to make sure no one was there. He kicked at the guard, whose lifeless body fell over backwards. The hefty weight of the guard falling backwards tore the cell door free from its hinges and landed on top of him. Flin cautiously exited the cell and then stripped the Grimgoblin of his cloak. He threw the black cloak high in the air, letting it settle over his entire body. It appeared as a big black bed sheet on his small frame.

"Aauh!" he gagged nauseously, scrambling desperately to find an air hole. "Didn't this, this, this *thing* ever clean itself?" He pulled the black mask free from the Grimgoblin's head. There, under the mask, was a large, pale-faced, filthy old man with oversized ears and a large, dirty black nose. He raised the soiled mask to his face and placed it on his thirteen-year-old head, which was much smaller than that of the Grimgoblin. Flin tried picking up the Grimgoblins mammoth club, but could only drag it behind him as he headed up and out of the cell area.

"Guard, guard!" called a pleading someone to Flin's back as he passed. Flin recognized the whiny voice at once. He turned and looked out of the two eye holes in his mask. It was Parcell.

"Guard! I'm ready to tell Blade where the treasure's hid now!"

Flin stood motionless for a moment, thinking. *Should I set Parcell free—or leave him?* Flin slowly raised the black hood from his face, revealing himself.

"*You . . . !*" snarled Parcell, his eyes filled with fire. "How'd you get free?" he continued to roar, showing that his anger was much greater than his desire to ask Flin to help set him free.

"Guards, GUARDS!" shouted Parcell at the top of his lungs screaming in the direction leading out of the cell area. "He's getting away!"

Flin pulled the mask back over his head, dropped the heavy club, and sprinted out of the cell area.

"Guards, hurry! Hurry, he's getting away!" Parcell's pleas continued from inside the cell.

As Flin swiftly made his way down the tunnel, he overheard two guards below talking. "Someone's yelling in one of the cells up there—go and see what it's all about!" Quickly, he backed into the shadows of the tunnel and into the dark. Seconds later, a seven foot tall guard stomped passed him. Flin's heart raced.

"What's all the yelling about?" shouted the guard as he entered the prison cavern.

Flin took off at a swift pace down the tunnel. He drew near the guard who had just given the orders to check on the cell.

"That didn't take long. So what was all the blasted yelling about?" asked the guard, his face looking down at some odd wooden chart used apparently for prison cell paper work. He assumed Flin was the guard returning. Flin was stumbling for what to say. The Grimgoblin looked up at Flin. "Hey, you're not the guard I sent up there!"

Flin took off down the tunnel at high speed. The guard stood up befuddled. "Who are you? Come back!"

Flin rounded the next corner with his black cloak skirting in the air behind him, which led to the exit. Two guards stood posted on the sides. He neared them with his heart in his throat.

"Identify yourself!" demanded the first guard, taking a step toward him.

"I've never seen a royal guard so small," said the second, with confusion.

"Stop him!" shouted the guard from up above, pointing at the back of Flin as he came dashing down the tunnel toward them.

"Didn't you hear the guard?" scolded Flin in the deepest voice he could conjure up. "He said to stop him. Were you two asleep? The human ran down this way!" Flin pointed out the tunnel's exit and ran passed the two confused guards.

The large guard made his way from up top toward them. "Idiots! You just let the human escape!" he snarled then backhanded them both.

Once Flin made it a ways out of the tunnel, he tore off the hood and cloak and sprinted through the thick, familiar woods. Fear gripped him again when he heard the sound of growling wolves chasing after him.

"They're gaining on me!" he screamed as he looked back over his shoulder to see the brush and small trees being trampled. *The tunnel! The tunnel's just up ahead!* He made a sudden change in direction, hoping to throw the wolves off course by running through a gray fog that lay on the ground like a thick blanket. As Flin ran through the blinding fog, his body unexpectedly plummeted deep into a pond of water. Desperately, he began to trudge through it.

Rabid growls and barking now quickly approached as he slowly paddled his way through the water. The wolves sprang out over the pond's bank, plunging not far behind him. He made it to the edge of the bank and climbed out. Uncontrollable shivers ran up and down his spine as he hunched over, trying to regain his breath. "I have it!" Flin leaned out over the edge of the pond and placed his hand down into it. He closed his eyes and urgently focused on freezing the water. The threatening growls grew louder, making it difficult for him to concentrate. He raised his eyes to see the wolves now bearing down on him as they swam for the bank. Again, he shoved his left hand into the water and closed his eyes. His fear intensified and sent chills racing up his spine, down his arm, then out the ends of his fingers and into the water.

Thunderous crackling shot up from the water, drowning out the grueling barks and howls that seconds ago littered the pond. Seconds later, only the echoes of the wolves snarling and growls remained in the air then swiftly faded away. There was instant silence. Flin opened an eye, then the other. There, just inches away from his face, stood a giant, frozen, black wolf with its mouth wide open, about to have bitten him.

He looked over the icy pond to see dozens of wolves frozen in place. Some were frozen high in the air, others deep in the pond with their heads barely poking out. "Yes!" Flin shouted triumphantly, flicking the long, white fang of the frozen wolf in front of him.

"There he is!" a gruff voice jolted Flin back to the present. He looked up to see several guards slipping across the frozen pond and making their way through the maze of frozen wolves toward him. He took off for the tunnel at a full sprint. It was now only a couple hundred feet away. As he entered the tunnel, he could hear the ice in the distance behind him beginning to crack and thaw and the sound of angry wolves fighting to break free. The tunnel dimmed the further he entered. *Dang it! I can't see a thing!* He heard the determined growls of wolves enter the tunnel below him.

"Great, wolves can see in the dark!" he said, stumbling over small boulders as he used his hands for eyes along the sides of the tunnel wall.

The sound of hostile wolves quickly grew nearer. He looked down the tunnel to see several pairs of blue eyes glowing back at him. His heart began to ache as it pounded hard against his chest. "A ledge!" he said, feeling a protrusion in the tunnel. Hastily, he climbed up it just as the group of angry wolves rushed below. He remained perfectly still for a minute then started to make his way back down, when he heard a rumble deep in the throat of one of the wolves just beneath him.

One of them was waiting for me! He thought as he quickly climbed back up. Then he saw them in the dark—two cold, electric blue eyes glaring up at him. The wolf snarled then lunged up after Flin, but was unable to get to him. The Daglid tried again, only this time he scratched frantically at the tunnel wall. Unsuccessful, the wolf began to howl. Flin was worried the other wolves would soon hear the howling and return. He felt a baseball-sized rock on the ledge and broke it free. He gripped it tightly in his hands and focused all his fear and anger into the stone. Seconds later, the rock made a tiny explosion in the palms of his hands and crumbled into tiny pieces that continued crackling until the rock had turned into a handful of fine dust. He waited for the wolf to leap up at him again, and then threw the fatal dust down at it. The dust slowly settled over its body, and the wolf began to yelp and violently bite at itself. Moments later, it fell to its side, staring up at him. Its blue electrified eyes gradually faded and went out.

Flin crept down, placed his hand to the tunnel wall and again took off at a jog. He spotted light further up, shining down onto the tunnel floor. Sounds below him echoed up from the disgruntled guards as they made their way up the tunnel towards him. He sprinted out of the tunnel and into the familiar cavern. He looked up at the beautiful, clear anemone as he ran then turned back to see the dreaded torchlight reflecting off the tunnel walls. He sprinted in the direction of the cathedral. *Why can't I see the giant petrified tree or the Snapdragon?* He rounded the cavern's wall and came to an unfamiliar orchard he had never seen before.

"Trees?" he said, perplexed. "Nothing looks familiar," he said, stopping and glancing around. He wondered if he had entered into the wrong cavern. "These trees look just like the one we cut down with the deadly black fruit on it! This is impossible! How could this orchard have gotten here?" he said, unsure of where he was.

He heard snarling wolves that had back-tracked and were coming toward him. He sprinted through the unkempt maze of trees, looking for a place to hide.

"He can't be much further ahead!" he heard one of the looming guards yell. "The Daglids sound like they've located him."

Flin knew he was unable to outrun the wolves through the open meadow. He darted back and forth looking for a place to hide. With no luck, he frantically climbed up one of the many nearby trees in the middle of the orchard and stood perched perfectly still on a branch full of leaves. Within seconds, the pack of wolves arrived and began circling just under him, sniffing viciously at the meadow grass. They began to howl.

"The Daglids are just up ahead!" shouted the tromping guard. The guards arrived to see the wolves sniffing uncertainly at the ground beneath the tree.

"What are they doing? They must have lost the human's scent!"

"Where do you think he could be, Talamus?"

"Anywhere in this blasted forest—there are thousands of trees!" he answered, smacking the trunk of the tree Flin was hiding in. Talamus looked up into the tree. He began to squint.

"What are you looking at?" asked Tuke, the other guard, who also looked up in the tree with interest.

"Look, up there!" Talamus said, pointing far up into the tree.

"What are you pointing at? Do you see him?" asked Tuke with roaming eyes.

"Can't you see that?"

"See what?" Tuke said, squinting through his mask.

"*That*, you idiot!"

"That black fruit way up there? I've never seen black fruit before, have you?"

"Oh, shut up, Tuke! Let's go back."

"Hey, I don't remember ever being in this cavern before, do you?"

"You dummy! If we'd known all this fruit were here, don't you think we'd have come here long ago?"

"You're right!"

"Of course, I'm right!"

"What about the human?" asked Tuke.

"He knew where to hide, right? He must live in this cavern, right? And if he lives here, this might be where he's hidden the treasure, right? Don't you think Blade will reward us well if we tell him about this?"

"Hey, you're right again!"

"Of course I'm right again, you fool. We'll tell Blade about all of this and come back for the human later. Once we catch him, he'll tell us where the treasure's hid—trust me!" Talamus said, pulling a sharp knife out from under his cloak and running his thumb across its blade.

Flin started to lose his footing. He shuffled his feet delicately on the branch, accidentally knocking a piece of black fruit out of the tree that fell and hit Tuke on the shoulder.

"Hey!" snarled Tuke as he glanced up into the tree suspiciously.

"What are you staring at now?"

"This piece of fruit just hit me!"

"And, you think the human threw it at you?" laughed Talamus.

"Yeah, maybe!"

"Idiot! Why would he blow his cover by throwing a dumb piece of fruit at you?"

"Hey, you're right again."

"Stop saying that! Now, let's go back and tell Blade about this."

"Alright, but first—" Tuke said, picking up the black piece of fruit and taking a bite. "It's juicy—Ow!"Tuke reached for his mouth.

"Now what!?"

"I don't know—my teeff feel like they're bein' eat'n away," he said in a slurred voice.

"Quit foolin' around and let's go!"

The black fruit dropped from Tuke's hand. His terrified movements became slower and slower until he stood perfectly still.

"I said stop messing around and let's go! Can't you hear me?" barked Talamus, walking over to Tuke and jerking off his mask. "What the *devil?*"Tuke's head had turned a dull gray, and the ailment that had caused this degeneration was rapidly spreading down his neck and traveling throughout the rest of his body. Within seconds, he became entirely consumed by the look of death and stood as a statue.

Talamus reached down and cautiously picked up the black fruit. He raised it close to his nose and sniffed at it. "AAARR!" he roared, then threw the fruit to the ground and stomped on it several times. Angry, he turned and gave the closest wolf a kick to the ribs, then stormed off back to the tunnel with the pack of wolves following distantly behind.

Flin spotted the cathedral from high up in the tree. He slid down its trunk and took off at a jog. Soon, he burst through the front door of the cathedral.

Inger was all by himself in the Entrance Hall when Flin entered.

"Flin?" muttered Inger in disbelief. "Is it really you? 'Tis you! Ever'one, Flin's returned!"

Immediately the room filled with people, including Cretchit, who limped over with a cast made from tree bark on his leg.

"You're alive?" Cretchit said surprised. "But, but, Pilt and I saw them drag you up and into that tunnel. How'd ya escape?"

"It's a long story; I'll tell you later."

"Flin!" shouted Pilt as he came running in from the kitchen with candy in both hands and frosting from head to toe.

"Is Head Revels around?" Flin asked urgently.

"No, he and Mr. Luftin haven't returned yet either," said Miss Lemons gloomily. She wrapped her arm around one of her students.

"Well then, is Principal Vespar around?" Flin asked, his eyes glancing about tensely.

"She and Voss Yeg went outside not too long ago. You had to have passed them coming in," replied Flowell, looking at Flin with concern. "Flin, why are you acting so weird? Is something wrong?"

"Yes—I mean no!"

"I don't get it! What do you mean yes and no?" Flowell grabbed Flin by the hands and drew close to his face, trying to capture his full attention.

"I'll tell you later," Flin said, then abruptly stood up and dashed out the front door. *"Principal Vespar! PRINCIPAL VESPAR!"* he yelled repeatedly as he ran down the path toward the garden and orchard. *"PrincipalVespar!"*

"Yes? What is it?" Her head popped up over the raspberry bushes. Principal Vespar could see even from a distance that Flin's face was full of exhaustion and stress.

"Where are you?"

"We're over here in the raspberry patch."

Flin stumbled over toward her.

"Flin, thank heavens you're safe!" she said, dropping her gardening supplies and making her way over to him to give him a smothering hug. "We've been worried sick! Pilt and Cretchit told us that awful story of how you'd been captured. They thought you'd possibly been killed!"

"Thanks for the concern, but *really*, I'm fine! I need to tell you something though. The men who captured me, they said they were going to return, and I think they meant with Blade's army!"

"Blade? Oh, you mean the awful, giant Pigman? What makes you say that?" Principal Vespar asked now tremendously concerned. She swiftly pulled off her gardening gloves, which were made from curtains.

"They're evil, like nothing I've ever seen before, and they don't have a problem with killing things—"

"Even people?"

"Even people! I'm telling you, they won't stop at any cost! Trust me on this!"

"Why would they come here? What is it that they're after?"

"It's some treasure that they call the Oliblish Treasure. They think I know where it is, and they said they were going to come back and get it. I'm telling you, Principal Vespar, they won't stop at any cost! They mean to kill!"

"Oh heavens, please no! This is terrible!" Principal Vespar said, placing her hand over her mouth and then over her heart. "I wish Head Revels were back!" she said with panic in her voice, looking around in every direction in desperation.

"Mrs. Yeg!" Principal Vespar called curtly.

"Yes."

"Perhaps the radishes are fine for the moment. I think we'd better return to the cathedral for now."

"Oh, alright then," said Voss Yeg, popping up from the radish plants and removing her gardening apron. She sensed the gravity of the situation. They briskly walked back up the trail and into the cathedral.

"Everyone, quick! Please, gather round!" called out Principal Vespar with much stress in her voice. "Flin has informed us of some recent disturbing news. It appears we may be in grave danger."

The room suddenly began to buzz with insecurities.

"Danger? What kind of danger?" asked one of the alarmed students.

"Well, it's not quite clear at the moment, but until Head Revels returns, no one is to leave the cathedral. Do I make myself clear on this? The cathedral door is to be locked at all times! Sheraton, you and Edgar go and make sure the bolt on the door is locked," she instructed, then walked over to Flin. "Come, I need you to tell me everything you know!"

Later that night, the cathedral sat quiet. At dinner, tension was high and even though Heppel had made an incredible meal, no one at the moment seemed very interested in eating. Flin had been asked by Principal Vespar to sit with the adults and bring them up to speed.

"Well, I never! I can't believe Mr. Sump would stoop so low!" said Voss Yeg, her nostrils flaring as she turned her head away in repulsion.

"What about the, the two boys, Parcell and the other one, oh, what was his name, Ruel?" asked Fig Tronsel, his mind going blank from fear.

"Well, I'm not sure about Ruel, but Parcell seemed to be fitting right in with Blade and his men," responded Flin.

"And Mr. Luftinand Mr. Revels, you last saw them when?" asked a concerned Miss Lemons, hoping for a different response than she'd already received.

"It's like Pilt and Cretchit said earlier. A couple of days ago, when we were still all together, the tunnel came to a fork, and we split up. They went to the right, and we went to the left."

Chapter Twenty-Three

WHY THE NAME FLINNIGAN HOVGARD IS SO GRAND

S hortly, Fezzy and Inger carried their plates of food over and sat across from Flin and started eating. Flin sat staring down at his food in deep thought, his mind consumed with Blade and his obsession with this Oliblish Treasure. Unaware, he started to mumble out loud, "What is it about greed and this hunger people have for wealth and treasure?"

"Treasure, ya say lad," said Fezzy as he snapped his bread in half, catching Flin off guard. "'tis whad makes man go, whad you say, oh… crazy. Talk of this treasure… Ay've seen haunting greed in their eyes… takes over their mind it does."

"What?" Flin asked in deep thought, glancing up from his food. "Oh, yeah. Tell me about it! My dad's told me a story hundreds of times of my crazy greatgrandfather who apparently always talked of some bizarre treasure that had sunk to the bottom of the ocean. He said that he knew where it was but could never get back to it!"

Inger's fork suddenly fell to the table. He stopped chewing, a leaf of lettuce hanging out of his mouth. He glanced over at Fezzy, who looked stunned as well.

Fezzy turned to Flin, "Dis *great* grandfather ya speak uf—do ya by chance know 'is name?"

"Of course, how can I forget? It's my name, too!" Flin was slightly embarrassed.

"Wella, whad 'tis it, lad?" Fezzy again asked.

"Hovgard— well, Flinnigan Hovgard Newby," Flin said quietly. He looked around, hoping no one had overheard, then went back to eating.

Fezzy and Inger's mouths both fell wide open as they turned to each other and then back to Flin. "Whad wus thot ya said, laddy?" Fezzy asked slowly, now starting to stand.

"My whole name?" he hesitated. "My whole name is, Flinnigan Hovgard Newby, why?"

Fezzy dropped his drinking mug, spilling his red punch all over the floor in front of him. "Did ya jist say, *Hovgard Newby….?*"

"Uh huh," Flin nodded, picking up his drinking goblet.

Both Fezzy and Inger jumped up from their stools, ran opposite directions around the table, grabbed Flin by the arms and started dragging him outside.

"What, what are you two doing? Fezzy, Inger, let me go!" Flin hollered. They set him free on the porch and both pointed up at the face of the cathedral. The moon's rays shone directly down on its hard surface, which was heavily covered in ivy. Inger and Fezzy quickly climbed up it and pulled back the vines from off its enormous trunk.

Fezzy whistled and hollered down, "Do ya see it?"

Curious and concerned, everyone had joined them on the deck and were staring up at the image of a man with a beard that was carved deep into the base of the tree.

Flin yelled up with a shrug of the shoulders, "Yeah, I see it! But who is he?"

"That there be **HOVGARD!** Your great grundfather."

"What? No, that can't be him!" said Flin, entirely confused. He stepped back, nearly falling off the deck. A low hum of whispers erupted around him.

Fezzy and Inger climbed back down and looked up at the long, lost face of Hovgard.

"Alright! We've been out here long enough," said Principal Vespar, looking out into the uncertainty. "Everyone, back inside!" She guided everyone into the cathedral like a mother hen and locked the door.

Fezzy and Inger sat down with Flin. "See lad, it twas yar great, grundfather's ship. It sank 'ere years ago. Heund sixty udder people were sunk to the bottom of the ocean, trapped in an air pocket in da cabin of da ship— 'tleast til it crashed inta da anemone wall. It twas yar great granddad who planted dis 'ere tree by accident, ur so he said."

Principal Vespar stood close by listening intently to the conversation. "But, it had to have taken hundreds, if not thousands of years for a tree this size to grow!"

"No, two days is ull," responded Fezzy, raising two of his short fingers. "Hovgard had dese seeds. He neber showed anyone, but he said that one day, one of um fell ta da cavern floor und jist about flooded de entire cavern as it tore through de anemone. For years after, water flooded down on da big tree until da anemone finely grew around da top of it. That's why da roots are outa da ground, da water from da ocean fell through the anemone and washed da dirt away. After da tree sat 'ere next ta da cavern wall for a couple of years, dey mined it out, convertin' it inta da grand cathedral ya see bifore ya taday. Dey lived 'ere fur abou' fifty years. Then one day, Hovgard found a way out, but he neber did come back fur da treasure," Fezzy finished.

"Treasure! Did you just say treasure?" sparked Pilt, who'd been sitting silently and absorbing every word they'd said. "So, there really is a treasure?"

"Oh, yis! He take some of da gold and gems from da treasure, und he melt it down. Fur years und years, he make lots uf different kinds uf rings from da treasure with da help of other Cobbles like ourself, and of course, Naja, who later we found ou' was an evil sorceress, but that's anudder story," said Inger, now looking down at Flin's finger with a confused expression.

"So, he's the one who started the whole family 'Destiny Ring' thing," mumbled Flin, looking sadly down at his naked finger.

"Hovgard said there would be one that would follow him years later, but if'n you be Hovgard's greatgrundson, where might yar ring be?" Fezzy asked, touching Flin's ring finger. "Ay was there and saw that very ring being made years and years ago. Oh… it was the great Cobble high council who put together the stones and symbols on yar ring and throughout the cavern. They said that ring in particular was a special ring. Powers it had too… Ay…remembers all this."

"Oh, I had a ring, but I lost it the night we helped the baby whale," Flin responded with disappointment.

"So, Flin really has a treasure?" Pilt's mind was now fully consumed by one thing, *treasure.*

"Oh, yis! 'Tis late— but tamarrow wu'll take ya ta what's left of da treasure," said Fezzy, his eyebrows bouncing on his forehead.

"So, you really think my greatgrandfather made this cathedral and everything?" asked Flin, looking around incredulously.

"Yis, fur sure!" Fezzy nodded.

"What about that wild orchard several hills away? Did he plant those trees as well?" asked Flin.

"Oh, yis, yis, bud dose trees were planted by sum more of his udder seeds!"

"But, when he left, why didn't he take the treasure with him?" asked Pilt, still consumed by the thought of wealth.

"Ay don' rightly know."

The once silent room was now hopping with whispers of Flin's greatgrandfather's treasure, which was soon to be his. Flin glanced at the giant faced clock and was surprised to see it was already one thirty in the morning.

BOOM! An unexpected and unnerving bang rattled the door.

"Don't anyone answer that!" hushed Principal Vespar, standing up with fright.

BOOM! BOOM! BOOM! There was thunderous pounding coming from outside the door.

"It's Blade and his men, I just know it!" whimpered Pilt, bumping into the others as he backed away from the door.

The pounding continued.

"I guess we should see who it is," said Principal Vespar, unsure. All eyes stared frightfully back at her. "Mr. Tronsel, would you please see who's at the door? Pilt and Flin, would you help him?"

"Yeah, sure," Flin replied. He looked over at Pilt, who was vigorously shaking his head in a definite *no*. "Come on, Pilt. She asked us to get the door."

Terrified, Fig Tronsel's long frame crept toward the door.

"You guys go ahead," said Pilt. All eyes now looked at the frightened Pilt as he inched forward from the back corner of the room. Pilt glanced over at Sam, who was shooting him a disapproving glare. She swung her chin toward the door, trying to coax him.

"Yeah, sure, what the heck, Flin," he said loudly. "Let's get the door!" He quickly walked up to the door with Fig and Flin and unlocked it. There came another pounding just as the latch came free. Flin pulled at the large wooden door. A dirty hand missing bits and pieces of its fingers reached in and grabbed Flin by the arm.

"Flin!"

"Mr. Luftin," Flin said with relief.

"Why is the door locked?" came the voice of Head Revels from outside.

The students, excited for their return, swiftly huddled to the door. The two of them looked exhausted as they entered.

"Quick, some of you take their packs," Voss Yeg pointed.

The two of them limped over to one of the tables and collapsed on a chair stump. "Someone, quickly run and grab them both a drink," said Principal Vespar.

"We think we may have found a way out," Head Revels said in a parched voice, excited to share the good news as he sat down. The room instantly filled with the anxious chatter of high hopes.

"We went deep into the earth for about a day. We were low on food and water and were about to turn back, when we noticed that up ahead the tunnel took a sharp angle upward. We decided to pursue it for several more miles. We eventually spotted a door about a quarter of a mile further up the tunnel with sunlight around the outside edges of it. Leaves from up top were lying all about the tunnel floor," he concluded optimistically and took a long, hard drink.

"Really? You could see sunlight around a door that leads out?" inquired Principal Vespar, intrigued. She refilled their drinks and sat close by.

"Oh yes! Looks very hopeful!" gasped Head Revels, finishing his drink for the third time.

Heppel, after hearing the news of the two men going without food, quickly came in with some simmering meats and other items.

"Why, thank ye, Heppel! 'aven't eaten a decent meal for days now!" said Mr. Luftin, causing Heppel to blush as she set down the food tray. Miss Lemons swiftly sat down next to Mr. Luftin. She gave him an unexpected warm smile and began buttering a roll for him.

Head Revels eagerly bent over his plate with a fork full of food. "Why again was the door locked?" he asked, then filled his mouth.

Flin explained, "Well, do you remember, Pilt, Cretchit, and I took the fork that went the other way?"

"Yes, and?" Head Revels asked, reaching his cold hand for the purple grapes as Heppel continued to bring out even more food.

"Well, we sort of ran into a bit of bad luck. That tunnel led to a dark secluded cavern, where we found Sump, Parcell, and Ruel. They had joined up with, well, very bad—" Flin recounted the entire story to Head Revels and Mr. Luftin. "So, the last I heard was the one Grimgoblin was going back to tell Blade where this cavern is, and then they were going to return for the treasure."

Head Revels stopped eating and wiped his mouth with a cloth. "Treasure? What treasure?"

"I'll explain about the treasure later."

"How long do you think it will take before they get here?"

"I'm not sure, but I think it will be soon. A day or two at the most."

"That doesn't leave us much time to prepare ourselves to leave and travel that new tunnel," he said pensively. "It will atleast take a day or two before we can gather up all the supplies will need."

The excitement of going home was shrouded by the fear of Blade and his men. Many sat huddled in groups discussing what the following day might bring.

Early the next morning, Fezzy and Inger came running into Flin's room. They grabbed him by the hands and pulled him out of his bed and onto the floor.

"Ow," he said, half asleep. He yawned and rubbed his hair.

"Hurry, Flin! Remember, we go und show ya yar greatgrundfather's treasure!" Fezzy said rubbing his hands together excitedly. He grabbed Flin some clothes out of the log dresser.

"Okay, let me get dressed, and I'll be right down," Flin said in a yawn as he stretched.

"Okee, but ya must 'urry!" Fezzy said as he and Inger scampered out of the room.

"I'm coming, too," yawned Pilt, letting his feet flop to the floor.

"Und me uz well," said Cretchit, gingerly climbing out of bed.

"You can't go—you've got a broken leg," said Pilt.

"I cun still walk! Besides, Voss Yeg thinks I only bruised it."

Flin, now nearly dressed, darted out of the room.

"Good morning, Flin," Head Revels said. "Fezzy's just finished telling me about how your greatgrandfather built this place. What a remarkable story it is, too! What are the chances of something like that happening—your greatgrandfather being down here before you? And, they say there's a big carving of his face on the cathedral. Did you see it?"

"Yeah, I saw it last night."

Pilt and Cretchit came running down the stairs. "Cretchit, you be careful," scolded Voss Yeg, pointing her aged finger. "You're going to injure your leg again if you're not careful."

"I'm fine! Doesn't really hurt no more!"

"Let's go see Flin's treasure!" burst Pilt with a big smile, as he jumped over the bottom two stairs. "I can't wait to see all that gold!"

"Flin, would it be alright with you if I also came along and saw this treasure of your greatgrandfather's?" asked Head Revels.

"Sure," replied Flin curtly.

"Okee, we go!" said Fezzy hurriedly as he scampered out the cathedral door and led them for a ways around the outer wall of the cavern.

"Fezzy, are we almost there yet?" said Pilt impatiently.

"Yis, almost dere!" responded Fezzy, walking through a patch of grass that towered high above his head. They walked down a steep hill for a few more minutes until the cavern floor was at its lowest point.

"Dere!" Fezzy said, pointing in the distance.

"Why, there really is an old ship!" Head Revels said, raising his spectacles closer to his eyes and scrunching up his nose.

"Yis!" Fezzy responded again proudly.

"Fezzy, where's the treasure?" Pilt looked around eagerly.

"Cum, I show you!" Fezzy replied, throwing his hands in the air.

They walked a few hundred more yards until they were at the base of the clear anemone wall. There, sitting on the ocean floor and split right down the midsection of the ship, was the clear anemone separating the front half of the vessel from the back half. The front half of the ship was in nearly perfect condition, preserved by being on the inside of the anemone. The ships green paint was slightly faded, and its bow had just a touch of dust on it. However, the rear portion of the ship, out in the water, was beginning to rot. It was covered in green thick moss with tiny sea creatures climbing all about the rear deck, inhabiting the rotted holes in the ship.

"Whoa . . . 'tis truly amazin' . . ." said Cretchit.

"Where's the treasure?" asked Pilt, standing on his toes with his nose flattened up against the anemone wall.

"Look dere," Fezzy said, pointing to the back of the ship. "De Oliblish Treasure!"

Just then a cloud departed from up above and the sun's rays shone brilliantly down through the ocean water landing on the gems on the back of the ship. Colored beams of light shot off the back of the ship in every direction, like lasers, lighting up the ocean water in a rainbow of colors. The group stood speechless, staring at the treasure.

"Wow, that really is some treasure!" said Head Revels.

"Why is half the ship out in the ocean and the other half in the cavern? And, why didn't Flin's grandfather get the treasure?" asked Pilt.

"'Cause Flin's greatgrundfather und da udders crashed inta the anenome. It leaked badly round da ship for several years. Flin's greatgrundfather din't want ta damage da anemone unymore, so he left what remained of the treasure right dere," he said, pointing.

"Fezzy, where's the treasure chest?" asked Pilt. "I can see gold and gems, but there's no chest? All treasures have a chest!"

"Yis! Dere was a chest, a big red one with brass straps, but then one dee, jis gone! Maybe it rot, ur big fish came'n ate it. Who knows?" replied Fezzy, shrugging his shoulders.

Flin stared silently through the anemone at the remaining shimmering treasure. "I think my greatgrandfather was a wise man not to risk flooding the cavern. And, he really wasn't crazy after all like everyone said he was. There really was a treasure."

"Well, Flin, I'm sorry. I wish there were some way we could get what's left of the treasure and take it back to the surface with us," said Head Revels regretfully.

Thoughts of what Flin might do with the treasure to lighten his parents' financial burden went through his mind. "Thanks, but its fine just the way it is," he said, knowing that flooding the entire cavern was way too high of a risk. Flin walked around to the front of the ship, examining it. Thoughtlessly, he grabbed hold of the ship's bow emblem.

"We took da chain und anchor back to da cathedral," said Fezzy.

"So, that's where the chain and the anchor came from for the clock. I wondered where it had come from. Ingenious, your Great Grandfather Hovgard," smiled an amused Head Revels.

"Yis, Hovgard used many parts of da ship for da cathedral."

The smooth, cold surface in Flin's hand caught his attention. He pulled his hand away to see a tarnished, brass green dolphin. "The dolphin from my ring," he muttered. "Hey look!" he said, excitedly pointing at it. "That dolphin ornament was one of the symbols on my ring—the third symbol, I think!" Head Revels pulled out his glasses to see if there was something significant about the dolphin.

"The second symbol that was on my ring, Cretchit and I saw in one of the wind tunnels. Didn't we, Cretchit?" Flin said excitedly. His mind suddenly returned to the night he'd received his ring. Now, for the first time, he truly realized that he was destined to be down under the ocean at this very moment.

"I wonder—" said a perplexed Head Revels, bending down and squinting at the icon.

"Wonderwhat?" asked Pilt, rubbing the dolphin, wanting to somehow be a part of this great mystery. Seconds later, he lost focus and went back to gloating over the shimmering treasure.

Head Revels continued, "Well, it's too bad that Flin's ring was lost, because it might have been some kind of map. Maybe, if we could follow the symbols, we could find our way out. If only we still had that ring. But, still, if I'm not mistaken, this recently discovered tunnel should atleast take us up to the surface."

Flin stared down disheartened at his finger where the destiny ring had once been. He knew that what Head Revels had said was true. He should have been more careful with his ring.

"Whoa!" Pilt shouted excitedly as a red beam of light shot off the back deck. "If that's what I think it is, it's worth a fortune! I'd atleast try getting that out."

"I agree!" Cretchit exclaimed, he too catching the infectious lust for treasure.

Gradually, they all somberly walked back to the cathedral.

Chapter Twenty-Four

THE DREADED ARRIVAL OF BLADE

Night was drawing near as Flin sat tensely in a leather chair next to the fire in the Entrance Hall. He knew that Blade and his men could be there at any time.

The wood burning in the fireplace that night was part of the multicolored tree they'd cut down. An orange glow flickered, barely lighting up the enormous room as the delicious smell of freshly baked peach cobbler wafted about. When the fire dimmed, Head Revels asked Flin if he would go and get more firewood.

"I'll help you, Flin!" said Pilt, jumping off the bridge.

"It's fine, Pilt, I can get it myself."

"I know it's fine, Flin, but I'm still going. That wood can get *really* heavy," he said quite loudly, hoping that some of the girls in the room would hear him as he poked out his chest.

Flin lifted the lock free from the door, and he and Pilt walked out of the cathedral and into a stiff, cold breeze.

"Looks like it's gonna rain tonight," Pilt mumbled, looking upward as they made their way towards the stacked firewood.

"Yeah, I heard Inger say this morning that he was going to go and open up the rain tunnel to water the gardens and vineyard!" hollered Flin over the gusting wind.

"This wind's awful!" shouted Pilt, folding his arms tight to his chest. "Wait a sec! I'm going back to get my jacket!"

While Flin waited for Pilt's return, he looked up at his greatgrandfather's face carved deep into the surface of the cathedral. Orange smoke billowed out of the chimney, dancing high into the air with the gusting wind before it rushed down after him like a swarm of bees. *I guess my Great Grandfather Hovgard wasn't crazy after all. Everything he said turned out to be true, and I kind of like the name, Hovgard — Flinnigan Hovgard Newby.*

Raindrops the size of large grapes began to pour down out of the clouds above. Just then, Flin somehow could sense confusion or anger. He stopped and looked off in the distance. He spotted the terrifying blue glow of several Snazzard's eyes glaring back at him from a far off tunnel.

He sprinted for the cathedral just as Pilt was exiting. "Pilt! No! Go back inside! Hurry, run!" screamed Flin.

Pilt caught sight of the distant unwelcome Snazzards slithering towards them through the trees. "But what about, you?" screamed Pilt through cupped hands.

"Just do it! There's no time!" Flin replied as he desperately sprinted toward the cathedral. He looked back to see two large Snazzards with dark cloaked Grimgoblins on their backs nipping at his heels.

"Flin! Flin!" screamed Head Revels, realizing what was happening and motioning helplessly at him from the porch. He could see there wasn't enough time for Flin to make it back to the cathedral.

Flin darted off the path and into the thickly wooded forest.

"We have no other choice!" Head Revels said disheartened as he closed the cathedral door behind him. "We need to lock the door and make sure the reinforcements are secure! I hope Flin's alright! Dang, if only we had more time!"

Snazzards slithered in and out of the trees, chasing after Flin. The outside of the cathedral was now swarming with dozens of Snazzards and Grimgoblins. Trees crashed down all around Flin, smacking into him and nearly knocking him to the ground. He spotted Blade across the meadow, charging out after him on the back of the biggest Snazzard he'd ever seen. It was deep purple with black, iridescent scales and silver, piercing eyes. Long, white fangs protruded out of its mouth.

Just then, there came an unexpected screech from the sky above, followed by a lingering hiss that thundered down through the clouds. A black streak vanished into the thick mist above him.

Flin had been forced to the edge of the grove, leaving only a small meadow with tall grass in front of him. Reluctantly, he darted out into it when he spotted Blade at the opposite end, driving the heels of his boots deep into the Snazzard's ribs and racing towards him. Another screech came from the sky above and caused Blade to jerk back on the reins and look up in terror.

Flin continued to dart across the meadow when he felt warm moisture on the back of his neck. He could smell the awful stench of Snazzard breath. Fear made his blood run cold when he realized exactly what it was. He looked over his shoulder and straight into the eyes of a giant, red Snazzard bearing down on top of him. It opened its mouth wide about to swallow him up.

Suddenly, a loud crash came from behind, shaking the earth and knocking him to the ground. Flin wondered what had happened. Tensely, he turned around to see. There, perched on top of the Snazzard, was a colossal cobra with eagle like wings which were the length of a large airplane's. The cobra's talons were latched deep into the now lifeless skull of the Snazzard.

The Grimgoblin that had been riding the Snazzard jumped from its back and took off running. The long neck of the cobra coiled back then struck out after the Grimgoblin, knocking him to the ground. The flying cobra turned to Flin, who stood frozen, unable to move. He knew that if the flying snake wanted to, it could strike at him at any time as well. Flin noticed that one of its eyes was missing and in its place was a large, shimmering diamond. The flying snake stared at him for a moment then let out an awful screech and released its talons from the Snazzard's head. The cobra spread open its wings and flew off in search of others. Flin fell to the ground confused. *Why didn't it kill me?*

Flin heard another ear-piercing screech come from the cobra. He watched as it straighten out its long body and tuck its wings to its side, like a massive arrow. It soared down through the clouds and crashed on top of another beastly Snazzard, this time an albino white Snazzard.

"There he is!" A startling shout diverted Flin's eyes from the diving snake above and back to his circumstances. Several Grimgoblins and Daglids were tromping their way through the tall grass towards him. He took off for the cathedral. The rain on the meadow grass caused Flin to slip out of control. He tripped several times over the maze of fallen tree branches as he desperately ran.

Head Revels spotted Flin through a crack in the door and opened it up. "Come on, Flin! You can make it!" he motioned with his arm.

"No, they won't quit! We'll be trapped inside!" yelled Flin.

Head Revels knew Flin was right. He shut the door and swiftly turned to Cretchit. "Cretchit!" shouted Head Revels.

"Yes sir!" responded Cretchit racing to his call.

"Take Pilt, and you two go and open those wind tunnel doors!"

Daglids now flanked both sides of Flin as he ran.

"Stop him!" Blade's thundering voice boomed from high up on top of the back of the purple Snazzard as it chased after Flin.

Flin ran frantically down the trail that headed directly toward the sunken ship. He took a sharp turn off the beaten path and into some thick brush in one last desperate attempt to lose Blade and his men. He was suddenly surrounded by several panting daglids that emerged from out of the tall grass and began circling him. Blade came barreling in, dropped the reins and slid down the side of his Snazzard.

"Tell me, human!" demanded Blade, pulling off his gray leather gloves. He walked over to the wheezing Flin, who fell exhausted into the grass. "Where is the Oliblish Treasure?"

Flin looked around in despair.

"I said, where is the treasure? Tell me or die!" erupted Blade.

Flin could see the ship out of the corner of his eye.

"Daglids!" commanded Blade, snapping his fingers and pointing down at Flin. "Food!" The wolves instantly dropped to their chests and began to growl as they crawled towards him.

"Okay, I'll tell you were the treasure is," Flin said begrudgingly as he pushed himself up from the ground.

"Gooood," Blade said, rubbing the palms of his hands together. "Where is this treasure?" The yellows of his eyes smoldered like sizzling embers, lighting up in a fire of greed.

Flin hesitated before answering. He knew that if he told Blade where the treasure was, he would risk flooding the entire cavern.

"You're stalling! Do we need the Daglids to jog your memory? Or maybe we should just let the Snazzards have you. Food!" Blade said, turning sharply again to the daglids.

"Okay! *Okay!* It's over there!" Flin, terrified, pointed just over the next ridge to the ship, which protruded halfway out of the water. "The treasure's over there," he sighed.

"That's no treasure. That's just an old wrecked ship!"

"It's in the back of the ship. You just can't see it from here."

"Bring him!" demanded Blade. Two guards grabbed Flin by the arms and dragged him over to the ship, followed by Blade and the rest of his men.

Hostile clouds from the open rain tunnel now filled the cavern with fury as bright flashes of lightning lit up the sky, followed by the pounding sound of thunder.

"Where is it? I see no treasure!" Blade said, glaring out into the ocean.

"It's in the back of the ship, the part that's in the water."

"Ohhh . . . I do see it! You! Come here!" Blade pointed to one of his guards.

"But if you try to get what's left of the treasure, you could flood the cavern," Flin feebly tried to explain.

"Only speak when spoken to, human. Now you!" barked Blade to the guard as he snapped his fingers. "Get on the deck of that ship, go through that door, and bring me back my treasure!"

The Grimgoblin struggled but finally climbed up on the bow. He pulled back the twisted ivy and clumps of moss that strangled the moist door and gave it a hard tug. "It won't open."

"Try pushing on it, you idiot!" Blade commanded. The Grimgoblin used the weight of his body to push against the door. As the door slightly opened, a wave of water came splashing into the cavern and the door was forced shut.

"Stop!" shouted Flin. "Once you get the door open, you might not be able to close it! The water will just keep pouring in until the entire cavern's flooded!"

"I said quiet, human!" said Blade impatiently. "Open the door further this time!"

The Grimgoblin pushed against the ship's door, allowing more water to pour in on the ship's bow. He forced his way through the narrow opening and into the cabin flooded by ocean water and the door slammed closed behind him from the force of the water. They all watched as the Grimgoblin traveled through the cabin windows until he made it to the back of the ship. Bubbles began to rise out of his nose and mouth. He slipped on the decades of moss on the deck while holding tight to the rotted rail to keep from floating away. As the Grimgoblin neared the pile of treasure, lust and greed could be seen burning in the eyes of Blade as well as all of his men who were now pressed up against the anemone wall staring out into the ocean.

In all the excitement of retrieving the treasure, the focus had moved from Flin to the treasure. He cautiously took a step backwards—then another—and another.

The Grimgoblin finally made it to the treasure. He dared to let go of the rotted rail with one of his hands and leaned out to the center of the deck to scoop up handfuls of loose gold coins and precious gems. Excitedly, he stuffed them down into his black cloak, which he discovered actually helped to weigh him down.

Confidently he began to stuff more and more of the treasure into his cloak. Then he leaned out and snatched up the last of the treasure that he could reach while still holding onto the rail. He turned and looked through the clear anemone at Blade.

"I want it all! Leave nothing!" screamed Blade through the anemone out at him.

The Grimgoblin released his anchoring hand from the rail and slowly started his way to the center of the deck. With every step he took, the shimmer of gold coins and jewels trickled out of the bottom of his cloak. He finally neared the bulk of treasure, his eyes wide with greed as his body began to rise up off the deck and float away. Frantically, he began waving his arms up and down in an effort to try and re-anchor himself. In all the panic, his movements caused even more gold coins and jewels to fall out of his clothes. Bubbles now poured from his mouth as coins and jewels floated all around him, eventually landing back on the deck. His eyes once filled with greed now bulged with panic and fear. He fruitlessly looked in at Blade and the men for help. He let out one last scream in a large bubble, then slowly floated up and out of sight.

"AARRGHH!" yelled Blade, kicking at the base of the anemone wall. He turned to see the back of Flin as he sprinted toward the cathedral. *"Get him!"* he shouted pointing.

The daglids and Snazzards were quickly on his tail as he made his way up the path. They trapped him against the outside of the cathedral, leaving him no place to go, but up. He desperately began climbing the rockhard tree, trying to avoid being captured.

"You'll all be sorry if he gets away again. After him!" Flin heard Blade yell from down below.

Flin used the vines from the wild ivy to pull himself up, slipping occasionally due to the rain pouring down upon him.

Cretchit and Pilt cracked open the front door and waited until the coast was clear. Then, they darted out of the cathedral and into the thickly wooded trees, headed for the wind tunnels.

From high up, Flin could clearly see the giant winged cobra, as it continued to dive down and pick off Snazzard after Snazzard.

Several Snazzards were now climbing up after Flin, their talons digging into the cracks of the cathedral as they pulled their way up toward him. Flin was several hundred feet in the air and nearing the top of the cathedral where it met the ceiling of the anemone. He pulled himself up the last couple of feet to where the anemone wrapped tightly around the petrified tree. He was pinned. He reached up and touched it.

I'm trapped! Flin panted, his heart pounding out of control. He watched the Snazzards gradually near him. *Dang it! What are my options?* He looked hastily around. *I have no options. Well, I have two options— both death! I can stay here and let the Snazzards get me, or I can jump! There's just got to be another way!*

He peered down at the approaching Snazzards, the smell of their horrible breath growing stronger as they closed in on him. He noticed an occasional slip from the Snazzards on the rock hard surface.

Thick clouds flooded the cavern sky, engulfing Flin in a gray fog that temporarily blocked out his view below. He placed both of his hands up to the cold damp anemone.

"That's it! I'll freeze the anemone! I can do it! I know I can do this!" he said as he secured himself to the ledge and placed his left hand against the cold ceiling then closed his eyes. Seconds later, he re-opened them. "Dang, nothing happened!"

A Snazzard's long tongue reached up and wrapped around one of Flin's leg, just about pulling him off the ledge. He knew he was running out of time. He closed his eyes again, knowing that deep within himself he had to truly become the emotion he was trying to create. "It's cold, Flin—it's ice cold! I'm freezing cold inside! In fact, I'm so cold, I'm an ice block! Chills are racing up and down my spine and I'm starting to get goose bumps," The cold wet rain that drenched him helped to magnify his truly cold emotions within. Uncontrollable shivers raced up his spine, and rushed through his arm, then traveled out the ends of his fingertips. The wet rain on the anemone ceiling instantly turned into thick sheets of ice that shot out from the ends of his fingertips and crisscrossed the dome. The temperature dropped drastically in the cavern and within seconds, the clear dome had turned a frosty white and appeared more like a giant igloo sitting at the bottom of the ocean. Flin opened his eyes to see the pounding rain had turned into large flakes of snow, which was swiftly piling up on the surface of the cathedral. The Snazzards footings became extremely unsure. They remained motionless, trying to keep from slipping off.

Flin could hear the far off sound of rushing wind. He looked down to see a small cyclone quickly growing from out of one of the tunnels.

"Yes! YES! Someone's opened up the wind tunnel doors!" he shouted joyfully then looked down into the eyes of the alarmed Snazzards clinging to the slick petrified rock.

The thick clouds that blanketed the ceiling began to thin as the giant tornado emerged from the wind tunnel and quickly grew into a ferocious typhoon. The Typhoon roamed about the cavern, aimlessly consuming all the snow and debris in the air. The white twister tossed back and forth, sucking up everything in its path. Flin watched as the giant flying cobra averted the twister and darted into an open tunnel to safety. The meandering cyclone was now making its way to the base of the cathedral. It sucked up many of the Daglids and Grimgoblins as they tried to escape, sending them spiraling through the air and down into the endless wind tunnel.

Flin watched as Blade's men fled Cobble Cavern. The few remaining Snazzards that clung to the tree dug their talons deep into the coarse surface. Flin placed his hand on the cathedral and closed his eyes. He focused on making the wet, snowy surface into sheets of ice. The snow began to radiate a vibrant blue then suddenly transformed into a huge sheet of ice that spread all the way down the trunk. The raging cyclone again roamed back toward the cathedral, this time pulling at the long dangling tails of the remaining Snazzards that hung about the cathedral's trunk. One at a time, the Snazzards were plucked off, sending them spiraling haphazardly through the air and into the tunnel and out of sight.

The open mouth of the twister made its way further up the tree, this time sucking violently at Flin. He held desperately to the ledge as the cyclone pulled at his legs, stretching his body out over the cavern. He started to lose his grip and was about to soar through the air with the last of the Snazzards, when the blustery cyclone lost its energy and disappeared into thin air. Flin scrambled back up onto the icy ledge and stared out over the snowy cavern. He saw the cathedral door open below as dozens of people burst out and immediately looked up. Head Revels frantically began to scan every inch of the cathedral, looking for Flin.

"Flin! Flin, where are you?" Head Revels shouted up with cupped hands.

"I'm at the very top!" He leaned out over the ledge and waved to be seen.

"Thar he be!" shouted Luftin with great relief, pointing hundreds of feet into the air.

"Where?" asked Flowell uneasily.

"Right up at the tippy top there. 'es usin' that there branch for a ledge!"

"Oh," she said as a smile quickly replaced the worried look on her face. "I see him now!" she said, bouncing on her toes and clapping.

"That blessed boy! Somehow he seems to keep getting himself stuck as high up in the air as he possibly can," sighed Principal Vespar, placing her trembling hand over her heart.

Flin waited for the ice to melt then started his way back down. The moon's rays shone beautifully through the melted anemone as Flin leapt from the last limb and down onto the secure cavern floor. Immediately, he was surrounded like a hero.

"Hey! Hey everyone!" shouted Pilt, as he and Cretchit came running up the path. "Did you see what I did? Hey!" he screamed loudly, only to be ignored by everyone as they smothered Flin with praise. "Did you see what I just did?" he shouted even louder. "I'm the one who opened the wind tunnel and sucked up all the bad guys!"

"*We*, Pilt, *we* sucked up all those bad guys!" Cretchit reminded him, patting his chest.

"Anyways, we pretty much saved the day," Pilt said, hoping for some praise of his own.

Principal Vespar saw Pilt's face desperate for praise and broke off from the rest of the group. She made her way over to both Pilt and Cretchit. "Well done, the both of you. Together you two did a great job!"

Pilt looked hard through the crowd that surrounded Flin to see if any of the girls had heard Principal Vespar applauding him for his bravery.

Sam made her way over to Pilt, "You did do a good job," she said, then gave him a hug.

After all the excitement finally died down, everyone went back into the cathedral. They were talking of Flin and how he'd single-handedly defeated Blade and his entire army.

Later that night, Flin, scraped and bruised, limped over to Fezzy, who was next to the fire. Fezzy was humming a merry tune and smoking his pipe while building another food cage out of roots. Flin sat and watched silently for a moment.

"Fezzy, what was that giant flying snake that saved me?"

"Ya saw 'er," he said without looking up from his work. "She's carved right out dere on the front door. 'er name's Xanthis."

"Yeah, now that you say that, I do remember seeing a snake with wings carved into the front door."

"Da Grimgoblins und Snazzards stole 'er unhatched eggs several times und took und ate 'em. She don' like dem. If she sees dem, she kill dem! Xanthis, she's our friend."

"Everyone! Please, your attention!" shouted Head Revels. He went and stood up on a wooden bench. "I think that the attack we had tonight only confirms the urgency for our dismissal. We still plan on setting out early tomorrow morning in hopes that our newly discovered tunnel will take us to the surface!"

The room fell silent with mixed emotions. An abrupt sob erupted within the crowd as Heppel could be seen running away with her head in her hands. For the first time, she went somewhere other than the kitchen.

Chapter Twenty-Five

GETTING OUT

The next morning, bags were stacked high by the front door, and students were gathered in the Entrance Hall of the cathedral. Flin stood somberly on the bridge, leaning over the rail and staring down at the fish.

"You know, Pilt, I'm really looking forward to going home and all, but I think I'm really going to miss this place," Flin said as he glanced around the mystical cathedral, watching a green cloud from the fire loom about the roomwhile the moon rocks provided a dim light.

"Yeah . . . I know exactly what you're saying. I'm going to miss all the girls. And, I'm especially going to miss Heppel's freshly baked blueberry pie— Oh! And, she never tells me I've had too much!"

Principal Vespar spoke. "Okay! Now does everyone have all that they brought?" she paused and glanced around the room at the students. Her eyes rested on Fezzy, Heppel, and Inger, who were all huddled together and staring back at her with big tears in their eyes. Immediately, Principal Vespar's eyes began to puddle up as well.

"Fezzy—Heppel—Inger—thank you so much from all of us. It's been a *great* pleasure being here with you all. I hope you know how much we've grown to love and value all three of you!" A mumbling of thank yous came from the students as well.

Head Revels briskly entered the room. "Okay then! Mr. Luftin, do we have all the food and water packed?"

"Yes, sir, believe so!" he said as he quickly double-checked. "Yipper! We shoud be good!"

"Good, then, we're off!" said Head Revels, taking a resolute step toward the door.

They headed out the front door, each person hugging Heppel, Fezzy, and Inger as they left. No one spoke as they started down the cobble path, but a great feeling of sadness hung in the air.

"Please . . . Head Revels," said Principal Vespar in a soft pleading voice, turning back at the cathedral. "May I take just a minute? I want to look at it one last time." A big smile covered her face. "Isn't it absolutely beautiful!" she said, wiping away tears with a handkerchief that Heppel had made her. "It's like a fairy tale down here."

Voss Yeg started to weep as well.

"Okay, we can go now." Principal Vespar and Voss Yeg put their arms around one another as they headed down the path.

They continued on, leaving the giant cathedral behind them. Hours into the tunnels, sleeping assignments were made. Unable to sleep, Flin watched as the torch's light danced upon the tunnel ceiling one last time. Instead of the soothing sound of crickets and frogs from the meadow serenading him to sleep, there came a far off trickle of dripping water in the burrow up ahead.

"Pst! Hey, Flin," whispered Pilt.

"Yeah," Flin responded, slightly annoyed.

"What do you think Fezzy's doin' about now?" asked Pilt.

"Uh, just a guess, but probably sleeping, Pilt! Like I'm trying to do at the moment!" Flin rolled over and faced the other direction.

"Yeah, I guess so," replied Pilt, staring up at the ceiling. "Tomorrow, I'll probably see my mom and dad."

There weren't many people sleeping throughout the night. The tunnel buzzed of talk of possibly seeing family and friends the next day. Finally, hours into the night, the tunnel fell silent. All slept, except Pilt, who sat close to the fire thinking he'd heard a Snazzard further up the burrow.

"Okay! Everyone up!" clapped Head Revels in an effort to wake the group. "Remember, if we hurry, we can make it out while it's still light outside."

After hours of hiking, Mr. Luftin burst out, "Look! Up ahead there! 'Tis light in the shape of a square only 'bout a half-miler ahead!" He could see the sun's rays coming from around the door.

"I see it now, too!" shouted Head Revels. "Let's pick up the pace," he said, stepping toward the lighted door with much enthusiasm.

"Oh, can't we just rest here for a minute more?" asked an exhausted Voss Yeg. She and Principal Vespar sat on a large boulder in the middle of the tunnel.

"My goodness, ladies," Head Revels said invigorated. "Once we're outside that door, we can rest all we want! Must get up!"

As they neared, the sun's beams shone brilliantly through the cracks around the door, inviting the group, including Voss Yeg and Principal Vespar, to sprint towards it.

Cretchit neared the door. "It looks like one of the wooden doors from down in the wind tunnel, except this door's much bigger and heavier!"

"Head Revels, I hate to be the one to sound pessimistic, but why on earth would someone go to all the effort of making such a big door like that? I don't understand the reasoning. I mean, you'd think they were trying to keep something from getting in rather than getting out!" said Principal Vespar while supporting the exhausted, Voss Yeg.

"I'm not sure why the door's there. I only know there's sunlight just on the other side of it, and that means we're to the surface!" said Head Revels, brushing away her concern.

"Triston, let me see that there torch," said Mr. Luftin, briskly taking it from his hands. "Now then, let's jus' see how this 'ere door's gonna open. Thot's strange—this door's got some kinda lock on 'er," he said, bending down with the torch to get a better look. "Und that there lock hus got ta be *thee* biggest lock I ever did see!"

"But, why'd someone be putting a lock on the inside of the tunnel? It doesn't make a lick a sense," said Fig Tronsel, his head nearly hitting the low ceiling. He tensely glanced around looking into the eyes of others, hoping for some kind of reassurance.

"I don't know. Maybe this was an old abandoned mine or something at one time, and maybe they didn't want kids getting in, so they put the lock on the inside," replied Head Revels, irritable and tired.

"But, if that's the case, how'd they get out after they put the lock on the inside of the door?" asked Pilt, staring intently at Head Revels, awaiting an answer.

"I don't know, Pilt, okay?" exploded Head Revels, due to all the pessimistic inquiries.

Mr. Luftin picked up a rock. He raised it high above his head and struck down at the lock several times. "I don' know," he said scratching his head and wiping the sweat from his brow with the sleeve of his shirt. "That there lock's on pretty darn good!"

Flin bent down to the lock. "I wonder?" he said in a loud whisper.

"Ya wonder whad, Flin?" asked Mr. Luftin, abandoning his search for a bigger rock.

"Oh, nothing," Flin replied. He waited until no one was paying attention to him and held the lock in his hands. He closed his eyes. His body began to shake. "Come on, stress metal, *stress!*"

"Flin! I don' think she'll open jis cause yar gettin' mad at 'er," chuckled Luftin. "Now 'ere's a serious lookin' rock!" Luftin took a large gray stone out of the hands of one of the Haunsdale students. Again, he raised the stone high above his head and struck down at the lock with all his might. Orange sparks flew in the air, lighting up the tunnel momentarily as the lock shattered into hundreds of small pieces.

"Good! Well done, Mr. Luftin," applauded an excited Principal Vespar. "Now some of you boys grab onto the door and help slide it open."

As the door rolled back into the dusty, cobwebbed niche, sunlight rushed in and onto the tunnel floor. Everyone rushed to the tunnel's exit to look out.

"Look, trees! And birds!" said Flowell cheerfully, standing on her toes and clapping.

"Alright!" Head Revels said, pulling back some of the excited students. "Just in case there's any possible chance of danger, I think the adults should go first!"

Mr. Luftin poked his head out of the tunnel and looked up. The unfiltered sun made him squint. "There be the sun, alright! Welp, it truly looks like the surface," he said as he took in a deep breath. "Und the air ou"ere smells fresh." He then proceeded cautiously out of the tunnel. "Looks fine. I cun see birds above, und over there went a deer into those trees jis yonder. I think it's fine for the young'ns ta come out!" he shouted, now a ways out of the tunnel.

The rest of the group stood huddled around the tunnel's exit. Warily, they crept out.

Sam happily jumped up and down. "We're really out!"

"Let's climb to the top of that hill over there and get a better feel for where we are," said Head Revels eagerly.

"Oh, Mr. Revels, if it's alright with you, I'd rather sit here and rest a moment. I just want to enjoy this glorious air until we know for sure which way we're headed!" said Voss Yeg with a pleading smile as she sat in the shade of a tree in the nearby meadow grass.

"That's fine. We'll check it out and then come back for you," replied Head Revels.

"I'll stay here with her as well," smiled Principal Vespar, joining Voss Yeg. She was relieved as well to finally get a chance to rest.

The group anxiously began their climb. They passed through a thick grove of Aspens and made their way up a steep hill.

"Why, look! Over yonder! It looks as if some'n started ta build a castle und never finished," hollered Luftin, pointing at an edifice that was nearly threestories high and made from white and black boulders. Similar rocks were scattered sporadically about the ground.

"That's interesting. Why would someone start to build something so grand and then never complete it?" said a puzzled Head Revels, staring over the hills at the mammothsized building.

"The vegetation round 'ere is strange as well. I've never seen uny of these 'ere types of plants before, 'tleast not in Ireland," said Mr. Luftin, looking around perplexed.

Pilt was the first to make it to the top of the hill. Head Revels stopped to catch his breath.

"What do you see up there, Pilt?" hollered Head Revels.

Even from afar, Pilt looked puzzled. "All I can see is water," he said. "There's water all around us!"

"All around us? It can't be!" said Head Revels in disbelief, quickening his stride. He and Mr. Luftin finally made it to the top.

"Impossible! It appears somehow we've come up and through an island!" he said, placing his hands on his hips. A look of discouragement was painted on his face. "There's no land anywhere. Hold it, I do see something! Is that the top of the cathedral I see? Look, way out into the ocean just over there!" he said, pointing. "Can you see tree branches poking up and out of the water?"

"Yeah . . . I believe yar right! That there definitely does look like the top of the cathedral," agreed Luftin.

"Head Revels! Look up there!" shouted Pilt, pointing above them in the air.

"What in the world? It can't possibly be! It looks like a pterodactyl! Those have been extinct for hundreds of years!" The pterodactyl flew circles directly over the group, squawking loudly the closer it got.

"I've read they couldn't fly very far, which is probably why it's still here, confined to this little island!" Just then, the pterodactyl tucked its wings to its sides and dove down after them. It let out a horrific screech as it skimmed the top of their heads.

"Okay, everyone down and off the hill right now!" ordered Head Revels.

As they neared the bottom of the hill, Flowell's frantic running slowed to a jog. Her eyes were fixed on a clump of nearby bushes just off the trail in front of them. "Aaa . . . Mr. Luftin!" she said in a high squeaky voice, her pointing finger shaking with terror. "Th, those bushes are moving, and I can see some big yellow eyes staring back at me!"

Just then, a ghastly roar erupted from within the bushes. A giant, black lion with bright orange stripes leapt out of the thicket and thundered down the path after them.

"Quick! Everyone, back into the tunnel. NOW!" shouted Head Revels, steering the students and adults back into the tunnel.

"Hurry! Faster!" shouted a frightened Principal Vespar, frantically ushering students in.

"It's almost here! I need help shutting the door!" screamed Head Revels, looking desperately around. Fig Tronsel stood frozen, staring out at the attacking lion. Mr. Luftin, Flin and some of the other boys rushed to the door and helped Head Revels roll it back into its channel just as the lion lunged into the air at them.

BOOM! The lion crashed into the back of the door just as it shut. Thick dust stirred around the cracks of the door. The room sat silent, except for heavy breathing and a few whimpers. Fig Tronsel glanced about the tunnel wide eyed and terrified, looking at the others as the torchlight danced upon their frightened faces.

"Now, tha' there is wha' cha call a close n'!" said Mr. Luftin, falling backwards into the wall and placing his hand over his heart.

The lion scratched wildly at the back of the door for a minute. Then, it let out one last angry roar and the tunnel fell silent.

"Well, I don't think we're getting out that way," said Head Revels, pulling out a hanky and wiping off his forehead.

"I think you're right!" replied Principal Vespar, who was cuddling a frightened Haunsdale girl as Miss Lemons attended to the rest of the dance students.

The tunnel sat silent for a short while.

Mr. Luftin spoke. "Wull, I'm not sa sure I speak fur the rests of ya's when I say 'twasn't ull that bad back there with Fezzy und the others in the cathedral. I mean a, I truly kinda miss'm ulready!"

"Here, here!" replied Voss Yeg briskly, looking around for support.

Head Revels stood, the torchlight reflecting on his discouraged face. "Well, here's how I see it," he said, holding his chin in deep thought. "We really only have but two choices." He started pacing up and down the tunnel floor. "One, we can go through that door again where we know we're not welcome! Or two, go back to the cathedral with the others, like Mr. Luftin said."

Principal Vespar spoke out. "I think we should put it to a vote! Who wants to go back out that tunnel door?"

Somehow the hushed tunnel fell even more silent, all but the sound of Fig Tronsel's rattling teeth.

"All those who want to return back to the cathedral, say aye!"

"Aye!" the unanimous response from everyone echoed for miles down the tunnel.

"It appears that we are headed back to the cathedral!" said Principal Vespar cheerfully. "Mr. Luftin, if you'd please lead us there."

"I cun do thot!" he said with a smile as he limped his way around to the front of the group. They traveled at a swift pace for several hours.

"We can either stay here for the night and sleep on the tunnel floor, or continue on?" asked Head Revels.

"Continue on!"

"Alright! We'll press on!"

Back at the cathedral, Fezzy was holding Heppel, consoling her as she cried.

"I miss 'em, Fizzy. Ay wished they din't haft ta go," she sobbed.

"I know 'eppel, but they hud ta go back home, my sweet. Ya know Ay'm a missin 'em, too!" Fezzy responded. "Inger lad, what cha doin' over there in da corner by yarself!" Inger's feet could barely be seen by the firelight.

"Justa thinkin' tis ull," he said as he twiddled his short, fat thumbs together.

BOOM! BOOM! BOOM! There came a loud pounding on the cathedral door.

"Oh, Fizzy, don' open it! Please! It's Blade und his men! They've cum back ta get uz!" Heppel covered her mouth and backed up the steps.

BOOM!

Inger crept to the door and placed his ear against it.

"Fezzy! Inger! Let us in!" A faint voice could be heard outside the door.

"'Tis them! They've come back!" Inger said excitedly, lifting the latch free from the door.

As the door flew open, Inger was practically stampeded by the rushing crowd. Heppel spotted Principal Vespar and ran to her with arms wide open and tears of joy streaming down her face.

"Ay missted you!" she said as she grabbed Principal Vespar tightly around the waist.

"And, I missed you, too, Heppel!" she said with a big smile. She bent down and gave her a hug and then a kiss on the cheek.

"It looks like we're home—for a while anyways, if that's alright with you three?" Head Revels asked with a subtle smile, looking at the three dwarfs for their approval.

"Oh, yis! Yis, yis! 'Tis more than ulright," said Heppel as she squeezed Principal Vespar's hand and smiled up at her.

Fezzy, Inger, and Heppel were practically mauled for the next half hour as everyone took turns hugging and kissing them.

A while later, after the excitement of returning had subsided, and the group had told of their adventure, they all dispersed back to their rooms. Flin went back up to his room and began to place what few items he had taken with him back into his dresser drawers. He smiled as he glanced around his room then up at the anemone with fish swimming overhead. He pulled open one of his hollowed out log drawers to put some of his items away.

"Oh, that's right, I almost forgot my boxes of pits!" Flin said, opening up one of the cigar boxes. "Hmm, that's strange—I don't remember ever seeing this pit before." He reached into the box and pulled out a peculiar purple pit the size of a golf ball with raised silver dots in the shape of shields and two large thorns at opposite ends. Just then, the dried flaking sheaths that covered the old tips of the thorns suddenly popped off, revealing two new, long, sharp burgundy thorns that began to squirm in the palm of Flin's hand. *"Oh great, now what?"*

CPSIA information can be obtained
at www.ICGtesting.com
Printed in the USA
BVHW050953181019
561475BV00025B/3397/P

9 780578 590233